I have been lucky enough to tour with several of the books in the Kate Burkholder series and I must say it has been one of the highlights of my career.

I'd like to dedicate this book to the booksellers, librarians, reviewers, readers, and bloggers who have attended my events, bought the books, written reviews, blogged about the books, and written me to share your thoughts. I very much appreciate each and every one of you.

Gone Missing

LINDA CASTILLO

PAN BOOKS

First published 2012 by Macmillan

This edition published 2012 by Pan Books
an imprint of Pan Macmillan, a division of Macmillan Publishers Limited
Pan Macmillan, 20 New Wharf Road, London N1 9RR
Basingstoke and Oxford
Associated companies throughout the world
www.panmacmillan.com

ISBN 978-1-4472-0215-8

Acknowledgements

A writer spends months on end writing a book, but there are many other behind-the-scenes individuals whose efforts, talent, dedication and heart go into the publishing of it. I'd like to acknowledge a few of the people who helped bring this book to fruition. First and foremost, I wish to thank my editor, Charlie Spicer, for sharing so much of his talent, being such a great listener, and always urging me to go that extra mile. I'd like to thank my agent, Nancy Yost, whose brilliance never ceases to amaze me. I've learned much from you. Many thanks to my editor in the UK, Trisha Jackson, for always making the books better. I'd also like to thank the entire team at St. Martin's Press for their continued support, confidence in me and in this series, for working so tirelessly to get the books into the hands of readers – and for making it fun! Sally Richardson. Andrew Martin. Matthew Shear. Matthew Baldacci. Sarah Melnyk. Hector DeJean. Kerry Nordling. April Osborn. David Rotstein. There are many more individuals who contributed much, but remain unnamed due to space constraints. I'm incredibly lucky to write for such a dynamic publishing house.

I'd also like to thank my critique group for all of those Wednesday night marathons when I kept you up late. Jennifer Archer. Anita Howard. Marcy McKay. April Redmon.

Heartfelt thanks to fellow authors, Ellie James and Catherine Spangler, for the years of friendship and support. You gals rock!

Last, but not least, I'd like to thank the love of my life, Ernest, for his unconditional love and support through all the ups and downs of cohabitating with a full-time writer.

Prologue

Becca had always known her life would end in tragedy. As a child, she couldn't speak to her certainty of her fate or explain how she could foresee such a thing. She believed in providence, and it came as no surprise when she realized she would also die young.

When she was seven years old, she asked her *mamm* about death. Her mother told her that when people die, they go to live with God. The answer pleased Becca immensely. It gave her great comfort, knowing what she did about her destiny. After that day, not once did she fear the closeness or inevitability of her mortality.

Now, eight years later, as she stood on the frozen shore of Mohawk Lake and stared across the vast expanse of ice, her mother's words calmed the fear that had been building inside her for days. Dusk had fallen, and the lake was a monochrome world in which sky and horizon blended to a gray smear, one barely discernible from the other. A dozen or more ice-fishing shanties dotted the lake's surface. Yellow light glowed in one of the windows. But the others were dark, telling her the *Englischer* fishermen had gone home for the day.

The wind scored Becca's skin through the covering of her wool coat as she stepped onto the ice. Blowing snow whispered across the jagged plane and stung her face like sand. The hem of her dress was frozen and stiff and scraped against her bare calves. She'd been walking for quite some time and could no longer feel her hands or feet. But those petty discomforts didn't matter. Soon she'd be home, and she didn't have much farther to go.

Becca loved this lake. Summer or winter – it didn't matter. When she was a little girl, her *datt* bought her and her brother ice skates and they'd spent many a winter afternoon playing hockey. By spring, she could skate faster than any of her Amish friends, even faster than her older brother. He hadn't liked being shown up by a girl. But her *datt* would laugh and clap his hands and tell her she could fly. His praise, such a rarity, always made her feel special. Like she mattered and her achievements, regardless of how small, were important.

The lake became her special place, her hideaway from the rest of the world, away from her troubles. It was the place where she learned to dream. No one could catch her when she was on the ice. No one could touch her. No one could hurt her.

Only he had.

When Becca was nine years old, her brother found her sitting on the stump, lacing her skates. He'd knocked her down and ground her face into the snow, and then he took her right there on the frozen bank. And from that day forward, Becca knew she was doomed.

Later, when her *mamm* asked about the cut on her cheek, Becca told her what her brother had done. It wasn't the first time and, as always, *Mamm* blamed Becca. *You should have fought harder. You should have prayed more. You should be more forgiving.* She ended the conversation by asking Becca to confess her sins to the bishop.

The memory brought tears to Becca's eyes. How could her

brother's actions be her fault? Had she somehow tempted him? Was there something wrong with her? Was God punishing her for being unable to forgive? Or was this simply her lot in life?

Snow crunched beneath her shoes as she made her way across the ice. Becca was nearly to the center of the lake when she stumbled over a fissure and went to her hands and knees. The cold bit into her skin with the intensity of a thousand blades. She knew it was stupid, but she began to cry. It wasn't supposed to be like this. She wasn't supposed to be scared, and she hadn't expected to feel so alone.

A little voice reminded her it wasn't too late to turn back. Her warm bed in her little attic bedroom waited for her at home. *Mamm* and *Datt* didn't have to know she'd ventured out. But Becca knew there were other things waiting for her at home. Bad things that had been happening to her since she was three years old, when her brother had slipped his hand into her panties and told her not to cry.

Becca knew what she was about to do was a sin. But she also knew God would forgive her. She knew He would welcome her to heaven with open arms and love her unconditionally for all of eternity. How could that be wrong?

Rising, she looked around to get her bearings. Behind her, the trees near the shore were barely visible. Farther out, the silhouette of an ice-fishing shanty shimmered like a mirage in the fading light. Brushing snow from her coat, she started toward the structure. Constructed of wood with a single window and tin chimney, the shanty reminded her of a tall, skinny doghouse. She knew sometimes English fishermen spent the night on the lake. But there was no telltale glow of lantern light. No ribbon of smoke rising from the chimney. This one was vacant. It would do.

Becca slogged through a deep drift and stumbled toward the front of the shanty. A padlock hung from the hasp, but it wasn't engaged. Shaking with cold, she shoved open the door. The interior was dark and hushed. The air smelled of kerosene and fish. Out of the wind, it was so quiet that she could hear the ice creaking beneath her feet.

Her breaths puffing out in clouds of white vapor, she pulled out the candle and matches she'd brought from home and lit the wick. The light revealed a small interior with plywood walls and a shelf covered with fish blood and a smattering of silver scales. A lantern sat on the shelf. A coil of rope hung on the wall.

Becca crossed to the shelf and set the candle next to the lantern. Turning, she surveyed the floor. Someone had covered the fishing hole with a square of plywood. Bending, she dragged the wood aside. The hole was about fourteen inches in diameter and crusted over with new ice.

She looked around for something with which to break it, but there wasn't much in the way of tools. A broken concrete block. A plastic box of fishhooks. Empty beer cans. Then she spotted the hand auger in the corner. Kneeling, she picked it up and used it to break the thin crust.

When the hole was open, Becca crossed to the bench, lifted the rope from its hook, and uncoiled it. It was about twelve feet long and frayed on both ends. Her hands shook as she tied one end of it around her waist. She didn't let herself think as she secured the other end to the concrete block.

Kneeling next to the hole in the ice, Becca bowed her head and silently recited the Lord's Prayer. She asked God to take care of her *mamm* and *datt*. She asked Him to ease their grief in the coming days. She asked Him to forgive her brother for what he'd done to her most of her life. Finally, she asked God to forgive her for the sin she was about to commit. She closed her eyes and prayed harder than she'd ever prayed in her life, hoping it was enough.

When she was finished, Becca rose, picked up the rope, and lowered the concrete block into the hole, watching it disappear into the black depths. She thought of the journey before her and her chest swelled – not with fear, but with the utter certainty that soon all would be right.

Standing at the edge of the hole, she closed her eyes, stepped forward, and plunged into the water.

ONE

My *mamm* once told me that some places are too beautiful for anything bad to happen. When I was a kid, I believed those words with all of my young heart. I lived my life in a state of ignorant bliss, oblivious to the evils that lurked like frothy-mouthed predators outside the imaginary gates of our small Amish community. The English world with its mysterious and forbidden charms seemed like a million miles away from our perfect little corner of the earth. I had no way of knowing that some predators come from within and beauty has absolutely nothing to do with the crimes men commit.

Ohio's Amish country is a mosaic of quaint farms, rolling hills dissected by razor-straight rows of corn, lush hardwood forests, and pastures so green that you'd swear you had stepped into a Bill Coleman photograph. This morning, with the sun punching through the final vestiges of fog and the dew sparkling like quicksilver on the tall grass of a hay field, I think of my *mamm's* words and I understand how she could believe them.

But I'm a cop now and not easily swayed by appearances, no matter how convincing the facade. My name is Kate Burkholder and I've been the police chief of Painters Mill for about three years now. I was born here to Amish parents in a one-hundred-year-old farmhouse set on sixty acres of northeastern

6

Ohio's rich, glaciated soil. I grew up Plain – no electricity, no motorized vehicles. Up until the age of fourteen, I was a typical Amish girl – innocent, God-loving, content in the way most Amish children are. My future, my very destiny, had been preordained by my gender and the religion bestowed upon me by my parents. All of that changed on a postcard-perfect summer day much like this one when fate introduced me to the dark side of human nature. I learned at a formative age that even on perfect, sunny days, bad things happen.

I try not to let my view of the world affect the way I do my job. Most of the time, I succeed. Sometimes I feel all that cynicism pressing in, coloring my perceptions, perhaps unfairly. But far too often, my general distrust of mankind serves me well.

I'm idling down Hogpath Road in my city-issue Explorer with my window down and a to-go cup of coffee between my knees. I've just come off the graveyard shift, having covered for one of my officers while he visited his folks in Michigan. I'm tired, but it's a good tired. The kind that comes with the end of an uneventful shift. No speeders. No domestic disputes. No loose livestock wreaking havoc on the highway. When you've been a cop for any length of time, you learn to appreciate the small things.

I'm thinking about a hot shower and eight hours of uninterrupted sleep, when my radio crackles. 'Chief? You there?'

I reach for the mike. 'What's up, Mona?'

Mona Kurtz is my third-shift dispatcher. She's been part of my small police department from day one, and despite her Lady Gaga-esque wardrobe and decidedly uncoplike manner, she's a good fit. A night owl by nature, she keeps things interesting when the shift is slow – which is usually the case – but when the situation calls for it, she's all business and a true benefit to the department.

'I just took a nine one one for some kind of disturbance,' she tells me.

'What's the twenty?'

'Covered bridge.'

Images of drunk and disorderly teenagers flash in my mind's eye and I groan inwardly. The Tuscarawas Bridge is a favorite hangout for some of the local youths to 'chill.' As of late, some of that so-called chilling has deteriorated to other unsavory activities, like underage drinking, fighting, and drug use – and I'm sure that's just the tip of the iceberg. A week ago, one of my officers busted the mayor's seventeen-year-old son with an ounce of weed and a meth pipe. The mayor hasn't spoken to me since. But I know *the conversation* is coming. Probably in the form of a request I won't be able to grant.

I glance at the clock on my dash and restrain a sigh. Eight A.M. 'They're starting early.'

'Or staying late.'

'Who called it in?'

'Randy Trask was on his way to work and said there was some kind of ruckus.'

Muttering beneath my breath, I swing right, hang a U-turn in the middle of the road, and hit the accelerator. 'Is Trask still there?'

'He left, Chief. Had to get to work.'

I sigh. 'I'm ten-seventy-six.'

'Roger that.'

The Tuscarawas covered bridge is a Painters Mill icon and of substantial historical significance. It was built in 1868, fell to ruin during the Depression, and was refurbished at the expense of the taxpayers and a donation from the Painters Mill Historical Society in 1981. Constructed of wood and painted barn red, it spans 125 feet across Painters Creek. The bridge is a tourist attraction and has been the topic of many a town council meeting, mainly due to the fact that a few local graffiti artistes have declared it fair game – and my department has yet to catch a single one. It's located on a little-used asphalt road that cuts through bottomland that's prone to flooding in the spring. The surrounding woods are dense with century-old hardwood trees and a summer's growth of underbrush – the perfect locale for a multitude of illicit activities.

It takes me five minutes to reach the bridge. I slow as I approach its yawning red mouth. To my right, I can just make out a footpath cut into the forest, and I know there have been plenty of people hoofing it down to the creek bank to fish or swim or whatever the hell it is they do there.

A jacked-up Chevy Nova with wide tires and a spoiler at the rear is parked on the gravel turnout, its oxidized paint glinting dully in the morning sun. Next to it, an ancient Bonneville with a patchwork of Bondo on the front quarter panel squats on the shoulder like some armored dinosaur. The driver's side door is open and the coarse echo of techno-rock booms out so loudly, my windows vibrate. I see two more cars parked on the other side of the bridge. I peer ahead and see, cloaked in the shadows of the covered bridge, the silhouettes of a couple of dozen young people grouped into a tight circle.

I pulse my siren a couple of times to get their attention. Some look my way. Others are so embroiled in whatever's going on, they don't even notice. Or maybe they don't care.

I park behind the Nova, shut down the engine, and hail Mona. 'I'm ten-twenty-three.'

'What's going on out there, Chief?'

'I'd lay odds on a fight.' I've just opened my door, when a scream echoes from within the bridge. 'Shit,' I mutter. 'Is Glock there yet?'

'Just walked in.'

'Get him out here, will you?'

'Ten-four.'

Racking the mike, I slip out of the car and hit the ground running. Several of the teens look up and scatter as I approach, and I catch a glimpse of two people on the ground, locked in battle. The agitated crowd throbs around them, shouting, egging them on, as if they've bet their life savings on some bloody dogfight.

'Police!' I shout, my boots crisp against the wood planks. 'Back off! Break it up! Right now!'

Faces turn my way. Some are familiar; most are not. I see flashes of surprise in young eyes alight with something a little too close to bloodlust. Cruelty in its most primal form. Pack mentality, I realize, and that disturbs me almost as much as the fight.

I thrust myself into the crowd, using my forearms to move people aside. 'Step away! Now!'

A teenage boy with slumped shoulders and a raw-looking outbreak of acne on his cheeks glances at me and takes a step back. Another boy is so caught up in the fight, he doesn't notice my approach and repeatedly jabs the air with his fist, chanting, 'Beat that bitch!' A black-haired girl wearing a purple halter top that's far too small for her bustline lands a kick at one of the fighters. 'Break her face, you fuckin' ho!'

I elbow past two boys not much bigger than I am, and I get my first unobstructed look at the epicenter of the chaos. Two teenage girls are going at it with the no-holds-barred frenzy of veteran barroom brawlers. Hands grapple with clothes and hair. Nails slash at faces. I hear animalistic grunts, the sound of ripping fabric, and the wet-meat slap of fists connecting with flesh.

'*Get off me, bitch!*'

I bend, slam my hands down on the shoulders of the girl on top. 'Police,' I say. 'Stop fighting.'

She's a big-boned girl and outweighs me by about twenty pounds. Moving her is like trying to peel a starving lion off a fresh kill. When she doesn't acquiesce, I dig my fingers into her collarbone, put some muscle into it, and haul her back. 'Stop resisting!'

'Get off me!' Blinded by rage, the girl tries to shake off my hands. 'I'm going to kill this bitch!'

'Not on my watch.' I put my body weight into the effort and yank her back hard. Her shirt tears beneath my hands. She reels backward and lands on her butt at my feet. She tries to get her legs under her, but I press her down.

'Calm down.' I give her a shake to let her know I'm serious.

Ignoring me, she crab-walks forward and lashes out at the other girl with her foot, trying to get in a final kick. I wrap my hands around her bicep and drag her back several feet. 'That's enough! Now cut it out.'

'She started it!' she screams.

Concerned that I'm going to lose control of the situation before backup arrives, I point at the most sane-looking bystander I can find, a thin boy wearing a Led Zeppelin T-shirt. 'You.'

He looks over his shoulder. 'Me?'

'I'm not talking to your invisible friend.' I motion to the second fighter, who's sitting on the ground with her legs splayed in front of her, her hair hanging in her face. 'Take her to the other side of the bridge and wait for me.'

I'm about to yell at him, when a girl with a pierced eyebrow steps forward. 'I'll do it.' Bending, she sets her hands on the other girl's shoulder. 'Hey. Come on.'

I turn my attention to the girl at my feet. She's glaring at me with a belligerent expression, breathing as if she's just come off a triathlon. A drop of mascara-tinged sweat dangles from the tip of her nose and her cheeks glow as if with sunburn. For an instant, I find myself hoping she'll take her best shot, so I can wipe all that bad attitude off her face. Then I remind myself that teenagers are the only segment of the population entitled to temporary bouts of stupidity.

'If I were you,' I say quietly, 'I'd think real hard about what you do next.'

I look around, gauging the crowd. They're still agitated, a little too close for comfort, and restless in a way I don't like, especially when I'm outnumbered twenty to one. Keeping my hand on the girl's shoulder, I straighten and make eye contact with a few of them. 'You have thirty seconds to clear out, or I'm going to start arresting people and calling parents.'

When they begin to disburse, I glance at the girl. She's eyeballing her friends, gesturing, sending them nonverbal messages teenager-style, and I realize she's enjoying her fifteen minutes of fame.

'What's your name?' I ask.

She gives me an 'Eat shit' look. But she's smart enough to know this is one standoff she's not going to win. 'Angi McClanahan.'

'You got ID on you?'

'No.'

I extend my hand to help her up, but she ignores it and jumps to her feet with the grace of a fallen figure skater going for the gold. She's a pretty girl of about sixteen, with blond hair and blue eyes, freckles sprinkled over a turned-up nose. Her build is substantial, but she carries it well, the way young women do. The sleeve of her T-shirt hangs off her shoulder. I see scratch marks on her throat, another on the inside of her elbow. There's blood on her jeans, but I don't know where it came from.

'Are you injured?' I ask. 'Do you need an ambulance?'

She gives me a withering look. 'I'm fine.'

'What happened?'

She jabs a finger in the direction of the other girl and her lips peel back. 'I was out here hangin' and that fuckin' ho jumped me.'

The words dishearten me, but it's the hatred behind them that chafes my sensibilities. I don't know when kids started talking this way, but I detest it. Don't get me wrong; I'm not naïve. I've heard worse words in the course of my law-enforcement career, many of which I've been the target of. But hearing that kind of rhetoric from such a pretty young woman somehow shocks me.

I reach for the cuffs tucked into a compartment on my belt, yank them out. 'Turn around.'

'*Dude.*' Her gaze slides down to the cuffs and she raises her hands. 'I didn't do anything!'

'Put your hands behind your back.' Grasping her bicep, I spin her around, snap one end of the cuffs onto her right wrist, and draw it behind her. 'Give me your other hand. Now.'

'Please don't . . .' She's upset now. On the verge of tears. Starting to shake.

I don't feel much in the way of compassion. Grabbing her free wrist, I snap the cuff into place and crank it down. The too-sweet scent of drugstore perfume mingles with the stink of cigarettes and comes off her in waves. Grasping the chain link between the cuffs, I guide her to the window. There, I turn her around, lean her against it, and put my finger in her face. 'Do not move from this place,' I tell her. 'Do not speak to anyone. Do you understand?'

Mouth tight, she refuses to answer and looks away.

When I turn my back, she mutters, '*Bitch.*' I let it go and start toward the crowd. Most of the teens have disbanded, but there are several stragglers, their eyes bouncing from me to Angi, hoping for more fireworks.

The crunch of tires on gravel draws my attention and I see

the Painters Mill PD cruiser pull up behind my Explorer. Relief flits through me when Officer Rupert 'Glock' Maddox emerges. A former marine with two tours in Afghanistan under his belt, Glock is my best officer, and I'm invariably glad to see him, especially when I'm outnumbered, whether by teenagers or cows.

The remaining teens give him a wide berth as he walks onto the bridge. He has that effect on people, though he doesn't seem to notice. 'Whatcha got, Chief?'

'A couple of Einsteins thought it might be fun to roll around on the ground and beat the shit out of each other.'

He glances past me at the handcuffed girl. 'Females?'

'It's the new thing, I guess.'

'Damn. That's just wrong.' Shaking his head, he slants a doleful look my way. 'Girls didn't fight when I was a kid.'

'Evidently, stupidity is an equal-opportunity condition.' I motion toward Angi McClanahan and lower my voice. 'See what her story is. If she gives you any shit, arrest her.'

He pats the Glock at his hip. 'Hey, I'm an equal-opportunity kind of guy.'

I withhold a smile. 'I'm going to talk to Muhammad Ali over there.'

I find the second fighter on the opposite side of the bridge, standing next to the girl with the pierced eyebrow. Both girls are facing away from me, staring out the window, elbows on the sill, smoking clove cigarettes.

'Put the smokes out,' I tell them as I approach.

Two heads jerk my way. The girl with the brow hoop turns to me, stubs out her cigarette on the sill, and then drops it to the floor. The one who was fighting flicks hers out the window to the creek below, then faces me. For the first time, I get a good look at her face. Recognition stops me cold. I know her. Or at least I used to, and I'm pretty sure she's Amish. For an instant, I'm so shocked that I can't remember her name.

'Hey, Katie,' she says sweetly.

I stare hard at her, racking my memory, unsettled because I'm coming up short. She's about fifteen, with gangly arms and legs and a skinny butt squeezed into jeans at least two sizes too small. She's got pretty skin, large hazel eyes, and shoulder-length brown hair streaked blond by the sun. She took at least one punch to the face, because I see a bruise blooming below her left eye.

She smirks, a shifty amusement touching her expression. 'You don't remember me.'

My brain lands on a name, but I'm not certain it's correct. 'Sadie Miller?'

She dazzles me with a smile that's far too pretty for someone who was on the ground and throwing punches just a few minutes ago. She's the niece of my sister's husband, and I almost can't believe my eyes. The last time I saw Sadie was at my mother's funeral, just over three years ago. She'd been about twelve years old, a cute little tomboy in a blue dress and white *kapp;* all skinny legs, scabby knees, and a gap between her front teeth. I remember her so well because she was sweet and social, with a natural curiosity that had appealed to me even through my grief. She was one of the few Amish girls who could hold her own with the boys and had no qualms about speaking her mind to the adults. I ended up spending most of my time with her that day, mainly because most of the other Amish refused to talk to me.

This young woman looks nothing like that cute little Amish girl. She's tall and beautiful, with a model-thin body. There's a wildness in her eyes that adds something edgy and audacious to an already bold appearance – at least in Amish terms anyway – and I know her early defiance of the rules has turned into something a hell of a lot more chronic.

'Do you need an ambulance?' I ask.

She laughs. 'I think I'll live.'

I make a point of looking her up and down. Her nails are painted blue. Her makeup is well done but heavy on the liner. She wears a silky black tank with bold white stitching. The material is so thin, I can see her nipples through the fabric. I hear myself sigh. 'Do your parents know you're here?'

'It's none of their business.' She flicks her hair off her shoulder. 'I'm on *rumspringa*.'

Rumspringa is the time when young Amish people are allowed to experience life without the constraints of the *Ordnung*, while the adults look the other way. Most teens partake in some drinking and listening to music – small infractions that are generally harmless. I wonder if this girl will be one of the 80 percent who eventually become baptized.

I stare at her, trying to reconcile the young woman before me with the sweet kid I met three years ago. 'You're kind of young for *rumspringa*, aren't you?'

'In case you haven't noticed, I'm not a kid anymore.'

'You didn't look very grown-up a few minutes ago when you were fighting.'

'I'm fifteen.' She looks away. 'Old enough to know what I want.'

'Half of the adult population doesn't know what they want,' I mutter drily.

She laughs outright. 'That's what I like about you, Katie.'

'You don't know me.'

'I know you break the rules.'

'Yeah, well, all that rule breaking isn't everything it's cracked up to be.'

'That must be why you left,' she says, her words saturated with sarcasm.

'Don't go there,' I warn her.

'I'm thinking about leaving the plain life,' she blurts.

Since I'm the last person who should be having this conversation with a young Amish woman, I take a moment to dig my notepad from my pocket. 'How do your parents feel about that?'

'They think the devil has gotten ahold of me.' She throws her head back and laughs. 'They could be right.'

Trying not to wince, I turn my attention to her friend, the girl with the gold hoop sticking out of her eyebrow. 'What's your name?'

'Lori Westfall.'

I scribble the name on the pad. 'You can go.'

Her eyes slide to Sadie. 'But . . . I'm her ride home.'

'Not anymore.' I point to the mouth of the bridge. 'Go.'

Huffing a grievous sigh, she turns and walks away.

'I guess all those stories I've heard about you are true,' Sadie says.

'I'm not going to respond to that, Sadie, so save your breath.'

She ignores me. 'Everyone says you're a badass.'

'Don't believe everything you hear.'

'I'm glad you cuffed that bitch.'

'If I were you, I'd start taking this a lot more seriously.'

She sobers, but I still discern the smile in her eyes.

'Who started the fight?' I ask.

Looking far too comfortable with the situation, she shrugs. 'I threw the first punch.'

'Why were you fighting?' I ask, hoping none of this is about drugs.

'Her boyfriend likes me more than he likes her, and she's the jealous type.'

'Who touched whom first?'

'She shoved me.' She glances down, peels at the nail polish on her thumb. 'So I slugged her.'

'Did she hit you back?'

She points to her eye. 'Hello.'

I frown. 'Don't get smart with me, Sadie. Just because you're family doesn't mean I won't take you to jail. Do you understand?'

'I got it.' But she gives me a sly grin. 'Angi McClanahan is a fuckin' ho.'

The words are so incongruous with the girl standing before me that I'm taken aback. 'Give it a rest,' I snap. But I'm acutely aware of the discomfort in my voice. 'You're too pretty to talk like that.'

'Everyone else does.' She looks at me from under long lashes, curious, testing me. 'Even you.'

'This isn't about me.'

'The old women still gossip about you, Katie. They talk about how you used to be Amish but left the plain life for the big, bad city.' She looks at me as if somehow what I did is something to be admired. 'Fannie Raber said you told the bishop to go to hell.'

'I don't see how that's something to be proud of.'

She shrugs. 'I'm tired of all the rules.'

The urge to defend the Amish way rises in my chest with surprising force. But knowing any such defense would be hypocritical coming from me, I hold my silence. 'Maybe you should discuss this with your parents.'

'Like they're going to understand.'

'Then the bishop—'

She barks out a laugh. 'Bishop Troyer is so lame!'

'Fighting is lame. Look at you. How could you disrespect yourself like this? You're going to have a black eye.'

Looking only slightly chagrined, she lowers her voice. 'I'm serious about leaving, Katie.'

Suddenly, I feel as if I'm tiptoeing through a minefield

without the slightest idea where to step. 'I'm not the person you should be discussing this with.'

'Why? Because you left?'

'Because I'm a cop, and I'm not going to discuss it. Do you understand?'

She holds my gaze. 'I've been thinking about it for a long time.' She lowers her voice. 'I don't fit in. I'm drawn to all the things I shouldn't be. Music and . . . art. I want to . . . read books and watch movies and see places I've never seen. I want to go to college and . . .'

'You can pursue all of those things without fighting and getting into trouble,' I tell her.

'I can't do those things and remain Amish.'

'You're too young to be making such an important decision.'

'I hate being Amish.'

'You don't know what you want.'

'I know exactly what I want!' she retorts. 'I'm going to design clothes. English clothes. For women. I know that sounds like some stupid pipe dream. Or according to my *datt*: devilment.' She does a decent impersonation of her father. 'He doesn't get me, Katie. I'm *so* good with the needle and thread. Just ask *Mamm*. She knows I could make a go of it. Only she won't admit it.'

She motions at the tank she's wearing. 'I made this! Look at it. It's beautiful, but *Mamm* won't let me wear it. She won't even let me sell it at the Carriage Stop. She says it's got too much ornamentation and that it's prideful.'

The words tumble out of her in a rush, too fast and falling over one another, as if she's been holding them inside and some invisible dam has burst. I recall a vague memory from a couple of months ago: My sister, Sarah, telling me about this girl's needlework. I hadn't paid much attention at the time; my sister and I have been dealing with our own issues. But Sarah had gone on about Sadie's talent. How she'd already sold a dozen quilts at one of the tourist shops in town and customers couldn't seem to get enough. There's a part of me that hates the idea of snuffing out that kind of passion. Too many people slog through their lives without it. It is a view, of course, that would not be welcomed by the Amish.

'So are you going to take me to jail?' she asks, looking a little too excited by the prospect.

'I'm going to take you home.'

Sighing as if jail is the better option, Sadie reaches into her pocket, pulls a brown cigarette from a pack, and lights up. I can tell by the way she does it, she's not a smoker.

'Put that out,' I tell her.

'Why, Katie? You smoke. I saw you. At the *graebhoff*. Why can't I?'

'Because you're fifteen and it's illegal.' I snatch the cigarette from her and toss it out the window.

She stares at me with clear, watchful eyes that don't miss a beat. It's strange, but I find myself feeling self-conscious because, for some crazy reason, this girl looks up to me. She's learning things she probably shouldn't, wanting things that, if she remains Amish, she won't ever possess. It's a recipe for heartache, and I want no part of it.

'I don't want to go home,' she tells me.

'Here's a news flash for you, Sadie. You don't always get what you want.' I glance over my shoulder. All but two of the kids have left. Glock is speaking with Angi McClanahan. She's flirting with him, probably trying to get him to remove the cuffs. He jots something in his notebook, steadfastly unaffected.

'Stay put,' I tell Sadie. 'I'll be right back.'

I start toward Glock. He glances up and meets me in the

center of the bridge, so that we're out of earshot of both girls. 'What do you think?' I ask him.

Glock shakes his head. 'Were we that dumb when we were teenagers?'

'Probably.'

He glances down at his notepad. 'Apparently, the two girls were fighting over some guy. McClanahan made contact first. Other girl threw the first punch.'

'I'm so glad I'm not a teenager.'

'I'd kinda like to be the guy they were fighting over, though.'

We grin at each other.

'So who're we taking to jail?' he asks.

'I'm going to let them off with a warning and have a chat with the parents.'

'Good call.' He nods his approval. 'Fewer reports to write.'

'Will you drive McClanahan home? Talk with her folks?'

'Sure.'

I glance over at Sadie Miller and sigh. She's leaning against the windowsill, her foot propped against the wall, smoking a clove cigarette, watching me. 'I can't believe kids still smoke those things,' I mutter.

Glock nods in agreement. 'They'll kill you, that's for sure.'

As I start toward the girl, I figure we both know there are far more dangerous ills facing our young people and that most of us are at a complete loss as far as how to keep them at bay.

TWO

Forty-five minutes later, I'm pulling out of the long gravel lane of the farm where Sadie Miller lives with her parents and four siblings. I'm adept at reading people, regardless of culture, and I'm pretty sure that when Sadie and I initially walked in, they thought *I* was the one who'd given her the black eye. Deserved or not, I've earned a reputation among the Amish.

I did my best to remain objective as I explained what had happened. Esther and Roy Miller listened quietly, but I saw the distrust in their eyes – perhaps even a little suspicion. I heard a lot more silence than questions. By the time I left, I was starting to doubt if they believed any of what I'd told them.

Had this been a non-Amish family, I'd still be in there, listening to the parents defend their child or, perhaps, deflecting cheap shots aimed at me and my department. Not so with the Amish. There was no finger-pointing or laying of blame or absurd rationalizations. Amish parents are generally strict with their children; obedience is ingrained at a young age and enforced with 'smackings' when necessary.

Sadie is past the age where a smacking would be effective. But I have no doubt she will be punished for her disobedience, more than likely by the assignment of some unpleasant chore. I wonder if it will be enough.

I'm tired, still thinking about Sadie, on my way to the station to file my end-of-shift reports when my cell phone chirps. Mild annoyance transforms into pleasure when I see Tomasetti's name on the display, and I pull on my headset. 'Morning, Agent.'

'I called earlier and got voice mail. Everything okay?'

'Sorry. Got tied up with a stop.'

'Cows?'

'Worse,' I tell him. 'Teenagers.'

'That *is* worse.'

'At least with cows, you know what you're getting.'

'Less bullshit anyway.'

John Tomasetti is an agent with the Ohio Bureau of Criminal Identification and Investigation in Cleveland. We met a year and a half ago, when he assisted with the Slaughterhouse Murders case. It was a tumultuous time for both of us, not only professionally but personally. His wife and two children had been murdered just nine months before, and he was an emotional basket case. He'd been taking some heavy-duty prescription drugs and mixing them with alcohol, a coping mechanism run amok that had put his career on the skids and sent his life careening out of control. There were probably other things going on as well that he didn't see fit to reveal. But then, people like us excel at keeping secrets, especially when they're big ones.

It was my first major case as chief, and my personal connection to the killer made for an extremely stressful investigation. The murders themselves were shocking and brutal – the things of nightmares. Somehow, in the course of all that depravity and blood, Tomasetti and I became allies. We became friends and, later, lovers. In the end, we broke that damn case wide open.

'Have you slept?' He knows I covered the graveyard shift last night.

'I'm heading home as soon as I file reports.' In the back of my mind, I'm wondering if he's going to drive down. If he's got the weekend off and wants to spend some time with me. It's been a month since I last saw him. Something inside me surges at the thought, but I quickly bank it. I'm still reluctant to trust any emotion that packs so much power and comes with such ease.

'I just got handed a case,' he tells me. 'I was wondering if you'd be interested in coming up to consult.'

For a moment, I'm too shocked to answer. The request is unusual in the extreme. I'm a small-town chief of police. I spend my days mediating domestic disputes, breaking up fights, and investigating the occasional theft. Small-town crime. Why would he need me when he has a plethora of sophisticated resources at his fingertips through BCI? 'This doesn't have anything to do with cows, does it?' I ask.

He chuckles. 'Missing persons. Two so far, but the case is developing.'

'That's not exactly my area of expertise.'

'It is if they're Amish.'

My curiosity flares. 'You've got my attention.'

'I have two missing teenagers from two towns within a one-hundred-mile radius. We're just now putting things together. I'm going on-site, and I'll need to conduct interviews with the families as soon as possible. I thought you might be able to offer some insight.'

No one is more aware than I am of the divide that exists between the Amish and English communities. It's a divide that runs even deeper when it comes to law enforcement, particularly an outside agency such as BCI. My intimate knowledge of the plain life, combined with my fluency in Pennsylvania Dutch, will go a long way with regard to bridging the gap and encouraging the Amish to speak freely.

I pull over in front of the Butterhorn Bakery and give the call my full attention. 'Where did these disappearances occur?'

'Latest was in Rocky Fork. Small town about fifty miles from Cleveland.'

I take a deep breath, trying not to be too flattered. 'I'm interested.'

'Interested enough to drive up?'

'You mean now?'

'Clock's ticking. I thought we could meet here in Richfield. Take care of the red tape. Introduce you to the suits. There'll be a formal briefing. Some forms to sign. They'll supply you with a temporary ID. You up for it?'

A sensation that's a little too close to excitement flashes in my chest. 'Let me tie up some things here. When's the briefing?'

'As soon as you get here. Call me.'

I start to give him a time frame, but he disconnects. I sit there for a few seconds, smiling stupidly, energized by the prospect of consulting for such a well-respected agency. But I know most of what I'm feeling has more to do with John Tomasetti than it does with BCI. I don't know if that's good or bad. But it's honest, and I resolve not to analyze it any more closely than that.

My mind jumps ahead to the tasks I need to complete before I leave. I'll need to brief my team, speak to the mayor, get my shifts covered. We're chronically understaffed in Painters Mill. But Skid – the officer I stood in for last night – is due back today. I was scheduled to have the weekend off. It could work.

Sleep forgotten, I hit my radio and hail Mona. She answers with a perky 'Painters Mill PD!'

'Hey, it's me.'

'What's up, Chief?'

'I want you to call the guys in for a quick briefing.'

'This morning? What's going on?'

I recap my conversation with Tomasetti. 'See if you can get everyone there within the hour. I'm going to swing by the house for a quick shower and to pack a bag.'

It takes me an hour to shower and pack enough clothes for a few days on the road. I'm no fashionista – not by any stretch of the imagination – so it takes me a good bit of time to figure out which clothes to take. Usually, I wear the old standby: my police uniform. We're talking basic navy with a leather shoulder holster. No frills. After three years of being chief, that's the way I've come to identify myself, at least with regard to style. This consulting stint promises to take me out of my comfort zone by a couple of light-years. That's not to mention the issue of Tomasetti. I may not be into the whole fashion thing, but I'm still a woman. I might have grown up Amish, but there's a small part of me that is vain.

I opt for business-casual and go with the khaki boot-cut slacks, black trousers, and a pair of blue jeans. A couple of blazers and a few camis, a blouse, some nice T-shirts. Impatient with myself for taking so long when I still have a one-hundred-mile drive ahead, I forgo jewelry, toss my toiletries into the bag, and head for the door.

I call Mayor Auggie Brock on my way to the station and break the news, going heavy on the 'This will improve our relationship with an important state law-enforcement agency' angle.

'How long will you be gone?' is, predictably, his first question.

'I'm not sure,' I tell him. 'Two or three days.'

He makes a noise that tells me he's not happy about the situation. But he knows he can't say no, because for three years I've forgone vacations and, most weeks, a day off. I'm well within bounds to push the issue if needed.

'You'll have to do this on your own time,' he tells me. 'I mean, you'll need to take vacation days. And of course we can't afford travel funds for you. We've got budget constraints.'

'They pay a daily stipend and expenses.'

'That's good.' I can practically hear him thinking this over, weighing all the pros and cons, trying to think of a worse-case scenario.

An awkward silence ensues. I'm trying to think of a way to end the call, when he broaches the one subject I'd wanted to avoid. 'Before you leave,' he says after a moment. 'I've been meaning to call you about Bradford. I mean, about the charges.'

'Auggie—'

'He's a minor . . . a good kid with his whole life ahead of him.'

'Everything's already been turned over to the county attorney. You know that.'

'You could . . . pull the charges.'

' "Pull the charges"?' Incredulity rings in my voice; this is nervy even for Auggie. 'We caught him with drug paraphernalia and an ounce of pot. He slugged one of my officers. T.J. had to get stitches, Auggie. There's no undoing that.'

'There were extenuating circumstances. Bradford was upset about—'

I don't know Bradford Brock, but I read the police report. The so-called good kid had enough marijuana on his person to supply the high school potheads for a month. The blood test that came back confirmed that he was high on methamphetamines, as well.

'Stress over a high school government exam isn't considered extenuating circumstances,' I tell him.

'Look, I'm finding it difficult to believe my son had an entire ounce of marijuana on him. Perhaps T.J. . . . . overreacted. Maybe you could . . . correct his report. At least with regard to the amount of pot.'

The conversation has taken a path I have no desire to tread. Uneasiness presses down on me. 'I don't think we should go there, Auggie.'

'I have to go there. He's my son.' He sighs. 'Come on, Kate. Work with me here.'

'What, exactly, are you asking me to do?'

'Nothing that doesn't happen every day.' He pauses. 'Come on. Reports get lost. Evidence gets lost. It happens all the time. It would mean the world to me and my wife if you could make this go away.'

'You're asking me to cross a line, Auggie.'

'Kate, I'm desperate. This situation has been a nightmare. If Bradford is tried as an adult and convicted, these charges could ruin his life. He'll have a record.'

That's when I realize this is an argument I'm doomed to lose. Auggie Brock is, indirectly, my boss. But he's also a father, and I know better than most that blood always trumps lesser loyalties, which include right and wrong.

'For God's sake, Catherine is going to have a breakdown over this. You should have called me instead of arresting him! Why didn't you let me take care of it?'

'*Take care of it?*' I take a deep breath, close my eyes briefly, remind myself Auggie is a good man who's been placed in an untenable situation by someone he loves. 'I'm going to pretend we never had this conversation.'

The line goes dead before I finish.

Shaking my head, I drop the phone onto the console. I feel compassion for Auggie and his wife. But there's no way I'm going to falsify police records or 'lose' evidence to keep his snot-nosed punk of a son out of jail. As far as I'm concerned, a stint in juvenile hall might be the kick in the pants the kid needs to get back on the right track.

A few minutes later, I arrive at the police station and park in my usual spot. The department is housed in a century-old redbrick building replete with drafty windows, noisy plumbing, and an array of unexplained odors, most of which are unpleasant. Mona and Lois hide air fresheners in creative places, but the reception area invariably smells of old plasterboard, rotting wood, and maybe a dead mouse or two. The decor looks like something out of an old *Dragnet* episode. And I don't mean retro cool, but truly butt ugly. The town council *did* spring for a new desk and computer for our dispatch station a couple of months ago. But only because the old computer went up in flames – literally.

My conversation with Auggie niggles at me as I enter. Mona Kurtz sits at the reception station, hunched over her computer with her headset on and the mouthpiece pushed aside. She's eating grapes out of a Baggie with her left hand, clutching the mouse with her right. As usual, the volume on her radio is turned up a little too high and she's tapping her fingers to a funky Linkin Park number.

I'm midway to her desk when she spots me. Offering a quick smile, she flicks off the radio and plucks a dozen or so pink slips from my message slot. 'You're a wanted woman this morning, Chief.'

'And it's not even ten A.M.'

'Ever think about cloning yourself?'

'Somehow, I don't think the world is ready for two of me,' I tell her.

Her hair is a slightly darker shade of black today, with a contrasting burgundy stripe on the left side of her crown. She's wearing skinny black pants with a snug T-shirt and a blue scarf that's tied around her neck like a noose. I'm glad I can't see her shoes from where I'm standing.

I page through messages. One from Tomasetti. Two from Auggie. Six from Kathleen McClanahan. It takes me a moment to place the name and then I realize she's the mother of Angi, the girl from earlier this morning. 'McClanahan mention what she wants?'

'You mean aside from your head on a stick?'

I chuckle. 'She's going to have to stand in line.'

'I swear, Chief, that woman can cuss. It was like being at an auction.'

'There's something to look forward to.' I start toward my office. 'Let me know when everyone's here.'

'Roger that.'

I grab a cup, fill it to the rim with coffee, and drink half of it down hot on the way to my office. Using my key, I open the door and flip on the light. The odors of paper dust and toner greet me when I walk in. It's a small space, not much bigger than a walk-in closet, with bad lighting and a dingy window that looks out over Main Street. It's jam-packed with a metal desk, a mismatched file cabinet, two hotel-fare visitor chairs, a half-dead ficus tree, and a bookcase upon which a broken coffeemaker sits. Shortcomings aside, this is my home away from home, and most days I'm unduly glad to be here.

Dropping my overnight bag at the door, I go directly to my desk and dial Sheriff Rasmussen's number from memory. I've known the sheriff for almost a year now. We've drunk a few beers together and butted heads a couple of times, but he's a decent man and a good cop. We worked closely together during the Slabaugh case last December. It was a difficult investigation, during which four people lost their lives, shattering a family and shaking everyone involved, including me. Especially me. It was the first time in the course of my career I used deadly force. I'm still dealing with the aftermath of that, mostly in the form of nightmares. On bad days, I still flash back to the moment I pulled the trigger, and I wonder if I could have done something different.

I keep tabs on the surviving children. Not as any kind of penance – that's what I tell myself anyway – but because I care. I want to make sure they have everything they need and every opportunity they deserve.

On the phone, I hear Rasmussen's voice telling me to leave a message, and I can't help but think, *Golf day*. I let him know I'm going to be out of town for a few days and ask him to look in on my department. I leave my cell number and tell him to contact Glock if he needs anything in my absence.

I'm in the process of hanging up when Mona buzzes me and lets me know my team has arrived. I hit the power button on my desktop to begin the lengthy process of booting up, then start for the conference room. Officer Chuck 'Skid' Skidmore meets me in the hall. He's about thirty years old, unmarried, and has a sense of humor most civilians don't appreciate. He's originally from Ann Arbor, Michigan, and had a promising career with the police department there – until he lost his job due to an off-duty DUI. I took him on, with the caveat that if I ever caught him drinking on the job, I'd fire him on the spot and do my utmost to make sure he never worked in law enforcement again. He's been with the department for three years now and has never breached our agreement.

Eight months ago, he was shot during a sting I set up to catch a killer. He sustained a nonpenetrating head wound, which left him with a concussion and a gash that required stitches. Every now and then, we still rib him about the thickness of his skull, but he takes it in stride. What I like most about Skid is that while he might be one of my less personable officers, I know that if things get dicey, I can count on him to back me up.

'How was the trip?' I ask.

'About two days too long.'

'You were only gone two days.'

'Yeah.' He grins. 'Thanks for covering for me, Chief.'

'Your parents doing okay?'

'They're fine. Glad to see me, if you can imagine that.'

A deep male voice cuts in. 'They were lying about being glad to see you, dude.'

Glock stops next to Skid. The two men shake hands and then Glock turns his attention to me. 'This guy told you he was going to Michigan?'

'That's a likely story,' Mona mutters as she squeezes past.

'He was probably down at the Brass Rail boozing it up,' Glock says with a grin. 'I'd fire his ass.'

'Who's getting fired?' comes a gravelly voice from behind us.

We turn, to see Roland 'Pickles' Shumaker shuffle toward us, his gnarled hands clutching mismatched mugs filled with coffee. At the age of seventy-five, he's my only auxiliary officer and works part-time – when I can get him to go home, that is. During the 1980s, Pickles single-handedly brought down one of the largest methamphetamine rings in the state. He's slowed down the last couple of years, but he's still a good cop. In fact, if it hadn't been for the pressure I received from the town council, he'd still be full-time. But several of the more vocal members felt he was too old to be an effective police officer – mainly due to an incident in which he shot and killed a rooster during a call. The case caused an uproar, not only from the dead rooster's owner but from some of the community, as well. I couldn't see letting Pickles go after nearly fifty years of service, especially over a dead chicken. So I met with him privately and asked him to go part-time. He pretended to be pleased about 'not working so damn many hours.' But I know he misses being in the thick of things.

Despite the fact that he's not on the clock this morning, he's wearing a uniform and his trademark pointy-toed cowboy boots are buffed to a high sheen. I suspect he'll still be at his desk in his cubicle when the sun goes down. . . .

'No one's getting fired,' I tell him.

'Good thing,' he grumbles. ''Cause I ain't shot no damn chickens lately.'

I keep walking.

At the podium, I set down my mug and scan the room. My eyes land on Mona and her counterpart, Lois, who are seated near the door so they can hear the switchboard and radio.

'Where's T.J.?' I ask.

'I'm here.'

T.J. appears at the door, looking dapper and fresh in his crisp blue uniform. At twenty-five, he's my youngest officer and the only rookie in the department. He receives a good bit of teasing, but he's a good sport and generally serious about his work. When I need someone for overtime, he's my go-to man.

'Sorry I'm late, Chief.'

I nod. 'I'll let it slide since this is – was – your day off.'

Chuckling, he takes the chair beside Glock.

I look around the room. 'I'm sorry to have called everyone in on such short notice this morning, but I wanted to let you know I'm going to be consulting for BCI for a few days. Apparently, there have been some disappearances in the northeastern part of the state. The reason I've been asked to consult is because the missing persons are Amish.'

A collective sound of surprise sweeps the room. I feel the rise of interest and continue before the questions come. 'As of now, the agency doesn't know if these disappearances are connected, but the speculation is that they are.' I glance at my watch. 'I'll be leaving in a few minutes.'

I give Glock a pointed look. 'You're in charge while I'm gone.'

He gives me a two-finger salute.

'I've got my cell and I'm available twenty-four/seven if anyone needs anything.' I survey my department, and a rolling wave of pride sweeps over me. 'Try not to shoot anyone while I'm gone.' I smile at Pickles. 'That includes chickens.'

THREE

I'm twenty minutes out of Richfield when Tomasetti calls. It's a good thing the town council approved wireless headsets for the department last month, because I've spent much of this trip on the phone. I've spoken once with Sheriff Rasmussen, once with Auggie – who apologized for his 'inappropriate' comments earlier – and I've had four decidedly unpleasant conversations with Kathleen McClanahan. Mona was right: The woman curses with the speed of an auctioneer hawking wares at an estate sale. McClanahan ended the call by threatening to sue me for 'roughing up' her little girl and then hanging up on me.

I catch Tomasetti's call on the third ring. 'I'm almost there,' I say by way of greeting.

'We've got another one,' he says. 'Fifteen-year-old female. Happened last night. Local law enforcement called ten minutes ago.'

'Where?'

'Buck Creek, a small town about an hour northeast of here.'

'She's Amish?'

'Family searched for her all night.'

'And they're just now contacting the police, because they thought they could handle it themselves.' My voice is bone-dry.

'See? I knew you'd be a benefit to the case.'

'Who's the vic?'

Paper rattles on the other end of the line, and I know he's paging through the file. 'Annie King. Parents sent her to a vegetable stand and she never made it home.'

He pauses and I sense he's champing at the bit and ready to go – and I'm holding up the show. The first forty-eight hours are the most crucial in terms of solving any case, but that's particularly true when dealing with a missing child. Two of the kidnappings are cold. This one is fresh; we're still within that golden period.

'I've got everyone rounded up here,' he tells me. 'We're just going to bring you in. Do the introductions. HR will have a couple of forms for you. Then we're on our way.'

'I'll be there in ten minutes.'

'I'll meet you at the door.'

It's just after noon when I turn onto Highlander Parkway. I'm not nervous, but an edginess creeps steadily over me as I draw closer to the BCI field office. Like Tomasetti, I'm keenly aware of the ticking clock and anxious to get started. I want to visit the scene and speak to the missing girl's family. I want to find the girl before something terrible happens – if it hasn't already.

I remind myself that I'm only going to be consulting, and I can't help but wonder what kind of parameters I'll be working within. I'm hands-on when it comes to my job. How difficult will it be to ride this out in the backseat?

To complicate matters, there's also the issue of my relationship with Tomasetti. We're walking a fine line, working together on a case while we're personally involved. Nobody knows, and for now we would be wise to keep it that way. I'm confident neither of us will let private feelings affect the case. But I'd be lying if I said I wasn't looking forward to spending some time with him.

I park in the visitor section of the lot, grab my overnight bag, and head toward the double glass doors at the front of the building. The uniformed security officer behind a glossy walnut desk stands as I approach.

'Can I help you?'

She's a trim African-American woman wearing a navy jacket, a chrome badge clipped to her belt, and a name tag that tells me her name is Gabrielle. 'I'm Kate Burkholder. I have an appointment to see John Tomasetti with BCI.'

'He's called twice. Hold on.' She's in the process of dialing when I hear my name. I turn, to see Tomasetti treading toward me with long, purposeful strides. Pleasure unfurls in my stomach at the sight of his tall frame. As usual, he's well dressed in a crisp blue shirt with a gray-and-burgundy tie and nicely cut charcoal slacks.

I can't help it; I smile. 'Agent Tomasetti.'

His expression softens. 'Chief Burkholder.' He glances at the security officer. 'Thanks, Gabby.'

She waves him off, but not before I see something in her eyes, and I realize I'm not the only one who likes my men dark and brooding and just a little bit on the shady side.

'How was the drive?' he asks, extending his hand.

'Uneventful.'

'Best kind, I guess.' We shake, and I notice several things at once. His palm is warm and dry. His grip is substantial. He's looking at me a tad too closely and perhaps with a little too much intensity, both of which I like. 'You look nice,' he says in a low voice.

'So do you.'

Amusement crinkles the outer corners of his eyes. He holds on to my hand an instant too long before motioning toward the bank of elevators. 'Let's get this show on the road.'

We head toward the elevator. He starts to take my overnight

bag but then thinks better of it, and I realize he doesn't want anyone getting the wrong impression about us, particularly his superiors. I heft the bag onto my shoulder and pretend not to notice the awkwardness of the moment.

We wait for the elevator in silence and without looking at each other. Then the doors swish open and we step inside. He taps the button for the second floor and the doors whisper closed. We're alone; the only sound is the Muzak flowing down from an overhead speaker, mangling an old Sting song. I'm keenly aware of Tomasetti standing next to me, but my mind has already jumped ahead to meeting his superiors, the impression I want to make, the benefits I will bring to the case. Less than a second into the ride up, Tomasetti turns to me, sets his hands on my shoulders. The next thing I know, my back is against the wall and his mouth is on mine. Shock punches me with such force that for an instant my knees go weak. The Muzak fades to babble, but my heartbeat becomes a roar in my ears. Vaguely, I'm aware of the car moving ever upward, the firm pressure of his lips against mine, the taste of peppermint and coffee and the man I've missed for weeks now. I'm about to put my arms around him, when he pulls back, gazes down at me. 'Welcome to Richfield,' he says quietly.

'You're all business this morning.' My laugh sounds nervous and my voice is breathy and thin. 'They don't have security cameras in these elevators, do they?'

'I checked.'

'So this was premeditated.'

'Cameras in the halls upstairs, though.'

'In case I feel the need to throw myself at you.'

'I thought you might have a hard time resisting.'

We smile at each other and then the doors swish open. No time to think about what just transpired. My heart is still riding high in my throat when we step into a well-lit hall lined with a dozen or so doors, most of which are open. Government-issue artwork adorns institutional white walls. I see an Ansel Adams photo in a black frame; a color photograph of Ohio's attorney general; a matted and framed mosaic of the great seal of the state of Ohio; a photo collage of agents killed in the line of duty. At the end of the hall, Tomasetti motions me to the right and we stop outside a door affixed with a chrome plate that says CONFERENCE ROOM 1.

'I'll try to make this as quick as possible,' he says.

I wipe my damp palms on my slacks. 'I'll try not to look like I just got waylaid in the elevator.'

He tosses me a sideways look, and then we're through the doorway and entering the conference room. Two men and a woman sit at a heavy oak table. They look up, their eyes skimming quickly over Tomasetti and then settling on me, curious, assessing, making judgments based on appearance and demeanor, psyching me out. I know the routine; I've done it myself to many a rookie over the years. I discern immediately the two men are law enforcement. Bad suits. Stares that are slightly too direct. The woman is in her early thirties, well dressed, with expensive jewelry and a nice manicure. I peg her as administrative but sense she prefers to hang with the guys.

Tomasetti doesn't waste any time. 'This is Chief of Police Kate Burkholder,' he says by way of introduction.

The men stand. A tall, lanky man with blue eyes and a bulbous nose threaded with broken capillaries extends his hand to me. 'I'm Lawrence Bates, the deputy superintendent.' He lowers his voice conspiratorially. 'Which basically means I have to put up with Tomasetti most days.'

I grin, liking him. 'Tough job.'

He chuckles as I turn my attention to the second man, and we shake. His grip is a little too firm and damp. 'Denny McNinch.'

His stare is calculating. There's baggage in his expression, perhaps even between him and Tomasetti. He's got a battered look about him that has nothing to do with physical scars. And I know that before he sat behind a desk, he spent a good bit of time on the street. 'Nice to meet you,' I tell him.

'Denny's out of the Columbus office,' says Tomasetti, clarifying.

Baggage, I think. Tomasetti worked out of the Columbus office after leaving the Cleveland PD. He'd had some problems there early on, nearly got himself fired. I can tell by McNinch's stare that he knows about it. I can also tell by the way he's looking at me that he's wondering if there's something going on between Tomasetti and me. Or maybe I just have a guilty conscience.

'Welcome aboard, Chief Burkholder,' he says, releasing my hand.

Bates takes command of the meeting and gets right to the business at hand. 'We're pleased you're here, Chief Burkholder. I'm sure John has already filled you in on the situation.'

I nod. 'I understand there's now a third person missing.'

'We just got the call from local law enforcement in Buck Creek,' Bates says. 'I know you're anxious to get started, so we'll keep this brief.'

McNinch motions to the woman, who has remained seated throughout the introductions but hasn't taken her eyes off me since I walked in. 'This is Paige Wilson, my assistant. She's got a couple of forms for you to sign, Chief Burkholder. We've got to keep all of this on the up-and-up with Uncle Sam.'

'Call me Kate.'

Nodding, he motions to the forms on the table. 'We pay a small stipend, plus mileage, expenses.'

The forms are in typical government triplicate. The pages that require a signature are marked with red flags. Everyone's in a hurry, so I give the forms a cursory read-through and scribble my name.

When I've finished, Bates says, 'I've wanted to meet you since Tomasetti assisted with the Slaughterhouse Murders. Hell of a case for a small town.'

'It was a tough one.' The very thought of that investigation and all its gnarly implications still makes the hairs on the back of my neck stand up. 'Agent Tomasetti was a tremendous help to the entire department.'

'He tells us you used to be Amish,' McNinch says.

That's always the thing everyone wants to know. They don't care about my résumé or law-enforcement background or my degree in criminal justice. They don't ask about my solve rate from when I was a detective in Columbus. They want to know if I was Amish; if I wore homemade dresses and rode in a horse-drawn buggy and lived my life without electricity and cars. 'I grew up Amish,' I say simply.

In my peripheral vision, I see the woman lean slightly to one side, and I wonder if she's checking to see if I'm wearing practical shoes.

'I understand you're also fluent in Pennsylvania Dutch,' McNinch says.

I nod. 'That's particularly beneficial, especially with regard to breaking down some of the cultural barriers.'

'So far we're batting zero in the way of garnering much useful information,' Bates says.

'Local law enforcement isn't getting much from the Amish families,' Tomasetti adds, clarifying the matter.

'Unfortunately, that's not unusual,' I tell them. 'There's a certain level of distrust between the Amish and the government, particularly law enforcement. We ran into that when we had a rash of hate crimes last December.' I don't look at Tomasetti as I speak. I'm afraid if I do, somehow these men will know that we're more than colleagues, more than friends. 'The Amish are also slow in making contact with us because of their tenet of remaining separate. But there are also cultural issues. Religious issues.' I think of the chasm that stretches between me and my siblings. I don't mention the fact that sometimes even if you're born into the plain life, you can still be an outsider. 'Generally speaking, once we convince the family we have only their best interest at heart, they'll open up, especially if the safety of a loved one is in question.'

'Excellent.' Bates slides a folder across the table toward me. 'We're still putting things together, Kate, so the file is sparse.'

Intrigued, I open the file and find myself staring down at three missing-person reports. Bates was right: The information is hit-or-miss. The missing consist of three females between the ages of sixteen and eighteen, all of whom are Amish.

'We think their being Amish is the key element here,' McNinch says.

'Do you think this is a serial thing?' I ask. 'And this is some kind of escalation?'

Tomasetti nods. 'Maybe.'

'What we can't figure is motive,' Bates says.

'No ransom demand,' Tomasetti puts in.

'Yet,' Bates adds.

'Anything come to mind off the top of your head?' McNinch asks.

I look up from the reports and make eye contact with him. 'I'm sure you've already considered this, but the first thing that comes to mind is that these are sexual in nature.' I think of the Plank murder case and all of the dark places the investigation took me. 'It could be fetish-related. An individual with an Amish fetish acting out some fantasy. His motivation has more to do with the victims' being Amish than anything else.'

'I didn't know such a thing existed,' McNinch comments.

'We're running queries through NCIC and VICAP,' Tomasetti says. 'We're still waiting for results.'

'There's also the hate angle,' I tell them. 'It's happened in Painters Mill. I know of cases in other towns, too.'

'I guess hate crimes don't have to make sense.' Bates scratches his head. 'But the Amish? Seems like they'd make pretty good neighbors.'

'Some people don't like the religion and see them as fanatical or cultlike. Some don't like them because the horse and buggies hold up traffic.' I shrug. 'You name it and there's probably some nutcase out there who thinks it.'

'Have you ever dealt with any kidnappings with regard to the Amish?' McNinch asks.

I shake my head. 'Suspects?'

Bates shakes his head. 'Nada.'

'Anything at any of the scenes?' I ask.

'We don't have a scene,' Tomasetti replies. 'These kids disappeared without a trace. We don't know where the actual kidnappings – if, in fact, that's what we're dealing with – took place.'

I look down at the file. The part of me that is a cop is intrigued by the puzzle. I want to know what happened and why. I want to find the person responsible, go head-to-head with whoever it is. I want to stop him. Bring him to justice. But the more human part of me – the part of me that is Amish and knows the culture with such intimacy – is outraged by what has been done and frightened by the possibilities. 'What about the victims? Aside from being Amish, do they share any other common threads?'

'Not that we've found, but we're still gathering information,' McNinch says.

'Analyst is looking at everything now,' Tomasetti adds.

'Once we arrive on-scene, we'll talk to the families. That's where you come in.'

I nod. 'That's where we're going to get the brunt of our information. The families. Friends.'

'We haven't been able to get our hands on photos,' Bates adds.

'Most Amish won't have photos of their children,' I tell him.

He stares at me blankly, and I realize he's probably not an Ohio native. 'Most Amish don't like to have their photos taken,' I tell him. 'They feel it's a vain display of pride. Some of the more conservative have biblical beliefs that keep them from having any kind of likeness done.'

'We've brought in the state Highway Patrol,' Bates says. 'They wanted photos, but all we could give them were physical descriptions.'

'If the parents will cooperate, we may be able to get a sketch done,' I offer as an alternative. But everyone knows a sketch takes time and isn't as helpful as a photo.

'Say the word and we'll get someone down there,' Bates says.

Tomasetti glances at his watch, and I know he's sending his superiors a not-so-subtle message to hurry this along so we can get on the road.

'Has local law enforcement talked to the parents?' I ask.

Tomasetti nods. 'I talked to the sheriff. He didn't get much. Apparently, the parents are as baffled as we are.'

McNinch scrubs a hand over his head. 'No reflection on small-town law enforcement, but I suspect these people are out of their league. You know, small departments with minimal resources. They're understaffed. The sheriff sold vacuum cleaners before he took the job, for Chrissake. No offense, Kate, but the majority of these guys just don't have the experience for this kind of investigation.'

'None taken.' I smile at him. 'Just FYI, I've never sold vacuum cleaners.'

McNinch chuckles. 'Then you're not out of your depth.'

I hope not, a small voice inside me whispers.

FOUR

Fifteen minutes later, Tomasetti and I are on the road in his Tahoe, heading east on the Ohio Turnpike toward Buck Creek, Ohio, where the most recent disappearance took place. The town is located near the Mosquito Creek Wilderness area in the northeastern part of the state. It's about an hour from the Richfield office, through pretty countryside dotted with small towns, farms, and miles of tall hardwood forest. Tomasetti drives well over the speed limit, which takes a bite out of the drive time. At Newton Falls, we cut north on Interstate 5 and pass through Cortland, then take a less-traveled state highway toward Buck Creek.

Fifteen minutes later, a sign welcomes us: THE HUNTING CAPITAL OF OHIO, POPULATION 1,200. The first thing I notice about the town are the trees. Ancient buckeyes, maples, and elms line the main drag, their massive trunks nearly obscuring the buildings from view. We pass a manufacturing park where Erie Overhead Door and Whittle Plastics share a gravel lot that's jam-packed with cars and trucks. The downtown area is quaint, with redbrick storefronts, hanging pots overflowing with petunias, and an old-fashioned cobblestone street. We pass half a dozen antiques shops, two sporting-goods stores, a bank that looks like something out of the Bonnie and Clyde era, and *The Early Bird* newspaper.

We turn left at the traffic light, pass a massive Lutheran church and the Buck Creek High School, home of the Fighting Panthers, and then we're on a twisty two-lane road, heading out of town. Trees encroach onto the shoulders of the road, the canopies blocking the sun, so that only the occasional shaft of light flashes across the windshield. It's cooler here, perhaps because of our proximity to the lake, and Tomasetti flicks off the air conditioning. I'm in the process of opening my window when his cell erupts.

He thumbs a button, then growls his name into his Bluetooth. 'Where?' he snaps after a moment. Then: 'We're on the way.'

He ends the call, then shoots me a look. 'Do you want the good news or the bad news?' he asks.

'Let's start with the good,' I reply.

'I just took a call from the sheriff. We have our first scene.'

'That is good news.' Other than catching someone red-handed, or finding the missing, having a scene from which to extract evidence is the best news we could receive at this point. 'What's the bad news?'

'There's blood. According to the sheriff, a lot of it.'

'Shit.'

'Yeah.'

'Anything else?'

'Locals are there, looking around. I'm going to get a CSU down here.'

'How far?'

'A couple of miles from here.'

'That's one of the things I like about small towns,' I tell him. 'Never far to the scene of the crime.'

A mile down the road, we turn onto a narrow asphalt track.

A quarter mile in, a Trumbull County sheriff's cruiser with its emergency lights flashing is parked on the gravel shoulder. Two additional cruisers straddle the road at haphazard angles, blocking both lanes. A uniformed deputy drops orange caution cones to divert traffic. Another strings yellow crime-scene tape, using the trees that grow alongside the road and the tops of the cones to cordon off the area.

Tomasetti stops a good distance from the scene and pulls onto the gravel shoulder. We exit simultaneously and head toward the nearest cruiser.

The air is cool and clean and filled with a cacophony of birdsong. We're in the midst of a forest that turns midday into twilight. The thick underbrush forms a seemingly impenetrable wall on both sides of the roadway. The area is shadowed and humid and has the feel of some vast wilderness – or a place where something bad could happen and no one would ever know. Aside from the occasional crackle of a police radio, it's so quiet, I can hear the buzz of insects.

'I'm sorry, folks, but the road's closed.'

I look up to see a large man in plainclothes striding toward us, his expression grim. He's about forty years old, with a military buzz cut and a handlebar mustache that looks touched up to cover the gray. He's wearing khaki trousers, a white shirt with the underarms sweated through, and a leather shoulder holster with a nice-looking Taurus .380 sticking out of its leather sheath. He looks more like the Hollywood version of a private detective than a county sheriff, and I get the impression he's a hit with the ladies – a fact that doesn't elude him.

He motions in the direction from which we came. 'You're going to have to turn around and take the township road.'

His voice trails off when Tomasetti holds up his identification. 'We're with BCI.'

The man's expression softens and I see a flash of relief. 'I thought you two looked kind of official.' Chortling, he sticks out his hand. 'I'm Sheriff Bud Goddard.'

Tomasetti makes the introductions, and I show my temporary ID, which was issued to me just this morning.

Goddard pumps my hand with a little too much enthusiasm, and I know he's genuinely glad we're here. 'You're that Amish police chief nabbed that serial killer a few years back.' His voice is as deep and melodic as that of a bass opera singer.

'Formerly Amish,' I tell him. 'Agent Tomasetti thought I might be able to lend a hand.'

'Well, them Amishers do prefer to keep to themselves.' He motions toward the scene, where a deputy is talking on his cell. I wince upon spotting what looks like dirty motor oil from a blown engine spilled on the road. But I know it's not. 'As soon as we finish up here,' he tells us, 'I'd like to drive out there and talk to the family. They don't have a phone. Sure would appreciate it if you came along. They're the damnedest lot to interview, if you know what I mean.'

The words come at me like a cockeyed blow, not a direct hit, but just enough to chafe my sensibilities. He's right, but that doesn't make me like the generality any less.

Tomasetti is staring in the direction of the stained roadway. 'Who discovered the scene?'

'Motorist spotted a bag on the road about an hour ago. When he got out to take a look, he found all that blood. He remembered hearing about the missing girl and called nine one one.'

'That's a lot of blood,' I say. *Too much*, a little voice whispers in the back of my mind.

The sheriff grimaces. 'If it's hers, I suspect that girl's either hurt bad or dead. Course, we got a lot of deer around here. Damn things get hit all the time. We looked around and didn't find a carcass, but I suppose it's possible it ran off. You guys got any kind of field test that will tell us if it's animal or human?'

Tomasetti nods. 'Not with me, but I'll call the CSU and tell them to grab an RSID kit. It's pretty quick, so we should get an answer right away.'

'That'd be a tremendous help. At least we'll know what we're dealing with.' Goddard looks toward the bloodstain and shakes his head. 'We think the bag belongs to the missing girl. During the initial interview, her parents said she was carrying one. We'll run it over there and see if they can ID it.'

As if by some unspoken mutual agreement, the three of us start toward the pool of blood. Around us, the tempo of the forest seems to increase, pulsing with birdsong, cicadas, and other insects. The *whoit whoit whoit* of a cardinal echoes off the thick canopy overhead. The air is heavy and still and smells of damp foliage. As we draw closer to the stain, I discern the buzz of hundreds of flies. They're feeding on the blood, I realize.

The stain is a red-black slick nearly four feet in diameter, mostly dry now, except for the center. I can smell the deep copper scent of it. At least one vehicle has driven through it, leaving a decent impression of the tread. The CSU will take tire-tread imprints, but my gut tells me that more than likely they were made by an inattentive motorist who simply didn't notice. At some point, some small animal left paw prints at a place where it may have lapped at the blood.

It's a macabre scene in the crepuscular light. Like the sheriff, I hope for some benign explanation – a deer struck by a car. But in my gut, I know it's human blood. I know something terrible happened here. In light of the fabric satchel lying a few feet away, I'm pretty sure it happened to the missing girl.

I look at Tomasetti. 'Is that a fatal amount?'

He grimaces. 'Hard to tell. Maybe.'

'She could have been walking alongside the road and got hit by a car,' Goddard says, but he doesn't look convinced.

'With that kind of scenario, it seems like internal injuries would be a more likely result,' I say.

'And there's no body,' says Tomasetti.

'Maybe whoever hit her put her in the car,' Goddard offers. 'Took her to the hospital.'

'No skid marks,' I say.

'Unless it wasn't an accident.' Tomasetti glances at the sheriff. 'Did you check area hospitals?'

Goddard nods. 'I've got my secretary checking.'

Around us, the forest goes silent, as if in reverence, due to the violence that transpired just a short time ago in this very spot.

Tomasetti scans the surrounding woods. 'Do you have the manpower to search the area?'

'I can probably round up some volunteers.' Goddard unclips his phone from his belt but then pauses to indicate the tire marks. 'What do you think about those?'

Tomasetti squats and studies the tread mark. 'CSU might be able to lift tread imprints. If we can match those to a manufacturer, we might catch a break.'

'How old do you think this blood is?' Goddard asks.

Tomasetti shakes his head. 'There's quite a bit of drying around the edges. Spatter is dry.' He looks up, and I realize he's trying to figure out how much sun gets past the trees. 'Doesn't get much sun here. It's humid. I'd say six or seven hours.'

The sheriff jerks his head. 'I'll get to work on those volunteers.'

Stepping away from the scene, Tomasetti pulls out his phone, punches in numbers, and begins speaking quietly.

I study the scene, trying to envision what might have

happened. The bag lies on the gravel shoulder, about four feet from the bloodstain. A couple of ears of sweet corn still wrapped in their husks have spilled out of it, looking out of place on the asphalt. I cross to the bag for a closer look. It's a satchel made of quilted fabric – an Amish print – and looks homemade. My *mamm* had a similar one when I was a kid; she used it when she went to the grocery store or into town for supplies.

Pulling a pen from my jacket pocket, I squat next to the bag and use the pen to open it and peer inside. I see green peppers, another ear of sweet corn, and tomatoes that have gone soft in the heat. Straightening, I cross to the sheriff. 'Is there a vegetable stand nearby?'

He blinks at me, as if realizing he should have already explored that angle. 'The Yoders run a stand a couple miles down the road.'

'You talk to the folks at the stand?'

'Not yet,' he says sheepishly. 'There ain't no phone out there.'

The statement sounds like an excuse, and he knows it. The last thing I want to do is ruffle local feathers. By all indications, he's competent and capable. Still, I'm surprised that hadn't occurred to him.

Looking chagrined, he pulls his phone from his belt. 'I'll get one of my deputies out there.'

I walk the scene, memorizing as much of it as I can. The location of the pool of blood, the proximity of the satchel in relation to the blood, the angle of the tire tread.

When he ends the call, I ask, 'Did you photograph the scene?'

'Not yet.'

'Have you checked registered sex offenders in the area?'

'My secretary is pulling it now.'

We study the scene for a minute or so and then I ask, 'What can you tell me about the family?'

'Girl's parents are Edna and Levi King. They're Old Order. Nice folks, though. I think they got about eight kids now, with Annie being the oldest. Anyway, they came into my office about eight this morning and told me she didn't come home last night.

'Evidently, they spent the night looking for her. Got the neighbors involved. Finally, they got so worried, they decided to involve the police.' He swats a fly off his forehead. 'I wish they'd come to me right away, so we could have gotten a jump on this.'

'You have a description of the girl?'

'They didn't have a photo.' He pulls a notepad from his back pocket, flips it open. 'Fifteen years old. Brown hair. Brown eyes. A hundred and fifteen pounds. Five feet five inches.' He grimaces. 'I seen her a time or two. Pretty little thing.'

A picture of her forms in my mind. I see a plain, slender girl with work-rough hands. Trusting. At 115 pounds, she would be easy to overpower. Easy to control. I pull out my own pad and jot down the information. 'Do you know what she was wearing?'

'Blue dress with a white apron. Black shoes. One of them bonnet things on her head.'

'Prayer *kapp*,' I tell him.

He gives me a 'Yeah, whatever' look.

'Does she have a boyfriend?'

'To tell you the truth, Chief Burkholder, the parents weren't very forthcoming about the girl's personal business. They kind of clammed up when I asked, and I got the impression they were uncomfortable talking to me.' He grimaces. 'I was thinking we could run out there so you could have a go at them.'

'Sure,' I tell him.

'CSU is on the way.'

We turn at the sound of Tomasetti's voice. He's striding toward us. 'Should be here in an hour or so.'

'I think we need to speak with the parents,' I tell him.

'Sounds like a good place to start.' He glances at Goddard. 'Do you have the manpower to protect the scene?'

'I'll tell my deputy to stay put until your crime-scene guy gets here.' He starts toward the young officer.

Tomasetti and I head toward the Tahoe. 'What do you think?' I ask as we climb in.

He grimaces. 'I think that blood is a bad fucking sign.'

I agree, but I don't say the words.

Ten minutes later, we turn onto a winding gravel lane bounded on both sides by cornfields, the shoulder-high stalks shimmering like some massive green mirage in the afternoon sun. A tangle of raspberry bushes grows along the wire fence on the north side. White dust billows from the tires of Sheriff Goddard's cruiser in front of us, tiny stones pinging against the grille of the Tahoe.

A quarter mile in, the track opens to a large gravel area. Two hulking red barns trimmed in white loom into view. Ahead, I see several smaller outbuildings, an old outhouse, and a rusty metal shed. On my left, a white farmhouse with tall, narrow windows and a green tin roof looks out over the land. I wonder about all the things the house has witnessed over the years and I know this place, like so many others in this part of the country, has stories to tell.

Beyond, several huge maple trees shade a manicured yard teeming with blooming peonies and tufts of pampas grass with spires as tall as a man. A scarecrow wearing a straw hat and suspenders stands guard over a garden abundant with strawberries and green beans. An Amish girl in a tan dress stops hoeing to watch us.

I recall reading, when I was in college, that sense memories can be a powerful trigger of flashbacks. The sight of this farm, combined with the smell of cattle and horses and that of summer foliage, elicits an intense sense of déjà vu. This farm is uncannily similar to the one I grew up on, and for the span of several seconds I'm transported back to the past. I see my *mamm*, a clothespin between her teeth, hanging trousers and dresses on the clothesline. Looking at the field behind the barn, I imagine my brother Jacob driving our team of Percheron geldings while my *datt* and the neighbor boy cut and bundle hay. I remember the frustration of being stuck in the house, scrubbing floors, when I desperately wanted to be outside on the back of one of those horses.

They were happy, innocent times, and though that part of my life was far from perfect, the memories evoke an uneasy sense of longing. It's not that I want to be Amish again or that I want to recapture my youth or a past I know is forever gone. But invariably when I remember those days, I can't help but think of all the things I left unfinished. Mostly my childhood, which was cut short long before its time. So many things I left unsaid, most of it to my family. But if I've learned anything in my thirty-three years, it is that no matter how badly you want a redo, life never makes such allowances.

I think of Annie King and I wonder if she was content living here with her family. If she found comfort in being part of this tight-knit community. Or was she like me? Perpetually discontent and pining for things she could never have. I wonder where she is at this very moment. If she's frightened and wishing she was back here with her brothers and sisters and the monotony of farm life. I wonder if years from now she'll look back and, like me, wish she'd done things differently.

'Looks like they've got company.' Tomasetti's voice snaps me out of my fugue.

Two Amish men in blue work shirts, straw hats, and dark trousers with suspenders stand at the barn door, watching us.

'They're probably neighbors,' I tell him. 'Here to help with the search or care for the livestock while the family deals with this.'

I follow his gaze. A few yards away, two Amish girls are trying to wrestle a large dog into a beat-up washtub. The girls are about ten years old. They're wearing plain green dresses, their mouse brown hair pulled into buns at their napes. Their feet are bare and dirty, and the dresses haven't fared much better. The simplicity and innocence of the sight makes me smile.

All children are innocent, but Amish children possess a particular kind of innocence. They believe the world is a good place, that their parents never make mistakes, that everyone they meet is their friend, and that if you pray hard enough, God will answer your prayers. It's particularly shattering for an Amish child when she realizes none of those things are true.

Tomasetti and I watch the girls for a moment, each of us caught in our thoughts. That's when it strikes me that these girls are about the same age his own would have been had their lives not been cut short by a career criminal who thought he'd make an example of a cop who crossed him. That was three years ago, and I know Tomasetti is still clawing his way out of that bottomless pit of despair. Most days, I think, he succeeds. But sometimes when I look into his eyes, I see the dark place in which he resides.

He cuts me a sideways look. 'I think the dog is going to win.'

'My money's on the girls.' I smile at him.

'Are you telling me I shouldn't underestimate the determination of an Amish girl?'

'Especially when she's got her sister to help her. Dog doesn't stand a chance. One way or another, he's going to get that bath.'

He parks adjacent to a rail fence next to the sheriff's cruiser and kills the engine. Neither of us speaks as we take the sidewalk to the porch and wait for Sheriff Goddard.

'Damn, it's humid.' Before he can knock, the door swings open. I find myself looking down at a little boy whose head comes up to about waist level. He's blond-haired and blue-eyed, with blunt-cut bangs that are crooked from a recent trim. His small nose is covered with a smattering of freckles.

'Hello there, little guy,' Sheriff Goddard says. 'Is your mom or dad home?'

The little boy squeals and runs back into the house.

'You've got a way with kids,' Tomasetti says.

The sheriff glances sideways at us. 'Same situation with women.' He looks at me. 'No offense.'

I withhold a smile. 'None taken.'

He's barely gotten the words out when an Amish man enters the mudroom and crosses to the door. He's tall – well over six feet – with muscled shoulders and the beginnings of a paunch, divulging the fact that, despite his fitness, he's a well-fed man. He's blond and has a brown beard that reaches halfway down his belly, telling me he's married. I guess him to be in his mid-forties. Dressed in black trousers, suspenders, and a vest over a white shirt, he is an imposing figure.

His eyes are the color of onyx beneath heavy brows, and they take in our presence with no emotion. 'Can I help you?' he asks, but he makes no move to invite us inside.

'Afternoon, Mr. King,' Sheriff Goddard begins. 'We'd like to talk to you about your daughter.'

The Amish man's expression remains impassive as his eyes move from Goddard to Tomasetti and me.

Goddard introduces us, letting him know which agency we represent. 'They're here to help us find Annie, Mr. King. We were wondering if you and your wife could answer a few questions.'

King's eyes narrow on me. I'm not sure if he recognized my last name as a common Amish one or if he's merely curious because I'm from Holmes County. He doesn't ask, turning his attention to Goddard. 'Do you have news of her?' he asks.

'We think we found her bag,' the sheriff tells him.

A quiver runs through King, as if hope and terror are waging war inside him. 'Where?'

'A couple of miles from the vegetable stand,' Goddard says. 'Have you had any luck on your end?'

The man's shoulders fall forward and he shakes his head. 'No,' he says, and opens the door.

We enter a mudroom with a scuffed plank floor and two bare windows, which usher in plenty of light. I see six straw hats hanging neatly on wooden dowels set into the wall. Muddy work boots are lined up on a homemade rug. An ancient wringer washing machine that smells of soap and mildew has been shoved into a corner. A basket filled with clothespins sits on the floor next to the machine.

King leads us through a doorway and into a large, well-used kitchen. The aromas of bread, seared meat, and kerosene greet me, and the same sense of déjà vu from earlier grips me. Light filters in from a single window over the sink, but it's not enough to cut the shadows. Dual lanterns glow yellow from atop a rect-angular table covered with a blue-and-white-checkered cloth. Scraped-clean plates and a smattering of flatware and a few drinking glasses litter the table's surface, and I realize that though it's not yet four o'clock, this family has just finished dinner. That's when I notice the one place setting that hasn't been touched. Annie's, I realize. It's a symbol of their hope that she will return, of their faith that God will bring her back to them and their prayers will be answered. It's been a long time since I put that kind of faith in anything. It makes me sad to think that this family might soon realize that some prayers go unanswered.

An Amish girl barely into her teens gathers dishes from the table and carries them to the sink, where an Amish woman wearing a dark blue dress, white apron, and a gauzy white *kapp* has her hands immersed in soapy water, her head bowed. She's so embroiled in the task, or perhaps her thoughts, she doesn't notice us until her husband speaks.

'*Mir hen Englischer bsuch ghadde,*' he says, meaning 'We have English visitors.'

The woman turns, her mouth open in surprise. I guess her to be at least a decade younger than her husband. I suspect that at one time she was beautiful, but there's a hollowed-out countenance to her appearance. The look of the bereaved. I doubt she's eaten or slept or had a moment's peace of mind since her daughter went missing. Despite her faith, worry for her child's well-being has begun eating away at her like some flesh-eating bacteria that can't be stopped.

'I'm Kate Burkholder,' I tell her. 'We're here to help you find Annie.' Before even realizing I'm going to move, I'm across the kitchen and extending my hand. I sense the collective attention of Goddard and Tomasetti on me, and I address her in Pennsylvania Dutch. 'Can we sit and talk awhile?'

The woman blinks at me as if I've shocked her. Out of sheer politeness, she raises her hand to mine. It's wet and limp and cold, and I find myself wanting to warm it. Her eyes sweep to her husband, asking for his permission to speak with me, I realize, and I try not to be annoyed with her. His gaze levels on me. I stare back, not missing the hardness of his expression or the mistrust in his eyes.

He gives her a minute nod.

'I'm Edna.' She raises her eyes to mine. '*Sitz dich anne un bleib e weil.*' Sit yourself down and stay a while. 'I'll make coffee.'

FIVE

Ten minutes later, Edna and Levi King, Tomasetti, Goddard, and I are sitting at the big kitchen table with steaming mugs of coffee in front of us. I can hear the children playing in another part of the house; a dog barking from somewhere nearby; the *jaay-jaay* screech of a blue jay in the maple tree outside; the whistle of a train in the distance. The mood is somber, laced with a foreboding so thick, it's tangible. I find myself hoping that none of us will have to tell this family that their little girl won't be coming home.

Goddard pulls the satchel that was found at the scene from an evidence bag and presents it to the parents. 'We found this earlier. We're wondering if it's Annie's.'

Edna stares at the bag for a moment, then takes it from him, her mouth quivering. 'It is hers.' She studies it, turning it over in her hands and appearing to search every inch of the fabric, as if the satchel holds the answers we all so desperately need. She raises her gaze, her eyes darting from the sheriff to Tomasetti and then to me. 'Where did you find this?'

The sheriff answers. 'Out on County Road 7.'

I'm relieved when he doesn't mention the blood. Until it's identified as human – or confirmed as Annie's – there's no need to torture this family with information that may not be relevant.

'We've been praying for her safe return.' Closing her eyes, Edna presses the bag to her chest. 'Perhaps this is a sign she will be coming back to us.' Her face collapses, but she doesn't make a sound. 'We miss her,' she whispers. 'And we're worried. We want her back.'

Levi sets his gaze on the sheriff. 'Was there any other sign of her?'

The sheriff shakes his head. 'We're going over the scene with a fine-tooth comb.'

A sound to my right draws my attention. I look up and see a little Amish girl, half of her hidden behind the doorway, peeking at us with one eye. She's wearing a blue dress that looks like a hand-me-down. Her bare feet are slender, tanned, and dirty.

Levi raises his hand and points. 'Ruthie, go help your sister in the garden.' His voice is firm but holds a distinctly sad note, which tells me the words have less to do with the garden than with his not wanting her to bear witness to this discussion.

The girl eyes us a moment longer, then darts away, her bare feet slapping against the oak-plank floor.

'How many children do you have, Mrs. King?' Tomasetti asks.

'Eight,' Edna tells him. 'God blessed us with four girls and four boys.'

As inconspicuously as possible, I pull out my notepad. 'How old are they?'

'David is our youngest. He's three.' She chokes out a laugh. 'I think you met him when you came to the door. He's shy with strangers, especially the *Englischers,* you know. Annie is the oldest.' Her voice falters, but she takes a moment, gathers herself. 'She's fifteen. . . . Lydia is thirteen. . . .' She lets her words trail off, as if there are too many children to name. 'They're worried about their sister.'

'When did you realize Annie was missing?' I ask.

The woman casts a glance at her husband, then looks down at her hands. They're red and chapped, the nails bitten to the quick. 'Yesterday afternoon. We sent her out for corn and tomatoes. She gets restless, you know. She's at that age.'

'What time was that?'

'Before supper.' She glances absently at the antique mantel clock on a shelf by the door. 'Two o'clock, I think.'

'Was she on foot?'

'Yes. She enjoys the walking.'

'When did you become worried?'

She looks at her husband, as if the answer is too much for her to bear, and he answers for her. 'We began to worry when she didn't make it home in time for the before-meal prayer,' he says.

'That Annie likes to eat.' Edna's laugh comes out sounding more like a sob.

'What did you do?' Tomasetti asks.

'I went looking for her, of course,' Levi responds.

'Alone?'

'My son and I took the buggy.' Levi sighs and shakes his head. 'We took the route she would have taken, but there was no sign of her. We talked to Amos Yoder at the vegetable stand, and he said she had been there earlier and she seemed fine.'

I look at Goddard. 'Is the place where we found the satchel between here and the vegetable stand?'

Goddard shakes his head. 'No.'

No one says it, but that means Annie either took a different route home or got into a vehicle with someone. 'What did you do next?' I ask Levi.

'I took the buggy to the bishop's house. He has a phone. We put together a search party.' A sigh slides between his lips, as if he's staving off an emotion he can't afford to feel. 'All of the able-bodied men and boys came out to help – some on horseback, some in buggies. Our English neighbors helped in their cars.'

'Why did you wait so long before calling the police?' Goddard asks gently.

'The *Ordnung* forbids our associating . . .' His words trail off. It's as if he realizes a missing child is the one time when there's no place for sectarian beliefs. 'I thought we would find her before now.' The words come out in a harsh whisper. 'If I had done over . . .'

Goddard nods understandingly.

'She didn't have anything to eat last night.' Edna's voice is barely discernible. 'She didn't have a bed to sleep in.'

I choose my next words carefully. 'Mrs. King, you mentioned Annie gets restless. Is there a possibility she didn't come home on purpose? Maybe there was an argument? Or she was upset about something?'

Levi shakes his head adamantly. 'No. She is a good girl. She would not worry us over something like that.'

Edna remains silent, not responding. Not even with a shake of her head. There are times when silence has a voice all its own. I mentally file the information away for later, wondering if she's privy to something her husband is not. Sometimes daughters confide in their mothers. . . .

'Have you had any problems with Annie?' I ask gently. 'Has she broken the rules? Has she seemed unhappy about anything recently?'

The look that passes between them is so subtle, I almost miss it. But I know there's something there, some scrap of information they don't want to reveal. 'We're not here to judge you,' I tell them. 'Or her.'

'We just want to find your daughter,' Tomasetti adds.

When neither of them speaks, I continue. 'Look, I know

that sometimes teenagers make mistakes. Even Amish teen-agers.' I feel Tomasetti and Goddard watching me, but I don't look away from Edna. 'Even good girls,' I finish in Pennsylvania Dutch, purposefully excluding the two men.

After a moment, Levi nods. 'Annie is very strong-willed.'

'She's a good girl,' Edna says quickly.

An alarm sounds in the back of my brain. Maybe it's because I know that when parents feel the need to emphasize the good-ness of their children, there's usually a reason. Like maybe the kid isn't quite as well-behaved as they'd like everyone to believe, and as they desperately want to believe themselves.

After a moment, Edna lowers her face into shaking hands. 'She is a good girl.'

The last thing I want to do is alienate them; at the moment, they are our best source of information. But I know if I don't push, I won't get what I need, and that is the truth – all of it.

I let the silence ride, giving them some time; then I return my attention to Edna. 'Have you spoken to Annie's friends?'

Edna raises her head. 'She keeps to herself mostly.'

'Does she have a best friend?' I press her, knowing that whether you're Amish or English, if you're a teenage girl, you have a confidante.

Edna perks up. 'She's been friendly with the Stutz girl. They went to a singing last week after worship. Amy is her name.'

I write down the name and turn my attention to the sheriff. 'Do you know where the Stutz family lives?'

He nods. 'Just down the road.'

I go back to Edna. 'Is there anything else you can think of that might help us find her?'

When the woman looks away, I turn my attention to Levi. The Amish man stares down at the tabletop. He knows some-thing, too; I see it in the slump of his shoulders, the cord of tension in his neck. I'm sure Tomasetti and Goddard sense it as well, and the only thing we can do at this point is wait them out and hope they open up.

For a full minute, the only sounds come from the hiss of the lantern's wick and the ticking of the mantel clock on the shelf. Then Levi raises his gaze to mine. 'She has been associating with some *Englischers*.'

Edna jerks her head his way. 'Levi . . .'

'What are their names?' I ask quickly.

'We do not know.'

'Does she have a boyfriend?'

The Amish couple exchange a look I recognize. A look I've seen before. One I understand all too well. One I saw in the eyes of my own parents. Shame. The need to secrete away the sins of their child. I know this because I was once that sinful child. This is the question they've been avoiding. The answer is one they don't want to divulge. A reality they don't want to acknowledge. Not even between them. Certainly not to us outsiders. But I also know it's the reason we've been invited into this Amish home.

Levi tightens his lips as if against words he doesn't want to utter. 'We think the English boy was courting her.'

'Did Annie tell you that?'

The Amish man shakes his head. 'Dan Beiler saw them together in town.'

'Do you know the boy's name?'

'No.' He looks everywhere except into my eyes. 'He has a car. She disappears sometimes and will not tell us where she's been.'

'Do you know what kind of car?'

'We don't know,' Levi spits out.

'She will not speak of him to us,' Edna says, choking out the words.

'We forbade her to speak to the *Englischers*,' Levi says. 'She would not listen.'

'Our Annie thinks she knows her mind.' Edna's voice cracks on the last word. 'When she wants something, there is no stopping her.'

'But her faith is strong,' Levi adds. 'She loves her family. She is kind and submits to God.'

I know that sometimes even the faithful find themselves face-to-face with the devil.

'Thank you, Mr. and Mrs. King. You've been very helpful.' I shake hands with both of them. 'We're going to do our best to find your daughter.'

Tomasetti, Goddard, and I stand as a single unit. As we start toward the door, I mentally add Amy Stutz to my list of possible sources of information. But the person I most want to speak with is the boyfriend. Any cop worth his weight knows that when a female goes missing, the first suspect is always the man who claims to love her.

Ten minutes later, Goddard, Tomasetti, and I are standing on the front porch of the Stutz house. Goddard has knocked twice, but no one has answered the door. 'We're batting zero,' he says with a sigh.

Tomasetti peers through the window as if expecting to discover someone lurking behind the shades. 'I thought the Amish spent their evenings at home,' he growls. 'Early to bed and all that bullshit.'

Goddard looks to me, the resident Amish expert. 'Any idea where they might be?'

'Visiting a neighbor, maybe.' I look around, taking in the long shadows of late afternoon.

'We could wait,' Goddard suggests. 'See if they show.'

'We need the name of the boyfriend,' Tomasetti mutters.

I drift to the porch rail and look out across the pasture, where eight Jersey cows and two young horses graze the lush grass. A thin layer of fog hovers in the low-lying areas. Twilight birds and crickets mingle with a cacophony of bullfrogs from the pond, where a profusion of cattails flourish. How many times growing up did I lie in my bed at night with the window open and listen to these very same sounds? How many times did I wonder what the world was like beyond the confines of the farm? I feel the memories pushing at the gate. But I don't open it.

Goddard clears his throat. 'Let's grab a bite to eat and come back.'

'Sounds like a plan,' Tomasetti says.

And then we're back in the Tahoe, following Goddard down the lane through plumes of billowing white dust.

I'm still thinking about the boyfriend. 'If Annie and her boyfriend are tight and he knows she's missing, why hasn't he come forward?'

'Maybe he's guilty of something.'

'Or they could be together.'

'Considering the blood at the scene, that would be a best-case scenario.'

We're nearly to the end of the lane when, in my peripheral vision, I notice a flash of blue through the dust. I glance over and see an Amish girl in a blue dress standing on the shoulder. Brown paper bag in hand, she's braving a thick bramble of raspberries. She's picking the berries, I realize.

'Stop,' I say abruptly.

Tomasetti hits the brakes hard enough to throw me against my shoulder harness. The tires grab and the Tahoe slides to an abrupt stop. He puts the SUV in park and tosses me a specula-tive look. 'Amy Stutz?'

'Age looks about right.'

A few yards ahead, Goddard's brake lights come on and he pulls over.

I open the door and start toward the girl. Her eyes widen when she realizes I'm coming toward her. 'Hi there,' I begin in my most friendly voice. '*Wei bischt du heit?*' *How are you today?*'

'*Ich bin zimmlich gut.*' *I'm pretty good,* but she's looking at me as if I'm an ax murderer, and I can tell she's thinking about making a run for the house.

'My name's Kate. I didn't mean to frighten you. I'm a police officer.'

'Oh. Hello.' It's a duty greeting. She doesn't want to talk to me, but she's too polite not to respond when she's been addressed by an adult, even if they're English. I guess her to be about fifteen years old. She's wearing a plain blue dress with a gauzy white *kapp* that's been left untied at her nape, and on her feet are a cheap pair of sneakers.

'I'm looking for Mr. and Mrs. Stutz,' I begin.

'They're visiting the Beiler family down the road. To see the new baby.'

'What's your name?'

'Amy.'

I make a show of looking at the raspberry bushes. 'How are the berries?'

'Juicy.' She peers into the bag. 'Not too many bugs.' She eyes the Tahoe. 'They're not for sale. *Mamm* makes jam.'

She's a pretty girl with hazel eyes and a sunburned nose. Her hands are dirty from picking berries and she's got a purple stain next to her mouth.

'Do you know Annie King?' I ask.

'*Ja.*'

I see scratches on her arms from the thorny bushes and I can't help but remember all the times my *mamm* sent me to pick raspberries or blackberries. I always returned scratched and bleeding, but it was always worth the pain because I ate as many as I harvested.

'Did you know she's missing?' I ask.

The girl's expression falls. 'I heard.'

'We're trying to find her.'

She looks down at the bag in her hand.

I spot a ripe berry growing low on the bush, pull it off, and eat it. 'They *are* good.'

'My *datt* says it's because of all the rain.'

I pluck a few more berries and drop them into her bag. 'I understand you and Annie are friends.'

'She's my best friend.'

I nod. 'Her *mamm* and *datt* told me Annie has some English friends. Did she ever talk about them?'

The girl steps away from me, as if the act of distancing herself will make me and my questions go away. 'I don't know anything about that.'

I tilt my head to make eye contact. 'Are you sure?'

She begins picking berries at a frantic pace, pulling off leaves and small branches and throwing them into the bag.

'You're not in any trouble,' I tell her. 'Neither is Annie. We just want to find her. Her parents are worried.' I pick a few berries and drop them into her bag.

The words seem to get through to her. She lowers her hand and gives me her full attention. 'She has too many English friends. She's been riding in their cars. Smoking. You know, *Englischer* kind of things. I told her it was against the *Ordnung*, but . . .'

I nod. 'Sometimes young people do things. They make mistakes.'

For the first time, she looks at me as if I might not be the enemy.

I'm aware of Tomasetti in the Tahoe a few yards away, waiting, watching us. 'Did Annie ever mention a boyfriend?'

She moves a branch aside and pulls off a big purple berry. '*Ja.*'

'Do you know his name?'

She stops what she's doing and looks at me. I see in her eyes a tangle of misery and confusion and the terrible weight of a fear she doesn't understand – all of it tempered by the hope that her friend is okay. 'She asked me not to tell.'

'We think Annie could be in danger.' I wait, but she doesn't respond, so I add, 'Honey, you're not in any trouble. Okay? We just want to find her. If you know something, please tell me.'

Her brows go together and for the first time I get a glimpse of the full scope of the war waging within her: the need to be loyal to her friend; the tenet to remain separate from me; the need to tell what she knows because Annie could be in danger. 'His name is Justin Treece,' she says finally.

'Thank you.' I pull out my pad and write down the name. 'Is there anything else you can tell me that might help us find her?'

She bites her lip. 'Annie has a phone,' she blurts. 'I saw her talking on it.'

'A cell phone?'

She nods. 'I'm scared for her.'

'Why?'

'I just am.'

I reach out to touch her, to reassure her and thank her for her help, but she snatches up her bag and pushes past the bushes with such speed that I hear the stickers snag on her dress. She runs toward the house without looking back.

I watch until she disappears around the side of the house, and then I slide into the Tahoe and tell Tomasetti what I've learned. 'Why are the parents always the last to know?' he growls.

'Probably because they don't ask enough questions.'

'Or maybe some teenagers are pathological liars.'

'Such a cynic.' I tsk. 'You should try having a little more faith in our youth.'

'I could, but there's this pesky little detail called reality.' He's already got his phone to his ear, calling Goddard. 'We got a name,' he says without preamble. 'Justin Treece.' Tomasetti's face darkens and he scowls. 'Shit. You got an address on him?' He listens for a moment and ends the call.

'That didn't sound good,' I say.

Tomasetti drops his phone onto the console and puts the Tahoe in gear. 'Treece did a year in Mansfield for beating the hell out of his mother.'

SIX

Justin Treece lives with his parents in a run-down frame house on the outskirts of Buck Creek. The neighborhood is a downtrodden purlieu of postage stamp-size houses with ramshackle front porches and yards with grass trampled to dirt. Several houses are vacant, the windows either boarded up with plywood or open to the elements. The roof of the house next to the Treece place is fire-damaged; a hole the size of a tractor tire reveals blackened rafters and pink puffs of insulation.

'Damn, looks like Cleveland,' Tomasetti says as we idle past.

'Welcome to the other side of the tracks,' I mutter.

A beat-up Toyota pickup truck with oversize tires sits in the driveway next to an old Ford Thunderbird. 'Looks like someone's home.'

In front of us, Goddard's cruiser pulls over to the curb two houses down from the Treece place, and we park behind him. Tomasetti and I meet him on the sidewalk.

'Vehicles belong to the parents,' the sheriff tells us. 'Trina drives the Thunderbird. Jack drives the Toyota.'

'What about the kid?' Tomasetti asks.

'Last time I stopped him, he was in an old Plymouth Duster.

Him and his old man tinker with cars, so it could be in the garage out back.'

'Exactly how bad is this kid?' I ask.

'He's only got that one conviction.' Goddard shakes his head. 'But it is a doozy. To tell you the truth, I think that little bastard is on his way. In ten years, he'll be in the major league.'

'Or in prison,' Tomasetti puts in.

Goddard motions toward the house. 'The whole lot of them are regulars with the department. Domestic stuff, mostly. Parents get drunk and beat the shit out of each other. Kids run wild. It's sad is what it is.'

Having been a patrol officer in Columbus for a number of years, I'm all too familiar with those kinds of scenarios. It's a sad and seemingly hopeless cycle, especially for the kids. Too many of them become victims of their environment and end up like their parents – or worse.

'Wouldn't surprise me if this kid is involved with this missing girl,' Goddard tells us. 'He's got a hot head and a big mouth.'

'Bad combination,' I say.

'They armed?' Tomasetti asks.

'We searched the place once a few months back and didn't find anything. But nothing would surprise me when it comes to this bunch.' Goddard divides his attention between the two of us. 'So are you guys packing, or what?'

'Never leave home without it,' Tomasetti replies.

I open my jacket just far enough for him to see the leather shoulder holster where I keep my .22 mini-Magnum.

'Well, lock and load, people.' He motions toward the house. 'Let's go see what Romeo has to say.'

We take a sidewalk that's buckled from tree roots and riddled with cracks. A tumbling chain-link fence encircles the front yard. I glance between the close-set houses and see a tiny backyard that's littered with old tires. Beyond, a detached garage with peeling yellow paint and a single broken window separates the yard from the alley.

'Light on in the garage,' I say.

'Kid hangs out there a lot. Listens to that weird-shit music loud enough to bust your fuckin' eardrums.'

'Do the parents work?' Tomasetti asks as we take the concrete steps to the front door.

Goddard nods. 'Jack Treece is a mechanic at the filling station in town. He's good, from what I hear. Probably where the kid got the knack. Trina works down at the bowling alley. Tends bar most nights.'

'What about Justin?' I ask.

He shakes his head. 'I don't think anyone around here would hire him to tell you the truth. He's got a rep. Most people steer clear.'

We reach the front door. A few feet away, a window-unit air conditioner belches water onto the concrete. Goddard knocks and then steps aside, as if expecting someone to shoot through the door.

The door creaks open. I find myself looking at a huge round woman with brown eyes and a tangle of black hair that reaches midway down her back. She's got the kind of face that makes it difficult to guess her age, but I'd put her around forty. It's obvious we wakened her, but she must have been sleeping on the sofa, because it didn't take long for her to answer the door, and she doesn't look like the type to move with any kind of speed.

She's wearing a flowered muumuu that doesn't cover as much of her as I'd like. Her calves are the size of hams and bulge with varicose veins. Swollen toes with thick yellow nails stick out of the ends of pink slippers.

She takes in the sight of us with a mix of hostility and

amusement. 'Sheriff.' Her voice is deep and slow, with a hint of the Kentucky hills. 'I heard you died.'

'Well, no one's told me about it yet.' Goddard shows her his identification. 'Hope that's not too much of a disappointment.'

'Things would get pretty boring round here without you cops fuckin' with us all the damn time.'

'Is Justin here?'

Her gaze slides from the sheriff to me and Tomasetti and then back to the sheriff. I see a cunning in its depths that reminds me of a big lumbering bear that can transform to a predator capable of tearing a man to shreds with no provocation or warning. She's got cold, empty eyes and an 'I don't give a shit' air, both of which tell me she has no respect for anything or anyone – including herself – and has a particularly high level of loathing for law enforcement.

'Who wants to know?' she asks.

'Me and these state agents.'

'State agents, huh?' She gives me the once-over and makes a sound of disdain. 'What'd he do now?'

'We just want to ask him some questions.'

'This about that girl gone missing?'

The collective surge of interest is palpable. The sheriff leans forward. I see Tomasetti, who is beside me, crane his head slightly, looking beyond her. 'Trina, we just want to talk to Justin,' Goddard tells her.

She makes no move to open the door. 'I know my rights, Bud. I'm the parent and I want to know why you want to talk to my son.'

Tomasetti shoves his identification at her. 'Because we asked nicely, and if we have to come back with a warrant, we won't be so nice.'

She's not impressed and doesn't even glance at his credentials. 'Who the fuck 're you?'

'I'm the guy who's going to fuck you over if you don't open the goddamn door.'

Goddard's mouth sags open wide enough for me to see the fillings in his molars. Trina Treece doesn't even blink. The flash of amusement in her eyes shocks me. Tomasetti is about as amusing as an autopsy. Most people do their utmost to concede to his wishes, especially if he's in a nasty mood. He might be a cop, but he possesses an air of unpredictability that keeps even the densest individuals from crossing him. This woman doesn't even seem to notice – and I don't believe it's because she's dense.

She smirks at the sheriff. 'Where'd you find this charmer?'

'If I were you, I'd just open the door,' the sheriff says tiredly. 'We really need to speak with your son.'

'Well, hell, all right.' Her triceps flap when she swings open the door. 'C'mon in. Wipe your damn feet.'

Tomasetti goes through the door first. He brushes by her without a word, his right hand never far from his holster, and he doesn't bother wiping his feet. I go in next, swipe each shoe against the throw rug at the threshold. Goddard brings up the rear, and actually looks down while he diligently wipes his shoes on the rug.

The interior of the house is hot and stuffy and smells vaguely of fish. A swaybacked sofa draped with a dingy afghan separates the small living room from an even smaller dining area. A floor fan blows stale air toward a narrow, dark hall. A sleek high-def television is mounted on the wall. It's tuned to an old Bugs Bunny cartoon, the volume turned low. From where I stand, I can see into a dimly lit kitchen with cluttered counters and a sinkful of dirty dishes. Beyond is a back door, its window adorned with frilly yellow curtains. A folded pizza box sticks out of the top of a stainless-steel trash can.

For a full minute, the only sounds are the rattle of the air conditioner and Trina Treece's labored breathing.

'Where is he?' Goddard asks.

'I reckon he's out back with that worthless old man of his.' But she's looking at Tomasetti as if trying to decide which buttons to push and how hard to push them. Tomasetti stares back at her with a blank expression that gives away absolutely nothing. *Oh boy.*

A sound from the hall draws my attention. Two girls, about ten years old, peek around the corner at us. I see shy, curious faces and young eyes that have already seen too much.

Trina hauls her frame around. 'I told you two idiots to stay in your room!'

Both girls have the same wild black hair as their mother. But all likeness ends there. The girls are thin and pretty and seemingly undamaged by the environment in which they live. Watching them, I can't help but to compare these kids to the girls at the King farm. Innocent girls whose lives are filled with promise but whose future will be determined by the guidance they receive from their parents and the vastly different worlds in which they reside.

I think of all the life lessons that lie ahead for these two girls, and I wonder if they'll be able to count on either parent to guide them through it. I wonder if they'll survive.

'Who are these people, Mama?' the taller of the two girls asks.

'This ain't your concern, you nosy little shit.' Trina crosses to the sofa, picks up an empty soda can, and throws it at the girl. The can bounces off the wall and clangs against the floor. 'Now go get your damn brother. Tell him the fuckin' cops are here.'

Next to me, Tomasetti makes a sound of reprehension, and I know he's on the verge of saying something he shouldn't. His face is devoid of emotion, but I know him well enough to recognize the anger burgeoning beneath the surface of all that calm, and I'm reminded that his own daughters were about the same age as these two girls when they were murdered.

'Let it go,' I whisper.

He doesn't acknowledge the words, doesn't even look at me. But he doesn't make a move. I figure that's the best I can hope for.

Unfazed by their mother's mistreatment, eyeing us with far too much curiosity, the girls start across the living room. No one speaks, as if in deference to their presence. The things we'll be discussing are not suited for young ears, despite the probability they've already heard far worse. They're wearing shorts with T-shirts that are too tight and too revealing for such a tender age. That's when I notice the Ace bandage on the taller girl's left wrist. My eyes sweep lower and I notice a bruise the size of a fist on her left thigh, a second bruise on the back of her arm, and I wonder who put them there. I wonder how integral violence is to this family.

The back door slams. I look up, to see a tall, dark-haired young man appear in the kitchen doorway. I know immediately he's Justin Treece. He's nearly six feet tall. Skinny, the way so many young males are, but he's got some sinew in his arms and the rangy look of a street fighter – one who knows how to fight dirty. He's wearing baggy jeans with a drooping crotch – perfect for secreting a weapon – and a dirty T-shirt. Well-worn Doc Martens cover his feet. Newish-looking tats entwine both arms from shoulder to elbow. A single gold chain hangs around his neck, and he has gold hoops in both ears. He's looking at us as if we've interrupted something important and he needs to get back to it ASAP.

'What's going on?' he asks, wiping grease from his hands onto an orange shop towel.

Trina twists her head around to look at him. 'I don't know what you did, but these cops want to talk to you.'

'I didn't do shit.' His gaze lingers on his mother, and for an instant I see a flash of raw hatred before he directs his attention to us. 'What do you guys want?'

Justin Treece is not what I expected. He's attractive, with dark, intelligent eyes that have the same cunning light as his mother's. Someone less schooled in all the wicked ways of the human animal might presume he's a decent, hardworking young man. But I've never put much weight in appearances, especially when I know they're false.

Goddard doesn't waste time on preliminaries. 'When's the last time you saw Annie King?'

An emotion I can't quite identify flickers in his eyes; then his expression goes hard. 'I was wondering when you were going to show up.'

Tomasetti flips out his identification, holds it up for Justin to see. 'Why is that?'

Justin gives him a dismissive once-over. 'When something bad happens around here, the cops come calling. I'm their go-to man.'

'When a girl goes missing, the boyfriend is usually one of the first people the police talk to,' Goddard tells him.

'That's your problem,' Justin says.

Tomasetti never takes his eyes from the teen. 'Stop acting like a dipshit and answer the sheriff's question.'

'I ain't seen her in a couple days.' He shrugs a little too casually, as if a missing girl is of no great concern, girlfriend or not. 'I heard she was missing, though.'

'You don't seem too worried,' Tomasetti says.

'I figured she left.'

'Why would you think that?'

Justin rolls his eyes. 'Anyone under eighteen with a brain

is thinking about leaving this fuckin' dump. Besides, she hates those Bible-thumping freaks.'

'You mean the Amish?' I ask.

He gives me his full attention. Curiosity flickers in his eyes. He's wondering who I am and why I'm here. I tug out my identification and show it to him.

'Yeah, man, the Amish. They treat her like shit, and she was sick of all their self-righteous crap.'

'She told you that?' I ask.

'All the time. They're always judging her, telling her what she can and can't do. She has no freedom and can't do shit without one of them pointing their holier-than-thou fingers.' That he's speaking of her in the present tense doesn't elude me. 'I'm glad she finally got out. Good for her.'

'How close are you?' I ask.

'We're friends. You know, tight.'

'Since you're so tight, Justin, did it bother you that she left without saying good-bye?' I ask.

The kid surprises me by looking down, and I realize the question hit a raw spot he doesn't want us to see. 'It's a free country. I always told her if she got the chance, she should take it.' He laughs. 'I figured I'd be the one to go first.'

'Did she mention a destination?' Tomasetti asks.

He thinks about that a moment. 'We used to talk about Florida. She hates the cold. Never even seen the ocean. But I can't see her just picking up and going with no apartment. No job.'

'Her parents are worried,' I tell him.

'They shoulda treated her better,' he shoots back.

'We think she could be in trouble,' Goddard says.

His eyes narrow on the sheriff. 'You mean like someone . . . hurting her?'

'That's exactly what we mean.' Tomasetti stares hard at him. 'Do you know anything about that?'

'What? You think I did something to her?'

'You ever lose your temper with her?' Tomasetti asks, pressing him. 'Ever hit her?'

Trina Treece heaves her frame up off the sofa with the grace of a gymnast. 'What kind of question is that?'

'The kind he has to answer.' But Tomasetti doesn't take his eyes off the boy.

Justin holds his gaze. 'I never touched her.'

'Did you buy her a cell phone?' Goddard asks.

'Her parents wouldn't do it, so I did. Last I heard, that wasn't against the law.'

'She use it?' I ask.

'Sure. We talk all the time.'

'When's the last time you heard from her?' Tomasetti asks.

'I dunno. A couple days ago.'

'Have you tried to contact her in the last twenty-four hours?'

Justin nods. 'Goes straight to voice mail.'

'Didn't that seem strange?' Goddard asks. 'Or worry you?'

'Hey, she's like that. Independent, you know?' The teenager shrugs. 'I figured she'd call me when she got to where she was going.'

Tomasetti pulls out his notepad. 'What's the number?'

Justin rattles it off from memory and Tomasetti writes it down.

'You got your cell on you?' he asks.

'Sure, I—' The kid's eyes narrow. 'Why?'

'Because I'm going to take it.' Tomasetti holds out his hand. 'Give it to me.'

The kid wants to refuse. I see it in his face and in the way he can't quite make himself reach into his pocket to get it out. But he must see something in Tomasetti's eyes, because after a moment, he produces the phone. 'That cost me plenty.'

'We're just going to take a look, see if it will help us with a time line.' He removes an evidence bag from his pocket and the boy drops the phone into it. 'You'll get it back.'

Justin doesn't believe him, and looks away. 'Whatever.'

'You know, Justin, it would have been helpful if you'd come to us when she first went missing,' Goddard says.

'So that's what you're calling it?' Treece looks from Goddard to me to Tomasetti. 'She's missing?'

'Her parents just filed a missing-person report,' I tell him.

'I figured she was fine,' the boy says. 'How was I supposed to know?'

'You could have tried using that thing between your ears,' Tomasetti tells him.

The teenager gives him a 'Fuck you' look.

'Does she have any other friends she might have taken off with?' Goddard asks.

Justin shakes his head. 'Most of her friends are Amish.'

'Did she have transportation?' I ask.

Another shake. 'Not that I know of. She couldn't afford a car.' He chuckles. 'I let her drive mine once and she took out old man Heath's mailbox.'

'So you just assumed she'd walked somewhere?' Tomasetti asks.

'Or took the bus.' His voice turns belligerent. 'Look, we're friends, but I ain't her fuckin' keeper.'

'How did you meet her?' I ask.

'She was walking along the road. It was raining, so I stopped and asked her if she wanted a ride. She got in.' He lifts a shoulder, lets it drop. 'I offered her a cigarette and she smoked it.' He smiles. 'It was funny, because she was wearing that old-lady dress – you know, the Amish getup. We hit it off.'

'Are you involved in a relationship with her?' Tomasetti asks.

'Well . . . we're friends . . . mostly.'

Tomasetti sighs. 'Are you sleeping with her, Justin?'

To his credit, the kid blushes. 'I guess. I mean, we did it a few times. But we weren't like boyfriend and girlfriend or anything like that. I'm not ready to get tied down, so I set the boundary right off the bat.'

Silence falls and all of us stand there, caught up in our own thoughts. The two little girls watch the scene from the kitchen, eating chips from a bag. Tomasetti's trying not to look at them, but he's not quite managing.

I look at Justin. 'If you wanted to get out of Buck Creek so badly, why didn't you go with her?' I ask.

He laughs. 'I don't think my probation officer would appreciate that.'

A few minutes later, Tomasetti and I are sitting in the Tahoe, waiting for Goddard to start rolling. Tomasetti is staring out the window, brooding and preoccupied. I'm trying to find the right words, when he beats me to the punch.

'What the hell are people doing to their kids, Kate?'

It's not the kind of statement I'm accustomed to hearing from him. He's more apt to spout off some politically incorrect joke than a serious philosophical question, and it takes me a moment to find my feet. 'Not everyone treats their kids that way.'

'Too many do.'

I want to argue. Only I can't, because he's right. So I let it stand. 'We do what we can, Tomasetti. We can't control everything.'

'That bitch in there doesn't deserve those little kids.'

'I know.'

'She's going to fuck up their lives the same way she fucked up her own.'

'You can't say that for sure.'

His laugh is bitter. 'Since when are you the optimist?'

'Don't get cynical on me, Tomasetti.'

'That's kind of like asking the ocean not to be wet.' But he doesn't smile as he stares out the window. 'We take so much for granted. I wish I had five minutes with my kids. Just five lousy minutes to say the things I didn't say when they were alive.'

Tension climbs up my shoulders and into my neck. This is the first time he's talked about his children with this level of intimacy, this kind of emotion. It's the first time he's mentioned regret or allowed me a glimpse of his pain. I don't have children. But I know what it's like to lose a loved one. I've been to that dark place and I know firsthand the toll it can take.

'That's human nature,' I tell him. 'We take things for granted. All of us do.'

He says nothing.

'I'm sure they knew you loved them,' I say, but I feel as if I'm floundering.

'When I was on a case, I'd go for days without seeing them. Even when I was home, when I worked late, I didn't kiss them good night. I didn't tuck them in. I barely looked at them some days. Half the time, I didn't even fucking miss them. What the hell kind of parent doesn't miss his kids?'

I glance over at him. He's gripping the wheel tightly, staring straight ahead, and I think, *Shit*. 'Tomasetti . . .'

He tosses me a sideways look. 'I don't remember the last words I said to them, Kate. I was in a hurry that morning. Had some big fucking meeting. Some meeting that didn't mean anything to anyone. I didn't know that the next time I saw them would be in the morgue.'

It's difficult, but I hold his gaze. 'You loved them. They knew it. That's what counts.'

'I didn't keep them safe.'

'You did your best.'

'Did I?'

I take a moment to calm down, rein in my own emotions. 'Tomasetti, are you okay?' I ask.

He gives me a wan smile. 'I'm not going to wig out, if that's what you're asking.'

I reach across the seat and take his hand. 'Just checking.'

For a couple of minutes, neither of us speaks. We watch Goddard get into his cruiser. The only sounds come from a group of little boys playing stickball in the yard across the street and a blue jay scolding us from the maple tree a few feet away.

'I wanted to take that bitch's head off,' he says after a moment.

'Now there's the Tomasetti I know and love.'

His mouth twists into a grim smile, and the tension loosens its grip. An instant later, his cell goes off. He glances at the display, makes eye contact with me, and answers it. 'What do you have?'

His eyes hold mine as he listens to the caller, but his face reveals nothing. 'Got it. Right. Check on that for me, will you?' He disconnects and clips the phone to his belt.

'What?' I ask as I buckle up.

He cranks the key and the engine rumbles to life. 'The blood is human.'

'Damn.' We both assumed that would be the case. Still, the news is like a hammer blow. 'Is it hers?'

'They don't know yet. Lab's backed up. They should have blood type tomorrow. DNA is going to take a few days.' He puts the Tahoe in gear and pulls onto the street behind Goddard.

'That was a lot of blood,' I say, thinking aloud. 'If it's Annie's, she's seriously injured.'

Or worse.

The unspoken words hover like the smell of cordite after a gunshot. Neither of us dares say them aloud.

SEVEN

Half an hour later, Tomasetti, Bud Goddard, and I are standing in the reception area of the Trumbull County sheriff's office with three uniformed deputies, a state trooper, and a single officer from the Buck Creek PD. Tomasetti and I were introduced upon our arrival as 'state agents here to assist,' which is usually well received by even the most territorial of law-enforcement agencies. We do a lot more than assist, but then, that's cops for you.

The sheriff's department is typical of most county-funded offices: small, cramped, and cheaply furnished, but functional. However, the computers look relatively new and the dispatch and phone system are state-of-the-art. I figure if Goddard is as good at policing as he is at politicking, the county is in pretty good hands.

We convene in an interview room, which is past the rest room, at the rear of the offices. The space is small and windowless, with barely enough room for the rectangular table, which looks like a donation from someone's garage, and a hodgepodge of folding and task chairs. A laminate podium with the seal of the great state of Ohio affixed to the facade demarks the head of the table. Goddard stands behind it, looking down at his notes. Behind him, a whiteboard as well as a terrain and road map of northeastern Ohio are tacked to the wall. Three red circles indicate the locations where the missing teens were last seen.

Tomasetti and I sit together on one side of the table. Across from us are the three deputies, one of whom is a female. Though she wears a sheriff's department uniform, she's armed with a steno pad instead of a Glock, and I realize with dismay that she's here only to take notes. The trooper and city cop sit one chair down from Tomasetti and me.

Goddard clears his throat. 'This is an informal briefing to bring everyone up to speed on a developing missing-person case.' He recites the names and agencies of everyone in the room. 'Trooper Harris, who's with the state Highway Patrol, and Officer Gilmore, a member of the local PD are here to assist the Trumbull County sheriff's department, as well.'

He turns to the whiteboard and writes: 'Missing' with a double underscore. Below that: 'Annie King, fifteen, missing thirty-six hours – Buck Creek. Bonnie Fisher, sixteen, missing two months – Rocky Fork. Leah Stuckey, sixteen, missing one year – Hope Falls.'

'That's what we got so far, folks, and it ain't much,' he begins. 'Three missing females. All three are Amish. All three are teenagers. Annie King is the only missing person from Trumbull County, but Agents Tomasetti and Burkholder believe these three incidents are related. At this point, we do not have a suspect. No motive. No body. So we're not exactly sure what we're dealing with.'

'The CSU got back to me on the blood,' Tomasetti interjects. 'It's human.'

'Shit.' Goddard grimaces. 'Hers?'

'Lab should have the type by tomorrow.' Tomasetti looks at Goddard. 'We'll need to get her blood type from the family, if they have it.'

'I'll check,' Goddard replies.

Nodding, Tomasetti continues. 'DNA is going to take a few days. Lab is backlogged.'

'There's a surprise for you.' Sighing, the sheriff looks down at his notes. 'We now have a crime scene, which is being processed now by a CSU from the state. We also have the King girl's cell phone number. Agent Tomasetti is working on gaining access to phone records and getting a triangulation going.'

Goddard looks at Tomasetti. 'Any idea how long that'll take?'

'We should know something tomorrow.'

'Keep us posted.'

No one mentions the possibility that Annie King might not have that kind of time.

I catch Goddard's eye. 'Do you have an address for the other families? I'd like to speak with the parents.'

'Got the Fishers' address right here.' He leans down and hands a sheet of paper to one of the deputies, who passes it to me. I glance at the type; it contains an address for Fisher's Branch Creek Joinery in Rocky Fork.

'What were the circumstances of Bonnie Fisher's disappearance?' I ask.

He looks down at his notes. 'Took her bicycle to work one morning at the joinery the family runs, but she never made it there. Bicycle was found a mile from the house.

I nod. 'What about the Stuckey family?'

The chief grimaces. 'They were killed in a buggy accident a couple of months ago.'

'They have kids?' I ask.

He shakes his head. 'No one survived the accident.'

Disappointment presses into me with insistent fingers. When someone goes missing, the family is almost always the best source of information. That's particularly true if the missing person is Amish, because most are so family-oriented. Of course, Goddard will have copies of interviews, but nothing contained in the file will be as helpful as a one-on-one with the family.

As if sensing my frustration, he adds, 'I'll get you copies of everything, Chief Burkholder.'

I nod my thanks, hoping the investigating department was thorough.

'Persons of interest.' Goddard recaps our meeting with Justin Treece. 'We don't have anything solid on this kid, but as most of you know, he's got a violent temper and didn't have any qualms about beating the hell out of his own mother.'

He gestures toward the papers stacked in front of each of us. 'Julie pulled a list of registered sex offenders for Trumbull County. We got sixty-eight perverts in the county. She broke it down by the ages of the victims. That narrows it down to twenty-nine offenders, which is a starting point.'

'Damn big starting point,' one of the deputies says.

Tomasetti speaks up. 'I'm running some VICAP queries to see if there are other cold cases that might be related.' He scratches a note on the pad in front of him. 'I started with the northeastern part of the state and will fan out from there.'

'Keep us posted.' Goddard nods. 'And if the nature of this case ain't bad enough, I think I got one more wrench to throw into the mix.' He directs his attention to the older deputy sitting across from me. 'You remember old Red Gibbons?'

The deputy guffaws. 'That sumbitch is kind of hard to forget.'

Laughter erupts from around the table. It seems everyone in the room is familiar with the aforementioned Red Gibbons.

Goddard directs his attention to Tomasetti and me. 'Red was sheriff before me. One of the more colorful characters to grace the office.' He glances at the deputy. 'He retired, what, about six years ago?'

The deputy nods. 'Thereabouts.'

'Red's been following the development of these cold cases.' All semblance of humor disappears. 'He called me this morning and told me about another kid went missing nine years ago in Monongahela Falls. Dot on the map up near Painesville.

'Eighteen-year-old Amish kid by the name of Noah Mast. I pulled the file. From all indications the kid walked away from the farm and no one heard from him again.'

'I remember the case,' another deputy says. 'Everyone thought he was a runaway.'

'The fact that he's a male stands out,' I put in.

'Was there a missing-person report filed?' Tomasetti asks.

'Eventually.' Goddard nods. 'I'll have copies made for everyone.'

'How far is Monongahela Falls?' I ask.

Goddard indicates the location on the map. 'About fifty miles north.'

'An hour's drive,' Tomasetti comments. 'Not too far.'

We watch as Goddard turns to the whiteboard and writes 'Noah Mast – nine years ago,' followed by a large question mark. He then circles a fourth location on the map: Monongahela Falls.

Tomasetti raises the next question. 'Are any of the sex offenders on that list convicted of assaults on a male victim?'

'One.' Goddard writes a name in bold letters without looking at the list, telling me he'd already considered the angle. 'Mike Campbell.' 'Forty-two-year-old white male. One conviction sexual assault on a minor. Victim was a thirteen-year-old neighbor kid.'

'Probably worth a look,' the deputy says.

'What's his location?' I ask, thinking of logistics.

'Sugar Bend.' The chief indicates the location on the map. 'About forty-five minutes southeast of here.'

'Do any of these offenders have an Amish connection?' I ask.

Goddard writes another name on the board: 'Stacy Karns.' 'Karns is some big-shot photographer. Lives out on Doe Creek Road, by the lake. Forty-four-year-old black male. Originally from Toledo. Anyway, he did six months on a child pornography charge. Case file says he photographed a fourteen-year-old Amish girl in the nude. Happened in Geauga County. I guess he won all kinds of awards. Everyone thought it was fucking art.'

'Except her parents,' Tomasetti says.

Goddard smiles. 'And the jury.'

'What about that cult over to Salt Lick?' the deputy asks.

'I'm getting to that.' Goddard turns to the whiteboard and writes another name: 'Frank Gilfillan.' 'Fifty-two-year-old white male. Clean record. Runs the Twelve Passages Church over in Salt Lick. They got about sixty followers now. Strange mix of people. Most are fanatical, and they're big into recruiting. The reason this group is of interest is because Gilfillan doesn't like the Amish. He's outspoken about it and makes an effort to recruit their young. A couple of Amish teens have joined the Twelve Passages Church. Don't know if any of that is related to our missing persons, but I thought it was worth a mention.'

I'm still thinking about the missing Amish boy. 'Has anyone talked to Noah Mast's parents recently?'

Goddard shakes his head. 'I didn't even think of the Mast disappearance until Red mentioned it. To tell you the truth, I'm not convinced it's related, what with the time gap and his being a male. Won't hurt if you want to run out there. They live in Monongahela Falls.'

'If I recall,' the deputy begins, 'Perry Mast was some kind of Amish elder or deacon.'

Goddard returns his attention to the group, looking from

person to person. 'A missing-person report has been filed on King. All of these girls are categorized as "missing endangered" and Amber Alerts have been issued.' He nods at the trooper. 'The state Highway Patrol has been notified. Info has been entered into NCIC. I also put the call into A Child is Missing, so the ball is rolling.

'Assignments.' Goddard flips to the next page, then looks at the young deputy. 'Lewis, I want you to talk to Mike Campbell. See if he's got an alibi and then check it. If something doesn't jibe, I want to know about it. And don't break any heads. You got that?'

Laughter ripples around the table, but the humor is short-lived. Goddard looks at the officer from the local police department. 'Dale, why don't you guys recanvass the area where the King girl disappeared. Talk to the neighbors again and see if anyone saw anything. And walk those woods again to see if we missed anything.'

Goddard's gaze lands on the older deputy. 'Clyde, you want to come with me to talk to Gilfillan?'

The deputy pats his shirt pocket. 'Got my holy water right here.'

Another round of laugher erupts.

The deputy named Clyde looks at me. 'Fisher place isn't too far from Karns's.'

'We're game if you want us to swing by,' Tomasetti offers.

Goddard and Clyde exchange cockeyed looks, as if they share some amusing secret. 'Might not be a bad idea,' Goddard says.

The deputy chuckles. 'Karns doesn't have much respect for small-town cops.' His gaze narrows on Tomasetti. 'If you don't mind my saying so, you kind of have that big-city look about you.'

'I also carry a sidearm,' Tomasetti says, deadpan.

The beat of silence lasts an instant too long; then everyone in the room breaks into laughter.

It takes Tomasetti and me almost an hour to reach Rocky Fork and locate the Branch Creek Joinery, the woodworking shop owned by Eli and Suzy Fisher. They build kitchen cabinets, desks, and other wood furniture, utilizing only old-fashioned methods and tools. According to Goddard, the business has been in the Fisher family for two generations.

Tomasetti parks in the gravel lot, where two draft horses are hitched to a wagon loaded with cabinetry.

'Looks like they're about to make a delivery,' I say.

'Damn nice cabinets.' Tomasetti shuts down the engine.

The joinery is housed in a nondescript gray building with small windows and a tin roof. We exit the Tahoe and start toward the entrance, which is a plain white door with no window or welcome sign. The absence of a sign, combined with the lack of customer accommodations, tells me they probably don't sell directly to the public, but to area builders and furniture stores.

The odors of freshly cut wood, propane, and diesel fuel greet us when we walk in. The shop is large, with high ceilings and two Plexiglas panels for added light. Several propane lights dangle from steel rafters. An Amish man wearing a light blue work shirt and dark trousers with suspenders taps a chisel against what looks like a headboard. A second Amish man, this one with a salt-and-pepper beard, his hands gnarled with arthritis, operates an ancient treadle lathe with his foot. Somewhere in the back, a generator rumbles.

For several seconds, we stand there, taking it all in. I feel like I've stepped back in time. My *datt* did a good bit of wood-working, making birdhouses and mailboxes, which he sold to one of the local tourist shops. When I was three years old, he made me a wooden rocking horse – against the explicit wishes of my *mamm*. It was painted red, and the rough edges chafed the insides of my thighs. That didn't matter to me; I loved that rocking horse, and my *mamm* couldn't keep me off it. I don't think she ever forgave my *datt* for setting me on the path to eternal damnation.

'May I help you?'

The softly spoken words drag me from my musings. I look up and see an Amish man wearing a light green shirt, dark trousers, and a dark hat approach. I guess him to be about forty-five years old. His full beard tells me he's married. The bulge at his belt indicates that his wife keeps him well fed.

I extend my hand to him, and Tomasetti and I introduce ourselves. 'We're looking for Eli Fisher.'

'I am Eli.'

'We'd like to ask you some questions about your daughter,' Tomasetti begins.

'Bonnie?' Hope leaps into his eyes, and I realize he thinks we're here with news. 'You have some news of her?'

Quickly, I shake my head. 'I'm afraid not, Mr. Fisher. We just want to get some information from you.'

'I have already talked to the police.'

'These are just a few follow-up questions,' Tomasetti replies easily.

Suspicion hardens Fisher's eyes. He knows this is no chance visit. 'It has been two months. What questions do you have now that you did not have before?'

There's a thread of steel in his voice. He's frightened for his daughter and frustrated with the police. He stares at us with direct, intelligent eyes, and I wonder how he was treated by local law enforcement in the agonizing days following her disappearance. I don't believe the sheriff's office had treated him callously, but I know that sometimes cultural differences can cause misunderstandings.

I notice the other man looking our way and lower my voice. 'Is there a place we can speak in private?'

He looks from Tomasetti to me as if trying to decide whether he should throw us out or let us rip his world to shreds one last time. He's wondering if we're there to help him find his daughter, or if we're just two more in a long line of bureaucrats.

After a moment, he nods. 'There is an office in the back.'

He takes us through the shop, past wood shelves filled with intricately carved bread boxes and dollhouses with tiny shutters and a chimney fashioned from cut stones. The workmanship is exquisite, and I find myself wanting to run my fingers over the wood to explore every detail.

'You have many beautiful things.' I say the words in Pennsylvania Dutch.

He gives me a sharp look over his shoulder. 'You speak the language well. How did you come to know it?'

'I was born Amish,' I tell him. 'Did you make the bread boxes yourself?'

'God bestowed upon me the gift of carving. My *datt* didn't see it as ornamentation, but an art form to be nurtured, like a crop. He saw to it that I didn't let it go to waste.'

Eli pauses outside a door and lowers his voice. 'My wife works here in the office. We have spoken to the police many times. It never gets any easier for her.'

'We'll do our best not to upset her,' Tomasetti tells him.

Nodding once, the Amish man opens the door.

The office is small and cluttered, with a single window that looks out over a cherry tree. A plump Amish woman of about forty sits behind a wooden desk, clutching a number 2 pencil as she transfers numbers from a form onto a columnar pad, her concentration intent. When the door clicks shut, she looks up and smiles briefly. I know it the instant she recognizes us as cops. Her hand stills. The smile freezes on her lips.

Her gaze goes to her husband and she slowly rises. 'Is it Bonnie?' she asks hopefully.

Eli shakes his head. 'They have questions for us.'

The woman seems to sink into herself. The hope that had lit her eyes just seconds before goes dark.

'I'm Kate Burkholder.' I cross to her, extend my hand. 'We're sorry to bother you on such a busy day.'

'I'm Suzy.' She returns the shake, but her hand is clammy and limp, as if the life has been drained from her.

'You have a very nice workshop,' I tell her. 'And some lovely things.'

'The Lord has blessed us with much work.'

I note the Rolodex on her desk and the wooden antique card files behind her. 'I see you have a state-of-the-art computer system.'

I'm speaking ironically, of course. While some of the younger Amish might sneak a cell phone and partake in texting or listen to music, the adults who have been baptized do not utilize any kind of electronic gadgetry.

The woman offers a weak smile. 'It contains the names and addresses of every wholesale customer we've had since Eli's grandfather sold his first bread box seventy-six years ago.'

Suzy lowers her eyes to the desktop, sets her hand over her mouth, and closes her eyes tightly. 'We pray every day for her safe return,' she whispers.

To my right, Eli rounds the desk and comes up behind his wife, sets his hand on her shoulder. 'What is it you want to know?' he asks us.

Tomasetti and I read the file before driving over. We know the particulars of the case: when Bonnie went missing, where she was last seen, who searched for her, whom she was last seen with, who was questioned. The local PD interviewed her friends and family. What we're looking for today are any details that, for whatever reason, either weren't included in the reports or that her parents failed to mention.

'In the weeks and days before Bonnie disappeared, what was her frame of mind?' I ask.

If my line of questioning surprises him, Eli doesn't show it. 'She was fine,' he tells me. 'The same as always.'

I look at Suzy. 'Was she troubled by anything? Was she having problems with any of her friends?'

The woman meets my gaze, shakes her head. 'She is a happy girl. Looking forward to helping teach the little ones in the fall.'

'Does she have a beau?'

Suzy's eyes skid right and she picks up her pencil. 'She does not have time for a beau. She stays busy with teaching the children.'

It is then that I realize Eli Fisher is either a better liar than his wife or is oblivious to the fact that his daughter was involved with someone. 'What about arguments? Did either of you have words with her?'

Eli shakes his head. 'Nothing like that.'

I don't take my eyes off of Suzy. Beside me, Tomasetti hangs back, gives me the floor. 'Is that true, Mrs. Fisher?' I ask gently.

'Of course.' But the Amish woman's breaths quicken. Her grip on the pencil tightens so much, her knuckles turn white.

Eli runs his hand lightly over her shoulder before letting it fall to his side. 'Why are you asking these things?' he asks.

'Because I want to find your daughter.'

'We have told the police everything.' He glares at me. 'Why do you come here now and ask the same things all over again?'

'I want to make sure no one left something out that could

be important.' I hold his gaze. 'Something that might help us find Bonnie.'

I feel Tomasetti's attention burning into me, but I don't look away from Eli.

'You think we have done something wrong?' the Amish man asks. 'You think we are guilty of something?'

'I think you're trying to protect your daughter.'

He opens his mouth, but no words come.

'You don't have to protect her from us,' I tell him. 'Please. I need the truth. All of it.'

Suzy raises her eyes to mine. I see a resolve within the depths of her gaze, something I hadn't seen before, and I know my suspicions are correct. She wants to come clean about something, but she doesn't want to speak in front of the men.

'Mr. Fisher,' I begin, 'I was wondering if I could buy one of those bread boxes from you?'

'We don't sell to the pub—'

He stops abruptly when Suzy reaches up and squeezes his hand. 'Sell her the bread box,' the woman says.

I glance at Tomasetti. With a nod, he moves toward the door. 'I know which one you want,' he says over his shoulder as he leaves the room.

Eli takes a final look at his wife. With a shake of his head, he follows.

When we're alone, I address Suzy in Pennsylvania Dutch. 'He's a good husband, isn't he?'

'*Ja.*' She nods adamantly, but her eyes are sad. 'A good father, too.'

I wait.

'But he is a man and there are certain things he cannot understand.'

I don't agree; men are as capable of understanding as women, but I let it go. I watch her struggle with the words; then she raises her gaze to mine. 'Bonnie had a beau,' she says.

'What was his name?'

'I don't know.'

'Was he Amish or English?'

'I do not know.'

'How do you know she had a beau?'

She looks down at the invoice to her left, transfers a number onto the columnar pad. 'Because she was with child.'

I've been around the block a few too many times for this news to shock me. Teenagers having babies is nothing new – even within the Amish community. The thing that does surprise me is that this information hadn't come out before now.

'How far along was she?' I ask.

'I don't know. She wasn't showing yet.'

'She confided in you?'

Her gaze skates away from mine, and I realize she's more hurt by the fact that her daughter didn't confide in her than she is by the out-of-wedlock pregnancy. 'I found the . . . plastic thing,' she tells me. 'You know, from the drugstore.'

'A pregnancy kit?'

'*Ja*. In the trash. She'd tried to hide it, but . . .' A sigh shudders out of her. 'That's when I knew.'

'You asked her about it?'

'She denied it at first, but when I told her I'd found the test, she . . . confessed.'

'Do you know who the father is?'

My question elicits a blank stare, as if it hadn't occurred to her to ask. But I know it had, and I realize with some surprise there's something else going on that she considers even worse than the pregnancy.

'Who's the father?' I ask again.

She transfers another number onto the columnar pad.

'Mrs. Fisher?' I say gently. 'This could be important. Who is he?'

The woman looks down at the desktop, folds her hands in front of her. 'Bonnie doesn't know,' she whispers.

'She had more than one partner?'

The woman jerks her head. 'I don't understand her. I don't understand why she does these things.'

'Do you know the names of the men she was with?'

Her face screws up, but she regains control before the tears come. 'She would not say.'

'Do you know how many there were?'

She puts her face in her hands and shakes her head. 'No.'

'Do you know where she met them?'

'She is . . . secretive about such things. She gets angry when I ask too many questions.'

I want to say something to comfort her. But I'm so far out of my element, I can't find the words. The things I know as a cop would be no comfort, and so I hold my silence.

'We did not teach her to be that way. I don't know how she knew. . . .'

I nod, give her a moment. 'Is there anything else you can think of that might help us find these young men?'

She shakes her head, as if she's too upset to speak. When she raises her gaze to mine, her eyes are haunted. 'Do you think one of the boys might have taken Bonnie?'

'I don't know,' I tell her. 'But I'm going to do my best to find out.'

Ten minutes later, I slide into the Tahoe beside Tomasetti. Neither of us speaks as he backs from the parking space. The two horses and the wagon filled with furniture are still there. Eli Fisher is helping a younger man load a cabinet into the back. He stops what he's doing to watch us. His eyes are shadowed by the brim of his hat, so I can't discern his expression, but he's not smiling and he doesn't wave.

'Mrs. Fisher isn't a very good liar,' Tomasetti says as he pulls onto the road. 'Did you get anything?'

'Bonnie Fisher was pregnant.' Only after the words are out do I realize I'm speaking of her in the past tense.

He glances away from his driving and makes eye contact with me. 'Who's the father?'

'She doesn't know.' I pause. 'Evidently, the girl didn't know, either.'

He cuts me a sharp look. 'Maybe her disappearance is some kind of jealous-lover situation. One guy finds out about the other and the girl gets the short end of the stick.'

'Or maybe lover boy decided he didn't want to be a dad.'

'Wouldn't be the first time.'

I think about that a moment. 'Two of the missing girls were involved in relationships.'

'I don't think that's unusual.'

'Undesirable relationships,' I say, clarifying. 'Especially in the eyes of the Amish.'

He nods. 'Might be something we need to add to the profile.'

I run all of that through my mind. 'Do you think she's dead?'

'Two months is a long time to be missing, Kate.' He grimaces. 'We need the names of the men she was involved with.'

'All we can do at this point is talk to the people she knew,' I tell him. 'Especially her friends.'

As we pull away, I try to put my finger on something else that's bothering me about our meeting with the Fishers, but I can't pinpoint it. I glance out the window and see Eli Fisher standing at the rear of the wagon, watching us, his mouth a thin, flat line.

'You know, Chief, that was pretty smooth, asking for one of those bread boxes.'

I glance over at Tomasetti and see one side of his mouth twitch, and I know he's messing with me. 'How much do I owe you?' I ask.

'I thought maybe you could buy dinner.'

I glance at the clock on the dash. It's almost 6:00 P.M. I wish I could reach out and stop time. 'Is later okay?'

'What do you have in mind?'

'I thought we'd drive up to Monongahela Falls and talk to the parents of the missing boy.'

He gives me a look of feigned disappointment. 'You're not trying to weasel out of dinner, are you?'

'Wouldn't dream of it.'

EIGHT

Irene and Perry Mast live on a mile-wide swath of farmland cut into national forest fifty miles north of Buck Creek. According to Goddard, the farm is over two hundred years old. During the Civil War, the house was part of the Underground Railroad, a stopping point for African slaves escaping to Canada. Now the Masts run a large hog operation and farm corn and soybeans.

Dusk has fallen by the time Tomasetti and I turn into the narrow gravel lane. It's bordered on both sides by vast fields of corn as high as a man's head. I catch the telltale whiff of hog manure as we speed toward the house. Most Amish farms are neat and well managed, the kinds of idyllic places photographers like to capture for postcards or coffee-table books. That's not the case with the Mast farm.

The lane curves right and a sprawling brick house with peeling white paint and a rusty tin roof looms into view. Ahead, a massive barn with red paint weathered to brown greets us like a grizzled old friend. Looking through the fence rails, I see a dozen or so Hampshire hogs rooting around in mud so deep, their bellies scrape the surface.

The farm has a depressed, overused look to it, as if the people who own it no longer have the will to maintain it. I wonder if the loss of their son nine years earlier has anything to do with it.

Tomasetti steers the Tahoe around deep ruts and parks adjacent to the fence. 'Damn place stinks,' he says as he slides out.

'Pigs,' I tell him as I start toward the house. 'Poorly managed manure pit.'

'Great.' We share a look, and I know he's thinking about the case we worked last winter, when three family members perished in the cesspit on their farm.

'There's a light in the metal building over there.'

His voice jerks me back to the present, and I follow his finger as he points. Set back a short distance from the barn, a large windowless steel building looks out of place among the older wood structures. The sliding door stands open about three feet and dim yellow light slants through the opening.

A narrow dirt path cut into knee-high grass takes us toward the shed. We're fifteen feet from the door when I notice several objects the size of soccer balls in the grass. At first, I think they're decorative rocks. I'm nearly upon them before I realize they're severed hog heads.

Tomasetti actually takes a step back, sends me a 'What the fuck?' look.

'They're probably slaughtering hogs,' I explain.

'Well, if the smell of shit isn't bad enough, let's just throw in a couple of severed heads.'

'You want to wait out here?'

He stares down at the heads in disgust. 'This is going to ruin the whole baby back rib thing for me.'

Grinning, I go through the door. 'Man up, Tomasetti.'

I grew up on a farm where the slaughter of livestock was a routine part of life. I bore witness to the process a dozen times before I was old enough to realize how much I hated it.

Sense memories, I think, and I'm surprised at how vividly those days come rushing back.

The smell of dirt and manure and the salty copper stench of blood assaults my senses when I enter the building. A lantern hangs from a wire strung between two rafters and casts yellow light in all directions. A buggy with a missing wheel is parked a few feet away, its dual shafts angling down to the floor. Steel livestock panels lean against the wall. Next to them, an aluminum trough is tipped onto its side. A dozen or more burlap bags filled with some type of grain are stacked neatly atop a flatbed wagon, a good bit of yellow corn spilling onto the floor. Beyond, a shadowy hall leads toward the rear of the building.

'Hello?' I call out as I scan the shadows. I notice the stairs to my right, which lead up to some type of loft. I'm about to call out a second time, when the unmistakable sound of a gunshot explodes.

Next to me, Tomasetti drops down slightly and draws his sidearm. 'Where did it come from?'

I pull my .38. 'I don't know. The hall, maybe.'

A guffaw of laughter draws our attention. I glance toward the hall, where I see a short Amish man with bowed legs emerge from the shadows. He wears a light blue work shirt with dark suspenders and a straw hat. A black rubber bib is tied at his waist, and he's laughing his ass off – at us.

'Can I help you?' He barely gets the words out before breaking into laughter again, bending at the waist and slapping his knees. When he straightens, I see tears on his cheeks.

I holster my .38 and try not to feel like an idiot. 'Mr. Mast?'

Tomasetti isn't amused, and he doesn't relinquish his pistol.

'I'm Benjamin Yoder.' Chuckling, wiping at the tears with his sleeve, the man hobbles over to us. 'My wife and I live next door. I'm helping Perry butcher the hogs.' He looks at Tomasetti, his eyes twinkling. 'You thought the hogs were shooting back, eh?'

Tomasetti holsters his weapon. 'For Chrissake.'

I can't help it; I laugh – a big belly laugh that feels good coming out. Yoder joins me, and I swear I hear Tomasetti chuckle.

After a moment, I extend my hand to Yoder. 'I'm Kate Burkholder.'

Wiping his eyes with his left hand, he pumps my hand with the other. 'Hello, Kate Burkholder. That's a good strong name.' He turns his attention to Tomasetti and the men shake.

'We're with the Ohio Bureau of Criminal Identification and Investigation,' Tomasetti tells him. 'Are the Masts home?'

Yoder's expression falls somber. 'You have news of Noah?'

'Just a few routine questions,' Tomasetti tells him.

We both know none of this is routine for the families of the missing.

'Come this way.' Yoder limps toward the hall. 'I'll take over so he can talk to you.'

I don't miss the revulsion on Tomasetti's face as we pass by a stainless-steel bin filled with severed hog hooves, and I know the slaughter room is the last place he wants to be. Of course he won't admit it, and he falls in next to me. But I suspect it might be a while before he indulges in those baby back ribs.

Yoder leads us down a short hall. Ahead, lantern light spills through a wide door. The stink of fresh manure and blood is stronger here. I can hear the pigs grunting and moving around in the chutes to my right, and I wonder if the animals know their fate. I'm aware of our footsteps on the concrete floor, my heartbeat thudding in my ears. I've never been squeamish, but my stomach seesaws when we reach the room.

Yoder enters first. Tomasetti and I stop at the doorway.

The room is about twenty feet square. The air is overly warm and unpleasantly humid. But it's the smell that unsettles me. Corrugated steel panels comprise the walls. In the center of the room, a dead hog hangs suspended by a single rear leg, a chain wrapped around the area between the hoof and hock. The chain is attached to a pulley affixed to a massive steel beam overhead. A second Amish man, presumably Perry Mast, stands next to the dead animal with a large knife – the sticking knife – in hand. There's a drain cut into the concrete floor and blood still drips from the hog's snout.

'Fuck me,' Tomasetti mutters.

'Maybe we can do this outside,' I hear myself say.

Yoder looks at the hog approvingly. 'That's a good bleed, Perry,' he says.

The other man doesn't even look up. With gloved hands, he shoves the giant carcass toward a massive steaming vat. I don't want to watch what comes next, but I can't look away. I remember my *datt* and brother doing the same thing. They called it 'the scalding tank.' Not bothering with gloves, Yoder jumps in to help guide the carcass toward the vat. He quickly checks an industrial-size thermometer and nods. Using the pulley and chain, they lower the carcass into the hot water.

'*Mir hen Englischer bsuch ghadde,*' Yoder says when the carcass is lowered. *We have non Amish visitors.*

Mast finally glances at us. '*Es waarken maulvoll gat.*' *There's nothing good about that.*

Yoder lowers his voice and, speaking in Pennsylvania Dutch, tells him about us drawing our sidearms. Yoder breaks into laughter again, unabashedly amused. Mast's reaction is more subtle. If I hadn't been watching him, I would have missed the whisper of a smile on his lips.

He motions toward the hog. 'When the hair slips easily, pull it out. I won't be long.'

Without looking at us, he peels off his gloves and removes his blood-spattered apron. He tosses both on the scraping table and starts toward us. Perry Mast is a tall, thin man with sagging jowls and hound-dog eyes. He wears black work trousers with a dark blue shirt, black suspenders, a black vest, and a flat-brimmed straw hat.

'I am Perry Mast,' he says by way of greeting.

Tomasetti and I introduce ourselves, letting him know we're with BCI. Neither of us offers our hand.

'Is this about my son?' he asks.

The question is clearly devoid of hope. And I wonder how many times during the last nine years he asked other law-enforcement officials the same question. I wonder how many times their answers tore the last remnants of hope from his heart.

'I'm sorry, no. There's a girl who's missing,' I tell him. 'An Amish girl. Annie King.'

'*Ja.*' He closes his eyes briefly. 'I heard.'

Tomasetti motions toward the door. 'Is your wife home, Mr. Mast? We'd like to speak with her, as well.'

Mast looks as if he's going to refuse; then his shoulders slump and he seems to resign himself to unavoidable unpleasantness. 'This way,' he says, and leads us through the door.

A few minutes later, Perry Mast, Tomasetti, and I are sitting at the table in their small, cluttered kitchen. The interior of the house isn't much neater than the exterior. Dozens of jars of canned fruits and vegetables cover every available surface on the avocado green countertops. A hand-painted bread box – perhaps from the Branch Creek Joinery – encloses a crusty loaf of bread. A well-seasoned cast-iron skillet sits atop the big potbellied stove. The open cabinets expose stacks of mismatched dishes – blue Melmac and chipped pieces of stoneware – and sealed jars of honey with chunks of honeycomb inside. Home-made window treatments dash the final vestiges of daylight, giving the kitchen a cavelike countenance. A kerosene-powered refrigerator wheezes and groans. The lingering sulfur stink of manure has me thinking twice about coffee.

Irene Mast stands at the counter, running water into an old-fashioned percolator. She's a substantial woman, barely over five feet tall, with thinning silver hair and a bald spot at her crown. She wears a light blue dress with a white apron and low-heeled, practical shoes. The ties of her *kapp* dangle down her back. She hasn't said a word since we were introduced a few minutes ago, but she immediately set about making coffee and bringing out a tin of peanut-butter cookies.

'I understand you're a deacon, Mr. Mast,' I say.

The man looks down at the plate in front of him, gives a single, solemn nod.

'It is a heavy burden,' Irene tells me.

'We'd like to talk to you about your son, Noah,' Tomasetti begins.

The woman's back stiffens at the mention of her son, but when she turns to us, her expression is serene. 'It's been nine years now.' She doesn't look at us as she pours coffee into cups.

That's when I notice the fourth place setting: a plate and silverware, a cup for coffee, a plastic tumbler for milk.

'Nine years is a long time,' I say.

Irene sets a plate with two cookies on it in front of me. 'At first, we hoped, you know. We prayed a lot. But after so much time . . . we've come to believe he is with God.'

'Do you believe he left of his own accord?' I ask. 'Or do you think something bad happened to him?'

The Amish man looks down at the plate in front of him. He's got blood spatter on his shirt, a red smear on the back of his neck. He didn't wash his hands when he came in.

'Noah got into some trouble,' Perry says. 'The way young men do sometimes.'

'What kind of trouble?' I ask.

'The drinking, you know. The listening to music. And he liked . . . the girls.'

'He confessed his sins before the bishop,' Irene adds.

In the eyes of the Amish, confessing your sins is the equivalent of a 'Get out of jail free' card. No matter how heinous the offense, if you confess, you are forgiven.

'The English police say Noah wanted to leave the plain life,' Perry says after a moment. 'I don't know who told them that. We don't believe it. We never did.'

'Noah loved being Amish.' Emotion flashes in Irene's eyes. 'He was a humble boy with a kind and generous heart.'

'What do you think happened to him?' Tomasetti asks.

Perry shakes his head. 'We don't know. The things the *Englischers* say . . .' His voice trails off, as if he's long since tired of saying the words.

I skimmed the file that had been amassed on Noah before leaving the sheriff's office. A missing-person report was filed. People were interviewed, searches conducted. The cops – and most of the Amish, too – believed the boy ran away.

'What did the *Englischers* say?' I ask gently.

The Masts exchange a look, and an uncomfortable silence falls. We let it ride, giving them some time.

'There were rumors.' Perry grimaces. 'And not just among the English. Some of the Amish young people . . . knew things.'

'Idle gossip.' His wife sends him a sharp look. 'All of it.'

Tomasetti trains his attention on Perry. 'Like what?'

The Amish man stares into his coffee. 'There is a man. Gideon Stoltzfus. He used to be plain, but he could not abide by the *Ordnung* and was put under the *bann*. I've heard he helps young Amish men leave the plain life.'

'He is a *Mennischt*.' Irene spits the word for Mennonite as if it has a bad taste.

'After Noah disappeared, we found out he'd been in touch with Stoltzfus.' Perry blows on his coffee and slurps. I see blood under his fingernails, cookie crumbs in his beard, and I look away. 'We believe Gideon may have filled Noah's young mind with untruths about the Amish.'

'The Mennonites recruit,' Irene says.

Being formerly Amish myself, I know men like Stoltzfus exist. There's a man in Painters Mill who helps young Amish leave the lifestyle. He runs a sort of Underground Railroad, giving them a place to stay while they transition. Contrary to what the Masts believe, these men are not the brainwashing monsters they're made out to be, but a bridge to an alternative lifestyle. But if Noah met with Stoltzfus, it wasn't in the file.

'Do you think Stoltzfus helped Noah leave?' I ask.

'I don't know what to believe.' Taking a final sip of his coffee, Perry gets to his feet. 'I need to get back to work.'

Tomasetti and I rise simultaneously. Neither of us touched the cookies or coffee.

'Thank you both for your time,' I say.

Without speaking, Perry, Tomasetti, and I start toward the door. I'm keenly aware of the silence in the house, broken only by the clink of dishes as Irene clears the table and the hollow thud of our boots on the floor, and I can't help but think that this is a very lonely house.

We're midway through the mudroom when Irene calls out, 'If you find our Noah, you'll bring him back to us, *ja*?'

Perry continues toward the door, not even acknowledging her. Tomasetti and I stop and turn. 'If we learn anything new, you'll be the first to know,' I tell her, and we step into the night.

Tomasetti and I are midway down the lane before speaking. 'What do you think?' he asks as he turns onto the highway that will take us to Buck Creek.

'Kid's been gone nine years and they still set the table for him.' I sigh. 'That's one sad, lonely couple.'

'Losing a kid . . .' He grimaces. 'Fucks up your life.'

There are a lot of themes running through this case, threads that hit a little too close to home for both of us. I think about the parallels, the jagged lines that connect us in so many unexpected ways. 'It's interesting that Noah Mast and Annie King had talked about leaving the Amish way of life,' I tell him.

'Do you think it's relevant?' He turns onto a township road, the headlights washing over tall rows of corn. 'Some kind of pattern?'

'I don't know. But it's unusual. Most Amish kids are content to remain Amish. They're happy and well adjusted. Tomasetti, something like eighty percent of kids go on to be baptized.'

'Maybe it's a connection.'

I glance at the dash clock. Another hour has flown by. It's already nine o'clock. 'Let's go talk to talk to Stoltzfus.'

Tomasetti cuts me a look, and in the dim glow of the dash lights, I see him smile. 'Get Goddard on the horn and get an address.'

I call Goddard for the address while Tomasetti pumps gas. According to the sheriff, the formerly Amish man lives a quiet life and keeps his nose relatively clean. I relay the highlights to Tomasetti as we enter the corporation limits of Buck Creek.

'Thirty-two-year-old white male. One arrest. No convictions. He's worked at the Martin-Bask Lumberyard for six years. Unmarried. No known children.'

'Sounds like a pretty boring guy.'

'Except he runs an Underground Railroad for young Amish people trying to leave the lifestyle and was known to speak to at least one Amish teen who is now missing.'

'Guess that excludes him from the boring category.' Tomasetti turns onto Township Road 5 and heads south. 'What was the arrest for?'

'Trespassing.'

'That's interesting.'

'Goddard remembered the incident. Apparently, a local Amish man discovered Stoltzfus in his barn at four o'clock in the morning, having sex with his son.'

'Bet that was a shocker. Son over eighteen?'

I nod. 'It was consensual. The Amish guy got in contact with the cops. They arrested Stoltzfus, filed a report. But once the complainant had a chance to think about the consequences – mainly, outing his son – he decided not to press charges.'

We zip past a mailbox at the mouth of a gravel lane, and Tomasetti hits the brakes. 'That was it.' Throwing the Tahoe into reverse, he backs up and pulls in. A minute later, we park next to a white Ford F-150. A single porch light illuminates a two-car garage with a door in need of paint. A cord of split logs is stacked neatly against the west side. The house is a small white frame structure with green shutters and a deck in the back.

We exit the vehicle and take the sidewalk to the porch. Tomasetti knocks and we wait, watching each other, not speaking. Then the door swings open and I find myself staring at a baby-faced young man with brown hair and matching eyes. He wears a Metallica T-shirt with faded jeans and dirty white socks. His hair is sticking up on one side, and I suspect we roused him from a nap.

'Can I help you?'

I can tell by his inflection that he grew up Amish. He's got that distinctive accent I recognize immediately.

'Gideon Stoltzfus?' Tomasetti presents his identification.

'Yeah.' He blinks at the ID. 'What's this about?'

'We're working on a case and we'd like to ask you a few questions,' I say. 'Can we come in?'

'Uh . . . sure.' He opens the door cautiously, as if expecting us to pounce on him and wrestle him to the ground.

We follow him to a small kitchen that smells of burned popcorn. The place is comfortable and relatively clean, but I can tell it's a bachelor pad. Knotty-pine cabinets line robin's egg blue walls. I see faux granite countertops. An obese dachshund lies on a grimy throw rug by the sink, probably deaf, because it didn't bark when we entered. There's a high-tech coffeemaker with a built-in grinder and timer. A tiny microwave sits on the counter, its door standing open. Cheap art hangs on the wall. Country music rumbles in another part of the house. I hear the yappy bark of a second dog, which has apparently been barred access to visitors.

At the counter, Stoltzfus turns to us and shoves his hands into his pockets. 'You want some coffee or something?' He motions to a small table that's not quite large enough for three people.

'We're fine.' Tomasetti's smile looks like a snarl.

Stoltzfus is an unassuming man with a quiet demeanor. He's wondering why we're here. His eyes shift from Tomasetti to me and he begins to fidget. I wonder why he's so nervous.

Tomasetti lets him sweat for a minute before asking his first question. 'I understand you run an Underground Railroad for young people wanting to leave the Amish way.'

'Underground Railroad?' Stoltzfus laughs, but it's a tight, tense sound.

Tomasetti glowers. 'What's so funny?'

Stoltzfus's Adam's apple bobs twice. 'I've never heard it put like that. It sounds kind of dramatic.'

'Why don't you clear things up for us and just tell us what you do,' I say.

His eyes flick again from Tomasetti to me. 'Am I in some kind of trouble?'

'We just want to know how you work.' I offer my best girl-next-door smile. 'Why don't you start by telling us how you find the young people who need help.'

My reassurance seems to bolster him and he calms down. 'Word of mouth, mostly. Buck Creek is a small town. People talk, and that includes the Amish. I usually hear about it when one of these kids wants to leave.'

'How do you make contact?'

'Usually, they contact me.'

'You used to be Amish?' I ask.

He looks down, and I realize whether he recognizes it or not, he's still conflicted. 'I've been gone ten years now.'

'Do you mind if I ask why you left?' I ask.

'I couldn't abide by the rules. I mean, living without electricity and a car was bad enough. But I wanted to go to college.' He shrugs. 'I didn't want to be a farmer. I didn't want that kind of future.'

'Any regrets?'

His eyes lock onto mine. 'I miss my family. I have four younger sisters. They looked up to me.' He gives a self-deprecating laugh. 'Hell, I still drive by the place. How pathetic is that?'

I find myself liking him despite my resolve to remain neutral. 'You see your siblings?'

He breaks eye contact, looks down at his stocking feet. 'Parents don't want me seeing them. They think I'm a bad influence, I guess.'

I nod, understanding more than he could know. 'What happens after a young person makes contact with you?'

'I offer him a place to stay. Lend him money if he needs it. Counsel him.' Stoltzfus likes to talk, I realize, and he's warming to us. 'It's harder than most people think. Leaving, I mean. You see, when you're Amish, your family is everything to you. It's like they're your whole *universe*. A lot of young people want to leave but don't because of their families. So I give them a neutral place, without judging them, and without the pressure of their families or the elders.'

'You're Mennonite now?'

He nods. 'The religious beliefs are similar, but you don't have to live your life as if it's the eighteenth century.'

I pause to give Tomasetti an opening. 'What can you tell us about Noah Mast?' he asks.

All semblance of tranquillity leaves Stoltzfus. His left eyelid begins to flutter. 'I didn't really know him. Noah was a few years younger than me, but I'd see him around. After I left, he got in touch with me and told me he wanted to leave. Asked me how to do it.'

'Did you help him?'

'I would have, but I never heard from him again.'

'At the time, had you been actively helping other Amish youths leave the lifestyle?'

'Well, I wasn't organized about it, not like I am now. But yeah. I helped a couple kids back in those early days. I mean, it had been so hard for me.' Another nervous laugh. 'I felt . . . compelled to help others.'

'What else can you tell us about Noah?' Tomasetti says the words amicably, but his stare is intense.

'Alls I remember is he told me he wanted out. I gathered he wasn't getting along with his folks. I offered to help him.' Stoltzfus shrugs. 'Next thing I know, he's missing.'

'Were you surprised?'

'Not really. I figured he'd just done it on his own.'

'Do you know Annie King?' Tomasetti asks.

His eyes go wide, and he begins blinking. He looks at us as if realizing he's wandered into a lion's den and his only escape is now blocked. 'You guys don't think I had anything to do with *that*, do you?'

'Did you know her?' Tomasetti repeats.

'No.'

'Did you have any contact with her?'

'No!'

'She didn't approach you? Ask you to help her?'

'Lookit, I never met her. Never talked to her. And that's the truth.'

NINE

'He's either a damn good liar or he's telling the truth,' Tomasetti says as he makes the turn onto the highway that will take us to the motel.

'I believe him,' I say. 'At least with regard to Noah Mast.'

'Seemed kind of nervous.'

'You were snarling at him.'

'I wasn't snarling.' But in the dim light of the dash, I see his mouth curve.

Feeling the drag of thirty-six hours without sleep, I look out the window. 'No one seems like a good fit.'

'Until we find someone more viable, we've got to go through the motions.' He glances away from his driving. 'You hungry? There's a restaurant down the road from the motel.'

'I saw it. The Flying Buck.' Having not eaten since last night, I'm starving. 'And it's a bar, Tomasetti, not a restaurant.'

'Since our restaurant choices are limited, we could probably have a beer with a burger without breaking too many rules.'

'No shots, though.'

'Suits would probably frown upon that.'

It's nearly ten o'clock when we pull into the gravel lot of the Flying Buck. Our headlights wash over a single vehicle, a nondescript Camry that looks as if it's just been waxed. The building itself is actually a double-wide mobile home painted in green camo. A hunting mural depicts two Labradors bounding through water and two orange-vested hunters taking aim.

A gravel walkway takes us to a covered porch scattered with tables for summertime dining. We enter through a thick wooden door capped with a set of twelve-point antlers. The interior is dim and smells like dozens of other bars where I've spent too much time – a combination of cooking grease, liquor, and cigarette smoke. An old Allman Brothers song about one more silver dollar crackles from a single overhead speaker. The bar is to our right, an ancient slab of wood that's seen more than its share of calloused elbows, slurred speech, and spilled beer. A hunched old man in a cowboy hat sits with his leg crossed over his knee, smoking a pipe. The rest rooms are in the back. A sign says SIT THE HELL DOWN. We choose a table at the rear.

Tomasetti pulls out my chair for me. I want to believe he's doing it because he's a gentleman. But I know he will never sit down in any public place with his back to the door. Some people might call that paranoid. Not me. Maybe because I know if some crazy shit walks in with a gun, Tomasetti will be ready.

A skinny waitress with blue-gray hair and bony legs rushes to our table and slaps down menus. 'Hi, folks. You here for dinner or drinks?'

'Both,' Tomasetti says. 'And not necessarily in that order.'

She chuckles. 'That's what I like to hear. What can I get for ya?'

We order two bottles of Killian's Irish Red and burgers with fries, and the waitress hustles away.

'What bothers me about Stoltzfus,' Tomasetti begins, 'is that he's put himself in the position of having access to disgruntled Amish teenagers.'

Something scratches at the back of my brain, but I can't quite reach it. 'Child predators operate much the same way.'

'And he's had contact with at least one of the missing.'

The waitress returns to the table with our beers and two frosty mugs. 'Be right back with those burgers.'

Tomasetti pours. We pick up the glasses and, watching each other over the rims, drink deeply. It's the first alcohol I've had since the Slabaugh case six months ago, and I don't want to acknowledge how good it goes down.

I'm still thinking about Stoltzfus when my cell vibrates against my hip. I glance down at the display, expecting another frantic call from Auggie. I'm surprised to see a number I don't recognize on the display.

I answer, saying, 'Burkholder.'

'This is Suzy Fisher.'

Surprise ripples through me at the sound of her voice. Not only is it unusual for an Amish person to use the telephone but it's also late – well past bedtime for an Amish woman. 'Hello, Mrs. Fisher. Is everything all right?'

'I'm sorry about the lateness of the hour,' she says breathlessly. 'But I couldn't sleep. I took the buggy to town to use the pay phone there.' She chokes out the words, as if her throat is too tight. 'Eli doesn't know.'

'It's okay,' I tell her. 'What is it?'

'I didn't tell you something today that I should have. I think it might be important.'

'About Bonnie?'

'*Ja.*' Only then do I realize she's crying. 'Bonnie loves babies. She loves children. She's so excited about teaching at the school in the fall.'

I wait, knowing there's more.

'Chief Burkholder, she was confused about the baby.'

'What do you mean?' But even as I voice the question, realization dawns. 'She didn't want the child?'

'We would have loved the child.'

'Mrs. Fisher, did Bonnie talk about terminating the pregnancy?'

'It goes against our belief system.' She begins to cry in earnest. 'I tried to talk her out of it, but she was so ashamed. So determined to do this thing. It was the last time I saw her.'

The words shock me. Most Amish believe abortion is murder. During my lifetime, I've known two Amish women who terminated pregnancies. One of them, though she confessed her sin before the congregation, felt so condemned by her peers, she ended up leaving the Amish way. The other committed suicide.

'Mrs. Fisher, I know it wasn't easy for you to come forward with this,' I tell her. 'Thank you. I think this could be important.'

'Please find her for us, Chief Burkholder. We don't care about her mistakes. We just want her back.'

'I'll do my best,' I tell her. 'I promise.'

The line goes dead. I take my time clipping my phone to my belt, then turn my attention to Tomasetti and recap the conversation. 'She never told her husband.'

'It sounds like these two girls – Bonnie Fisher and Annie King – were behaving way outside of Amish norms,' Tomasetti says after a moment.

I nod in agreement, thinking of the third girl, whose family was killed in the buggy accident. 'It would have been helpful to talk to Leah Stuckey's parents to see if she was somehow acting out, too.'

'Might have helped us figure out if their behavior somehow ties in to their disappearances.'

'We both know certain kinds of behavior can put people at risk.' I shrug. 'But does it connect the cases?'

'We've got too many threads, and none of them ties to anything.'

We pause when the waitress sets our burgers in front of us. We both look down at our plates. The food looks good and smells even better. We dig in with gusto.

'Let's put everything on the table,' he says.

I go first. 'Maybe there's a religious angle.'

'The Twelve Passages Church,' he says. 'According to Goddard, they don't like the Amish.'

'That could tie in. Annie King had an English boyfriend. Bonnie Fisher was pregnant, had multiple partners, and was considering an abortion.'

'That's enough to piss off any self-respecting religious fanatic.' Tomasetti's tone is bone-dry.

'So we keep everyone with ties to The Twelve Passages Church on our list of suspects.'

We concentrate on our food for a couple of minutes. Tomasetti finishes the last of his Killian's. I look down at my plate, drag a fry through catsup, running everything we know about the case so far through my head.

'Do you think Noah Mast's disappearance is related?' Tomasetti asks after a moment.

'I don't know,' I say honestly. 'According to Stoltzfus, he talked about leaving.' I think of the place setting for him in the Mast kitchen. 'You're checking into other missing-person cases? Cold cases?'

He nods. 'If there's something else out there, VICAP will kick it out.'

'If it's been reported.'

He gives me a sharp look. 'Do you think Amish parents might not file a missing-person report if one of their kids went missing?'

'Most would,' I tell him. 'Initially, they might try to handle

123

it themselves. But I think eventually, when they got scared and the reality of the situation sank in, they'd turn to the police.' I think about that for a moment. 'That said, there's a large faction of Amish who believe God will take care of them. If you combine that with a general mistrust of the English, particularly the English police, then I could see a family not making an official report.'

'Something to keep in mind.'

I nod, move on to other possible scenarios. 'What about the photographer Goddard mentioned?'

'Stacy Karns.'

'That conviction and the fact that his victim was a young Amish female definitely puts him on the list.' I glance at my watch. 'We could pay him a visit.'

'I think he'll keep until morning.' He gazes steadily at me. 'You look tired, Kate. Have you had any sleep?'

'Not much.'

He lays a couple of bills on the table. 'What do you say we call it a night and check out the Buck Snort Motel?'

The Buck Snort Motel is located on the main highway two miles outside Buck Creek. Set back from the road in a heavily wooded area, the motel is comprised of a dozen or so cabins replete with picnic tables and a community pit barbecue. Lights burn in two of the cabins. As we pull into the gravel lot, I see a group of kids sitting at one of the picnic tables. The motel office is a larger cabin with a huge front window and the requisite red neon sign that blinks VACANCY. A smaller sign boasts FREE MOVIES.

Tomasetti parks adjacent the office and kills the engine. 'I'll check us in and grab the keys.'

Without waiting for a reply, he's out of the Tahoe and striding toward the office. I watch him, vaguely aware that I'm admiring the way he moves, when it strikes me that I have no idea what kind of sleeping arrangements have been made – or how the night is going to play out. When we've worked together in the past, our relationship has never been an issue and we've never let it interfere. The investigation always takes precedence. This case is different in that both of us are away from home base, and I can't help but wonder if it's going to get in the way.

The door swings open, startling me. Tomasetti slides in, then cranks the engine. Without looking at me, he drives to the farthest cabin and parks. 'I'm in cabin twelve. You're in eleven.'

'So we're neighbors.' Without looking at him, I reach into the back for my overnight bag.

He stops me. 'I'll get that for you.'

'Sure. Thanks.' I make my exit before I start blabbering and watch as he opens the rear door and pulls out both our overnight bags.

We walk to cabin 11, and he unlocks the door, then passes me the key. The first thing I notice is the bed. It's a full with a camouflage pattern spread and a headboard made of deer antlers. A night table holds a single lamp, the base of which is constructed of antlers. Camo curtains. Hunting art on the walls – ducks and deer and Labrador retrievers. But the room is neat and smells of clean linens and cedar.

'I believe this is the most antlers I've ever seen in one place,' I say.

'Might be a problem if you're a restless sleeper.'

I laugh. 'Better than mounted heads on the walls.'

'Heads are probably in my room.' Chuckling, he sets my bag on the bed, then quickly checks the bathroom. 'Coffeemaker in the bathroom,' he tells me when he emerges.

On the small table near the window, a handwritten sign tells me the room is equipped with free Wi-Fi. I see a hookup for a laptop and a pad of paper printed with the motel's name and logo. 'All the comforts of home.'

An awkward silence falls. The rise of tension is palpable. I look at Tomasetti and find his eyes already on me. For the span of a full minute, neither of us speaks, and neither of us looks away.

'So how are we going to do this?' he asks after a moment.

The question needs no clarification. 'I don't know,' I say honestly. 'I'm kind of out of my element here.'

'Me, too,' he says. 'I'm used to traveling alone.'

'I'm used to you sneaking into my house through the back door in the middle of the night.'

He laughs.

Time freezes for the span of several heartbeats. I feel the weight of his stare, the power of my attraction to him. I sense the importance of this moment, the discomfort between us.

We've slept together before in the course of an investigation. We work well together despite our personal relationship. But this is my first consulting gig, and it feels different. It feels . . . premeditated.

'I don't want to screw this up,' I say after a moment.

'You won't,' he says quietly. 'You can't.'

'Maybe we should just take it slow.'

He nods and steps back. Some of the intensity leaches from the moment, and I can breathe again.

Bending, he brushes his mouth against mine. 'Careful with that headboard.' He walks to the door and turns to face me. 'Get some rest, Chief, and I'll see you in the morning.'

I stand there vibrating and breathless for a full minute after he closes the door, not sure if I'm relieved he's gone or disappointed I let him go.

Finally, I turn on the television, find the local news, and listen with half an ear as I unpack my clothes and put them away. I try to focus on the case as I set up my laptop and log onto my e-mail account. But the encounter with Tomasetti has left me unsettled. Combined with thirty-six hours without sleep, I can't concentrate and I'm too tired to be productive. I answer a few e-mails and head for the shower.

The truth of the matter is, I don't know where our relationship is heading. I enjoy being with him, working with him. My trust in him is absolute. I respect him on every level, and I believe those sentiments run both ways.

The long-distance aspect of our relationship has worked for both of us. We're too independent for anything too cozy. But I know that no matter how hard we try to keep things simple, relationships have a way of becoming complicated.

There are times when I think I love him. I want to be with him when I'm not. He's constantly in the periphery of my thoughts. When something amazing happens, he's the one I want to share it with. I honestly don't know if that's good or bad. Truth be told, it scares me. I can't seem to get past that little voice in my head that tells me what we have is too good to last.

I know my own heart, but so much of Tomasetti remains a mystery. Three years ago, he was married and had children. I don't know if he was happy or discontent or, like the rest of us, somewhere in between. He rarely speaks of his past. But I know he loved them. I know he loved another woman and had children with her. And I know the loss of them nearly killed him.

Sometimes, when he's untouchable, when I can't reach him, I wonder if she's the one he wants to be with. I wonder if he's still in love with her. I wonder if I'm with him because she isn't, if I'm competing with a dead woman.

*

The sound of my cell phone drags me from a deep and dreamless sleep. I fumble for it on the night table, flip it open, put it to my ear. 'Burkholder,' I rasp.

Even before I hear Tomasetti's voice, I know it's bad. When a cop is awakened in the middle of the night, it's never good news.

'We've got a body,' he says without preamble.

I sit bolt upright, disoriented, my heart pounding. The room is pitch-black, and for an instant, I can't remember where I am. Then the case rushes into my brain, the missing Amish teens, the blood on the road, and I'm out of bed and reaching for my clothes.

'Is it Annie?' I ask as I jam my legs into my slacks.

'I don't know.'

'Give me five minutes.'

TEN

The glowing red numbers of the alarm clock tell me it's 3:53 A.M. when I go through the door. Tomasetti has already pulled the Tahoe up to the gravel area outside my cabin and is leaning against the passenger side's front fender, talking on his cell phone. The night is humid and still, and I smell rain in the air.

He cuts his call short as I climb in. A moment later, he's behind the wheel and we're idling across the parking lot. 'Hell of a way to start the day,' he growls.

'Tell me what you know,' I say.

'Not much. There's no positive ID yet. But apparently, the victim is a young female.'

I think of a young life cut short, the parents who will be notified in the coming hours, the family that will be shattered by the news. I feel the familiar rise of outrage in my chest.

The tires spew gravel as we pull onto the highway. Beside me, Tomasetti scans the darkened storefronts and black shadows of the foliage as we cross a bridge and head toward town. He's in cop mode, I realize, already hunting for the perpetrator.

'Where's the body?' I ask.

'In a creek, evidently. Guy out fishing found her.'

I cringe at the thought. Murder is always horrific, but water somehow always makes it worse. In terms of evidence, it has just made our jobs exponentially more difficult. 'Anyone on-scene?'

'Goddard's en route.' He tosses me a grim look. 'We're closer.'

'Coroner?'

'There's a team from Youngstown on the way.'

I glance at him. He looks grim and tired and not quite friendly. He's not a good sleeper, and I suspect last night wasn't any different.

We pass through Buck Creek and head north on a narrow two-lane road that cuts through a heavily forested area. A few miles in, we come to a rusty steel bridge. A big Dodge Ram is parked on a gravel turnout. Tomasetti parks behind the truck, kills the engine, and grabs a Maglite off the backseat. 'There's another one in the door panel.'

I find the flashlight and swing open my door. The night sounds – crickets and bullfrogs and nocturnal animals – emanate from the thick black of the woods.

Tomasetti is already walking toward the truck. 'Where the hell's the driver?' he mutters.

I look around, but there's no one in sight. I set my hand on my revolver as we start toward the Dodge. Chances are, this call is exactly as it seems: a citizen who's stumbled upon a terrifying scene. But we're all too aware of the fact that where there is murder, there is also a murderer. More than one cop has been ambushed when he thought he was walking into a benign scene.

Lightning flickers on the horizon as I reach the truck. Tomasetti tries the driver's door, but it's locked. Using the Maglite, he checks the interior, sets his hand on the hood. 'Still warm.'

I drop to my knees, shine my beam along the ground. 'No one underneath.'

We're checking the truck's bed when I hear something large crashing through the brush on the other side of the bar ditch twenty yards away. At first, I think it's some kind of animal – a rutting buck or a black bear – charging us. Adrenaline skitters through my midsection. I raise my sidearm and spin to face the path cut into the trees.

Tomasetti rounds the front of the truck and comes up beside me, his Glock leading the way. 'Police!' he shouts. 'Stop! Identify yourself!'

A man bursts from the darkness, stumbles, and goes to his hands and knees in the grass. Both Tomasetti and I take a step back as he scrambles to his feet and lunges toward us. I catch a glimpse of a bald head and a tan flannel shirt.

'Jesus Christ!' he cries as he uses his hands to scale the incline.

'Hold it right there, partner,' Tomasetti says. 'I mean it.'

His voice is deadly calm, but the man doesn't seem to hear him. He's either high on drugs or terrified out of his mind. Considering the nature of the stop, I'm betting on the latter.

I maintain a safe distance as the man regains his footing and stumbles up the side of the bar ditch. He's breathing so hard, he's choking on every exhale. He's slightly overweight and falls to his hands and knees in the gravel ten feet away.

Tomasetti dances back, keeps his weapon trained on the center of the man's chest. 'Get your hands where we can see them.'

The man is so out of breath, he doesn't raise his hands. 'For God's sake, don't shoot! I'm the one who called the cops.' He gulps air, chokes on his own spit, and begins to cough.

Scowling, Tomasetti lowers his weapon, but he doesn't holster it. 'What happened?'

'There's a fucking dead body down there!' the man chokes out.

Tomasetti's eyes dart to the woods. Using his left hand, he shines the beam of the Maglite on the trailhead. Nothing moves. It's as if the forest has gone silent to guard the secrets that lie within its damp and murky embrace.

'Is there anyone else down there?' Tomasetti asks.

'I didn't see no one except that fuckin' body.' He coughs, taking great gulps of air. 'Just about gave me a heart attack.'

'What's your name?' I ask.

'Danny . . . Foster.' The man raises his head and squints at us. 'Who're you? Where's Sheriff Goddard?'

I pull out my identification and hold it out for him to see. 'You got your driver's license on you?'

He straightens and, still on his knees, digs out his wallet and thrusts it at me with a shaking hand.

Tomasetti comes up beside me and glances at the wallet, then frowns. 'What are you doing down there?'

'F – fishing.'

'At four o'clock in the morning?'

'Well, I gotta be at work at eight,' he snaps.

Tomasetti holsters his sidearm, and I do the same.

The man looks from Tomasetti to me. 'Can I get up now?'

'Sure,' I say.

He hefts his large frame and struggles to his feet. He's a short, round man wearing oversize khaki pants, a flannel shirt, and a fishing vest. From ten feet away, I see that his crotch is wet.

'What happened?' Tomasetti asks.

'I was fishing by that deep hole down there, about a quarter mile in.' Swallowing hard, Foster jabs his thumb toward the path from which he emerged. 'I'd just put my line in when I noticed something on the bank, tangled up in some tree roots.' He heaves a phlegmy cough. 'I thought it was one of them mannequins, like at the department store down there at the mall. I put my light on it and got the shock of my life. Scariest damn thing I ever saw.'

'You sure she's dead?' Tomasetti asks.

'Her eyes were all fuckin' glassy and looking right at me.' He blows out a breath. 'She's dead all right.'

Tomasetti digs out his cell phone, hits speed dial. I listen with half an ear as he explains the situation to Goddard and asks him to set up a perimeter with roadblocks around this part of the creek.

'What did you do after you found the body?' I ask.

'I puked my guts out; then I called nine one one.' He takes a deep breath, blows it out. 'Then I got the hell out of there.'

The flash of blue and white lights on the treetops announces the arrival of a law-enforcement vehicle. I glance behind me and see a sheriff's department cruiser park behind the Tahoe.

'Where, exactly, did you find the body?' Tomasetti asks.

Foster thrusts a finger toward the mouth of the path. 'Take the trail. You'll hit the creek a quarter mile in. Go another thirty yards and you'll see it on your right. There's a tree grows into the bank. Floods washed out the soil and the roots are exposed. She's jammed up in all them roots.'

Beyond where Tomasetti stands, I see Sheriff Goddard slide out of his Crown Vic, his Maglite in hand, its beam trained on the fisherman. 'Danny?' he calls out. 'That you?'

'Yeah, Bud.' The man heaves a huge sigh. 'I'm here.'

The sheriff nods at Tomasetti and me, then turns his attention to Foster. 'What the hell you doing out here this time of the morning?'

'Fishing, like I always do. There're large-mouth bass down in that deep hole. I don't know why everyone keeps asking me that when I done answered already.'

'Well,' the sheriff drawls, 'you know how cops are.'

I see sheet creases in his face and I know he was also ripped from his bed, the same as Tomasetti and I, and he's not in a very good mood.

Goddard shines his light on Foster's clothes. 'How'd you get that mud all over you?'

Foster looks down at his pants, realizes his crotch is wet, and pulls out his shirttail to cover it. 'I got so shook up when I found that woman down there, I dropped my flashlight and got off the trail. I fell down in some bramble.'

Tomasetti looks at Goddard. 'You get a perimeter set up?'

Goddard nods. 'I got two deputies out there. State Highway Patrol's on the way. We're covered, but barely.'

'We'd like to take a look at the scene, if it's all right with you,' Tomasetti says.

The flash of relief that crosses the chief's face is palpable. Most cops are, to a degree, adrenaline junkies. When something big goes down, most want to be in the thick of it. Some, I would venture to say, have an overstated sense of morbid curiosity. Goddard seems to break the mold on all counts. 'Probably best if a bunch of us don't trample the scene,' he says. 'You two go on, and I'll wait for the coroner.'

With Tomasetti in the lead, we descend the steep shoulder, cross through the bar ditch, and enter the path cut into the woods. The canopy closes over us like a clammy, smothering hand. Around us, the woods are dark and damp and alive with insects and nocturnal creatures. Mist swirls along the ground and rises like smoke from the thick undergrowth. Neither of us is dressed for wet conditions – no boots or slickers – and within minutes the front of our clothes is soaked.

The redolence of foliage and damp earth and the dank smell of the creek curl around my olfactory nerves as we move deeper into the forest. Dew drips from the leaves of the brush growing along the path and the treetops overhead. Mud sucks at our shoes. The low rumble of thunder tells me conditions are probably going to get worse before they get any better.

Tomasetti's Maglite penetrates the darkness like a blade. But the path is overgrown in areas and difficult to follow. Twice he veers off the trail and we have to backtrack.

'There's the creek.'

I follow the beam of his flashlight and catch a glimpse of the green-blue surface of slow-moving water. We continue for a few more yards, and I spot the tree Foster mentioned. An ancient bois d'arc grows out of the steep bank, its trunk leaning at a forty-five-degree angle. 'There's the tree.'

My heart taps out a rapid tattoo as we approach the water's edge. Vaguely, I'm aware of the flicker of lightning overhead and the patter of rain against the canopy above. Tomasetti stops where the ground breaks off and shines the beam downward. The dead are never pretty, but water does particularly gruesome things to a corpse. I come up beside Tomasetti and my eyes follow the cone of light.

I see the glossy surface of the muddy bank, the spongy moss covering the rocks, and the spindly black veins of roots. My gaze stops on the gauzy fabric flowing in the current like the gossamer fin of some exotic fish. I see the white flesh of a woman's calf, a slightly bent knee, a waxy thigh. Lower, the foot is swallowed by the murky depths below. She's clothed, perhaps in a dress, but the current has pushed the skirt up to her hips, exposing plain cotton panties – the kind a young Amish woman might wear.

She's faceup; her left arm is twisted at an awkward angle and tangled in the roots. My eyes are drawn to the pallid face. Her mouth is open, as if in a scream, and full of water and leaves. A cut gapes on her lower lip. Her eyes are partially open, but the irises are colorless and cloudy.

'Fuck me,' Tomasetti mutters.

Looking at the body, watching her long hair ebb and flow with the current is surreal. Neither of us moves or speaks. The tempo of the rain increases, but I barely notice. I don't feel the wet or the cold. I can't stop looking at the dead girl, and I wonder how her life came to this terrible end so long before her time.

I pull myself back to reality. When I speak, my voice is level and calm. 'How long do you think she's been there?'

'She's intact. No deterioration that I can see.'

I wait for him to elaborate, but he doesn't. 'No visible wounds,' I say, thinking about the blood we found on the road that afternoon.

'Still wearing her underclothes.'

But we both know it's no guarantee that a sexual assault wasn't committed. Perpetrators have been known to re-dress their victims. 'No makeup or jewelry. Nails are unpainted. Tomasetti, that dress is an Amish print.'

'Goddamn it.'

I look upstream, toward the bridge, but it's too dark to see anything. 'You think someone dumped her here? Or at the bridge?'

He shines the beam on the ground, illuminating several footprints, ours and a waffle stamp that may or may not be Foster's. But there are no broken branches. No crushed grass. No blood. 'No obvious sign of a struggle,' he growls. 'We're going to need to get tread imprints from Foster's shoes.'

He trains the beam on the steep bank directly below us, then shines it across the surface of the water. The creek is about twenty-five feet wide. It looks deep, but I can hear the gurgle of a shallow bottleneck a few yards downstream. 'He could have dumped her upstream. Current carried her down.'

'Or stopped on the bridge and threw her over,' I say.

'Shit.' Pulling out his phone, Tomasetti calls Goddard and

asks him to cordon off the bridge. 'Tire-tread impressions are a long shot,' he says as he snaps his phone closed.

'We might get lucky.'

Neither of us believes that. It's extremely difficult to extract meaningful evidence from an outdoor scene that's spread over a large area, especially if it's been left unprotected or trampled. Or rained on.

For several minutes, we stand there, using our flashlights, getting a sense of the scene. I wish for a camera, but we're going to have to hoof it back to the Tahoe to get it. I make a mental note of the time and memorize as much as I can – the location and position of the body, the slant of the tree, the erosion of the bank, the profusion of roots at the water's edge, the victim's clothes. But I know it's her face that will stay with me.

'We need to go back, get the camera, and a generator and lights,' Tomasetti says after a moment.

'I hate leaving her like that.' I know it's a stupid comment; we can't move the victim until the scene has been documented. But I hate the idea of leaving her in the water, where it's murky and cold and her flesh is at the mercy of the aquatic creatures whose domain has been invaded.

Abruptly, Tomasetti jerks the beam from the body, clicks off the flashlight, and stalks away. Surprised, I glance over at him. In the gray light seeping down from the canopy, I see him set his hand against a tree and lean against it, close his eyes. And I realize that even though he is a veteran witness to this kind of violence, he is as outraged and repulsed as I am.

After a moment, he scrapes a hand over his jaw and pushes away from the tree. 'I'm going to get a CSU down here before the rain destroys what little evidence is left.' Turning on the flashlight, he runs the beam along the steep, tangled bank of the creek. 'They might be able to pick up some footwear imprints.'

But he doesn't pull out his phone. He stands motionless between the path and the creek bank, the beam focused on the ground. His back is to me and his shoulders are rigid. I can't see his face, but I sense he doesn't want questions.

I give him a minute before asking, 'Do you want me to make the call?'

Slowly, he turns. I can just make out his features in the peripheral light from the beam. The shadows reveal lines in his face I never noticed before, something in his eyes I understand because I know he's seen the same thing in mine.

'I'll do it.' He looks away. 'I'm fine.'

'Don't take this the wrong way, but you don't look fine.'

His eyes meet mine. 'Five years ago, a scene like this would have pissed me off, and that would have been the extent of my emotional response. I would have felt nothing for that dead girl or her family. All I cared about was catching the fucker responsible. It was an added bonus if I got to take his head off in the process.'

'Don't beat yourself up for being human,' I tell him.

'That's the problem, Kate. I wasn't human. I didn't feel shock or sadness or remorse because a girl was dead. Sometimes I didn't even feel outrage. It was a game. All I felt was this driving need to catch the son of a bitch who'd done it. Not because of some noble desire for justice, but because I knew I was better than him and I wanted to prove it.'

'That's a protective mechanism built into all of us.'

'Now I know what's it's like to hear someone tell you everyone you've ever loved is dead.'

I cross to him. Before I realize I'm going to touch him, I set my palm against his cheek. 'I'm sorry.'

Setting his hand over mine, he brushes his mouth across

my palm, then pulls it away from his face. 'Let's go catch this motherfucker,' he says, and we start down the path.

An hour later, the township road swarms with sheriff's deputies, state Highway Patrol officers, and paramedics. The red and blue lights of half a dozen emergency vehicles flicker off the treetops. The area has been cordoned off with yellow caution tape. The state Highway Patrol has set up roadblocks, barring all through traffic from the bridge. Two ambulances from Trumbull Memorial Hospital are parked outside the secure area, their diesel engines rumbling in the predawn light.

Rain slashes down from a low sky as three technicians from the Trumbull County coroner's office struggle to carry the body up the incline of the bar ditch. Tomasetti snagged us a couple of county-issue slickers from one of Goddard's deputies, but we were already wet, and though the temperature hovers in the sixties, I feel the cold all the way to my bones.

I'm standing at the rear of the ambulance when the gurney is brought up. I can see the outline of the body within the black zippered bag.

'Any idea who she is?' Tomasetti asks.

'No ID,' replies one of the technicians. He's about thirty years old, with a goatee and wire-rimmed glasses. 'We preserved as much of the scene as possible, but the bank got pretty trampled.'

'Cause of death?' Tomasetti asks.

'No visible injuries.' The technician grimaces. 'Tough to tell with the water, though. We won't know until the autopsy.'

'How long will that be?' Tomasetti asks.

'Well, we're not backlogged. Maybe tomorrow morning.'

Tomasetti passes him his card. 'Keep us in the loop, will you?'

'You got it,' he says, and they load the body into the rear of the ambulance.

A fist of outrage unfurls in my gut as I watch the vehicle pull away. 'I was hoping this would have a better end.'

Tomasetti sighs. 'The case isn't exactly coming together, is it?'

'Chief Burkholder. Agent Tomasetti.'

We turn as Sheriff Goddard approaches. He's wearing a yellow slicker and holding two McDonald's to-go cups of coffee. I'm unduly thankful when he shoves one at me.

'Is it Annie King?' I ask.

'No one recognized her.' The sheriff shakes his head. 'And we don't have a photo.'

I tell him about the Amish-print dress, the lack of nail polish and jewelry. 'I think she might be Amish.'

Goddard's expression darkens. 'It's probably her. Timing's right. Damn it.' He heaves a grievous sigh. 'We're going to have to bring in the parents to identify her.'

'Who's the Amish bishop for this church district?' I ask.

Both men look at me.

'Even though we're only bringing in the parents to identify the body, if it's her, the bishop should be there,' I say.

Goddard nods. 'That'd be Old Abe Hertzler. He and his wife live out on River Road.' He lowers his voice, gives a single grim nod. 'I'll go get him. Can you two oversee things here? We can meet up at the hospital in Warren in a couple of hours. That's where our morgue facilities are.'

Notifying next of kin is a responsibility no cop relishes. I would venture to say it's one of the most difficult aspects of being a chief of police. Regardless of the manner of death, whether it's a traffic accident, a drowning, or the result of foul play, breaking the news to a loved one can affect a cop profoundly.

Goddard starts to turn away, but I stop him. 'I'll do it.'

He casts me a slightly incredulous look. 'Aw, Chief Burkholder, I can't put that on you.'

'It might help that I used to be Amish,' I tell him.

I'm aware that Tomasetti's watching me, but I don't look at him. I'm not sure I'm succeeding with the 'I'm not affected' persona I'm striving to project. 'That's why I'm here,' I add.

I don't mention the fact that most Amish are not only suspicious of the English but also of Amish who are from a different area. Not to mention those who have been excommunicated, like me.

The relief on his face is palpable. 'To tell you the truth, I'm a little out of my element when it comes to the Amish,' he says sheepishly.

'She knows the territory,' Tomasetti puts in.

'Where can we find the bishop?' I ask.

The sheriff gives us directions to the bishop's house, which is only a few miles to the south. 'I'll see you at the morgue in a couple of hours.'

ELEVEN

'Are you sure you're up to this?'

Tomasetti doesn't ask the question until we're turning into the gravel lane of the farm where Bishop Abraham Hertzler, aka 'Old Abe,' and his wife, Ruth, reside.

'I'm sure.' I don't look at him as I reply, because I know he's far too astute to miss the trepidation that's plastered all over my face. 'I'll do a better job than Goddard.'

'I could have just run over you with the Tahoe.'

I can't help it; I laugh and glance over at him. 'You're not trying to subtly tell me I'm a glutton for punishment, are you?'

'The thought crossed my mind.'

But I know he won't try to talk me out of it; he knows I'm right.

The eastern horizon is awash with Easter-egg pastels as he parks adjacent a ramshackle barn, next to an old horse-drawn manure spreader. We exit the Tahoe without speaking. I notice the yellow glow of lantern light in the window, telling me the Hertzlers are awake. We're midway to the porch when the door swings open.

An old Amish woman with a braided rug draped over her arm looks at us through bottle cap-lensed glasses. She's wearing a plain black dress with a white apron. Her silver hair is pulled severely away from her face and covered with the requisite prayer *kapp*. 'Who goes there?' she asks in a gravelly voice.

'Mrs. Hertzler?' I call out.

'I can't see you. Who are you?'

'I'm Chief of Police Kate Burkholder and this is Agent Tomasetti with the Ohio Bureau of Criminal Identification and Investigation.' We reach the porch and show her our identification. 'We're assisting the police department in their search for Annie King.'

The woman squints at our IDs. Her eyes are rheumy and huge behind the lenses of her glasses. But I see within their depths a sharp mind and a foreboding that wasn't there before. The police don't show up at your back door at 6:00 A.M. for idle chitchat.

'Is the bishop home, Mrs. Hertzler?'

'*Was der schinner is letz?*' *What in the world is wrong?* She asks the question as she opens the door wider and ushers us inside.

Tomasetti and I step into a small kitchen. I see a homemade wooden table for two, rustic shelves mounted on the wall, an old-fashioned potbellied stove. The smell of coffee and scrapple laces the air. A bent old man, as thin as his wife is plump, sits hunched over a cup of steaming coffee. He's clad wholly in black, the shock of white beard and hair contrasting severely against his jacket. Their dress tells me they are conservative Amish, and I wonder if they'll agree to ride in the Tahoe, or if we'll have to follow their buggy to the King farm, which will add hours to the identification process.

'*Guder mariye,*' I say, bowing my head in respect as I bid them good morning.

Both people look at me as if I just beamed down from another planet. The last thing they expected was for an

Englischer to walk into their kitchen and greet them in Pennsylvania Dutch.

'*Kannscht du Pennsilfaanisch Deitsch schwetzer?*' the bishop asks after a moment, surprised I speak Pennsylvania Dutch.

I explain to them that I'm from Holmes County – leaving out the part about my excommunication – and am assisting with the Annie King case. 'The body of a young woman was found this morning.'

Mrs. Hertzler gasps, but I don't stop speaking. 'We need Mr. and Mrs. King to tell us if it's Annie.' I look at the bishop. 'I thought you might be a comfort to them.'

The room falls silent. The only sounds are the hiss of the lantern and the rain dripping from the eaves. The air is hot and stuffy, but neither the bishop nor his wife seems to notice.

'*Mein Gott,*' Mrs. Hertzler whispers. 'God be with that poor child. God be with her family.'

'We need to speak with the family as soon as possible, Bishop Hertzler,' I tell him. 'I don't want them to hear the news from someone else. Will you come with us?'

The old man reaches for the cane leaning against the back of his chair, grips it with a gnarled hand, and pushes unsteadily to his feet. 'Bring me my Bible.'

The drive to the King farm is silent and tense. By the time we pull into the gravel lane, it's nearly 7:00 A.M. The sun sits on the eastern horizon like a steaming orange ball, burning away the final vestiges of the night's storm.

Despite the early hour, the King farm is abuzz with activity. Two children – little girls clad in matching blue dresses – are on their way to the barn when we park next to a flatbed wagon loaded with a single milk can. They stare at us as Tomasetti and I help the bishop from the Tahoe, but they don't stop to chat. More than likely, they've got cows or goats to milk before school.

A big black dog with white paws bounds over to us, tongue lolling. Tomasetti bends, stepping between the animal and the bishop to keep the dog from knocking the old man off balance.

We're midway up the sidewalk when the screen door squeaks open and Levi King steps onto the porch. He looks gaunt and exhausted. His eyes settle on Bishop Hertzler, and I see a recoil go through his body.

'Has something happened?' he asks, starting toward us. 'Is it Annie? Did you find her?'

'Mr. King—' I begin, but he cuts me off.

'Bishop?' Desperation rings in King's voice. He stops a few feet away and stares at the old man, as if Tomasetti and I aren't there. 'Tell me. Why are you here?'

'We found a girl's body,' I interject. 'There was no ID. We need for you to come with us and tell us if it's Annie.'

King looks at me as if I just rammed a knife into his abdomen and gutted him. His mouth opens. His lips quiver. 'It isn't Annie. It can't be.'

In my peripheral vision, I see Tomasetti glance toward the Tahoe, and I wonder if he's reliving the moment when someone told him about the deaths of his own daughters, the death of his wife.

The bishop maintains his grip on the younger man's arm. 'Be faithful, Levi, and leave the results to God.'

The screen door slams. I look up, to see Edna King standing on the porch in her plain dress and *kapp*, a threadbare dishcloth in her hands. There's no way she overheard the conversation. But she knows this is about Annie. She knows it's bad.

The dishcloth flutters to the ground, and then she's running toward us. 'Is it Annie?' she asks. 'Did something happen?'

Levi steps back into himself. When he turns to his wife, his face is resolute and calm. 'There was a girl found,' he tells her. 'It may not be Annie.'

'A girl?' She covers her mouth with both hands. 'She is alive?'

Her husband sets both hands on her shoulders, shakes his head. 'God will take care of Annie,' he says with conviction.

'Edna, there is much comfort in that,' the bishop adds.

I see the struggle waging within her, the war between absolute faith and the terror of knowing something horrific may have happened to her daughter. 'It cannot be Annie,' she whispers. 'Not Annie.'

Tomasetti snags my attention and motions toward the Tahoe. I take a step back and we start down the sidewalk.

'I have to go with them,' Levi tells her. 'Be strong, Edna. Get breakfast for the children. I'll be back before you've washed the dishes.'

'Levi . . .'

I hear her crying softly, but the Amish man turns away. Stone-faced, staring straight ahead, he starts toward the Tahoe.

Behind him, his wife falls to her knees, clenches handfuls of grass in both hands, and cries out her daughter's name.

The drive to Trumbull Memorial Hospital takes twenty-five minutes, but it seems like hours. The sense of dread inside the vehicle is palpable. Bishop Hertzler and Levi King ride in the backseat and spend much of that time in silent prayer or speaking quietly. Mostly, they talk about Annie – her youth and goodness, her love of God and family, the possibility that the body isn't hers and that another family will be needing their prayers. Levi returns to that theme again and again, and I know he's clinging to that hope with the desperation of a man trying to save his own life. In a way, he is.

By the time we park in the garage across the street from

the hospital, the men have fallen silent. No one speaks as we disembark. The two Amish men draw some attention as the four of us take the skyway from the garage to the hospital. It's always hard for me to believe there are people living in Ohio who've never seen an Amish person. Once inside, we take the elevator to the basement, where the morgue is located.

The elevator doors open to a reception area with pale yellow walls, a blue sofa and chair, and a couple of large areca palms. The coffee table holds a vase filled with silk peonies. A flat-screen television mounted on the wall is tuned to the Fox News Channel. As I take in the decor, I can't help but think that someone tried a little too hard to make a dismal place seem normal.

A middle-aged woman in a fuchsia skirt and jacket sits behind a glossy oak desk with a headset on. She offers an appropriately somber smile. 'Can I help you?'

Tomasetti steps ahead of us and shows his identification. 'We're here for a viewing.'

'We're expecting you. I think they're ready back there.' She eyes the two Amish men as she hands him a clipboard. 'Just sign at the bottom.'

Tomasetti scribbles an illegible signature on the form and returns the clipboard to her.

She rounds her desk. 'This way, please.'

With Tomasetti and I behind her and the two Amish men trailing, she takes us around the corner. We pass by a window-less gray door marked AUTHORIZED PERSONNEL ONLY. Above the door, a sign printed in an Old English font reads MORTUI VIVIS PRAECIPIANT. It's not the first time I've seen those words. I don't read Latin, but I know the translation by heart: 'Let the dead teach the living.'

The hall opens to a small, starkly furnished room painted an eye-pleasing beige. A sofa table holds a small lamp and a box of tissues. Above the table, a cheap southwestern print in an oak frame is hung a few inches too high. A ceiling-to-floor curtain drapes the fourth wall. Next to it, a small round speaker with a red button is set into a niche. Behind the curtain, I know, is the viewing window.

'I'll let them know you're here,' the woman tells us.

Bishop Hertzler and Levi King stand near the sofa table, looking out of place, not making eye contact with Tomasetti or me. Neither man acknowledges the curtain, as if pretending it isn't there will make whatever's on the other side disappear.

The urge to move, to pace the confines of the small space, is strong. I stand there waiting, impotent.

'Never doubt in the dark what God has shown you in the light,' the bishop says. 'He will take care of His children.'

No one responds. No one knows what to say. Those of us in law enforcement know that sometimes God sits back and lets Fate have her way. We know sometimes God's children die before their time.

Levi shoves his hands into his pockets and looks down at the floor. A few feet away, Tomasetti stands near the curtain, looking as if he might tear it aside himself if it doesn't open soon.

'Agent Tomasetti? Are you ready?' A male voice crackles from the speaker set into the wall.

Tomasetti looks at Levi. The Amish man nods. Tomasetti turns back to the speaker and depresses the red button. 'Let's do this.'

An instant later, a motor hums and the curtain glides open. Levi King leans forward, his eyes seeking. I'm standing slightly behind him. I make eye contact briefly with Tomasetti. He looks as grim and tense as I feel.

I see a small rectangular room tiled completely in white.

Stark light rains down on a stainless-steel gurney covered with a light blue sheet. I can just make out the shape of the body beneath. A young technician in green scrubs stands at the head of the table, looking out at us. He peels away the sheet. I see brown hair combed away from a slack, pale face, blue lips that are partially open, slender shoulders with blue-white skin.

The sight of the dead is always a terrible thing. But knowing the promising life of a young woman was cut short by violence is worse. Sometimes the senselessness and injustice of that is almost too much to bear.

Next to me, Levi King makes a noise. A quick intake of breath. From where I stand, I can see his mouth quivering. His shoulders begin to shake. Bishop Hertzler reaches out and squeezes his arm, but Levi doesn't seem to notice, and I know there will be no comforting.

In the Amish culture, grief is a private thing. Levi King doesn't have that option. The sound that erupts from him is so unsettling, the hairs at the nape of my neck stand up. His cry of grief cuts through me like a blade. In the periphery of my vision, I see Tomasetti turn away. The bishop wraps his arm around the other man's shoulders. 'She is with God,' the bishop says. But the words aren't convincing.

I glance at Tomasetti. He's standing a few feet away from the window, staring through the glass at the dead girl. His expression is dark and inscrutable. 'Is it your daughter?' he asks.

Levi King turns his face to Tomasetti, jerks his head once. Tears stream down his face and run unchecked onto his shirt.

It is a scene in which I've participated a dozen times in the course of my career. When I was a rookie, I always believed it was my inexperience that made it so damn hard. The truth of the matter is, it never gets easier. You don't get tougher or harder or colder, at least not in any way that counts. Every time, bearing witness to another person's grief cuts out a piece of you.

'Who could do this terrible thing?' the Amish man whispers.

No one answers.

TWELVE

Two hours later Tomasetti and I are back in the Tahoe, on our way to see local photographer and winner of the Ohio Photographic Arts Award, Stacy Karns. We haven't spoken much since dropping Bishop Hertzler and Levi King at their respective farms. We've fallen back into cop mode, a role we both find infinitely more comfortable than the white elephant of the scene back at the morgue.

'What do you know about Karns?' I ask.

'Forty-four years old. Self-employed. Convicted four years ago. Did six months at Lake Erie Correctional Institution. Five-thousand-dollar fine. Five years probation.' He rattles off the information from memory, which tells me he stayed up late reading the file.

'What was the charge?'

'Illegal use of a minor in nudity-oriented material.'

'Child porn.' The words taste bitter coming off my tongue.

'Some people rushed to his defense, especially during the trial phase.' His voice is powder-dry. 'You know, that fine line between art and child pornography.'

'I guess if you enjoy looking at pictures of naked Amish girls, those lines could get a little blurry.'

Fifteen miles northwest of Buck Creek, we turn onto Doe Creek Road. It's a narrow two-track that cuts through river bottomland and dead-ends at a sparkling creek-fed lake. We're less than a mile in when I spot the mailbox. There's no name, but the number matches the address Goddard gave us.

Tomasetti makes the turn and then we're barreling down the lane, leaving a billowing cloud of dust in our wake.

The lane carves a swath through a hardwood forest with trees so tall, the canopies block the sun. We make two twisty turns, climb a hill, and the trees fall away, revealing a magnificent Spanish-style mansion with stucco walls, a barrel tile roof, and a massive portico. A profusion of wildly blooming lilac bushes and peonies adorn the front yard. A neat row of pine trees demark the property's edge.

'Not bad for an ex-con,' Tomasetti comments.

'Photography must pay pretty well.'

'He's got a couple of coffee-table books out, too.'

I know Tomasetti is being facetious; it's his way of dealing with some of the more frustrating aspects of police work. Like when the bad guys make good. Having spent the last few hours in the morgue, I can't conjure a smile. 'You can dress it up, but a piece of shit is still a piece of shit.'

'You sound like you might have some preconceived notions about this guy,' Tomasetti says lightly.

'You might be right.' As far as I'm concerned, Karns took advantage of an underage Amish girl and then capitalized on it. He turned the negative publicity into fifteen minutes of fame, and the controversy made him a wealthy man.

Tomasetti drives around to the rear of the house, where gravel gives way to terracotta-colored paving stones. Outside a four-car garage, a teenage boy in swim trunks and flip-flops is washing a green Jaguar XJ6. Looking to my left, through the trees, I see the shimmering blue water of the lake. There's some kind of observation tower, and, lower, a boathouse and dock.

Tomasetti kills the engine and frowns at the kid. 'Wonder if his mom and dad know he's here.'

'I wonder if they know Mr. Karns likes to take photographs of naked teenagers.'

'Goddard says he's a pseudocelebrity around here.'

'That's wrong on so many levels.'

He mutters an unflattering adjective beneath his breath as we exit the vehicle. The boy stops washing the car and stares at us as we traverse the flagstone walkway to the house.

Stone stairs usher us to a large veranda that wraps around the front of the house and looks out over the forest beyond. A dozen or more Boston ferns hang from baskets. Clay pots overflowing with red geraniums and larger pots filled with lush palms lend a tropical feel.

We reach the massive front doors – mahogany with beveled skylights on both sides – and I press the doorbell. For the span of a minute or so, we just stand there, taking in the view, listening to the birds, gathering our thoughts. Despite the pressure of the case, the murder of Annie King, the impending interview with Karns, standing in the midst of such tranquil beauty, I find myself starting to relax.

I'm reaching for the bell a second time when one of the doors swings open. A tall African-American man with blue eyes and short-cropped hair that's going gray at the temples looks at us as if we're a couple of solicitors in need of being turned away. He's wearing gray khakis and a white polo shirt, no shoes. He's movie-star attractive, with the kind of face that compels people to stare. I'm not exactly sure what I expected Stacy Karns to look like, but this isn't it.

'Stacy Karns?' Tomasetti asks.

'That's me.' His voice is deep and pleasant, with just a hint of a northeastern inflection. 'How can I help you?'

We pull out our IDs and hold them out for him to see.

Surprise flashes across his features. 'Wow. Bureau of Criminal Identification and Investigation. That can't be good.' His gaze flicks first to Tomasetti and then lingers on me. 'What's this all about?'

'We'd like to ask you some questions,' Tomasetti tells him.

I watch him closely – his eyes, facial expression. I see an instant of confusion, followed by realization, and a flash of disbelief. On the surface, it's the perfect reaction – the response of an innocent man. But I'm well versed in the wicked ways of deception and I know he's putting forth exactly what he wants us to see.

'I just heard on the radio they found the missing Amish girl,' he says somberly. 'Is that why you're here?'

I give him points for innovation. When it comes to discussing an unpleasant topic like murder – especially with the police – most people try delay tactics. They beat around the bush. Or play dumb. That Karns got right to the point tells me he guessed we would show up.

'We're assisting with the investigation,' Tomasetti tells him.

'May we come in?' I ask.

Karns takes my measure and I see a glimmer of curiosity in his eyes. 'Of course.' He opens the door wider and motions us inside, a king inviting a couple of scruffy peasants into his castle. 'Would you guys like some coffee? Or iced tea?'

'We're fine, thanks.' Tomasetti gives him a bad imitation of a smile.

Karns notices, but he looks amused. With the ease of a man who has nothing to hide, he takes us through a foyer with gleaming hardwood floors and a console table that holds a striking glass vase filled with fresh-cut peonies. I smell the sweet scent of the flowers as we walk by. A set of French doors opens to a massive living room with a stone hearth and parquet floors. A wall of floor-to-ceiling windows looks out over the forest beyond.

While the room is beautifully appointed, it is the dozens of framed photographs on the walls that draw the eye. The majority are black-and-white shots. Stark, minimalist, dramatic and yet somehow subtle at once. Karns's talent is undeniable.

I stroll to the photographs for a closer look. Most of them feature some element of Amish life: an old farmhouse with a leaning brick chimney, a buggy and young Standardbred horse trotting through the gray swirl of morning fog; two barefoot girls holding hands as they skip down an asphalt road; a harvest moon rising over a cut cornfield; an Amish cemetery as the backdrop for a procession of black buggies.

'You're very talented,' I say after a moment.

He smiles, and I notice that his teeth are very white. 'If you're softening me up for some tough interrogation, it's working.'

In the periphery of my vision, I see Tomasetti roll his eyes. Ignoring him, I stroll past the windows to the wall next to the hearth. It is there that I see the other photographs: a naked baby crawling on an Amish quilt; an Amish woman with her skirt blown up past her hips, à la Marilyn Monroe; an Amish boy standing naked on the bank of a creek, preparing to dive into the water. None of the photos are sexually explicit, but they are disconcerting. There's a voyeuristic quality to Karns's work. Looking at them, I feel as if I've interrupted a private moment, seeing something I'm not supposed to see.

'Did you know most Amish object to having their photos taken?' I ask conversationally.

'I'm aware of that.' He keeps an eye on Tomasetti as he

peruses the photos on the other side of the hearth. 'I strive to be as respectful as possible.'

'As long as you get the shot,' Tomasetti mutters.

'Most cite religious reasons,' I continue. 'The prohibition of graven images. Some believe pictures are vain displays of pride. Some believe the snapping of a photo can actually steal one's soul.'

'With all due respect to the Amish, I think that's a little melodramatic,' he says. 'Don't you?'

'I think if you respected them, you wouldn't take photos of them without their knowledge.'

For a moment, I think he's going to argue. Instead, he smiles. 'Stealing someone's soul isn't against the law.'

I don't smile back.

After a moment, he shrugs, a diplomat conceding a point for some greater good. 'Everyone is entitled to their opinion.'

Tomasetti stops opposite a photograph of two preteen girls standing topless in the hip-deep water of a creek, shampooing each other's hair. 'You seem to have a real penchant for photographing naked children.'

Karns comes up beside him and looks at the photo. 'Most of these photos were taken from afar, some with a telescopic lens. I've found that my subjects are more . . . uninhibited when they don't realize they're being photographed. The facial muscles are more relaxed. I strive to be as unobtrusive as possible.'

'So they have no clue they're being photographed,' I say.

'Actually, many of my subjects give me permission.'

'And the ones who don't?'

'There are ways around that. Photographically speaking, I mean. For example, I can smudge the features so that they are unrecognizable.'

'The Amish aren't exactly a litigious society,' I say.

He smiles, turning on the charm. 'Well, I have to admit, I've never been sued by an Amish person.'

Tomasetti turns away from the photographs and gives Karns his full attention. 'You have, however, been convicted of the illegal use of a minor in nudity-oriented material.'

'I see.' Karns grimaces, as if his tolerance has reached its limit. 'And this is the point of your visit?'

'When a young girl turns up dead, the sex offenders are the first people we talk to,' Tomasetti says.

'With all due respect, I am not a sex offender,' Karns says with some heat. 'I resent the implication.'

Tomasetti meets his gaze head-on, completely unapologetic. 'Not technically or legally. But in my book, child pornography ranks right up there with sex offender. I don't differentiate between the two.'

Karns sighs. 'Look, I'm sure both of you know the story behind that so-called conviction.'

'Evidently, the jury didn't see the photo as art,' Tomasetti says.

'A lot of people did,' he tells us. 'There's nothing remotely sexual or inappropriate about my work.'

I listen to the two men debate the issue as I peruse the final wall of photographs. I'm about to join them, when a photo snags my attention. I know instantly it's the shot that cost him six months in prison. It's a stark black-and-white photo of a young Amish girl sitting cross-legged in an aluminum tub of water. She's nude except for a white prayer *kapp*. Her tiny pointed breasts are exposed. Her head is bent and she's bringing handfuls of water to her face.

The photo is a blatant invasion of the girl's privacy. She has no idea she's being photographed. I bet neither she nor her family has any idea the photograph was taken – or that it was the center of a controversy that cost a man jail time and set his career on a course that made him infamous and wealthy.

The photograph is powerful, with a grittiness that makes me squirm. I feel dirty just looking at it. And something begins to boil under my skin, an emotion that's gnarly and edgy and sets off an alarm in my head that tells me to rein it in. And I realize that despite this man's charisma and apparent talent, I have no respect for him and zero tolerance for what he does.

I make my way over to the two men and turn my attention to Karns. 'Did you know Annie King?'

He doesn't react to the name. 'I didn't know her.'

'Did you ever photograph her?'

'No.'

'Did you ever meet her or her family?'

'Not that I know of.'

'Where were you two nights ago?'

'I was at an art show in Warren. One of my friends had her first exhibit and I was there supporting her.'

'Can anyone substantiate that?'

'A dozen or so people.' He laughs. 'My credit card. I spent nearly four thousand dollars.'

I'm aware of Tomasetti watching me as I pull out my notepad. I let Karns hang for a moment while I make notes. 'What's the name of the gallery?'

'Willow Creek Gallery.'

'I'll need the names of three witnesses.'

He recites the names with the correct spelling and contact information, and I jot everything down. 'Do you know Bonnie Fisher?'

Karns's brows knit. 'I don't think so.'

'What about Noah Mast?' Tomasetti asks.

Karns shakes his head. 'I'm sorry, but I don't.'

He doesn't ask who they are and we don't offer the information.

Ten minutes later, Tomasetti and I climb into the Tahoe and head down the gravel lane toward the highway.

'Slick guy,' Tomasetti says.

'Except we're too jaded to buy into his bullshit.'

He slants me a look. 'You think he's lying about something?'

'I hate to see a guy like Karns rewarded for repugnant behavior.'

He pulls onto the highway. 'Maybe he made contact with her, photographed her without her parents' knowledge, and things went too far.'

'Or he initiated sexual contact and didn't want her talking about it,' I put in.

'I don't know, Kate. I think Annie's murder is related to the other disappearances,' he says, surmising.

'Maybe there's more to Karns than meets the eye.'

That's one of the reasons Tomasetti and I work so well together. He's never taken in by appearances and believes everyone is capable of deeds far removed from what they are. When he disagrees with me, he holds his ground.

After a moment, he sighs. 'I think he's a sack of shit, but I don't like him for this.'

I'm not ready to let Karns off the hook. 'The common denominator is that the missing are young and Amish and behaving outside the norm.'

'Karns's photos depict the Amish within normal parameters.'

'That doesn't rule him out.'

'We can't make the pattern fit if it doesn't.'

I don't respond.

THIRTEEN

An hour later, Tomasetti and I are back in the interview room of the Trumbull County sheriff's department. He's slumped in a chair, looking grouchy and bored, pecking on the keyboard of his laptop. I'm standing at the rear of the room with my cell phone stuck to my ear, listening to Auggie Brock lament the injustice of his son's ongoing legal saga. I make all the appropriately sympathetic noises, but I know what he wants and there's no way I'm going to compromise my ethics because his seventeen-year-old son has the common sense of a snail.

The rest of the deputies are out in the field, working various angles. I can hear Sheriff Goddard in his office down the hall. He's loud when he's on the phone, and now he's embroiled in a conversation that involves securing a warrant for the home of Frank Gilfillan, the leader of the Twelve Passages Church. Evidently, the judge on the other end doesn't see things the way the sheriff does, and Goddard isn't taking it well. So far, we're batting zero and the frustration level is rising.

'Kate, for God's sake, are you listening?' Auggie asks.

'I'm listening,' I reply, lying.

'My son's life is at stake here. If he's tried as an adult and convicted, his life is all but over.'

For an instant, I entertain the notion of telling him I'll do what I can, just to get him off the phone. Then Sheriff Goddard comes through the door, looking like he's had the crap beaten out of him, and saves me from stepping into that particular pile. 'Look, Auggie, the sheriff just walked in. I've got to go.'

'Will you at least think about what I said?'

I hit END and frown at Goddard.

He frowns back. 'Looks like your day might be heading in the same direction as mine,' he says.

'You mean to hell?'

'Thereabouts.'

I smile. 'Any luck with the warrant?'

Goddard sighs. 'Judge says the Twelve Passages is a church and they got the right to worship any way they see fit.' Another sigh. 'It's a damn cult, if you ask me.'

'Judge isn't a member, is he?'

Goddard gives me a look, as if I might be serious, and then erupts with a belly laugh. 'I don't think so, but I swear to God, nothing would surprise me these days.'

'Did you talk to Gilfillan?'

'We did, and let me tell you he's a weird son of a bitch. Got a weird belief system and bunch of damn weird followers. A lot of them aren't much older than our missing teens. He's recruited some Amish young people, too.'

That snags my attention. 'Does he have a record?'

'Not even an arrest.'

'Hard to ignore the Amish connection.'

'Well, it ain't over till it's over.' He glances at Tomasetti. 'You guys have any luck with Karns?'

'He's worth keeping on the radar,' I tell him. 'He shoots nude photos of kids, has an unusual interest in the Amish.'

'Maybe I'll have better luck getting a warrant for his place.'

'Judge isn't an art fan, is he?'

He chortles. 'Chief Burkholder, you've got a mean streak.'

A few feet away, the pitch of Tomasetti's voice changes, drawing our attention. I glance over at him and find his eyes already on me. I can tell by his expression that he's got something. I wait while he thanks the person on the other end of the line and sets down his phone. 'Remember those queries I put into VICAP?' he asks. 'Analyst found a cold case with the same MO.'

Goddard looks baffled. 'We checked similars,' he says. 'Ran a search through OHLEG. Nothing came up.'

'That's because it didn't happen in Ohio,' Tomasetti explains. 'Happened in Sharon, Pennsylvania.'

'That's just across the state line,' Goddard says.

'How old is the case?' I ask.

'Four years. Fifteen-year-old Amish female.' Tomasetti glances down at his notes. 'Ruth Wagler. She was selling bread alongside the highway and disappeared. Body was never found.'

'Suspects?' I ask.

'Sheriff's office looked at her boyfriend. Looked at her stepfather. But nothing panned out and no arrest was made.'

I look at Goddard. 'How far is Sharon from here?'

'Forty-five minutes in traffic, and there ain't no traffic.'

'We need to talk to the parents.' Tomasetti looks at me. 'You up for a trip?'

'Yeah.' My cell phone vibrates against my hip, inducing a flash of annoyance. Expecting Auggie Brock, I glance down. Surprise slips through me when Glock's name appears on the display.

Turning away from the two men, I answer. 'I'm glad you're not Auggie.'

'Not as glad as me.' He doesn't laugh, and I feel some internal radar go on alert. Some instinct that tells me he's not calling to chat. 'I just took a call from the Amish bishop, Chief.

Your sister and her husband are at his place. William Miller's niece is missing.'

Something akin to an electrical shock goes through me. My surroundings fade to gray. The voices of Tomasetti and Goddard dwindle to babble. 'Sadie Miller?' I ask.

'Right. Fifteen-year-old Amish female.'

His words barely register. I see Sadie as she was the day on the bridge – so defiant of society's rules, so sure of herself, and so utterly certain the world would be hers if she just had the chance to conquer it. Simultaneously, the image of Annie King's body tangled in the tree roots on the creek bank flashes in my mind's eye.

'When?' I hear myself ask.

'Sometime last night.'

'Goddamn it, why are they just now calling?' I know better than to take my frustration out on Glock, but the words are out before I can stop them.

My phone beeps. I glance down and see Troyer's name on the display. 'Put out an Amber Alert,' I tell Glock. 'Bring in the SHP. Call Rasmussen. Get everyone out looking. See if you can find someone with tracking dogs.'

'I got it.'

'I'll be there in a couple of hours.' I take the incoming call with a growl of my name.

'Katie, it's Sarah.' High-wire tension laces my sister's voice. 'Sadie is missing.'

'I just heard.' I don't cut her any slack. 'Why didn't you call me right away?'

'We didn't realize she was missing until this morning.'

'It's now afternoon, Sarah. Why didn't you call me the instant you realized she was gone?'

'It was William. . . .' I hear her breathing on the other end and I know she's struggling to control her emotions. 'He did not want to involve—'

'That's bullshit. I'm sick of it, Sarah. Do you hear me?' I'm shouting now and keenly aware that Tomasetti and Goddard are staring at me. I know I'm not helping the situation, that I'm alienating my sister, and I struggle to check my temper. 'How long has she been gone?'

'We believe she went out through her bedroom window last night.'

'Last night.' I lower my head, pinch the bridge of my nose between thumb and forefinger. The urge to tear into her verbally and denigrate the tenet of separation I loathe burns through me. I want to ask my sister how she could allow her belief system to endanger her young niece. Somehow, I manage to rein in my fury. 'Do you think she ran away?' I ask.

'I don't know. Katie, I'm scared. Sadie has been so rebellious and angry.'

I glance at my watch, knowing that even with my emergency lights flashing, it'll take two hours to get back to Painters Mill. 'I'm going to send Glock out to Roy and Esther's farm. Can you meet him out there?'

'Yes, of course.'

'Sarah, I want you to speak with them and tell them to cooperate with the police. Tell them we're their best hope of finding Sadie. Do you understand?'

'Yes. I will do my best.'

I want to say more. I want to tell her I love her, but I'm too angry. Instead, I snap my phone closed and shove all of those useless emotions into a compartment to deal with later.

'What happened?'

I turn to Tomasetti, who's standing directly behind me, staring at me through narrowed eyes that see a hell of a lot more than I'm comfortable with.

Quickly, I recap my conversation with my sister. 'The missing girl is my brother-in-law's niece.' The words don't begin to convey what I feel for that girl. I want to explain to him the connection Sadie and I share. The way she looks up to me. How I see in her all the good parts of myself. But there's no time and the words dwindle on my tongue.

'Kate, is it a runaway situation, or do they suspect foul play?'

The question rattles me anew. I look at Tomasetti, struggle to get a grip. 'She fits the profile of these victims,' I tell him. 'Troubled. Rebellious. The age is right.'

'The timing is off,' Tomasetti says. 'This is too close to the previous disappearance.'

I think of the pool of blood on the road, of Annie King's body tangled in those roots, and I can barely bring myself to answer. 'I have to go back.' I stride to the table, close my laptop without shutting it down, and slide it into its sleeve. 'I need the Tahoe.'

Tomasetti reaches into his pocket and retrieves the keys, hands them to me. 'I'll ride with Goddard to Sharon. Pick up another vehicle later.'

I take the keys. Tomasetti frowns when he sees my hand shaking.

Goddard comes up beside me. His hand on my shoulder is unexpectedly reassuring. 'Let us know if you find something that links this one to the others, Chief.'

Tomasetti unplugs the power cord of my laptop and hands it to me. 'Be careful.'

I stop what I'm doing and look at him. More than anything at that moment, I want to feel his arms around me. I want to know he's going to be there – not only in terms of the case but for me, too.

I loop the strap of my laptop case over my shoulder. 'I'll call you when I know something.'

And then I'm through the door and rushing toward the Tahoe.

There are a thousand reasons why a cop should never work a case in which he or she has a personal connection. Ask any veteran and they will tell you that a cop who is personally motivated will fuck things up faster and more thoroughly than any rookie. When the stakes are high – when someone you care about is at risk – everything changes.

I want to believe I can handle it, muscle my way through, conventional wisdom be damned. But already I can feel the gnarly beast of emotional involvement riding my back, goading me into territory in which I have no business venturing. I know going into this that I'm at a disadvantage. I'm vulnerable to making snap decisions and taking risks I might not normally take. It would be smarter to hand this case off to someone else. Only there is no one else.

It takes me just under two hours to reach Painters Mill. I employed emergency lights and siren and hit ninety miles per hour once I reached the highway. Still, those two hours seemed more like days and a thousand terrible thoughts ran through my head the entire time. I don't know for a fact that Sadie Miller has been kidnapped. As far as any of us know, she could have made good on her promise to leave the Amish way and taken off for greener pastures. But I know all too well how quickly a runaway situation can become a missing-person case.

Or a homicide.

It's early evening by the time I pull into the gravel lane of the Miller farm. I park the Tahoe in the long shadow cast by the house, ever aware that the day is drawing to a close. I see Bishop Troyer's buggy parked by the barn, the old Standardbred horse tethered to a tie post near the main door. Glock's cruiser is a few yards away. A Crown Vic from the sheriff's office sits at a haphazard angle behind Glock's car. There's another buggy I don't recognize next to the bishop's.

I've known the Millers since I was a teenager. They're a conservative Amish family, and there were many times growing up when they didn't approve of the choices I made or the things I did. Back then, I thrived on that kind of controversy. I thumbed my nose at the rules, and I didn't give a good damn that they looked at me as if I were something that needed to be mucked out of a stall with a pitchfork.

As an adult, I know they'll never approve of the decisions I made that put me on the path to where I am now. But this isn't about me or a past that's long gone. I hope their disdain for me doesn't affect the level of cooperation my department receives with regard to Sadie.

My legs are stiff from the drive, but I hit the ground running and head toward the back porch. I'm hoping Sadie has been found and I made the drive for nothing. I'm hoping for the chance to scold her and then throw my arms around her and tell her how glad I am to see her. But when the door swings open and Sarah and her sister-in-law rush out, my hopes are dashed. Both women wear light blue dresses with white aprons, white head coverings, dark-colored hose, and practical shoes. Their faces are blotchy from crying and their eyes are haunted.

One look at my sister and the anger I felt toward her earlier evaporates.

'Oh, Katie.' Her voice breaks on my name.

I go to her and try not to feel awkward as I put my arms around her. She smells of clean clothes and summertime, the way my *mamm* used to smell, and for a split second I find myself longing for all the hugs I never received. I can feel my sister shaking within my embrace. 'Any news?' I ask, easing her to arm's length.

She shakes her head. 'No.'

I turn my attention to Sadie's mother. Esther Miller is a stout woman with a round, freckled face and a port-wine birthmark the size of a quarter on the left side of her nose. Her brown hair is streaked with silver and pulled into a severe bun at her nape. When we were teenagers, she was funny and opinionated and had a rebellious attitude that appealed greatly to my own sense of dissent. We spent many an afternoon at Miller's Pond, smoking cigarettes and talking about things we shouldn't have been talking about, most of which revolved around boys and makeup and all the mysteries that lay ahead – edgy stuff for a couple of Amish girls. Then came the day she walked up on me as I was making out with Jimmie Bates, and that was the end of my first friendship. Esther told her *mamm* and, of course, her *mamm* told mine. It was my first brush with betrayal, and it hurt. In the end, Esther's mother forbade her to see me, and we never spoke again.

As I look into my former friend's eyes and offer my hand, I find myself searching for the young rebel I'd once known so intimately, the girl who could put me in stitches no matter how dark my mood. But time has erased all traces of that girl. Instead, I see a stern, frightened woman whose eyes are filled with mistrust. 'Katie, thank you for coming,' she says. 'Come in.'

I follow her through a narrow mudroom, past an old wringer washing machine, a row of muck boots lined up neatly on the floor, and three flat-brimmed straw hats hung on wooden dowels set into the wall. We go through a doorway and enter a large kitchen that smells of sausage and yeast bread. Sheriff Rasmussen sits at the table, talking to Roy Miller, Sadie's father. He looks up when I enter, and I think I see relief in his expression.

'Chief Burkholder.' Rising, Rasmussen crosses to me and extends his hand. 'Welcome back.'

I give his hand a firm shake. 'Where's Glock?'

'He's talking to the bishop.'

'Chief.'

I turn at the sound of Glock's voice and see him and Bishop Troyer enter the kitchen. Bowing my head slightly in respect, I greet the bishop first in Pennsylvania Dutch. Then I focus on Glock and Rasmussen. 'Bring me up to speed.'

The sheriff responds first. 'The parents think Sadie slipped out of her bedroom window sometime last night after seven. When Mr. Miller went into her room this morning at four-thirty, she was gone.'

'Have you talked to neighbors?' I'm aware that the bishop and Esther and Roy Miller are watching me, and I glance their way, letting them know they should jump in with any additional information.

'We interviewed neighbors on both sides,' Glock replies. 'No one saw anything.'

I look at Esther. 'Are any of her clothes missing?'

The Amish woman shakes her head. 'I checked her room. There is nothing missing.'

'Is it possible she had some English clothes stashed somewhere?' I ask.

'Sadie would not,' Esther tells me. 'She is modest.'

The last time I saw Sadie, she was wearing painted-on jeans and a shirt tight enough to squeeze the air from her lungs. I wonder how these parents could be so out of touch. But I know that's not fair. Amish or English, plenty of teens partake in behavior their parents will never comprehend.

'Sadie was wearing English clothes the day I brought her home,' I say.

Roy Miller looks down at the floor.

Esther stares at me as if I'm purposefully adding to their anguish. 'We don't allow English clothes in this house,' she tells me.

I turn my attention to Glock. 'Amber Alert is out?'

'About two hours ago.' He glances at his watch. 'State Highway Patrol has been notified. We called everyone we could think of, Chief. Skid's putting together some volunteers to search the greenbelt to the north. T.J. and Pickles are canvassing.'

'We got dogs coming in from Coshocton County,' Rasmussen adds.

I catch both men's eyes and gesture toward the next room. As inconspicuously as possible, I sidle into the living area and they follow. When we're out of earshot of the parents and Bishop Troyer, I lower my voice. 'We found the body of the missing girl in Buck Creek.'

'Aw shit,' Rasmussen mutters. 'Homicide?'

'The coroner hasn't made an official ruling yet, but we think so.'

Glock narrows his gaze. 'You think this is related?'

Considering the outcome of Annie King's disappearance, that's the one scenario I don't want to consider. I'm still hopeful Sadie left of her own accord and we're dealing with a runaway situation instead.

I sigh. 'I think we need to treat this as a missing endangered.'

'Painters Mill is farther away than the towns where other girls went missing,' Rasmussen says.

'Maybe he's expanding his area,' Glock offers.

'Did Sadie's parents mention any problems at home?' I ask them. 'A recent argument or disagreement? Anything like that?'

Rasmussen shakes his head. 'They said everything was fine.'

'What about a boyfriend?' I ask.

'They say no.'

The parents are always the last to know. Tomasetti's words float through my mind. I hate it, but he's right.

'The parents probably don't have a clue,' I say quietly, and

I realize the two men are looking at me as if I'm the proverbial expert on out-of-control teenage Amish girls.

'Sadie was considering leaving the Amish way of life,' I explain. 'It might be that she's with a boy her parents don't know about. Or maybe she took off to teach all of us idiots a lesson.'

'We need to talk to her friends,' Rasmussen says.

'I've got some names we can start with.' I look at Glock. 'Pick up Angi McClanahan. Matt Butler. And Lori Westfall. Take them to the station. Parents, too. No one's in trouble, but I want to talk to them.'

'I'm all over it.' Glock starts toward the door.

Rasmussen and I fall silent, both of us caught in our own thoughts. 'I'm going to talk to the mother,' I tell him. 'Take a look at Sadie's room.'

'You want some help?

'Might be better if I do it alone.'

'Gotcha.'

Roy and Esther glance up from their places at the table when I return to the kitchen. They look broken, sitting in their chairs with their hollow eyes and restless, unoccupied hands. It's only been a few days since I last saw them, but they look as if they've aged ten years. Roy is a tall, thin man with a long red beard that reaches to his belly. He's wearing black work trousers with a blue shirt and suspenders.

'I'd like to see Sadie's room,' I tell them.

For a moment, they stare at me as if I'm speaking in some language they don't understand. Then Esther looks at her husband. 'We could show her,' she says.

Impatience coils inside me. The Amish are a patriarchal society. The men make the rules and usually have the final say in matters. While most wives have a voice and their opinions are generally respected, they usually submit to their husbands' wishes.

I direct my attention to Roy. 'It's important,' I tell him. 'There might be something there that will help us find her.'

After a moment, he nods. 'Show her the room.'

Esther rises and motions toward the hall. 'Come this way.'

The steep, narrow stairs creak beneath our feet as I follow her to the second level of the house. Sadie's room is at the end of the hall. It's a small space with a twin bed, a night table, and a pine chest with four drawers. A white *kapp* and a black sweater hang from a single dowel on the wall above the bed. A window covered with gauzy curtains peers out over the front yard.

The room is cozy and neat. It might have been the bedroom of any typical Amish girl, but all semblances of plain end with the vast display of needlework. A green-and-white quilt utilizing several types of fabric that alter the texture in interesting ways covers the bed. Contrasting pillows, fabric layered with lace, and even a crocheted coverlet are piled against the headboard. The walls are white, but there's nothing plain about them, because they're plastered from floor to ceiling with fabric wall hangings. I see dark purple velvet layered with pink lace; red and purple fabrics sewn together with the avant-garde eye of an artisan – colors that are frowned upon by the Amish. Yet her parents allow her this small expression of individualism.

'Sadie loves to sew.' Esther says the words as if her daughter's needlework requires justification. 'She's been doing the needlework since she was six years old.'

I can't stop looking at the yards and yards of fabric, so painstakingly designed and sewn by the hands of a young girl with a passion her parents haven't been able to eradicate or contain. In the back of my mind, I'm remembering my conversation with Sadie that day on the bridge. *I'm drawn to all the things I shouldn't be. Music and . . . art. I want to . . . read books and watch movies and see places I've never seen. I want*

to go to college and . . . I'm going to design clothes. I'm so
good with the needle and thread. . . .

'She's right,' I whisper.

Esther tilts her head. 'What?'

'She's very talented.'

Esther looks embarrassed as she crosses to the bed and picks
up a pink-and-red pillow. 'Perhaps we should not have allowed
her so much individual expression.'

'Sometimes this kind of passion can't be quelled.'

She looks unbearably sad, standing there holding the pillow.
'We don't approve of the colors. Sadie takes too much pride
in her quilting. She's willful. She can be disrespectful.' Yet she
brings the pillow to her face and breathes in the scent of the
daughter she misses so desperately.

The words, the reproach they contain, conjure an Amish
proverb my *mamm* told me many times as a girl, especially
when she was trying to get a recalcitrant me to do my chores.
'Pride in your work puts joy in your day,' I whisper.

Tears spring into Esther's eyes. She puts the pillow against
her face as if to hide her tears and looks at me over the top of
it. 'She is a special girl with a good heart. A big heart.' She
chokes out a laugh. 'Perhaps too big.'

'I'll do my best to find her.'

She sinks to her knees, as if her legs no longer have the
strength to support her. Tears run unchecked down her cheeks
as she lowers her face into her hands and begins to sob.

I give her shoulder a squeeze and then turn my attention
to the room. There's not much to search; the bedroom of a
teenage Amish girl bears little resemblance to those of their
English counterparts. I begin with the night table, finding a
copy of *Es Nei Teshtament*, a Bible that's written in both
Pennsylvania Dutch and English. In the next drawer, I find a
plain hairbrush and comb, a candle, a carved wooden bear.

Finding nothing of interest, I move on to the chest. The top drawer is filled with Walmart cotton bras and panties. There are also old-fashioned bloomers, a winter head covering in need of mending. I move to the next drawer and find several hand-sewn Amish dresses. In the bottom drawer, I find a pair of blue jeans tucked into the back, where no one would notice them unless she was looking.

Standing, I step back and look around, spot the sweater hanging on the dowel set into the wall. I check the pockets but come up empty-handed. I kneel and look beneath the bed, check the insides of the sneakers and leather shoes.

'Come on, Sadie,' I mutter as I cross to the bed.

I'm not sure what I'm looking for. The name of a boyfriend written in a notebook. A cell phone number or address scribbled on a scrap of paper. A letter with some helpful information. A diary. I lift the mattress and run my hand along the box spring. My fingers brush against paper. I pull out a *Cosmopolitan* magazine and stare down at the busty model in a low-cut red dress on the cover. The smile that emerges feels sad on my face.

'Where are you?' I whisper.

And I tuck the magazine back into its hiding place.

FOURTEEN

I'm at the police station, standing in the hall outside the conference room with Sheriff Rasmussen. Inside, it's a full house.

Angi McClanahan and her mother sit together at the table, eyeing us like a couple of pissed-off cats. Matt Butler and his father, Andy, sit one chair away from the McClanahans. Andy looks impatient and put out as he thumbs his BlackBerry. His son, Matt, is hunched over his own device, texting and grinning with equal fervor. On the opposite side of the table, Lori Westfall sits alone, trying to look tough. Despite the too-tight jeans, black eyeliner, and pierced eyebrow, she's not doing a very good job.

'We need to split them up,' I say to the sheriff. 'Talk to each of them separately. We can use my office. Let the rest of them stew in here.'

He nods. 'Which one is the friend?'

I indicate Lori Westfall. 'I don't know how close they are, but she was with Sadie that day at the bridge.'

'Any idea where her parents are?' Rasmussen asks. 'They should be here for this.'

I shake my head. 'When I called her mother and told her I needed to speak with her daughter, she didn't seem too interested. I think she dropped her off and went back to work.'

'Nice.' He sighs. 'Maybe we'll get lucky and she'll tell us the Miller girl is at some tat shop in Wooster, getting her goddamn eyebrow pierced.'

We both know the outcome of this isn't going to be as cut-and-dried.

When I step inside, the room goes silent and all eyes land on me. Rasmussen hangs back, giving me the floor. 'I know everyone is busy, but I appreciate your coming.'

'Like we had a choice,' Angi McClanahan mutters.

Ignoring her, I turn my attention to Matt Butler, who's so embroiled in texting that the building could be crumbling around him and he wouldn't notice until a chunk of concrete hit him in the head. 'The first thing I'm going to ask you to do,' I say, 'is put away the cell phones. That includes you, Matt.'

The boy looks up, blinking, as if he's been awakened from a dream, then powers down. His father tosses his BlackBerry and it clatters onto the table in front of him, letting me know in no uncertain terms that he's an important man and doesn't appreciate being pulled away from his day.

Too bad.

'What's this all about, Chief Burkholder?' he asks.

'She's got it out for our kids.' Kathleen McClanahan casts me a spiteful look. 'They're easier to bully than us adults.'

I don't take the bait. 'We have a missing teenager in Painters Mill. Fifteen-year-old Sadie Miller. She's Amish and disappeared sometime last night.' I watch the reactions of each person as I relay the news, paying particular attention to Lori Westfall and Angi McClanahan.

Andy Butler looks appropriately appalled. 'My God, I had no idea.'

Lori Westfall goes stone-still, her eyes looking everywhere except at me. I try to read her body language, her facial expressions, but she's so stiff and unnatural, I can't. Does she know something? Or is she as shocked and frightened as the rest of us and simply doesn't know how to absorb the information?

Kathleen McClanahan doesn't react. When I look at her daughter, Angi, some of the toughness falls away. Before her eyes skate away from mine, I see a flash of guilt, and I wonder about its source. Does she have a guilty conscience because she fought with Sadie? Or does she have another reason to blame herself? It wouldn't be the first time bullying took an ominous turn.

I scan the group. 'I need to know right now if any of you know where she is.'

'Is it possible she ran away?' Andy asks me.

'Anything is possible at this point,' I tell him.

He looks at the other two teens in the room as if they have the answers, not his son.

I remain silent, waiting, watching.

At the door, Rasmussen remains unobtrusive. But his eyes are watchful and sharp, and I'm glad he's here to help me gauge reactions.

When no one speaks, I turn my attention to Lori Westfall. 'You're first,' I tell her. 'Come with me.'

'Wh—where are you taking me?' she asks in a tremulous voice.

Without replying, I start toward my office.

Once inside, I slide behind my desk and extract a legal pad, pen, and an antiquated tape recorder from the drawer. Lori lowers herself into the visitor chair across from me, nearly jumping out of her skin when Rasmussen closes the door and leans against it.

I turn on the tape recorder and recite the date, time, and the names of all present. Then I turn my attention to the girl. 'Why don't you start by telling me about your relationship with Sadie.'

The girl stares at me as if I've come at her with a knife. 'She's my best friend,' she mumbles.

My interest surges. I knew the girls were friends, but I didn't realize they were *best* friends. That's unusual, since Sadie is Amish. It's been a while since I was fifteen, but one thing I know will never change is that best friends tell each other everything.

'How did you meet her?' I ask.

'We met at the bridge. Last summer.'

'So you've known her for about a year?'

She nods.

'How is it that you became friends, when she's Amish?'

'Most of the time, Sadie doesn't *seem* very Amish.' The girl offers a pensive smile that reflects true affection. 'She wears jeans and smokes and cusses. Sometimes I forget she's different.'

'You don't seem to have much in common with her.' I prod, hoping she'll relax and elaborate and give me something – anything – useful.

Lori looks down and her hair falls forward, covering the sides of her face, as if she's trying to hide behind it, and I realize this girl is painfully shy. 'We just hit it off,' she tells me. 'I mean, we're both kind of outsiders, you know? Sadie because she's Amish. Me because I'm not into the whole social clique thing.' She shrugs. 'We don't fit in, but when we're together, that doesn't matter.'

'When's the last time you saw her?' I ask.

'Yesterday. Six o'clock or so. At the bridge.'

'How did she seem?'

'Same as always.' A ghost of a smile touches her mouth but vanishes quickly. 'She was complaining about not having a car. She, like, wants wheels bad.'

'Why does she want a car?'

'She mainly just wants to cruise around.'

'Did she ever talk about leaving Painters Mill?'

'We're always talking about getting out. But it's like something we're going to do in the future, you know? She's got all these big plans to move to New York and design clothes.'

'Has she mentioned New York recently?'

She shakes her head adamantly. 'She wouldn't go without me.'

'Has she had any problems at home?'

She nods. 'Her parents totally don't get her.'

'Did she have an argument with them?'

'They don't argue, exactly. But her parents have pretty much laid down the law about Sadie's art. It's like they don't understand that it's part of her, you know?' She frowns. 'They think it's worldly or something.'

I recall the needlework in Sadie's bedroom, and I feel a pang in my gut, because I know her art isn't condoned by her Amish peers. Like so many other things, her art is something she'll be forced to give up when she's baptized.

'What about the rest of the Amish community?' I ask. 'Any problems she's mentioned?'

'No.' Lori gives me a knowing look. 'But she's always talking about leaving. She's tired of the way they live. And she's struggling with the whole getting baptized thing.'

'Did she tell you that?'

'All the time. She says the Amish are always whispering behind her back, judging her. If she gets baptized, she'll have to give up everything. Her cell phone. Any dream of owning a car or going to New York. She'll have to give up her *art*. That sucks, you know?'

Rumspringa is the time when Amish teens are allowed to experience life without all the constraints of the *Ordnung*, while the adults look the other way. It's an exciting time of personal discovery and growth before a young person commits to the church. Was Sadie so conflicted, the pressure so intense, that she fled?

'Did she ever talk about running away?' I ask.

The girl hesitates. 'Sometimes.'

'Do you think that's what happened?'

She bites her lip. 'She would have told me.'

I mentally shift gears, move on to my next question. 'Does Sadie have a boyfriend?'

She shakes her head. 'She thinks the guys our age are jerks.'

'Let's go back to the bridge for a moment, Lori. Have you seen any vehicles or buggies you don't recognize? Any strangers hanging out?'

'Just the usual crowd. You know, from school.'

I push the legal pad and pen at her. 'I want you to write down the names of everyone you've seen there over the last couple of weeks.'

She picks up the pen. 'That's a lot of names.'

'I've got a lot of paper.' I smile at her.

She smiles back. Putting her tongue between her teeth, she starts writing.

'So what do you and Sadie do when you're at the bridge, anyway?' I ask conversationally.

'We drink beer and smoke.' She glances over her shoulder at Rasmussen and hastily adds, 'Cigarettes, I mean.' Her gaze lands on me. 'You're not going to tell my mom, are you?'

'We'll deal with that after we find Sadie, okay?'

The girl stares at me, as if the gravity of the situation is starting to sink in. 'Do you think something bad happened to her?' she asks.

'That's what we're trying to figure out.'

Ten minutes later, Angi McClanahan slides into the visitor chair adjacent to my desk. Rasmussen drags in an extra chair for her mother and then takes his place at the door.

I turn on the tape recorder, recite all the obligatory information, and turn my attention to Angi. 'When did you last see or hear from Sadie?'

'I guess it was the day I beat the shit out of her.' The girl's mother snickers, but I don't look away from Angi. She's pleased with herself. Pleased with the temerity of her answer and the fact that she has an audience.

'Why were you fighting?' I ask.

'Because she put her hands on my boyfriend.'

'What's his name?'

She raises her hand to look at her nails and begins to peel polish off her thumb. 'I don't remember.'

The urge to reach across the table, grab her by the collar, and slap that 'I don't give a shit' attitude off her face is powerful. Of course I don't, since I'm pretty sure it would be considered unbecoming behavior for the chief of police.

I turn my attention to Kathleen McClanahan. 'I suggest you encourage your daughter to cooperate.'

'Angi didn't do nothing to that little Amish troublemaker. Whatever trouble Sadie Miller met with, she brought down on herself.'

'I need his name,' I say. 'Right now.'

Tossing a sideways look at her mother, Angi crosses her arms over her chest. 'Dave Westmoore.'

I write down the name, recalling that the parents live near Millersburg. 'So you were angry because Sadie touched your boyfriend?'

'She was doing more than touching him. That slut had her hands all over him.'

'Jealousy is a powerful emotion.'

Something ugly flashes in the girl's eyes. 'I am *not* jealous of that bitch.'

'What would you call it?'

'Protecting my territory.'

'How far are you willing to go to protect what's yours?'

She shoots me an incredulous look. 'Are you kidding me? I didn't do anything to her!'

'You threatened to kill her,' I say.

'I didn't mean it literally.'

'Or maybe you planned a little revenge.'

Her mother lurches to her feet. 'This is bullshit.'

I give the woman a hard look. 'Sit down.'

When she does, I continue. 'Your daughter was one of the last people to speak with Sadie before she disappeared. They had a physical confrontation. Angi threatened to kill her in front of witnesses, including me.'

I turn a cold look on Angi. The scratch marks on her throat are healing, but they're still visible, so I use them to my advantage. 'Where did you get those marks on your throat?'

The girl raises a hand, her fingers fluttering at her neck. 'They're old. I got them that day on the bridge.'

'How did you get them?' I repeat.

'That psycho Amish girl attacked her,' her mother interjects.

'I'd like to hear that from Angi,' I say, never taking my eyes from the teenager.

'She ain't saying nothing without a fucking lawyer, you goddamn Nazi bitch.'

Holding Angi with my gaze, I lean back in my chair. 'Thank you for your time. That'll be all for now.'

'That was fun,' Rasmussen says.

It's half an hour later, and Rasmussen and I are in my office. I'm sitting behind my desk, trying to resist the urge to pound my head against its surface.

'She didn't run away,' I tell him. 'Someone took her.'

My phone rings, and I put it on speaker. 'What's up, Lois?'

'I just took a call from Elaina Reiglesberger out on County Road 14, Chief. She claims her daughter was out riding and saw Sadie Miller get into a car yesterday.'

Hope jumps through me and then I'm on my feet and reaching for my keys. 'Tell her I'm on my way.'

Rasmussen is already through the door. 'Here's to a witness with good recall.'

I'm on my way to talk to the purported witness when the call from Tomasetti comes in. 'I hope you're calling with good news,' I say in lieu of a greeting.

'I wish I was.'

'Shit, Tomasetti, you're not going to ruin my day, are you?'

He sighs. 'Coroner says Annie King sustained a fatal stab wound. She bled to death.'

Something inside me sinks, like a rock tossed into water and dropping softly onto a sandy bottom. 'Goddamn it.'

It's times like this when that voice in my head tells me I'm not cut out for police work. I've done this before. Receiving this kind of news shouldn't be so hard.

Tomasetti says something else, but I don't hear the words. I pull onto the shoulder, brake with so much force that the tires skid. For several seconds, I sit there, trying to get a grip. I want to punch something; I want to rant and rave at the unfairness of death. Because I'm terrified the same fate awaits Sadie.

'What kind of a monster does that to a fifteen-year-old girl?' I whisper.

He knows I don't mean the question literally; it doesn't require an answer. What he also understands is that I need to find the person responsible and stop him. 'Sooner or later, he'll fuck up,' he tells me. 'They always do. When that happens, we'll get him.'

For a moment, neither of us speaks; then he says, 'Anything on your end?'

I take a deep breath, and slowly the world around me settles back into place. My window is down and I hear a dove cooing from the fence outside. A small herd of Hereford cattle graze in the pasture beyond. The sun slants through the windshield, warm on my face, and I remind myself that no matter what happens, life goes on. Life always goes on.

'We might have a witness.' I tell him about the girl riding her horse. 'I'm on my way to talk to her now.'

'A break would be nice.' He pauses. 'You okay?'

'Better,' I tell him. 'Thanks.'

'If I can get things tied up here, I'll head your way.'

'I'd like that.' I start to tell him I miss him, but he ends the call before I get the words out.

FIFTEEN

The Reiglesberger family lives on a small horse property located at a hairpin curve on County Road 14. They breed Appaloosa horses and have boarding facilities for people who don't own land. I've met Elaina Reiglesberger several times over the years, but just to say hello. The only things I know about her are that she gives riding lessons to kids and that she runs a therapeutic riding program for special-needs children.

I pull into the gravel lane, drive past a double-wide trailer home, and park adjacent to the horse barn, next to Rasmussen's cruiser. It's an old building in need of paint; the pipe pens are rusty and bent, but the place is well kept.

I exit the Tahoe as two dogs of dubious breeding bound up to me, tongues lolling. I reach down to pet them, and I'm greeted with a barrage of wet kisses. The sliding door of the barn stands open and I can see the silhouettes of several people and at least one horse in the aisle. Wiping my slobbered-up hands on my slacks, I start toward the door.

The smell of horses and manure and fresh-cut hay greet me when I step inside. Five heads turn my way, one of which is Sheriff Rasmussen's. He's surrounded by several young girls in riding breeches and helmets, along with a plump, competent-looking woman wearing jeans and a yellow golf shirt. The horse is a big shiny bay in cross-ties and looks as if he's enjoying the hubbub. I suspect the bag of carrots lying on a nearby lawn chair might be part of the reason.

As my eyes adjust to the dim interior, I recognize the woman as Elaina Reiglesberger. She's a pretty thirtysomething with shoulder-length hair that's pulled into a ponytail and tucked into a Starbucks cap. Her shirt is covered with specks of hay. Something dark and gooey mars the right hip of her jeans. But she has a wholesome, centered look about her. She smiles at me as I approach.

'Hi, Chief Burkholder.' Muttering something about her hands, she wipes them on her jeans before offering a handshake. 'Terrible about the Miller girl.' She glances at the sheriff. 'You guys have any idea what happened?'

Her accent broadcasts Kentucky. She's got a straightforward countenance and a quiet confidence that tells me she's probably a good role model for these young riders. 'We're working on it,' I say noncommittally. 'I understand someone here thinks they might have seen something.'

'Mandy, my oldest. She was riding down the road yesterday, the day Sadie Miller disappeared, and thinks she might have seen her. She didn't think anything about it until she was watching the news and saw the story.' Elaina turns, takes one of the girls by the shoulders, and moves her toward me. 'Mandy, honey, tell the chief what you saw.'

The girl is pretty, with dark brown hair and wide, guileless eyes. I guess her age to be about twelve. She's still more interested in horses than boys, and isn't nearly as happy as the horse to be the center of attention.

'Hi, Mandy.' I extend my hand and we shake.

'Hi.' The girl's palm is wet with sweat, telling me to tread lightly if I'm to loosen up her memory and pry something – anything – useful out of her brain.

I run my hand down the horse's neck. 'Is this big boy yours?'

A grin overtakes her face. 'That's Paxton.'

'Hey, Paxton.' I give the horse a pat. 'What do you do with him?'

'We just started barrel racing.'

'I bet that's fun.'

'Except when she hits the barrel,' a girl who is a younger version of Mandy blurts out.

Mandy rolls her eyes. 'At least I don't fall off like you.'

'Girls.' Elaina sets her hand on the younger girl's shoulder and starts to play with her hair. 'Let the chief ask her questions.'

I turn my attention back to Mandy. 'Can you tell me what you saw yesterday?'

The other girls inch closer, as if they don't want to miss a word. Mandy swallows. 'Sometimes I take Paxton down the road after we practice barrels to cool him off. I saw that Amish girl walking along the road down by that old barn, and this car drove up next to her. She walked over and started talking to someone.'

'Did you see who she was talking to?'

'No.'

'What kind of car was it?'

'It was just old and kind of gross-looking.' Her eyes dart left as she tries to recall. 'Dark. Blue, I think.'

I glance at Rasmussen and see him jot something in his notepad; then I turn my attention back to Mandy. 'Do you know what time that was?'

'Around seven-thirty.'

I glance through the door toward the gravel lane. 'When you go down the road, do you go left or right?'

'Left. We usually ride down to the bridge.'

I'm familiar with the bridge. It's about a half a mile down the road and spans a small stream and greenbelt that separates a soybean field from a cornfield.

'Was the driver a man or a woman?' I ask.

Her eyes slide toward her mom, who gives her an encouraging nod. 'I couldn't tell.'

'Did Sadie get into the car?' I ask.

She knows where I'm going with my line of questioning; I see it in her eyes. And for the first time, the girl looks scared. 'I don't know.'

'Did you notice which direction the car went?'

'It was still there when I left.'

I give her a smile. 'You did great, Mandy. Thank you.' I turn my attention to Elaina and hand her my card. 'If she remembers something later, will you give me a call? My cell number is on the back. I'm available day or night.'

The woman gives me a firm nod and lowers her voice. 'God bless you guys. I hope you find that girl safe and sound.'

A few minutes later, I'm back in the Tahoe, idling past the bridge where Mandy Reiglesberger claims to have seen Sadie Miller talking to someone in a vaguely described vehicle. It's not much to go on – not *enough* to go on – but it's all I've got.

I've called Tomasetti and asked for a list of individuals in Holmes and Coshocton counties who own dark-colored cars more than three years old. But we both know extracting any useful information is a long shot. Still, I could whittle down the results to pedophiles or males convicted of a sex crime in the last five years. It's a start.

I park on the gravel shoulder a few yards from the bridge. Looking in my rearview mirror, I see Rasmussen pull over behind me. We exit our vehicles and meet on the shoulder.

He looks toward the west, where the sun has already sunk

behind a purple bank of clouds. 'It's going to be dark in half an hour.'

Trying not to feel as if we're wasting our time, I motion left. 'I'll go east and you go west. Let's see what we can find.'

He nods and we start in opposite directions.

There isn't much traffic along this deserted stretch. Two miles to the east, the road dead-ends at the county dump, which is chained off except on Saturday mornings. The asphalt is pitted and narrow, with a centerline that's been scoured by tires and the elements. I walk the narrow shoulder, my eyes skimming the grassy bar ditch, the fence, the soybean field, and the macadam on my left. I'm not sure what I'm looking for. Anything that seems out of place. Signs of a struggle. Skid marks. None of those things is indicative of a crime. But sometimes building a case is akin to putting a puzzle together. Alone, the pieces mean nothing. But when you arrange them in a meaningful way, a picture emerges.

Several minutes pass with no luck. I'm ever aware of the fading light, birdsong being replaced by a chorus of crickets in the woods. Near the bridge, I find a beer can and the ragged remnants of a paper towel. There's a plastic Baggie that looks as if it's been ripped to shreds by some animal. Twenty yards past the bridge, I notice horse hoof marks in the gravel. There are more in the grass, along with a pile of horse manure. I know now that this is where Mandy Reiglesberger rides.

I'm about to turn back, when I notice a single skid mark from a short, hard stop. It's not unusual to see rubber marks on any roadway. People brake for animals. Teenagers, armed with new driver's licenses, perform peel-outs to flaunt their horsepower and show off for their friends.

These particular skid marks are fresh. My heart jigs when I spot a thin brown cigarette lying in the gravel. It's smoked halfway down and it's been run over at least once. Pulling a glove from a compartment on my belt, I slip it over my right hand. I'm an instant away from picking it up when I discern the scent of cloves. And I have proof – at least in my own mind – that at some point Sadie was here.

I glance over my shoulder, see the sheriff wading through knee-high grass fifty yards back. 'Rasmussen! I think I found something! Bring the camera!'

Nodding, he starts toward his vehicle.

I return my attention to the skid mark. Cursing the swiftly falling darkness, I follow the direction of the skid to a disturbance in the gravel and a place where the grass has been flattened by a tire. It's as if someone made a U-turn in the middle of the road. There's no identifiable tread. Five feet from the skid mark, I find the one thing I didn't want to find: a dark, irregularly shaped stain. I know immediately it's blood.

'Goddamn it,' I mutter, staving off a crushing sense of helplessness.

'Looks like blood.'

I turn at the sound of Rasmussen's voice.

He pulls a Mini Maglite from his belt and sets the beam on the stain. 'Might not be hers.' He looks around, his eyes going to the wooded area at the bridge. 'Could be from an animal that got hit. Raccoon or possum that came up from that creek.'

'Maybe.' But I don't think that's the case. More than likely, if an animal had been struck by a car, the carcass would be lying nearby. I motion toward the cigarette butt a few feet away. 'Sadie Miller smoked clove cigarettes.'

We kneel next to the stain. There's not enough blood to form a pool like the one in Buck Creek. This one is elongated and looks more like a smear, or a scrape.

Wishing for a magnifying glass, I lean close. I see what looks like bits of flesh that have been abraded by the rough surface. My eyes land on something in the center of the stain, sending a scatter of goose bumps over my arms. 'A hair,' I hear myself say.

'Human?'

'I don't know. It's long. Same color and length as Sadie's.' I straighten, look at him. 'I'm going to call Tomasetti and get a CSU out here.'

He looks around. 'Kate, I hate to say this, because this could turn out to be nothing. But it almost looks like a hit-and-run involving a pedestrian.'

A dozen arguments spring to mind. We're overacting. Reading things into this that aren't there. Chances are, a deer or dog or a fucking raccoon got hit. But considering everything we know, his theory is solid. Too damn solid.

'He ran her down,' I whisper. 'And he took her.'

He tilts his head to catch my eye, then holds my gaze. 'I know you have a connection to this girl. If you want me to—'

'I can handle it.' I know he's thinking about the Slabaugh case and the fact that I used deadly force. I guard my secrets well, but he knows I'm still dealing with the aftereffects.

He nods, but his eyes are knowing. 'I'll get a roadblock set up and get some photos.'

I unclip my phone, surprised that my hands are shaking. Impatient with myself, I punch speed dial to get Tomasetti. He answers with his usual growl and I fill him in on Mandy Reiglesberger's sighting of Sadie Miller and the scene Rasmussen and I discovered.

'You sure the hair is human?' he asks.

'I've never met a raccoon with long hair.' Neither of us laughs. 'I was wondering if you could send a CSU.'

'I can have someone there within the hour.'

'I owe you one.'

'I'll remind you of that next time I see you.'

I almost ask him when that will be, but I don't want to sound needy. Maybe because, at the moment, I am. 'Anything on your end?'

'We have a witness who claims Gilfillan with the Twelve Passages Church had contact with Annie King, targeted her for recruiting. Goddard brought him in for questioning.

In terms of the case, unearthing that kind of connection is huge. 'You don't sound too excited.'

'Witness is a flaky son of a bitch. Known meth user. Disgruntled because he was kicked out of the church.'

'So he's got an ax to grind.'

'Maybe.' But his voice is uncertain. 'Or maybe Mr. Meth is telling the truth and Annie King didn't want to be recruited and things went sour. I'm working on a search warrant now.'

I think about Gilfillan in terms of Sadie's disappearance. 'Does he have an alibi for last night?'

'He claims he was home. Alone.'

The need to be there, to talk to Gilfillan myself, burns through me. Is it possible the self-proclaimed pastor is preying on Amish youths who are confused about the religious path they want to follow?

'Keep me posted,' I say.

'You know I will.'

SIXTEEN

One of the most difficult aspects of a long-term investigation – especially a case in which someone's life is in jeopardy – is knowing when to call it a night. I know it's a self-defeating mind-set; everyone needs sleep. But I invariably feel as if I'm turning my back on the victim when I go home. The truth of the matter is, I don't know how to stop being a cop. How can I go home to eat or sleep or sit on my sofa and watch TV when a young girl is depending on me to find her?

The answer is a simple matter of human endurance. No one can work around the clock indefinitely. If people try, there will come a point when they'll become ineffective, or, worse, a detriment to the investigation. They reach a point where exhaustion and emotions cloud the decision-making process, reaction time, and good old-fashioned common sense. I'm loathe to admit it, but I've been there. I'm not the least bit proud of the way I handled some aspects of cases past. The only positive gleaned is that I learned my limits.

It's nearly 1:00 A.M. when I unlock the door of my house and step inside. The aromas of stale air and the overripe bananas I left on the kitchen counter greet me.

Flipping on the light, I carry my overnight bag to the bedroom and drop it on the floor outside my closet. Physical exhaustion presses into me as I peel off my clothes and toss them into the hamper. But while my body is crying for sleep, my mind is wound tight, and I know sleep will not come easily.

In the bathroom, I crank the water as hot as I can stand it and step under the spray. I soap up twice, knowing I'm trying to wash away more than just the dirt of the day. I haven't let myself think of Sadie in emotional terms. I haven't let myself think about how this could turn out or what she might be going through at this very moment.

Now that I'm alone with my thoughts, all of those gnarly beasts come calling. I can't help but compare Sadie's disappearance to the murder of Annie King. The possibility that the outcome will be the same terrifies me. Another young life snuffed out long before its time. Another family shattered. And all I can think is that I can't let that happen.

In the bedroom, I pull on an old T-shirt from my Academy days and a pair of sweatpants. Padding barefoot to my office, I flip on my computer. While it boots, I pull out my Rand McNally road atlas and turn to a map of northern Ohio. Tearing out two pages, I take both to the bulletin board I keep on the wall adjacent to the desk and pin them up side by side. With a black marker, I circle the location of each disappearance. Monongahela Falls. Sharon, Pennsylvania. Rocky Fork. Buck Creek. Painters Mill. I draw a larger circle encompassing all the towns.

Leaning over my desk, I open the pencil drawer and pull out a red Sharpie, snap off the lid, and go over to the map. I circle Buck Creek, where Stacy Karns, Gideon Stoltzfus, and Justin Treece are located. I circle Salt Lick, where Frank Gilfillan and the Twelve Passages Church are located. I draw a larger circle to encompass each location and go back to my desk.

I stare at the map. The two large circles overlap each other and include much of the same area. All of the towns, the locations of the victims and suspects, are roughly within a one-hundred-mile radius. In rural terms, that's less than a two-hour drive. Chances are, the killer resides somewhere within that circle.

'Why do you do it?' I whisper.

I turn to the whiteboard and write, <u>Why?</u> with a double underscore. Then '<u>No ransom demand. Sexual in nature? Fetish related?</u>' I think of Annie and Sadie and write, '<u>Vulnerable? Runaways?</u>' Then I add, '<u>Blood found at scenes.</u>'

'Where are they?' I'm thinking aloud now, letting my mind run with random thoughts and undeveloped theories. 'Why did we find Annie King's body and not the bodies of the others?'

I divide the board in half with a bold line. Below the delineation, I write, '<u>Suspects: Stacy Karns, Frank Gilfillan, Gideon Stoltzfus, Justin Treece.</u>' Finally, I write, '<u>Unknown perpetrator.</u>'

'We don't know you yet,' I say.

I circle '<u>Unknown perpetrator.</u>' Next to it, I write, '<u>Motive?</u>' And then add, '<u>Why?</u>'

'Why do you take them?' I say aloud.

And I know that once we know why, we will find the who.

The sound of pounding drags me from a deep and dreamless sleep. A hard rush of adrenaline sends me bolt upright. For an instant, I'm disoriented, uncertain about the source of the noise. Then I realize someone's at the door. My mind registers that the doorbell didn't ring. Back door, I think, and something else niggles at my brain. A glance at the alarm clock on my night table reminds me that 3:00 A.M. visitors are almost always the bearers of bad news.

Jerking the robe from the chair next to my bed, I work it over my shoulders and tighten the belt. I open the top drawer of the night table and snag my .38, cock it. Holding the weapon low at my side, I pad silently to the kitchen, sidle to the back door, and peer through the curtains.

John Tomasetti stands on the porch with his hands in his pockets, looking out over the backyard as if his being here in the middle of the night is the most natural thing in the world.

I turn the bolt lock and swing open the door. 'Don't tell me,' I begin. 'You were in the neighborhood.'

He turns to me, hands still in his pockets, his face deadpan, and for a split second I'm terrified he's come here with some dire news about the case. 'Actually, I drove a hundred miles, against my better judgment and without telling my superiors, to sleep with you.'

I laugh, but it's a nervous sound. 'Well, that's pretty subtle.'

'That's me. Mr. Subtle.' His lips don't move, but I see the smile in his eyes. 'Pink robe goes nicely with that thirty-eight.'

Feeling only slightly self-conscious, I glance down at my threadbare robe, then open the door the rest of the way. 'Tomasetti, you are so full of shit.'

'Yeah, but you're still glad to see me.'

The truth of the matter is that he looks damn good standing there in that crisp shirt and those charcoal-colored trousers. Not a good key indicator for a prudent outcome to all this.

I motion him inside. 'Is everything okay?'

'Definitely looking up.'

His presence fills the kitchen the instant he steps inside. It's as if the air itself becomes charged with some electrical energy I feel all the way to my core.

'I'm sorry I woke you,' he says. 'I know sleep is tough to come by right now.'

'Sleep is always hard to come by when we're together.'

'I was talking about the case.'

'That, too.' Before I turn away from him, I see his eyes

sweep the length of me. Trying not to let that rattle me, I set my gun on the kitchen table and flip on the light.

'Anything new on the case?' I ask.

Shaking his head, he crosses to the table, works his jacket off, and drapes it over a chair back. I watch as he slides his Glock from his shoulder holster, unfastens the buckle, then sets both on the table. 'We got the search warrant for Stacy Karns's house. By the time the judge signed off, it was too late to get out there. Sheriff's office wanted to wait until morning to execute it.' He turns to me. 'I'll need to get out of here early.'

'It's already early,' I say.

'I've got a couple of hours to kill.'

'You're such a sweet talker.'

'That's what all the female chiefs of police tell me.'

I've known Tomasetti for about a year and a half now. After a shaky start and a little bit of head butting, we became friends – something that doesn't occur naturally for either of us. Maybe because we have so much in common. Or maybe because not all of the things we share are good.

Trust is hard to come by for people like us. But he's the closest thing to a best friend I've ever had. We've never discussed it; the truth of the matter is, neither of us is very good at the whole male–female relationship thing. We're even worse at communicating, especially when it comes to talking about our feelings. This is new ground, I suppose, but I like it. He keeps coming back for more. I keep letting him.

I go to the living room and switch on the stereo. I've always loved music, even when I was Amish and it was one of many forbidden fruits. Once, I stole a CD player from an English girl's car when I sneaked out to the mall. It was filled with a mishmash of genres – rock, mostly – and I couldn't get enough. I listened to those songs over and over until my *datt* caught me and made me return it. As an adult, there's not nearly enough music in my life. I choose Frank Sinatra's *Fly Me to the Moon* and my nerves begin to smooth out.

I find Tomasetti standing at the doorway of my office, looking at the map and whiteboard I worked on earlier. He gives me a long look when I come up beside him. 'You've been busy,' he says.

'Couldn't sleep.'

He turns his attention back to the whiteboard. 'Maybe you're right. Maybe we don't know the suspect.'

We study the whiteboard for a full minute, neither of us speaking. 'I think we're missing something,' he says finally.

'Like what?'

'I don't know yet.' He walks over to the map and reads aloud what I've written. 'Once we figure out the motive, we'll figure out the who.' He turns to me. 'The overriding question being: Why the Amish?'

'Not just the Amish,' I remind him. 'Young Amish who have considered leaving that way of life.'

He nods. 'Who would be offended by that? I mean, offended so profoundly that he'd go to extreme measures?'

'Someone who is devout.' I toss out the first thing that comes to mind, playing off his question, brainstorming. 'Someone who disapproves of the way these young people are living their lives. Someone who believes they should be punished.' I look at Tomasetti. 'Frank Gilfillan and the Twelve Passages Church.'

'Is he trying to punish them? Recruit them? Or redeem them?'

'Maybe all three.'

'So the fact that these Amish teens are confused about their religious beliefs makes them vulnerable. That's a benefit to Gilfillan. That's how he finds them.'

'Maybe Annie King refused to be recruited,' I venture.

'That could fit,' Tomasetti says.

'I'm starting to like Gilfillan for this.' I find myself wanting to return to Buck Creek with him in the morning, so I can be there when they execute the warrant. But I can't leave with Sadie missing. Not when the last missing girl turned up dead.

An image of Sadie flashes in my mind's eye. I see her as she was that day on the bridge in her skimpy tank top, with her long brown arms and reckless, engaging smile. Sadie with a can of beer in one hand, a cigarette in the other. Sadie rolling around on the ground and throwing punches with the abandon of a born street fighter.

'Tomasetti, I don't want to lose this girl,' I say quietly.

'I know.'

'Sadie is . . .' I don't know how to finish the sentence. I almost said 'special,' but I know in my heart she's no more special than the others. All of them are someone's daughter or son or brother or sister. All of them are loved.

'We'll get him,' he says.

'She's hard to handle. She won't acquiesce.' I stare at the whiteboard, but I no longer see the words. 'She might not have much time.'

'Kate, we're doing everything we can.'

That's one of the things I admire about Tomasetti; he'll never prop me up with false hope. He'll never make promises he can't keep, no matter how desperately I need to hear them.

He crosses to me. 'I know what you're thinking.'

I smile, but it feels crooked on my face. 'That I wish I wasn't on the wagon?'

He's standing so close, I can smell the remnants of his aftershave, feel the heat radiating from his body against mine. I see the five o'clock shadow on his jaw, the capillaries in eyes that are red from lack of sleep and too many hours on the road.

He frowns, but not in a serious way. 'You're beating your-self up because you're not out there looking for her.'

The urge to argue is strong. But I don't. Mainly because he's right. 'Do you want me to lie down on the sofa so you can ask me how I feel about that?'

'I know this is going to be a stunning revelation for you, Kate, but you and I need sleep and downtime, just like every-one else.'

'You're not trying to tell me we're human, are you?'

He offers a wan smile, but his eyes remain serious. 'I wish I could tell you we're going to go out there tomorrow and find her and bring her home. That we're going to get this guy. We both know it doesn't always work out that way.'

When I look away, he puts his fingertips under my chin and guides my gaze back to his. 'The one thing I can tell you is that we're doing our best. That's all anyone can do. That's got to be enough.'

I don't intend to reach for him. But one moment, I'm stand-ing there, feeling shredded and unbearably guilty. The next, my arms are around Tomasetti's shoulders and his mouth is fastened to mine. The power of the kiss makes my head spin. My body surges to life with an intensity that shocks me. I'm caught in a flash flood and tumbling out of control. . . .

He grasps my biceps, and then my back is against the wall. His mouth trails kisses down my throat. His hands fumble at my belt and my robe falls open. His hands find my breasts. I hear myself gasp as callus-rough palms brush against sensitive skin. I'm having a difficult time catching my breath.

Somewhere in the back of my mind, a tiny voice shouts a warning. It tells me anything that feels this good can't possibly be real or true or lasting.

I don't listen.

He's got the robe off my shoulders when I realize if I don't stop this right now, we're going to have sex either on the floor or on my desk, neither of which appeals.

I sidle right. Tomasetti follows and we stumble down the hall and into my bedroom. Dropping my robe on the floor, I draw back the covers and get into bed. Clothes rustle as he works off his shirt and steps out of his trousers.

And then he's sliding into bed beside me. The familiar rush of what I can only describe as joy fills me when he puts his arms around me. My worries about Annie King and Sadie Miller and the case that has refused to come together fade into the background. And for a short time, we shut out the rest of the world. We take refuge in each other's arms and this safe harbor we've built.

I wake, to find Tomasetti standing beside the bed, naked, his hair still wet from a shower. I have no idea how long I've been sleeping.

'What are you doing?' I ask, stretching.

'I've got to go,' he whispers. 'Go back to sleep.'

'What time is it?'

'Almost five. I'm late.'

But he climbs into the bed beside me. I snuggle against his shoulder, reveling in the solid warmth of him, the feel of his arm around me, the smell of soap and aftershave and his own distinct scent.

'There's never enough time,' he says.

'You're always sneaking away in the middle of the night.'

'Not by choice. I've missed you.'

Surprised by the seriousness of his tone, I raise up on an elbow and look at him. 'Same goes.'

'We could make this a little more permanent.'

Shock rattles through me with such force that for an instant I can't speak. 'What do you mean?'

He surprises me by laughing. 'For God's sake, Kate, don't look so terrified.'

I feign punching his shoulder. 'I'm not.'

He sobers, looks away, then finally meets my gaze. 'I found a house,' he says. 'In Wooster. It's old and big, with four bedrooms and a barn. It's set on a couple of acres with a pond and lots of trees.'

The statement hits me like ice water splashed in my face. 'Wooster?' I repeat dumbly as my brain struggles to sift through the implications.

'It's less than an hour from the Richfield office. An easy commute for me. And thirty minutes from Painters Mill.'

'You want to buy a house?'

'I want to live with you,' he says firmly, but he's watching me carefully. 'The house doesn't matter, Kate. It doesn't matter where we live. We can rent. Whatever you want.'

'That's a big step, Tomasetti.'

'It is. But we have something good.' His expression softens and he kisses my temple. 'You look like you're about to bolt.'

I try to laugh, but my throat is too tight. 'I didn't know you were thinking about . . . moving in together.'

'It would allow us to spend more time together.' He shrugs. 'Less commuting for me.'

'More time for sex,' I say with a laugh.

'There is that.'

I stare at him, trying to digest everything he's just laid on me. Admittedly, there's a part of me that's excited and flattered at the prospect of living with this man who is such a big part of my life, a man I admire and am wildly attracted to. But another part of me is terrified it would change things, bring something unwanted to a relationship that's good the way it is.

Knowing Tomasetti has enriched my life in ways I never imagined. In ways I never believed possible. I'm a better person because of him. I try harder because I know he will judge me, and I can't bear the thought of not measuring up. In a world that's stingy with friendship and trust, I've found a deep well of both with the most unlikely of sources.

I've never been in love, but I'm pretty sure I've found that with Tomasetti. I love him every way a woman can love a man. I love the part of him that is damaged and complex and difficult.

Does he love me? He's never said the words. He's never given me any indication as to the seriousness of his feelings for me. But is that proclamation some kind of unspoken prerequisite to shacking up? I don't know the answer to that, either.

What I do know is that three years ago, Tomasetti went through a horrific ordeal when his wife and children were murdered. He's come a long way since. He's recovered as much as a man can after something like that. But is he ready to love another woman?

'You're thinking awfully hard,' he says.

'I'm trying not to screw this up.'

'Nothing to screw up,' he tells me. 'Either you want to live with me or you don't.'

'It's not quite that black and white,' I tell him. 'We're in a good place right now. I don't want to ruin that.'

Leaning close, he brushes his mouth against my cheek and slides from the bed. 'You don't have to decide in the next ten seconds. I have to go.'

I watch as he steps into his trousers, jams his arms into the same shirt he wore the night before. 'Tomasetti—'

'I left the rental parked in your driveway.' He doesn't look at me as he buttons the shirt and cuffs. 'I'm going to need the Tahoe.'

'Keys are on the counter by the fridge.' I sit up, find my robe at the foot of the bed, and slip it on.

'Go back to sleep.' He starts toward the hall.

'Tomasetti.' I follow him, barefoot, knotting the belt as I go. 'We need to talk about this.'

I catch him in the kitchen just as he snags the keys off the counter. 'I get it, Kate. It's okay.'

'I'm terrible at this,' I blurt. 'I'm a coward.'

'No you're not.' He opens the door, pauses with his back to me. 'On both counts. I have to go.'

'I need to know if we're okay,' I say.

'We are,' he tells me, and closes the door behind him.

SEVENTEEN

I arrive at the station just before 7:00 A.M. Mona is sitting at the dispatch station with her headset around her neck and a grape Popsicle sticking out of her mouth. She's wearing a pink-and-red-striped shirt with a black skirt that's barely long enough to cover her . . . equipment. Black-tipped fingernails move deftly over her keyboard. She did something with her hair, but I can't put my finger on exactly what.

She glances up when I walk in and smiles. 'Morning, Chief.' She hands me a massive stack of pink message slips. 'Sorry. They've been piling up since about six.'

'You looked different yesterday,' I tell her as I page through messages.

'Hair.' She indicates her head. 'Added some burgundy.'

'I like it.'

She beams. 'Any news on the Miller girl?'

'Hoping something will break today.' I start toward my office, mentally reviewing all the things I need to get done, but an afterthought stops me and I turn back to Mona. 'Are you busy?'

'If you can call a Popsicle busy, I'm swamped.'

I start toward her desk, pulling my notepad from my pocket. 'Can you research something for me?'

Her eyes light up, and I forgive her for the miniskirt. 'I'd love to.'

I reach her desk and flip through my pad. Finding the sheet I'm looking for – a page on which I've written down the names of everyone involved with the disappearances – and I tear it from the pad. 'Take these names and hit a few search engines. See what pops.'

'You looking for anything in particular?'

'A written confession on some blog would be nice,' I mutter.

She hefts a laugh. 'That might be just a tad optimistic, Chief.'

I motion toward the paper in her hand. 'Some of the people on the list aren't directly related to the disappearances, but I still want to look at them.' Sometimes those are the people whose names eventually make their way to the top.

'Tax records?' she asks.

'Sure. Anything you can think of.'

'When do you need it by?'

'Yesterday.'

I spend an hour catching up on administrative tasks and following up on queries I put out the previous day. The CSU working the scene where Mandy Reiglesberger saw Sadie Miller calls at 8:00 A.M. and informs me the blood found at the scene is indeed human. As is usually the case, the lab is backlogged and the blood typing and DNA will take a few days. But at least now I'm relatively certain we're dealing with a crime scene. Not the news I wanted to start my day off with.

Tomasetti calls midmorning and I relay the news.

'Damn.' He sighs. 'I wanted to let you know we executed the search warrant for Stacy Karns's house and property. Get this: We found a photograph of Annie King.'

Shock punches me hard. 'Karns shot the photo? It's his work?'

'He's not talking. But it looks like his style. You know, black and white and kind of noir. There's a definite sexual element.'

'That son of a bitch lied to us.'

'Makes you wonder what else he lied about, doesn't it?'

'It makes me wonder if he had a relationship with her.'

'Does he have an alibi for the night Sadie Miller disappeared?'

'He's not talking. Asked for a lawyer. We're waiting for him now.'

'Bastard.' I realize I'm grinding my teeth and make myself stop. 'That makes him look guilty. Like he's hiding something.'

'I don't know if it will stick, but we took him into custody on an obstruction charge. He's cooling his heels here at the county jail.'

I think about what this means in terms of the case, in terms of finding Sadie. 'Tomasetti, the photo you found. Is it pornographic?'

'She's topless. Her back is turned to the camera, but part of one of her breasts is visible.'

Fury stirs in my chest, but I tamp it down. I can't afford to let those emotions out of their cage. I know from experience they can suck the energy right out of you. 'So we've got him,' I say harshly. 'Even if we can't get him on murder, we've got him on child porn.'

'Second offense, so he'll do time,' he tells me. 'As soon as I get a scan of the photo, I'll e-mail it to you.'

'An underage Amish girl.' I spit the words. 'What kind of man does something like that?'

'Pedophile. Sociopath. Self-important prick. Take your pick. If I get the chance, I'll take a shot at him for you.'

'I hate to admit it, but you're actually making me feel better.'

'That's my girl.'

'What really pisses me off about this is that he'll use this as publicity to promote his photographs and books.'

'Nothing we can do about that.'

'Do you think he killed Annie King?' I ask.

The miles between us hiss; then he says, 'I don't know. Initially, I didn't think so. I still don't, really. But, Kate, that photograph and the fact that he lied to us are hard to ignore.'

The connection between Karns and Annie King is undeniable. So why don't I feel better about it? 'Have you found a connection between Karns and any of the others?'

'Nothing yet, but we've confiscated his computer. We've got a lot of material to comb through.'

The silence that follows lingers an instant too long and I sense our thoughts have ventured back to this morning. 'What about you, Kate?' he asks. 'Everything okay there?'

'The CSU finished processing the scene.' I'm well aware that he wasn't asking about the case, but I fall back into cop mode anyway. Safer ground, I realize, and not just for me. 'There wasn't much.' Thinking of the blood, I sigh. 'The traffic-accident specialist tried to piece together what might have happened, but he didn't have enough for a definitive scenario. He suspects the victim may have been struck by a vehicle and received abrasions from the asphalt.'

At this point, that's a best-case scenario, but neither of us says it.

'Are you driving up here?' he asks.

'I hate to leave with Sadie still missing, but I'm spinning my wheels here.'

'Kate . . . I wanted to tell you I know I shouldn't have laid all that on you this morning,' he says. 'I mean about moving in together.'

'It's okay,' I say quickly. 'You just caught me off guard.'

'Bad timing on my part.'

'It was just . . . unexpected. Things are a little muddled for me right now. I mean with the case. I think I just need a little space.' I cringe, hating the way the words sounded, wishing I could somehow take them back.

He sighs. 'They're getting ready to interview Karns. I've got to get in there.'

In that instant, more than anything else in the world, I want to be there. I want to be with Tomasetti. I want to be there when they question Karns. If the man is guilty of murdering Annie King, there's a high probability he's involved with the disappearance of Sadie Miller.

'Tomasetti?'

'Yeah?'

A hundred words dangle on my tongue. I want to say something that will make all of this awkwardness between us go away. I want to let him know we're okay, that things really aren't muddled and the problem is that I suck at honest communication, especially when there's so much at stake.

'I'm thinking about it,' I blurt.

The statement needs no explanation. 'Okay,' he tells me.

I close my eyes. 'Let me know how it goes with Karns.' And I hit END before he can respond.

I've barely hung up when my cell goes off. I look down and see Auggie's name on the display and groan inwardly. For several seconds, I debate whether to answer, because I already know the direction in which the conversation will go.

'Kate, look, I just wanted to let you know I've talked to the county attorney about the charges against Bradford.' He begins the conversation as if my only thought in the world is the state of his son's life. 'I also spoke with Judge Seibenthaler. They suggested I speak with you. I thought we could discuss it and perhaps get the charges bumped down.'

'Auggie, I've got my hands full with the Sadie Miller case.'

'I'm not asking you to drop the charges. . . .'

He drones on as if I'm not there, and I realize that no matter how I handle this, I'm going to lose. I hit END, grab my keys off the desk, and leave my office.

In the reception area, I find Glock standing at Mona's station. 'I could shoot him for you,' he offers without preamble.

'Might not go over too well with the town council,' I say.

Mona snorts. 'On the other hand, it might help get that new budget passed.'

'You know I could charge both of you with conspiracy to commit murder, right?'

The three of us break into laughter, and another layer of stress sloughs off my back.

'You heading back to Buck Creek?' Mona asks.

I tell them about my conversation with Tomasetti and the photo found at Stacy Karns's home. 'I hate to leave with the Miller girl still missing. But it looks like Karns might be our guy.'

'She could be in Buck Creek,' Glock puts in.

I sigh. 'How do you feel about putting together some volunteers and searching the woods near her house again?'

'I'm all for it. I think Rasmussen is trying to get some dogs out there again, too.'

I turn my attention to Mona. 'Anything interesting on any of those names?'

She looks up from her computer and shakes her head. 'The only thing I've found so far is a piece from *The Early Bird* newspaper. Apparently, the Mast farm is historical. One hundred and fifty years ago, it was a stop on the Underground Railroad.'

'Probably not too helpful in terms of the case.'

'Interesting, though,' Glock puts in.

Mona hits a few keys. 'I'm just getting started, so maybe something will pop.'

I start toward the door, wishing I could be as optimistic. 'Call me if you need anything.'

Two hours later, I'm in the Explorer, heading north on Ohio 44. I'm ten minutes from Buck Creek when my cell phone chirps. I glance down, half expecting to see the mayor's name on the display. I'm relieved to see it's Mona.

'What's up?' I ask.

'Hey, Chief, I wasn't sure if I should bother you with this, but I think I found something interesting on that Amish couple in Monongahela Falls.'

'The Masts?'

'Did you know they lost a daughter, Rebecca?'

'I know their son disappeared.'

'Right. Noah. I was reading about the son when I found another story the *Pittsburgh Post-Gazette* did, like, ten years ago.'

'What happened to the daughter?' I ask.

'She went missing. Local PD conducted a search and found a suicide note in her room.'

'Suicide?' In the back of my mind I wonder why the Masts didn't mention it.

'A year before Noah Mast disappeared,' I say, my mind scrambling to make sense of the news, draw some kind of connection. 'Did they find her body?'

'Four months later, when they dragged a nearby lake.' More keys click. 'Evidently, she'd jumped through an ice-fishing hole on Mohawk Lake. Official manner of death was suicide.'

Tomasetti and I drove past the lake on our way to the Mast farm.

'Do you think this is relevant?' she asks. 'I mean, connected to the missing teens or that murdered girl?'

'I don't know.' Even as I say the words, I know that lying by omission can be as deceptive as an outright lie. 'But I'm going to find out.'

EIGHTEEN

Frustration rides my back as I speed past densely forested countryside interspersed with farmland and rolling, lush pastures toward Monongahela Falls. I'm annoyed because once again I've been pulled away from where I need to be: Buck Creek. I don't know why the Masts failed to mention their daughter's suicide; I don't believe its relevant. Nor do I believe they're involved in the disappearances. Nonetheless they've got some explaining to do.

I've spent the last two hours racking my brain, trying to hit on some common denominator that connects the missing teens: Annie King, Bonnie Fisher, Ruth Wagler, Sadie Miller, and, finally, Noah Mast.

Aside from being Amish, what did these five young people have in common? We haven't been able to determine if they knew one another or if they'd been in contact with one another. In all probability, mainly due to the physical distance between them and limited transportation options, they did not. As far as we know, none of the teenagers had access to a computer or laptop, so they probably didn't meet online. Of course, they could have used a public computer – at a library, for example – but I don't think that's the case.

The most obvious characteristic they shared was that they

were Amish. Second, all were between fourteen and eighteen years of age. I think about what events take place during that period of time in the life of an Amish teenager. Since most only go to school through the eighth grade, they would have finished by age fourteen and already have been considering joining the church. Some were already working, either on the farm or, depending on where they lived, outside the home. Some had entered *rumspringa,* which is basically a period of one or two years when the teenager is granted the freedom to experience the outside world before being baptized.

My gut tells me that while age is key, the element that connects these teens is more personal. Something unique to these particular teenagers. But what? What are we not seeing? Why the hell doesn't anything about this case feel right?

I know, perhaps better than most, that the Amish keep secrets. Even conservative Amish families do. My own family, while not exactly Old Order, were conservative. My *mamm* and *datt* held my sister and brother and me to some pretty high standards, even in terms of the Amish. Jacob and Sarah fared well beneath that kind of iron-fist parenting. Neither strayed beyond the parameters of the *Ordnung*.

But I floundered within those constraints. Even as young as twelve, I resented the restrictions imposed on my life, even though I had no inkling of the concept of freedom. I remember feeling as if every aspect of my life was being micromanaged – by my parents, by our bishop, by society and the Amish culture in general. I recall begrudging my brother because he – and Amish males in general – had more freedoms than I and my female peers did. Even then, the unfairness of that chafed my sensibilities.

All of that discontent came to a head when I was fourteen and an Amish man by the name of Daniel Lapp walked into our farmhouse when I was alone and raped me. I learned the meaning of violence that day. I learned to what lengths I would go to protect myself. And I learned that I was capable of extreme violence. I learned what it meant to hate – not only another human being but myself. Especially myself.

When my parents discovered I'd shot and killed my rapist, I learned that even decent, God-loving Amish break the law. I learned they're capable of lying to protect their children. And, in the eyes of the angry teen I'd been, I knew that underneath all those layers of self-righteous bullshit, they were sinners, just like everyone else.

I spent the following years rebelling against any rule that didn't suit me – and few did. I defied my parents. I railed against all those rigid Amish tenets. I rebelled against myself, and against God. I disrupted the lives of my siblings. Embarrassed my parents. Disappointed the Amish bishop. When *Mamm* and *Datt* began to worry that I was a negative influence on my siblings, I knew it was time to leave. The thought terrified me, but I would rather have died than admit it. Instead, when I turned eighteen, I left Painters Mill for Columbus, Ohio.

In the back of my mind, I always thought I'd fail. That I'd run back to Painters Mill with my tail between my legs. But I didn't. *Mamm* traveled to Columbus when I graduated from the Police Academy. Sadly, I never saw my *datt* again. He died of a stroke six months later. I finally returned to Painters Mill to be with *Mamm* after she'd been diagnosed with breast cancer. She'd forgone conventional medical treatment, opting instead for Amish folk remedies. Those remedies did little to help, of course, and she suffered a terrible end. Even after all these years, sometimes those old regrets sneak up on me.

In terms of Amish youth, I was an anomaly. But it's my only perspective and I can't help but compare my life with the lives of the missing teenagers. Do we share a common thread?

The only teen in the group I know personally is Sadie Miller.

Pretty, troubled Sadie. The last time I saw her, she'd been dressed in painted-on jeans and a revealing tank top. Wearing too much makeup and smoking cigarettes. Cursing because she'd discovered the power of shock value. Sadie and her love of fabric and art and all of her big plans for the future. Sadie, the rule breaker.

The rule breaker.

Something clicks in my brain.

'Shit,' I say aloud. 'That's it.'

I spot an exit for a rest area and swerve right. Then I'm down the ramp and parking in front of a picnic area. For an instant, I sit there, gripping the wheel, my thoughts reeling, and all I can think is, *Why didn't I see this until now?*

Getting out of the Explorer, I start toward the nearest picnic table, unclipping my phone as I go. I hit speed dial and begin to pace. One ring. Two rings. In the back of my mind, I'm already wondering if Tomasetti is avoiding me. Relief swamps me when he picks up.

'I found the connection,' I say without preamble. 'The missing teenagers were breaking the rules. They were misbehaving. Acting out.'

'Run with it,' he says, and I do.

'Someone's targeting troubled Amish teens. Bonnie Fisher was sexually active. She'd had multiple partners. She was pregnant out of wedlock and contemplating an abortion. Annie King had an English boyfriend, a bad boy, and she was known to run with a tough crowd. She was having doubts about her faith and was thinking about leaving the Amish way of life.'

The words tumble from my mouth in a rush. 'Sadie Miller is prideful and individualistic. She wears makeup and tight jeans. She smokes cigarettes, drinks beer, hangs out with the English. She values all the things she shouldn't, like her fabric art. She gets into fights, for Chrissake. She was entertaining thoughts of leaving the Amish way.'

There's a pause and then Tomasetti says, 'I'm playing devil's advocate here, Kate, but every one of those so-called vices could be considered typical behavior for a huge percentage of American teenagers.'

'Not if you're Amish. Sure, you hear about Amish kids misbehaving during *rumspringa*. But something like eighty percent of them go on to be baptized and join the church. These missing kids aren't simply misbehaving. They're breaking major Amish tenets and they're completely impenitent. They're anomalies and someone has taken it upon himself to do something about it.'

'It's tenuous,' he says. 'What about Ruth Wagler? Noah Mast?'

'I don't have it all figured out, but I think it's worth exploring.' I think about that for a moment. 'Did Ruth Wagler's parents mention having any problems with her before she disappeared?'

'No, but they weren't exactly forthcoming.'

'I want to talk to them.'

'Makes it tough when no one has a damn phone,' he grumbles.

I sigh, relived he's on board – or at least halfway in the boat. 'I don't know if I'm right but it feels . . . close.'

'It's not like you're an expert on breaking the rules or anything.'

The words dangle for a moment; then I clear my throat and tell him about Irene and Perry Mast's having lost a daughter ten years earlier.

'Odd that they didn't mention it,' he says.

'I'm on my way to Monongahela Falls now.' I pause. 'If you can hang tight for a couple of hours, I'd like to go with you when you speak to the Wagler girl's parents.'

'I'll wait.' He goes back to my earlier assertion. 'Keeping your rule-breaking theory in mind, what do you think about Gideon Stoltzfus? Do you think he figures into this angle somehow?'

All red hair and freckles, Gideon Stoltzfus looks about as harmless as a Labrador pup. But Tomasetti is right about appearances. Sometimes it's the most benign-seeming individuals who are capable of the most heinous acts. 'He's put himself in a position to make direct contact with young people who are considering leaving the Amish way of life.'

'What about motive?' he asks.

I mull over the question and something ugly pushes at the door, trying to slip into the mix. 'He's been excommunicated. His family won't talk to him. They won't take meals with him. His parents won't let him see his siblings. Those things can cause a lot of stress. A lot of anger. Rage, even.'

'Especially if your family is the center of your life.'

'For most Amish, it is,' I tell him. 'In every sense.'

A pause ensues. I sense that we're both working through the possibilities.

'So he's pissed off at the Amish,' Tomasetti says after a moment. 'He sees other young people getting away with all the things he couldn't. His life is ruined. He's had to join another church. Maybe he sees this as a way to get back at them. Hurt the Amish as a whole.'

'I don't know,' I say. 'Murder seems extreme.'

'Rage is an intense emotion. Add insanity and/or sociopathy to the mix and you have a fucking time bomb.'

'How does he find them?'

'When we talked to him, he told us most people had heard of him through word of mouth and contacted him.'

'How does he know about the teenagers from other towns?'

'Maybe he's got some kind of network in place,' he tells me.

The scenario isn't a perfect fit. A lot of unanswered questions remain. But I know there are times when crimes simply don't make sense, at least not in the mind of a sane person.

'Do you think this is enough to get a search warrant?' I ask.

'I'll see what I can do to get things rolling.'

'We need to talk to some of the teens he's helped in the past,' I say. 'See if Stoltzfus sent up any red flags.'

'I'll get to work on getting some names,' he replies.

More than anything, I want to turn around and help him with those names, but I'm nearly to the Mast place. Better to get this out of the way while I'm here. 'I'll finish up as quickly as possible and head your way.'

I barely notice the smell of hogs or the tall cornstalks encroaching onto the narrow gravel track as I turn the Explorer into the lane of the Mast farm. My mind is still working over my conversation with Tomasetti. The more I consider the possibility of Gideon Stoltzfus's involvement with the missing teens, the more convinced I am that he's a viable suspect.

Child predators and other deviants go to great lengths to cultivate prospective victims, doing their utmost to become caregivers or counselors. Stoltzfus puts himself in direct contact with Amish teens who are considering leaving the Amish way of life. I know from experience that a good number of those teens are, at the very least, discontent, or, at worse, troubled – the type of teen that fits the profile of the missing. They would be vulnerable to someone who claims to have the answers to all of their problems.

The grapevine is a powerful means of communication in the Amish community. It's general knowledge that Gideon

Stoltzfus helped young people leave the plain life. He's built that reputation by taking in troubled teens, gaining their trust, and helping them start new lives. He lends them money, gives them food and a place to stay. He counsels them and helps them find jobs. What if all of those things are a front for a more sinister agenda? What if Gideon Stoltzfus has discovered the ultimate stratagem for hunting prey?

The question sends a scatter of gooseflesh down my arms. The scenario fits – and neither Tomasetti nor I saw it until now. What I haven't been able to figure, however, is motive. As far as we know, there is no sexual element to the kidnappings. To complicate matters, Stoltzfus, whose reputation is above reproach, has indeed helped a handful of teens leave the Amish way without a single complaint that we know of. Are there other victims who've never come forward? Is it possible he helps some and simply does away with others? How does he decide which teens to help and which ones to eliminate?

In the Amish community, when someone does something deemed immoral, he or she is expected to confess before the congregation and ask for forgiveness. If the accused follows that protocol, despite the seriousness of the mistake, that person is redeemed in the eyes of the community.

What if this is about redemption? What if, using some twisted logic, Gideon Stoltzfus takes it upon himself to cull the 'bad Amish' from the community? In a perverse, fanatical way, it makes sense. Deliver the salvageable. Expunge the unredeemable.

I park behind a black four-wheeled buggy and kill the engine. The stench of the hogs washes over me like a wave of stagnant water when I get out. The afternoon has grown hot; humidity presses down like a wet blanket. The wind has gone still and a row of black clouds roil above the treetops to the west, telling me I'll probably be driving to Buck Creek in the rain.

'Terrific,' I mutter as I look around. The farm is so quiet, I can hear the hogs grunting and milling about in the pen on the other side of the barn. A lone blue jay scolds me from the branches of a maple tree in the side yard as I start toward the house. I ascend the steps to the porch and knock.

I wait a beat and knock a second time, using the heel of my hand. Frustration creeps over me when no one answers. *Damn it.* Cupping my hands, I peer through the window, but the mudroom is silent and dark. Shoving my hands into my pockets, I turn and scan the area, wondering if they could be feeding the stock or be baling hay in the field. Not for the first time, I curse the Amish people's aversion to modern conveniences. A phone would make this so much easier.

Leaving the porch, I take the sidewalk back to the Explorer. I reach for the handle, yank open the door. For an instant, I stand there, undecided. I need to get to Buck Creek, hopefully before the sky opens up. But the death of the Mast's daughter ten years ago must be delved into.

'Shit.' Slamming the door, I start toward the barn. I pass the slaughter shed, where Tomasetti and I talked to Perry Mast just two days ago. The severed hog heads are gone, but I can see the indentations in the grass, the oily smears of blood. The door is closed, so I continue on toward the barn. I pass by a chicken coop with an attached wire aviary where a dozen or so hens scratch and peck the ground.

The smell of the hogs grows stronger as I near the barn. To my right, several pink snouts poke between the boards of the fence, and I know the pigs are watching me, hoping for a snack. I slide open the big door and step inside, giving my eyes a moment to adjust to the dim light. The interior is shadowy and smells of moldy burlap and pig shit. Dust motes float in the slant of murky light coming in from a grimy window on the west side.

'Hello?' I call out. 'Mr. and Mrs. Mast?'

A pigeon coos from the rafters above. An antique-looking manure spreader stands next to a big hay wagon that's missing a wheel. A rusty hand auger leans against the wall. A leather harness hangs from an overhead tack hook. I can smell the saddle soap from where I stand. Several empty burlap bags lay scattered on the floor in the corner. Kernels of corn glow yellow against the dirt floor.

'Hello? Mr. Mast? It's Kate Burkholder.'

I cross to the window at the back and look out. Below, a small pen houses a dozen or more Hampshire hogs. Some are lying on their sides in the shade; others root around in a shallow mud puddle. To my right, in a larger pasture, two old draft horses and a sleek Standardbred gelding stand beneath the shade of a walnut tree, half-asleep, swatting flies with their tails.

I turn my attention to the field beyond the pasture, hoping to see someone cutting hay, but there's no thresher or wagon or team of horses. The Masts aren't home, and now I'm going to have to hang around before heading to Buck Creek.

'Damn,' I say with a sigh, knowing the day is going to be a bust.

I leave the barn. I'm closing the door behind me when I notice the greenhouse to my right. Some Amish use them to get a head start on their seedlings until the soil is warm enough to plant. I head that way on the outside chance someone's there, but I know it's wishful thinking. I've already decided that instead of waiting here for the Masts to return, I would be better off speaking to someone at the sheriff's office and, if I can find him, to the Amish bishop. Hopefully, someone will be able to shed some light on the death of Rebecca Mast.

Midway to the greenhouse, I pass by a fire pit surrounded by a low stone retaining wall. A steel fifty-gallon drum vented with bullet holes stands upright in the center of the pit. Growing up, we handled our trash much the same way, by putting everything that couldn't be composted into a big drum and burning it. If we were lucky, *Datt* would let Jacob and Sarah and me roast marshmallows.

Thunder rumbles like the long, low growl of a cross dog. The wind has picked up just enough to turn the maple leaves silver side up, their shimmering surfaces contrasting sharply against the black sky. I smell the acrid scent of ash and something else that gives me pause.

I breathe in deeply, trying to place the smell. It's earthy and spicy and slightly exotic. It reminds me of Christmas ham at the farm. Clove, I realize, and my heart begins to pound. Turning, I walk back to the fire pit, step down off the retaining wall, cross to the drum, and peer inside. It's half-full of partially burned trash. I see part of a cereal box, a melted bread wrapper. The smell of clove is stronger, definitely emanating from inside the barrel.

Using my foot, I shove the drum onto its side. Ash flies as the contents spill out on the ground. Looking around, I spot a charred branch and use it to poke through the ashes. I uncover an old piece of garden hose, a plastic flowerpot. Bending, I upend the barrel. That's when I notice the partially burned pack of cigarettes.

Clove cigarettes.

For the span of several heartbeats, all I can do is stare while my mind scrambles to make sense of what I see. It's the same brand Sadie was smoking that day on the bridge. What are the odds of an Amish couple having a pack of clove cigarettes in their trash? *The same obscure brand that a missing girl was known to smoke?*

I pull out my phone and dial Tomasetti. 'I think I have something,' I say by way of greeting.

'Lay it on me.'

I tell him about the cigarettes. 'Sadie Miller smoked the same brand.'

'Where are the Masts?'

'There's no one here.'

We fall silent, and I know he's running this new information through his brain, seeking that elusive connection that will make everything click. 'Tomasetti, I think they might be involved.'

'Kate, another kid went missing last night,' he tells me. 'A boy. Sixteen years old.'

'Shit,' I mutter. 'Where?'

'Alexandria. About fifty miles north of here.'

'Amish?'

'Yeah.'

'Troubled?'

'He's had a couple of scrapes with the law. We're still gathering information.'

'He fits the pattern,' I hear myself say.

'Get out of there.' He says the words easily, as if they are a suggestion that has just occurred to him. But I sense he's worried about my being here alone. 'I'll get started on a warrant.'

A clap of thunder makes me jump. 'Look, the sky's getting ready to open up.' I start toward the Explorer. 'I'll give you a call from the sheriff's office.'

'Be careful.'

'You know it,' I say, but he's already disconnected.

Smiling, I shake my head. 'Tomasetti,' I mutter, and reach for the door handle. I'm sliding behind the wheel, stabbing the key into the ignition when I notice the door to the slaughter shed is standing open.

NINETEEN

For an instant, I can't believe my eyes. I walked past the slaughter shed on my way to the barn when I arrived, and I'm certain the door was closed. Had it been open, I would have noticed. Of course, it's possible the wind blew it open, but I don't think so.

So how did the door get open?

'Only one way to find out,' I mutter as I get out of the Explorer. I stand beside the vehicle for a moment and scan the area. Aside from the wind, everything is silent and deserted. But I can't shake the prickly sensation between my shoulder blades.

My senses rev into hyperalert as I start toward the shed. I'm still holding my cell phone in my left hand. I'm aware of the holster beneath my jacket pressing reassuringly against my ribs.

I reach the door and peer inside. The interior is dark and smells faintly of old blood, manure, and stale air. I glance around for something with which to prop open the door, but there's nothing handy. I turn my attention to the hasp and realize it's the kind that could have blown open if not properly closed. But did it?

For a full minute, I stand there and listen for any sign of

movement. But the only sounds are the moan of the wind, the dry scuttle of leaves across gravel, and the low rumble of thunder.

The urge to step inside and take a look around is powerful, but I know that any impropriety on my part could become an issue if this ever goes to court. I'm miles out of my jurisdiction. Tomasetti is working on a search warrant. All I have to do is wait this out at the sheriff's office, and by day's end an army of agents and crime-scene technicians will search this property from top to bottom.

None of that changes the fact that Annie King is dead and that I have a fifteen-year-old missing Amish girl on my hands who may be facing the same fate. I don't know how or why, but my gut is telling me the Masts are involved. And I can't help but think that while I'm being herded through this case like an obedient cow being prodded onto a truck, Sadie Miller is somewhere nearby, fighting for her life.

Or she's already dead.

'To hell with it,' I mutter, and snap open my cell. The 911 dispatcher answers on the second ring. Quickly, I identify myself, letting her know I'm law enforcement. 'I'm out at the Mast farm on Township Road 405, and I need for you to send a deputy as soon as possible.'

'What is your emergency, ma'am?'

'I've found evidence of a crime that's related to a case I'm working on.'

I hear the clatter of fingernails against a keyboard. 'What's your location, ma'am?'

I recite the address from memory.

'I've got a deputy en route.'

'What's the ETA on that?'

'Twenty minutes.' She pauses. 'Are you in imminent danger, ma'am? Would you like me to stay on the line until he arrives?'

'Thanks, but I'm fine.' I disconnect and clip the cell to my belt.

Overhead, rain begins to tap on the roof, fat drops hitting the shingles like nails from a nail gun. A gust of wind sends a scatter of dry leaves around my feet. The door slams. The sound is like a shotgun blast, and even though I saw it coming, I jump.

Crossing to the door, I twist the knob and shove it open. There's no one there, just the wind and the storm and the weight of my own tripping suspicion. And all of it is shadowed by the doubt that I'm wrong about the Masts and that when the deputy arrives, I'm going to have some backpedaling to do.

Pulling my Mini Maglite from my pocket, I turn away from the door and start toward the corridor that will take me to the slaughter room. It's the same route Tomasetti and I took the night we were here. Everything looks different now as the cone of light plays over the dirt floor. It's as if some unseen threat lurks around every corner.

Using my foot, I shove open the door to the slaughter room, shine my beam inside. Light from an overhead Plexiglas panel reveals an empty space that smells vaguely of bleach and manure. The bench where the carcasses are dressed is clean and dust-free. The boiling drum is empty and dry. Cutting tools gleam from hooks on the wall. Above, the chain used to lower the carcass into the vat is rusty but free of contaminants. Perry Mast runs a clean operation. Only I found a half-burned pack of clove cigarettes in his trash. . . .

The velocity of the rain against the roof increases to a deafening drumroll. It's so loud, someone could fire a gun and I wouldn't hear it. I back from the slaughter room and continue down the corridor. I come to a door on my right and open it. It's a small shop with a workbench against the wall. A big floor sink with a bar of homemade soap next to the faucet and a towel draped over its side is set against the wall. I see a

227

container of bleach on a shelf. Cloth towels have been folded neatly on a shelf below. A cattle prod hangs from a nail that's been driven into a two-by-four. A knife the size of a machete lies next to a sharpening stone on a workbench.

Glancing at the other side of the room, I see a large piece of equipment covered with a tarp. I cross to it and pull off the tarp. Dust flies, but I barely notice because I'm transfixed by the sight of the dark blue Ford LTD. I almost can't believe my eyes. What the hell are the Masts doing with a vehicle? A vehicle that matches the description of the car Mandy Reiglesberger described near where Sadie Miller was last seen.

Leaving the tarp on the floor, I start toward the door, my heart pounding. Next to the door is a plastic fifty-gallon drum. The top has been sawed off and it's being used as a trash bin. No liner. Using my flashlight, I peer inside. I see a crumpled bag of cat food, chunks of hog hooves, the broken handle of some garden tool. The sight of the bloody rags gives me pause. I lean closer, noticing a few red-black flecks on the side of the drum. I remind myself this is a butchering shed; the rags may have been used to clean or disinfect the equipment.

It's not an unusual find, but I pull an evidence bag from my pocket anyway. Snapping it open, I use it to pick up the smallest rag I can find, stuff it inside. I'm in the process of sealing the bag when I spot another piece of fabric at the bottom of the barrel. The fine texture of the fabric tells me it's not a rag. It's dirty and torn and covered with chaff. I pull out a second bag – my last – and use it to pick up the scrap. It's about six inches long and frayed. I level my beam on it and lean forward to blow away the chaff. The hairs at the nape of my neck prickle as I take in the bold white stitching against black silk. I recognize it immediately as a piece of the tank top Sadie Miller was wearing that day on the bridge.

Adrenaline rips across my midsection. I run my beam around

the room, but there's no one there. Nothing moves. Rain hammers against the roof; I can't hear shit. Quickly, I tear the scrap into two pieces, drop half back into the barrel – evidence for the CSU – and stuff the other piece into the evidence bag. I push both bags into my back pocket and start toward the door.

Then I'm rushing down the corridor, anxious to get out. A right turn will take me back to the main door. I shine my beam left, spot yet another door at the end of the hall, next to what looks like a holding pen for the doomed hogs. I vacillate an instant, then take a left. Four strides and I reach the door. I reach for the knob, find it locked.

Cursing under my breath, I shine my beam into the holding pen. It's constructed of steel pipe. I see a concrete water trough, which is dry. The dirt floor is covered with a mix of wood shavings and straw. No trace of manure. On the outside wall, a small half door is closed, and I suspect it leads to the outer hog pen.

I'm about to make my exit, when I notice an irregularity on the pen floor. Thrusting my flashlight through the pipe rail, I train the beam on what looks like a sheet of plywood that's partially covered with wood shavings and straw.

Curious, I slide the pin aside. Steel creaks as I open the gate and step into the pen. I'm midway to the object when my boot thuds hollowly against the floor. Kneeling, I brush away the shavings – and realize I'm standing on a sheet of plywood.

It's about four by six feet and three quarters of an inch thick. Kneeling, I slide my fingers beneath the edge. Dust flies as I lift. It's heavy and requires a good bit of effort. But I muscle it aside. I almost can't believe my eyes when I realize I've uncovered some kind of stairway or pit.

'What the hell?'

Ancient brick steps lead down to a dirt floor and a narrow passage. The walls are constructed of wood beams and crumbling brick. At first glance, I think I've stumbled upon a storm shelter or old root cellar. But as my beam reveals details, I realize this is neither. It's some kind of tunnel.

Questions hammer my brain. *Why in God's name is there a tunnel beneath the Masts' barn? Where does it go? Who uses it? And for what?*

A glance at my watch tells me it's only been ten minutes since I called 911. That means a deputy won't arrive for another ten. Pulling my phone from my belt, I punch the speed-dial button for Tomasetti. One ring. Two. I don't want to admit it, but there's a small part of me that doesn't want him to answer. I tell myself I don't want him to worry. But the truth of the matter is, I know he'll try to convince me not to go down there – and I know that would be a pretty good piece of advice.

He answers on the fourth ring with a nasty growl of his name.

'The Masts are involved.' Quickly, I tell him about the car and the scrap of fabric. 'She was wearing that tank top the day of the fight.'

'Where are you?'

It's difficult to hear him above the din of rain against the roof. 'I'm at the Mast farm.'

'Is someone from the sheriff's office there?'

'He's en route.'

'Are you alone?'

I start to hedge, but he cuts me off. 'Goddamn it, Kate—'

'Tomasetti, there's some kind of underground tunnel beneath the slaughter shed. It's the perfect place to hide someone.'

'What's the ETA on that deputy?' The tone of his voice changes, and I visualize him grabbing his jacket and keys as he rushes toward the door.

'Ten minutes.'

'Call them again. In the interim, will you do me a favor and stay the hell out of that goddamn tunnel?'

He disconnects without saying good-bye. Shaking my head, I hit END, then dial 911. I get the same dispatcher and quickly identify myself. 'I need the ETA of that deputy.'

'He's ten minutes out.'

'Get him on the radio and ask him to run with lights and siren.'

'Will do.'

I thank her and snap the phone onto my belt, then shine the beam into the mouth of the tunnel. The passageway looks ancient; it was probably here long before this barn was built. That's when I notice the footprints in the dust on the steps, and I realize someone has been down there – recently.

I've nearly talked myself into walking outside to wait for the deputy when a scream rings out over the pounding rain. It's female and the power behind it unnerves me.

I yank my .38 from my shoulder holster. 'Shit.' With my left hand, I fumble for my phone, hit REDIAL with my thumb.

Two rings and the dispatcher answers. 'Nine one one. What's—'

'I've got a possible homicide in progress. I need assistance right now.'

'Ma'am, the deputy is seven minutes—'

The rain is like thunder on the roof and drowns out the rest of the sentence. All I can think is that whoever's down there doesn't have that kind of time. 'Call the Highway Patrol—' Another scream echoes from the depths. 'Send an ambulance.'

It's an awful sound and rattles me to my core. 'Goddamn it.'

'Ma'am?'

And in that instant, I know I'm not going to follow protocol. There's no way I can stand here and do nothing while God only knows what happens to a young woman just out of sight. 'Tell the deputy there's some kind of underground passage in the slaughter shed. I'm going down there.'

Snapping my phone closed, I clip it to my belt. I shine my beam into the mouth of the tunnel and start down the steps.

TWENTY

There are some decisions you make that you know will affect the rest of your life. Decisions where the line between right and wrong is blurred by circumstances. There's no time to weigh consequences or rein in emotions you should have left out of it. And while my intellect tells me it would be wiser to turn around and wait for that deputy, the part of me that is a cop tells me to go get that girl.

The odors of damp earth and rotting wood fill my nostrils as I descend the stairs. The temperature seems to drop with every step. The pound of rain against the roof diminishes, only to be replaced by hushed air compressed by the tons of earth above and the rapid-fire beat of my heart. Adrenaline becomes a buzz in my ears, an electrical storm wreaking havoc on my muscles, making them jump beneath my skin.

My palm is wet against the grip of my .38. I hold the Mini Maglite in my left hand and pray to God the batteries will last. For the life of me I can't remember the last time I replaced them. The beam isn't as powerful as my full-size Maglite, which I keep in the Explorer. The only reason I'm carrying this one now is because it fits in my pocket.

I've never been claustrophobic, but by the time I reach the base of the stairs, I feel the weight of it pressing down on me, as cold and dank as the flesh of a long-dead corpse. The tunnel is about three feet wide and just high enough for me to stand upright. Tree roots dangle from the ceiling like snakes. Sweeping the beam left to right, I start down the corridor.

Another scream stops me. This one is primal and raw and seems to go on forever. I discern terror in the voice, and pain, hopelessness. It is the sound of a human being who's been reduced to an animal. For the span of several heartbeats, I stand there unmoving, my every sense attuned to the darkness ahead. I listen for footsteps or voices, anything to indicate what I'm dealing with. All I hear is my own elevated breathing and the hum of blood through my veins.

I notice the beam of my flashlight shaking and order myself to calm down. I glance over my shoulder. The square of light from the opening is still visible, and I realize I've gone only twenty feet or so. I start walking, my footfalls silent on the dirt and brick floor. I've only taken a few steps when the smell assails me. I want desperately to believe it's manure that's leached through the layers of soil overhead, but I've smelled this particular stench too many times not to recognize it. There's something dead down here, and I don't think it has anything to do with farm animals or manure.

'Goddamn it,' I whisper as I shine the beam in a semicircle.

I've barely gotten the words out when I notice the niche to my left. My flashlight beam illuminates a small alcove with crumbling brick walls and an arched ceiling with a splintered wood beam. The sight of the body on the floor sends a shock wave through me, and I take an involuntary step back. Even in the dim light of the beam, I can tell it's a female. I see blue jeans, a filthy tank top that once was white, beat-up leather sandals. I note the horribly bloated torso, a mottled blue face with eyeballs that have long since liquefied. One arm sticks straight up. I see a black clawlike hand. At first, I think the position is due to rigor; then I notice the chain and I realize she was shackled to the wall.

'Shit. *Shit.*' My first thought is that it's Sadie. But the hair color is different, and the hair is shorter. Not Sadie, I realize, and a strange sense of relief sweeps through me.

I cross to the body and kneel. This person has been dead for a few days. Judging from the condition of the body, it wasn't an easy death; she suffered a good bit of abuse beforehand. I shine the beam on the shackle. It's constructed of heavy chain welded to some type of steel band that clamps around her wrist. It looks homemade. I can tell by the dried blood on her arm that she struggled – violently enough for the band to have cut flesh. I don't see any other visible injuries – gunshot or stab wounds – but there's so much dirt and deterioration, it's difficult to tell. After a minute, the stench drives me back. I'm loath to leave her, but there's nothing I can do for her now. Except find her killer.

Holding my sidearm at the ready, I turn and sidle back to the main corridor. I glance right. I can barely make out the gray light from the opening now. I wonder if the deputy has arrived. Putting the flashlight in my mouth, I pull out my phone, hit 911. The phone beeps and *Failed* appears in the display.

'Damn it,' I mutter, clipping it to my belt.

Sweeping my beam left, I step into the darkness. The sensation of being swallowed by some massive black mouth engulfs me, and I stave off a crushing wave of claustrophobia. I concentrate on my surroundings, listening for any sound, any sign of life – or danger.

I've traveled only about ten feet when my toe brushes against something. I jerk my beam down – half-expecting to see a rat – and find myself staring at a sneaker. I kneel for a closer look. It's a woman's shoe. The fabric once was pink, but it's covered with dirt and spattered with blood now.

I rise and, flashlight at my side, stare ahead into the black abyss. If there's someone there, he can see me. If he's armed, I'm a sitting duck. For the first time, I feel exposed, vulnerable. I consider turning off the flashlight and trying to make my way in the dark. But that could prove to be even more dangerous. I could encounter stairs or a pit – or someone equipped with night-vision goggles.

Raising the flashlight, I set the beam on the walls and ceiling. If someone is using this tunnel on a regular basis, he may have installed electricity or be using an extension cord. Sure enough, my beam reveals an orange cord that's affixed to the ceiling with galvanized fencing staples. I track the cord with my beam, realize it runs along the ceiling as far as I can see.

I pick up my pace, keeping my eye on the cord, sweeping the beam left and right. Traversing a tunnel of this size and scope is surreal. It's like a nightmare where you think you're about to reach the end but never do. Another few yards and I trip over a step and go to my knees. I scramble to my feet, fumble with the flashlight, and find a railroad tie sunk into the floor. To my right, an ancient door constructed of crumbling wood planks is set into the wall. I see a newish hook-and-eye lock, a floor-level wooden jamb. Above me, the cord makes the turn and disappears behind the door.

Averting the beam of my flashlight, I edge right and listen. The muffled sound of sobbing emanates from beyond. I set my ear against the wood. Not just sobbing. This is the sound of human misery, an unsettling mix of keening and groaning. Female, I think. I can't help but wonder if Sadie is on the other side of the door. I wonder if she's alone, if she's injured. I wonder if there's someone in there with her, hurting her, waiting for me.

Gripping my .38, I stuff the flashlight, beam up, into my waistband and use my left hand to ease the hook from the eye.

Metal jingles against the wood when it snaps free. The sobbing stops, telling me whoever is on the other side has heard it. I kick open the door with my foot, lunge inside.

The door swings wide, bangs against the wall. Dust billows in a gossamer cloud. I'm standing in a small antechamber. Movement straight ahead. I drop into a shooter's stance, train my weapon on the threat. 'Police,' I snap. 'Don't fucking move.'

For an instant, I can't believe my eyes. Shock is a battering ram against my brain. Three girls, teenagers, dirty and clad in little more than rags, sit on the floor, spaced about three feet apart. Two of the girls are little more than skin and bones, with sunken, haunted eyes. I see tangled, greasy hair, faces smudged with grime, bare arms covered with scabs and cuts.

The room is about six feet square and as damp and dank as a grave. The smell of urine and feces and unwashed bodies wafts over me as I move closer. The girls are chained to the wall, their wrists shackled with rusty steel bands and smeared with blood. *What in the name of God is going on?*

For the span of several seconds, three pairs of eyes stare at me as if I'm some kind of apparition. I see in the depths of those eyes a tangle of primal emotions I can't begin to name.

'I'm a cop.' I whisper the words, put my finger to my mouth in a silent plea for them to remain silent. 'Shhh. I'm here to help you. But I need for you to be quiet. Do you understand?'

'Katie?' The girl farthest from me lunges to her feet, the chain at her wrist clanging. 'Katie? Oh my God! *Katie!*'

Sadie, I realize. She's barely recognizable because of the dirt. 'It's going to be okay,' I tell her. 'But you have to be quiet.'

'*I'm scared,*' she whispers.

'I know, honey.' I move toward her, my eyes taking in details I don't want to see; details I'll be seeing in my nightmares for a long time to come. The steel band around her wrist has cut to the bone, exposing the ulna. Her hand is swollen and streaked with blood. The wound is bad; it's worse that she doesn't seem to notice.

'How badly are you hurt?' I ask.

'They're starving us. I've cut my wrist.' She motions toward one of the other girls. 'There's something wrong with her. She's feverish and out of her mind.'

Without warning, the girl she indicated lets out a blood-curdling screech. 'Awwwwwwwwwer,' she wails. 'Awwwwwwwwwer . . .'

Those were the screams I heard earlier. Quickly, I cross to her and bend. 'Be quiet,' I whisper. 'I'm here to rescue you.'

The girl scrambles away, yanks against her chain, screams again.

'Shut up!' Sadie hisses, and lashes out at the girl with her foot. 'Shut her up! She's going to get us all killed.'

Tossing Sadie a warning look, I holster my weapon and grasp the screaming girl by the shoulders, give her a shake. '*Quiet!*' I make eye contact with her. 'Please. Be quiet. Do you understand?'

Blank eyes stare at me from a face that's black with grime. *Dead eyes,* I think. And I know that while this girl might be physically alive, something inside her has been snuffed out.

'It's going to be okay.' Gently, I lower her to the ground, run my hand over her head. 'What's your name?'

She curls into herself, like some soft sea creature that's been prodded by a sharp stick.

'I think her name's Ruth,' Sadie whispers. 'She's crazy.'

Ruth Wagler, I realize. Four years gone and still alive.

I turn, find Sadie looking at me. Despite her ragged appearance, there's a fierceness in her eyes, as if she's ready to tear into the first person who walks through that door, the chain on her wrist be damned.

'Who did this to you?' I ask.

'The deacon,' the second girl hisses.

'Deacon?' I repeat.

'A man,' Sadie tells me. 'He's old.'

'A couple,' the other girl cuts in. 'A married couple.'

'The Masts?' I ask.

'That's it!' Sadie cries.

'They're fucking crazy,' the second girl chokes out.

I turn my attention to her, trying not to wince at the sight of the weeping sores around her mouth. 'What's your name?' I ask.

'Bonnie Fisher.'

The girl who disappeared two months ago, I realize. 'Your *mamm* and *datt* miss you.'

She slaps her hand over her mouth as if to smother a cry. Her eyes fill. But she doesn't utter a sound.

'Where's the couple now?' I ask.

'I don't know,' Sadie tells me. 'They haven't been down here for a while.'

'Are they armed?'

'He has a rifle,' Bonnie says.

Uneasiness creeps over me, like a big spider with cold, spindly legs creeping up the back of my neck. I glance toward the door. 'Is there anyone else down here?'

The two girls exchange looks. 'Leah,' Bonnie says.

Leah Stuckey. I recall the name from that first briefing with Sheriff Goddard. Sixteen years old. From Hope Falls, Ohio. Missing one year. Her parents were recently killed in a buggy accident.

'They took her,' Sadie adds. 'Two days ago.'

I think of the body a few yards outside the door and I wonder if it's Leah's. 'Where did they take her?'

'We don't know,' Sadie replies.

'They hated Leah,' Bonnie tells me. 'They were mean to her

because she was mouthy and cussed a lot. They tried to make her read the Bible, like for twenty-four hours straight.' She chokes out a sound that's part laugh, part sob. 'Leah told them to get fucked.' She closes her eyes tightly, as if trying to ward off the memory. 'They used a cattle prod on her.'

'They took her once, and when they brought her back, she got really sick. You know, bleeding . . .' Sadie bites her lip. 'Down there.'

'I think she's dead,' Bonnie whispers. 'They're going to kill us, too.'

'No, they're not,' I say firmly. 'I'm going to get you out of here. But I need for you to stay calm and be quiet.'

Sadie nods. The other girl jerks her head, but she doesn't look convinced. I hope they can hold it together long enough for me to figure out how to handle this.

I look at the band around Sadie's wrist. 'Is there a key?'

'The old man keeps it in his pocket.'

I glance around the chamber, looking for something with which to break the chain. 'Help me find something to break that chain,' I say. 'A rock or a brick.'

The two girls look around. A single bare bulb dangles from the ceiling and doesn't reveal much. I see an empty water bottle, a crumbled paper towel. A book lies facedown on a small table. I cross to it, read the embossed words on the spine *Es Nei Teshtament*. The New Testament.

'There's nothing here,' Bonnie says.

'Shoot it off.' Sadie motions toward my sidearm and raises her wrist.

I don't reply; I know she doesn't want to hear my answer. The chain is too heavy to sever with a bullet. The cuff is too close to her wrist. Not only would it require multiple firings and risk a ricochet but I'd probably run out of ammunition before the job was done, and then I'd have no weapon at all.

I pull out my phone. A lone bar appears on the display. I hit 911 anyway and get another *Failed* message. I try Tomasetti's number and get the same result.

Clipping my phone to my belt, I look at the two girls. They're standing a few feet apart – as close to me as their chains will allow – staring at me as if I'm their last breath of air. 'I have to go for help,' I tell them.

'*What?*' Bonnie looks at me as if I'm a traitor. 'You can't leave us!'

'*No!*' Sadie chokes. 'Don't go! You can't!'

'There's a deputy out there,' I tell them. 'Just stay calm and I'll get you out of here.'

The girl lying on the floor bellows an animalistic cry that echoes off the walls. Sadie whirls toward her. 'Shut up!' she hisses.

'What if they come for us while you're gone?' Bonnie whispers.

'They're not home,' I say firmly. 'I checked.'

'Don't leave us down here!' she cries.

'They'll kill us,' Sadie says.

I cross to her, set my hands on her shoulders, and give her a shake. 'Everything's going to be okay. But I need for you to be strong. Do you understand?'

Sadie jerks her head.

'Good girl.' I turn my attention to Bonnie.

Her face crumples. Sagging against the chain, she begins to sob. 'I can't believe you're leaving us. Please don't. *Please!*'

Reaching out, I set my hand on her shoulder and squeeze. 'I'll be back,' I say firmly. 'I promise.'

As I turn my back on them and start toward the door, I pray it's a promise I can keep.

TWENTY-ONE

Their cries follow me through the door and into the corridor. Then I'm moving at a jog, heading toward the hatch from which I entered. I'm looking for daylight, anxious to get the hell out of this godforsaken tunnel and get those girls to safety.

The beam of my flashlight carves a murky path through the darkness. I'm kicking up dust, and in the periphery of my vision, it hovers like mist. I can hear myself breathing hard, a mix of adrenaline and physical exertion. I catch a glimpse of a small wooden door to my right, and I realize there's yet another passage I overlooked on the way down. I have no idea how extensive these tunnels are; there could be many more passages and rooms. There could be more missing.

More bodies.

I keep moving as fast as I dare. I'm fifteen yards from the hatch. I'm running full out now, my mind jumping ahead to the things I need to do. I want to call Tomasetti and let him know three of the missing are alive. He'll expedite the search warrant for the house and property. The body will need to be retrieved. The families notified. Arrest warrants issued for Irene and Perry Mast.

The blow comes out of nowhere, like a baseball bat slamming against my chest. The impact knocks me off my feet. For an instant, I'm suspended in space. Then my back slams against the ground. My head rocks back, sending a scatter of stars across my vision. At first, I think I've been shot. I can't breathe. Terrible sounds grind from my throat as I try to suck oxygen into my lungs.

For what seems like an eternity, all I can focus on is breathing. I turn onto my side, manage a small gulp of oxygen. But pain zings all the way up to my collarbone. I'm aware of dim light above me. Dust motes are flying all around. I feel around for my .38, but it's gone. I've dropped my flashlight, as well. But I can see. Where's the light coming from?

My vision clears, and I find myself staring up at a bare bulb dangling down like some bizarre Christmas tree ornament. Turning, I look around. My flashlight lies on its side a few feet away. A man stands above me, his face obscured by shadows.

'Don't get up, Chief Burkholder.'

Perry Mast steps into the sphere of light from the bulb. He's holding a shovel in one hand, a rifle in the other, and the full gravity of my predicament hits home with all the stunning force of the blow.

'I don't think I will just yet.' The words come out on a groan. I shift, make a show of wincing, use the opportunity to look around, take stock of my injuries. Broken ribs, probably. But in some small corner of my brain, I know that those injuries are the least of my worries. My .38 is nowhere in sight. I must have dropped it, and he picked it up. My chest hurts, but at least I can breathe. If I can keep him talking until the deputy finds us . . .

'You shouldn't be down here,' he says. 'You shouldn't have come back.'

'Mr. Mast,' I begin, 'what are you doing?'

'I know you found the young people,' he tells me. 'I know you spoke to them. You should not have done that.'

How does he know? Has he been watching me since I arrived? Was he lurking outside the room, listening? Or maybe he's installed cameras or listening devices. Whatever the case, I decide, the less I profess to know, the better off I'll be. 'I don't know what you're talking about.'

'I'm afraid you've placed yourself in a tight spot.'

'This doesn't have to end badly. It doesn't matter what you've done. We can end this now.' I try to rise, but he sets the shovel against my shoulder and pushes me down.

'You're not going anywhere.'

I stare at him, my mind racing. 'We can walk out of here right now and get this straightened out.'

'I do not wish to leave this place.' Leaning the shovel against the wall, he moves closer and looks down at me. 'I will not abandon the work God has assigned me.'

For the first time, I get a good look at his face. His expression is serene. I see the wheels turning in his mind as he works through the predicament of my having discovered his underground secret. In that moment, I realize that cold, hard sanity is infinitely more frightening than madness.

'I'm a police officer,' I tell him. 'You can't get away with this. Stop now and I'll do what I can to help you.'

He's holding the rifle in his right hand. It's a .22 hunting rifle, a deadly weapon to be sure. But a long rifle can be unwieldy in tight quarters – like this tunnel. If this turns into a physical confrontation, that could work to my advantage.

'I will not stop my work here, Chief Burkholder. It is God's will and it will be done. Nothing you say or do can change that.'

'Mr. Mast, people know I'm here. Someone from the sheriff's office is aboveground, looking for me. It's over.'

'No one knows about the tunnels.'

'I told them. They'll find my vehicle. It's only a matter of time. Do yourself a favor and give it up.'

Mast stares at me as if I'm some unpleasant chore that must be completed. There's no hatred, no passion in his eyes. I'm not a person to him, simply an impediment to his mission. There's no doubt in my mind he means to harm me. Kill me. Or maybe chain me down here with the others.

'No more talking,' he tells me. 'My work here is larger than you or me, and I will not let you interfere. I will not let you stop me.'

I stare back, my brain scrambling for some way to get through to him. But my earlier calm has transformed into a twitching mass of nerves. The truth of the matter is, I'm in trouble. He's got the upper hand and we both know it.

Mast isn't a large man – maybe six feet tall, 170 pounds. He's thirty years older than I am, so I've got the advantage of youth. I'm physically fit and fairly adept in the arena of self-defense. But I'm injured; he's got fifty pounds on me and a lot more muscle.

Cautiously, I ease myself to a sitting position, try a different tactic. 'God would never ask you to hurt anyone. He is benevolent. He wouldn't ask you to harm another person.'

'He that spareth the rod hateth his son.'

'Thalt shall not kill.'

Mast sighs, as if none of this is his pleasure, but a burden placed upon him by a merciless God. 'I took no pleasure in that. Annie King was an accident. She ran . . .' He shrugs, his words trailing off. 'It made my heart heavy. But it is a burden I must bear. A sacrifice I have been asked to make.'

I want to tell him that's a total crock of shit, but I hold my tongue. 'You're hurting people,' I whisper. 'This is not what God wants you to do.'

'The young people have lost their way, Chief Burkholder.

Surely you see that in your line of work. Our youth have become morally corrupt. Spiritually destitute.' He shakes his head, a parent ravaged by disappointment. 'Ruth Wagler had become a slave to the white powder. She sold her body, her very soul to get it. Bonnie Fisher murdered her unborn child. Leah Stuckey seduced her own uncle. Young Sadie Miller lies with the English boys. She gives freely of her body. She drinks alcohol and her head is filled with prideful ideas.

'The Lord has burdened me with the task of punishing the disobedient and sinners, and when they manifest repentance, He will receive them back.' Fervor rings in his voice. 'I bring them back to the Amish way. Back to the Lord. In essence, Chief Burkholder, I save their souls.'

'By torturing and murdering?'

'It is extreme,' he admits. 'But they have strayed far. In time, they will be thankful.' For the first time, I see the glint of insanity in his eyes. 'Leah Stuckey was beyond redemption. But she did not die at my hand. God took her into His loving hands and returned her to the earth.'

I stare at him, knowing God had nothing to do with it. She died a slow death of starvation, exposure, and neglect.

Knowing there will be no negotiating, that his thought processes are beyond reason, I steal a quick glance around. The shovel leans against the wall, four feet away. I wonder if I can reach it before Mast brings down the rifle and gets off a shot.

'Did you dig these tunnels?' I ask, though I vaguely recall someone telling me this farm was once part of the Underground Railroad.

'These passages have been here since the Civil War. For the African slaves, you know. They could flee the house and hide in the forest—'

I lunge at the shovel, grab the handle above the spade. Pain rips up my side as I swing. The steel spade smashes against

Mast's chest. A guttural sound tears from his throat. His knees buckle and the rifle falls to the ground. I clamber to my feet. He lunges at me, but I lurch back, scramble out of reach. I look around for my weapon, but it's nowhere in sight. *Where the hell is my gun?*

The next thing I know, his arms clamp around my thighs. He's trying to knock me off balance, get me on the ground so he can overpower me. I raise the shovel, bring the spade down hard. The blade strikes his shoulder. Yowling, he reels backward, lands on his ass. I lunge at the flashlight a few feet away, but he reaches out and his hand closes around my ankle. I hit him with the shovel again, but my angle is bad and the blade only grazes his elbow. I lash out with my other foot, catch him in the chin. The impact snaps his head back, but he doesn't let go. If he gets me on the ground, I'm done. The rifle lies on the ground, three feet away. Even if I get away and run, he'll shoot me in the back.

I glance up, my eyes seeking the bulb. It's too far away for me to reach. But the cord is right above me. I upend the shovel, stab the cord as hard as I can. Sparks fly as the blade severs it. Electricity cracks and darkness descends. Working blind, I drive the shovel's spade in the direction where I last saw Mast, hear it make purchase. He releases my ankle. But I feel him grapple for the shovel. I thrust it at him but lose my grip as I stumble away. The blade grazes my hip. He's swinging it at me, trying to hit me.

And then I'm running, completely blind, arms outstretched, feeling my way along the walls. I planned to exit the tunnel the same way I'd entered, but Mast is blocking my way. I think I'm heading in the general direction of the house, which is sixty yards from the slaughter shed.

I've gone only a few strides when my shoulder brushes the wall. The impact spins me around. Barely maintaining my balance, I reorient myself and keep going. Dirt crumbles beneath my fingertips. Cobwebs stick to my hands. I want to try my phone, but I don't dare take the time. Mast has my flashlight and my .38. Not to mention the rifle. There's no doubt in my mind he'll fire blind to stop me.

Light flashes in my peripheral vision. I glance over my shoulder, see the flashlight beam behind me, and I know Mast is closing in. My foot strikes something solid. I stumble, land on my hands and knees, but in an instant, I'm back on my feet,

Keeping my left arm extended in front of me, I reach for my cell with my right, flip it open. Relief flits through me when two tiny bars glint up at me, and I hit the speed dial button for Tomasetti.

He picks up on the first ring. 'Kate.'

I can tell by his tone that he's been trying to reach me. He knows something's wrong. 'I'm in trouble.' My voice is breathless and high.

'Where are you?'

'Mast farm. There are underground tunnels. Mast is armed.'

No response.

'Tomasetti?'

Nothing.

'Damn it.' I look down and see that the call has been dropped. Cursing, I snap the phone onto my belt.

My shoulder scrapes the wall, knocking me to one side. I slow to a walk, reach out with both hands, and touch the walls to orient myself. I hear Mast behind me, his footfalls heavy on the ground. He's breathing hard, muttering words I can't make out. I jerk my head around, see a misty beam of yellow light. He's just yards away.

'*Shit.*' A hot burst of adrenaline catapults me back into a run. I stumble over a step, nearly lose my footing, somehow manage to stay on my feet. I don't know how far I've traveled or how far I have yet to go. I'm not even sure where I'm going or if I'll be able to escape when I get there. But I have no choice but to continue and pray for an exit. If Mast catches me, he'll kill me.

The tunnel veers left. I hear a sound behind me, but I don't dare turn to look. That's when I spot the small square of light a dozen yards ahead. The outline of a door, I realize. A hatch.

I barrel toward it, running as fast as I can. Definitely a hatch. Closed. But I can see the frame of light slanting through at the seams.

I'm a few feet from the stairs when a gunshot rings out.

TWENTY-TWO

The bullet ricochets off a brick a foot from my head. Fragments of brick sting my face. I throw myself onto the steps, clamber up them, using my hands. At the top, I ram the hatch with my shoulder hard enough to jar my spine. The double wooden doors fly open. I scramble up the remaining steps, look around wildly. I'm in a basement or cellar with a dirt floor and stone walls. I see shelves filled with canning jars. Gardening tools. Wood steps twenty feet away.

Another shot rings out. Bending, I slam the doors closed. They're heavy, fabricated of ancient wood planks with old-fashioned handles on the outside. There's no lock, and I have scant seconds before Mast climbs the steps and jams that rifle in my face.

Spotting a sickle hanging on the wall, I rush to it, yank it down, and dash back to the hatch. I jam the blade through both handles.

An instant later, the doors rattle as Mast tries to pound his way out. I back away, praying the sickle will hold, and grapple for my cell. Relief flits through me when I see four bars. I hit 911 as I dart toward the stairs.

'Nine one one. What's your emergency?'

Quickly, I identify myself. 'Shots fired at the Mast farm! I've got an armed suspect! One fatality!'

'Ma'am, the deputy is ten-twenty-three.'

Ten-twenty-three means he's arrived on-scene. If that's the case, where is he? I reach the steps and look up. A horizontal line of light bleeds from beneath the door. I lower my voice. 'Get another deputy out here. Perry Mast is armed with a rifle. I'm under fire.'

'Stand by.'

I hear the *pop* of a gunshot, spin toward the hatch behind me, see a chunk of wood fly. Mast is shooting his way through. I end the call, clip the phone to my belt, and take the stairs two at a time to the top. I have no idea if Irene Mast is waiting for me on the other side with a rifle. The one thing I do know is that if I want to live, I have to get the hell out of here.

I open the door a crack. I see a hallway with plank floors, a homemade rug. To my right is a small living area. Looking to my left, I can see the linoleum floor of the kitchen. If I can get through the kitchen and out the back door, I'll be able to take cover until backup arrives.

I listen for sirens. For Perry Mast pounding up the basement stairs. All I hear is the hard thrum of my heart and my survival instinct screaming *Run!*

Easing open the door, I step into the hall. Another layer of relief goes through me when I spot the skeleton key sticking out. Closing the door behind me, I twist the key. I know the lock is no match for a rifle, but it's one more barrier between me and Perry Mast. It might buy me some time.

My boots are silent against the floor as I start toward the kitchen. The smell of cooking tomatoes hangs in the air. Pots rattle on the stovetop, and I realize Irene is in there, canning vegetables, a chore my own *mamm* did a hundred times when I was growing up.

I stop short of the doorway and peer into the kitchen. Irene Mast stands at the stove, her back to me. The faucet is running. She's holding a towel in her left hand, has another slung over her shoulder. She's lowering a rack of mason jars into a large steaming pot.

The sight is so utterly benign that I can barely reconcile it with the scene that just transpired in the tunnel. I stand frozen in place, wondering if she knows about the missing girls. Has she been kept in the dark? Has she turned a blind eye because she can't handle the truth? Or is she part of it?

She's so intent on her chore that she doesn't hear me enter. I've gone only a couple of steps when it strikes me that if the deputy had indeed arrived, she wouldn't be in here canning tomatoes. She'd be outside, answering some disturbing questions about missing girls and how her husband spends his spare time.

I'm about to call out to her, when I spot the rifle leaning against the cabinet. It's an older .22 lever action with a scuffed walnut stock and a pitted barrel. The hairs on my neck stand straight up. *She knows,* a little voice whispers in my ear.

I'm ten feet away from her. She's standing between me and the rifle, the weapon within easy reach. All she'd have to do is bend and pick it up. I measure the distance to the back door, wonder if I can reach it before she snatches it up and shoots me in the back.

The Amish woman turns. Her eyes find mine, but her expression doesn't change. There's no shock. No realization of culpability. No anger or fear. It's as if she knew I was here all along. The only thought processes I see are intent and a cold conviction that chills my blood. And in that instant, I know she's part of this. I know if I don't act quickly, she'll kill me.

'Don't fucking move,' I tell her. 'Keep your hands where I can see them.'

Unfazed, she reaches for the rifle with the calm of a woman picking up the broom to sweep the floor. . . .

I lunge at the weapon just as she's bringing up the muzzle. I grab the barrel and yank it toward me. At the same time, I try to ram my knee into her abdomen, but there's too much space between us. She's a heavy woman; she's got a better grip and maintains her balance. Her mouth contorts as she wrenches the rifle toward her. I stumble forward, and for an instant, we engage in a tug-of-war, the rifle between us. She's got the advantage of weight. But I have training and youth on my side. I shove the rifle upward as hard as I can. The stock strikes the base of her chin, snapping her teeth together. Growling, she steps forward and slams her body into mine. The momentum knocks me off balance, but I come forward quickly, get beneath the rifle, jam it upward again. The stock hits her left cheekbone this time, hard enough to open the skin.

A guttural sound tears from her throat as she yanks back on the rifle. I catch a glimpse of her eyes. The rage reflecting back shocks me. The next thing I know, she's charging forward, using the rifle to drive me backward. My backside hits the table. The legs screech across the linoleum. I twist the rifle, but she doesn't release it. When I get her close enough, I bring up my knee, ram it into her abdomen.

The breath rushes from her in a sound that's part roar, part scream. She lets go of the rifle, reels backward into the stove.

'Do not move!' I shout. '*Do not fucking move!*'

I'm checking to see if there's a bullet in the chamber when she turns toward the stove.

'I will shoot you!' I scream. 'Get down on the floor!'

She yanks the pot from the stove. Water sloshes over the side as she spins toward me. The jars clank together as she hurls the pot at me. Boiling water spews onto my clothes, my face and neck. I know I'm being scalded, but there's too much adrenaline for me to feel pain. I use the rifle like a bat, slam it against the side of her head with such force that she's knocked off her feet.

Somewhere in the periphery of my consciousness, I hear a mason jar shatter as it hits the floor. Blood spatters the counter as Irene Mast goes down. The sensation of heat streaks down my neck, my right shoulder, my breast.

Irene Mast is lying on her side, not moving. Glass crunches beneath my feet as I cross to her, nudge her with my toe. She's deadweight. Her eyes are open, but she's not quite conscious. The blow opened a gash the size of my index finger just in front of her ear.

My hand shakes as I reach for my cuffs, only I'm not wearing my uniform belt. I look around for something with which to secure her hands, spot a towel on the floor. Using my teeth, I tear it into three strips and tie them together. Kneeling, I roll her over, pull her arms behind her back. As I secure her wrists, I glance toward the basement door behind me, half-expecting an armed Perry Mast to burst out shooting. I don't think I'm in any condition to go another round.

I get to my feet, give Irene Mast a final look. 'Don't go anywhere,' I mutter. Picking up the rifle, I start toward the back door.

Midway through the mudroom, I pull out my phone, punch 911. Standing to one side, I move the curtain with the muzzle and peer out. I notice two things simultaneously. My Explorer is nowhere in sight. And a Trumbull County Crown Vic is parked in the same place my Explorer had been parked just a short time earlier. Where the hell is the deputy?

'Nine one one. What's your emergency?'

Once more, I identify myself and tell her the sheriff's cruiser is here but that there's no sign of the deputy. 'He could be down. Perry Mast is armed with a rifle and shooting at cops.'

'Ten-four. Stand by.'

The cruiser is too far away for me to discern if the deputy is inside, injured or otherwise. He could be in the barn or one of the outbuildings, searching for me. Unless Mast shot him . . .

I look down at the rifle in my hands. It's an old Winchester with a tubular magazine. There's no quick way to tell how much ammo is inside. When I pump the lever, I see a single bullet move into place. Better make it count.

'There's another deputy en route,' says the dispatcher.

'What's the ETA?'

'Six minutes.'

It's not an unreasonable amount of time for a rural call. But a lot can happen in six minutes.

Clipping the phone to my belt, I peer through the window again. The yard between the house and barn is deserted. No sign of the deputy. No sign of Perry Mast. I hate not knowing where he is. It would take only a few minutes for him to double back and exit through the slaughter shed. He could be anywhere.

I open the door and step into a light rain. Feeling exposed, keeping low, with the rifle at the ready, I descend the porch steps and jog toward the cruiser. The headlights and wipers are on, but the engine is off. I'm twenty feet away when I notice blood spatter on the passenger window. From ten feet away, I can make out the silhouette of the deputy. He's slumped over the steering wheel, still wearing his hat.

'Shit,' I mutter, my steps quickening. '*Shit.*'

Keeping an eye on the barn, the slaughter shed, listening for any sound from the house behind me, I try the passenger door, but it's locked. I sidle around the front of the car. The hood is warm, the engine ticking as it cools. I approach the driver's side. The window is shattered. I look inside, see blood and glass on the deputy's shoulders. There's more on the head-rest, on the sleeves of his uniform shirt.

I reach through the broken window, unlock the door, and open it. The deputy's hands are at his sides, knuckles down. Blood covers the steering wheel and the thighs of his uniform slacks. Chunks of glass glitter on the seat. The scene is almost too much to process.

'Deputy,' I whisper. '*Deputy*. Can you hear me?'

No response.

The stench of blood assails me when I reach in and remove his hat. The bullet penetrated his left jaw. His face has been devastated. Most of the flesh of his cheek has peeled away. Some of the teeth have blown out, along with part of his tongue. The cup of his ear is filled with blood and has trickled down, soaking his collar. Even before I press my finger against his carotid artery, I know he's dead.

'*Goddamn it.*'

Under normal circumstances I wouldn't touch anything at a crime scene or risk contaminating evidence. But with an armed suspect at large in the immediate vicinity, I'm in imminent danger. I need a weapon. Unsnapping the leather strap of the deputy's holster, I slide a .40-caliber Glock from its nest and back away from the vehicle.

Using the lever, I eject six bullets from the rifle, drop them in my pocket, and toss the rifle on the ground. I look toward the house. No movement. Aside from the steady rap of rain against the car, the muddy slap of it against the ground, the farm stands in absolute silence. But I know I'm being watched. I feel it as surely as I feel the rain streaming down my face. Did Mast double back and exit through the slaughter shed? Or is he watching me from the house, his finger itchy on the trigger?

The sound of tires on gravel draws my attention. Relief skitters through me when I see a Trumbull County cruiser barrel up the lane, lights flashing. I wave, and the vehicle veers toward me, skids to a halt a few feet behind the other cruiser. A male deputy lunges from the car, a shotgun aimed at me. 'Drop that fuckin' gun! Get your hands up!'

'I'm a cop! I called.'

He keeps his eye on the house, the shotgun trained on me. 'Show me your ID.'

Slowly, I reach into my pocket, pull out my badge. 'I'm with BCI.'

He's a solid, muscular guy with sandy hair and a handlebar mustache. He takes a good look at my badge and lowers the shotgun. But his attention has already moved on to the other cruiser. 'What happened?'

'He's down.'

'Aw, man.' He dashes to the cruiser and peers through the passenger window. 'Fuck!' He stares at the body, his face screwing up. 'Walker! Fuck!' He spins toward me, his expression ravaged. 'What happened?'

'Perry Mast shot him. He's armed with a rifle. In a tunnel belowground. He's got hostages down there.'

He looks at me as if I'm speaking in a foreign language. '*What?*' He fumbles with his lapel mike, his hand shaking. 'Six-nine-two. I got shots fired at the Mast farm. Walker's down. I need backup.'

A gunshot rings out. Simultaneously, we drop to a crouch.

'Where the fuck did that come from?' he snarls.

Another shot snaps through the air. A tinny *whack* sounds and I see a hole the size of my pinkie tear into the cruiser two feet away. 'Barn!' I shout.

Staying low, we circle around, take cover on the opposite side of the car.

'Shots fired!' he shouts into his mike. 'Possible ten-ninety-three,' he says, referring to the hostages. 'Male suspect armed with a rifle.'

'Ten-four,' comes the dispatcher's voice. 'HP is en route. Stand by.'

Behind him, the radio inside the dead man's cruiser lights up with a burst of traffic. It's a welcome sound, because I know every cop within a twenty-mile radius, regardless of agency, is on the way here. It's one of the things I love about being a cop. That blue brotherhood. When an officer is down, you drop everything and go.

The deputy looks at me, wipes rain from his face with the sleeve of his uniform. 'Is the house secure?'

I tell him about my altercation with Irene Mast. 'I left her on the kitchen floor.'

'She in on this, or what?'

'She tried to blow my head off.'

'I'll take that as a yes.'

I turn my attention back to the house, feel that uneasy prickling sensation again. 'I jammed the tunnel hatch in the basement, but I don't know how long it will hold.'

'He could be anywhere.'

'That about covers it.'

He glances toward the lane. 'Where the hell is backup?'

The question doesn't require an answer.

'I'm Kate, by the way.'

He looks at me, nods. 'I'm Marcus.' We don't set down our weapons to shake.

I raise myself up slightly, glance over the hood of the cruiser toward the barn. 'If Mast goes through the tunnel to the house and gets through that hatch, we're sitting ducks here.'

We're on our way to the rear of the cruiser when the sound of a vehicle draws our attention. I glance left and see an Ohio Highway Patrol car barrel up, engine revving, lights flashing. Tomasetti's Tahoe brings up the rear. Both vehicles grind to a halt twenty yards away.

'There's the cavalry.'

I look at Marcus. 'Let's go.'

Keeping low, weapons at the ready, we sprint to the nearest vehicle, the HP cruiser. The trooper is already out, and he's left his door open for added cover. He's wearing a vest, his weapon at his side. He motions us to the rear of the vehicle.

'Where's the shooter?' he asks as he opens the trunk.

We crouch behind the raised trunk, and I give the trooper a condensed version of everything that has happened. 'He's armed with a rifle and has three hostages.'

'What about the female?'

'I left her in the kitchen, tied.' I shake my head. 'If Mast got through the hatch in the basement, he could have untied her.'

'Well, shit.' The trooper pulls out two Kevlar vests and hands one to me, the other to the deputy. 'Looks like we might be in for a standoff.'

As I slip into the vest, secure it at my waist, I see Tomasetti striding toward us, his cell phone pasted to his ear. He's holding his weapon in his right hand, down by his side, but he's not looking at the house or the barn. His attention is focused on me. His expression is as hard as stone and completely devoid of emotion. But it's like we're looking through a vacuum at each other; in the short distance between us, nothing else exists.

'Can't leave you alone for ten minutes, can I?' he mutters.

I try to smile, but I can't. 'Evidently not.'

He turns his attention to the trooper. 'Negotiator is on the way, along with the mobile command center. ETA thirty minutes.'

'I got a SWAT team en route.' The trooper looks at his watch. 'We might be in for a wait.'

I tell the men about the hostages, about my having to leave them behind. They listen intently, their expressions grim.

'You're lucky,' the trooper tells me.

I don't feel very lucky. The truth of the matter is, I feel guilty for having left those girls at the mercy of a maniac. 'I'm afraid he'll kill them,' I say.

'We're not equipped to go down in those tunnels,' the trooper tells me.

'What was Mast's frame of mind?' Tomasetti asks.

'Cold. Determined. Calm.' The word *murderous* floats through my mind, but then, that's a given.

The trooper glances toward the house. 'What about the wife?'

'Bat-shit crazy.'

The two men exchange looks and I know they're thinking the same thing I am. Do we go in and retrieve the Amish woman? Or do we wait for the command center and negotiator to arrive?

The trooper's radio cracks. Hitting his mike, he breaks away to take the call.

Tomasetti turns his attention to me. 'I told you to stay out of that tunnel.'

'You know how it is with me and authority.'

'Kind of like oil and water.' But his expression softens. 'You okay?'

'I promised those girls I'd come back for them,' I say.

'We'll get them.' His eyes skim down the front of me and I know he's looking for blood, injuries. I know it the instant he spots the scald on my neck. He raises his eyes to mine. 'How did you get those burns?'

I want to tell him the burns are not the source of my pain. That what ails me is the thought of Mast killing those girls. . . . 'Irene Mast threw a pot of hot water on me.'

His mouth tightens, and he motions toward the Tahoe. 'I've got a first-aid kit in the back. Think I have some burn gel.'

'I don't want to be fussed over.'

He sighs. 'Kate.'

'Those girls are chained to the wall like animals,' I whisper. 'Sadie's down there.'

He waits, as if knowing there's more. He knows me too well.

'They're running out of time,' I say.

'You can't rush in there like some rookie.'

'Mast knows it's over. He's going to kill them.'

'You go into that tunnel, he'll kill you. Or me.' He jams a thumb at the trooper. 'Or that young cop over there. Is that somehow better?'

'That's what we're trained to do.'

'Our training doesn't include taking crazy risks.'

I turn away and start toward the trooper's vehicle with no real destination in mind. I know I'm being unreasonable; the intellectual part of my brain knows he's right. It would be foolhardy to venture into that tunnel. But I saw the terror on the faces of those girls. I saw the cold determination in Perry Mast's eyes. And I know if we don't do something, he'll execute them.

I've gone only a couple of strides when Tomasetti sets a hand on my arm and stops me. 'Wait.'

I turn to him, struggling to control my temper and the fear that's squeezing my chest, making it hard to breathe.

'Kate.' He says my name roughly and with a good deal of reproof. 'We have to follow protocol on this one.'

'Sometimes I hate fucking protocol.'

'Welcome to law enforcement,' he snaps, unsympathetic.

I focus on the line of trees growing along the length of the lane, saying nothing.

After a moment, he sighs. 'Come here.'

I let him guide me to the rear of Tahoe. There, he turns to

me, backs me against the door. Gently, he shoves my collar aside and looks at my neck. 'Those look like second-degree burns.'

Without asking for permission, he unbuttons the top two buttons of my shirt and slips my bra strap aside. It feels too intimate for the situation, when there are two other cops in close proximity. Somehow, he makes it seem appropriate, and I allow it.

'It doesn't hurt,' I say.

'It will once the adrenaline wears off.'

He touches my arm, brings it up for me to look at. I'm shocked to see a swath of bright pink flesh that's covered with blisters.

Turning away, he retrieves his keys from his pocket and opens the back of the Tahoe. I watch as he pulls out a field first-aid kit, flips it open, and begins to rummage.

By the time he turns to me, my mind is back on the girls belowground. 'The shots came from the barn,' I say. 'He doubled back. That means he would have passed by the chamber where the girls are being held.'

Instead of responding, Tomasetti pours alcohol over both of his hands, letting it drip onto the ground, then unfastens another button on my blouse. I barely notice as he tears open a small pouch of gel and smears it over my burns. I don't want to acknowledge it, but the pain is coming to life: a tight, searing sensation that spreads from my collarbone, upper arm, and breast. It's strange, but I'm almost thankful for the distraction. Anything to keep me from imagining the scene belowground.

'You scared the hell out of me,' he says after a moment.

'I'm sorry.'

'No, you're not.' But he leans toward me and gives me a quick, hard kiss.

I think of the family he lost – his wife and two little girls

– and suddenly I feel guilty for doing that to him when he's already been through so much. The *pop* of a gunshot ends the moment.

On instinct, we duck slightly, look toward the house. At first, I think the deputy or the trooper has taken a shot. But they're also looking for the source.

'Where did it come from?' Tomasetti growls.

'The house, I think.'

Another shot rings out.

'The house!' The deputy shouts the words from his position behind the trooper's vehicle.

A woman's scream emanates from inside. At first, I think Mast has brought one of the girls topside. That he's going to use her for leverage or cover to blast his way out. Or kill her right in front of us to make some senseless point.

But the scream is too deep, too coarse to have come from one of the girls. 'That was Irene Mast,' I hear myself say.

Tomasetti's eyes narrow on mine. I can tell by his expression that he knows what I'm saying. 'What the hell is that crazy son of a bitch doing?'

A third shot rings out.

The house falls silent. We wait. The minutes seem to tick by like hours. Around us, the rain increases. No one seems to notice. I hear sirens in the distance, and I know the fire department and medical personnel are parked at the end of the lane.

'There he is!'

I don't know who shouted the words. I turn and see Perry Mast exit the house through the back door. He's holding a rifle in his right hand, my .38 in his left.

The trooper, armed with a bullhorn, calls out, 'Stop right there and put down the guns.'

Mast stares out at us as if he's in a trance. His face is blank and slack, completely devoid of stress and emotion. He's snapped, I realize. Mentally checked out. It's a chilling scene to see an Amish man in that state, knowing what he's done, what he's capable of.

'Drop those weapons!' the trooper says. 'Get down on the ground.'

The Amish man doesn't move, doesn't even acknowledge the command.

I look at Tomasetti. 'Do you think he'd respond to Pennsylvania Dutch?'

'Worth a try.'

Staying low, keeping the vehicles between us and the shooter, we start toward the trooper.

'She knows Pennsylvania Dutch,' Tomasetti says.

The trooper sends me a questioning look.

'I used to be Amish,' I tell him.

He passes the bullhorn to me. 'Might help.'

'Mr. Mast, it's Kate Burkholder.' I fumble for the right words, hoping to land on something that will reach him. 'Please put down the guns and talk to me.' I wait, but he doesn't respond.

'Violence isn't the way to handle this, Mr. Mast. Please. Lay down the—'

My words break off when Perry Mast shifts his stance. For an instant, I think he's going to acquiesce. That he's going to step off the porch and give himself up. Instead, he raises his left hand, sets the muzzle of the .38 beneath his chin, and pulls the trigger.

TWENTY-THREE

Mast's head snaps back. Blood spatters the door behind him, like red paint spattered violently against a canvas. His knees buckle and he falls backward, striking the door on his way down.

'Shit,' Tomasetti hisses.

And then we're on our feet, running toward the house.

'Irene Mast is inside!' I shout. 'She's armed!'

Marcus, the deputy, reaches the porch first. He's holding his Glock in his right hand, keeping his eyes on the window and door. I'm behind him. Tomasetti is beside me – so close that his arm brushes against mine.

I try not to look at Mast. He's lying on his back, his head propped against the door. The bullet entered beneath his chin. The entry wound is small. But I know enough about weapons to know the kind of damage a .38 will do when it exits. I don't see a wound, but a pool of blood the size of a dinner plate spreads out on the concrete beneath him. His eyes are open and seem to stare right at me. And even though I know he's beyond feeling any kind of emotion, I swear I see an accusatory glint.

We need to go through the door, but Mast's body is in the way. The trooper bends, sets his hands beneath the corpse's shoulders, and drags him aside, leaving a smear of blood on the concrete. Marcus yanks open the door. I go through first, the Glock at the ready, Tomasetti right behind me.

'Police!' I shout. 'Put your hands up and get on the floor!'

My heartbeat roars like a freight train in my chest as I step into the kitchen.

'Blood,' Tomasetti says, and motions left.

A pool of it shimmers black in the dim light slanting through the window. I see the strips of cloth I used to bind the Amish woman's hands. Then I spot the drag mark.

'Shit!' whispers the deputy as he steps in behind us.

A whimper sounds from the hall. It's a terrible sound in the silence of the house. The cry of a dying animal. My Glock leading the way, I follow the blood trail through the kitchen and into the hall. There, I see Irene Mast lying on the floor. Her hands are free. She's using her elbows to drag herself toward the basement door. With each movement, that terrible sound erupts from her mouth. It's as if she's a mindless thing that must reach some destination before she can die.

'Stop right there.' My throat is so tight, I barely recognize my own voice. 'Stop.'

She continues on as if she hasn't heard me, hands and elbows pulling her body along. Her hands are clawing at the hardwood floor, that terrible sound squeezing from her throat with every inch of progress.

In the periphery of my mind, I hear the deputy's radio crack; he's speaking into his mike, giving the paramedics the go-ahead to come up the driveway.

'Mrs. Mast?' I repeat. 'Stop. There's an ambulance on the way.'

She's sustained at least one bullet wound to the head. I don't know how it is that she's still conscious. That she somehow survived that kind of trauma. Her *kapp* and the hair beneath it are blood-soaked. Her left ear is missing. She's lost a lot of blood. But she doesn't stop. Her hand claws at the floor, a mindless, brain-damaged action. Her nails are broken to the quick. Her legs remain unmoving, part of a broken body being dragged along behind her.

I kneel next to her, set my hand on her shoulder. 'There's an ambulance on the way.'

That's when I notice the bullet hole in her back. It's small and there's not much bleeding. I wonder if the bullet struck her spine and that's why her legs aren't moving.

'Mrs. Mast, hold still. Help will be here any moment.'

She uses her left hand to turn onto her side. A sound squeezes between her lips as she rolls onto her back. Her eyes find mine, and I realize she's cognizant. She knows she's been shot. She knows I'm here.

'Who did this to you?' I ask.

Her eyes focus on mine. Her mouth opens and blood and saliva form a bubble between her lips. She whispers something unintelligible and then the breath rushes from her lungs. Her body jerks twice and goes slack. I hear the paramedics come through the door, but I know they're too late.

'She's done,' Tomasetti says.

I stare down at her for a moment, watching the life drain from her eyes. I remind myself that just minutes ago, she tried to kill me; I shouldn't feel anything except gratitude that I'm alive and she's lying there dead instead of me. But the fact of the matter is, it's not easy to watch someone die. In this case, Irene and Perry Mast left too many questions unanswered.

'Kate.'

It takes me a moment to realize Tomasetti is speaking to me. I have no idea what he's saying. I turn to him, pretending I wasn't somewhere else.

'The tunnel, Kate. Where is it?'

The sheriff's deputy stands next to him, barking something into his lapel mike, but his attention is on me.

'Basement,' I say. 'This way.'

Then I'm striding down the hallway, vaguely aware that my legs are shaking. The basement door stands open, the wood around the lock shattered. Evidently, Perry Mast used the rifle to blast his way out. I stop at the door, look down the steps into the basement. It seems like hours since I was down there, though in reality it's only a matter of minutes.

I start down the steps. The temperature drops as I descend. The odor of rotting wood and wet earth close around me like a dirty, wet blanket. Gray light oozes in from a single window at ground level, but it's not enough to cut the shadows.

My boots are silent on the dirt floor as I cross to the hatch. Tomasetti walks beside me, shining his Maglite from side to side. I hear the deputy behind me. He's breathing heavily, which tells me his adrenaline is flowing. The fact of the matter is, we don't know what we'll find down here. We don't know if there are other people, if they're armed, or if they mean us harm. We don't know if the girls are alive or if Mast killed them before coming out and turning the gun on himself.

'They ran electricity to the tunnel,' I say as I take them to the hatch.

'So much for all those Amish rules,' Tomasetti mutters.

'I cut the extension cord.'

We reach the hatch. The sickle I used to lock Mast in lies on the floor, a few feet away. One of the double doors lies next to it; the other hangs at a precarious angle by a single hinge.

'He shot off the hinges,' says Marcus stating the obvious.

Tomasetti shines his light down the steps leading into the tunnel. 'What the fuck is this?'

Marcus trains the beam of his flashlight on the steps. 'House used to be part of the Underground Railroad.'

'No shit?' Tomasetti says.

'Newspaper did a story a few years ago.'

'Did you know about the tunnels?' Tomasetti asks.

'No one mentioned tunnels.'

'Now you know why,' I mutter.

The deputy sweeps his beam along the brick walls of the tunnel. 'Creepy as hell, if you ask me.'

Dread scrapes a nail down my back as I stare into the darkness. My heart is a drum in my chest. The last thing I want to do is go back down there. Not because I'm afraid of some unseen threat, but because I don't know what we'll find. If Mast shot and killed his wife, chances are good he also killed the girls. . . .

'We need a generator and work lights.' Tomasetti glances my way, keeping his voice light. 'You want to get that going, Chief?'

He's giving me an out, I realize. As much as I appreciate the gesture, there's no way I can stay behind.

'I need to go down there.'

'Let's go.' Drawing his weapon, he starts down the steps.

Descending into the tunnel is like being swallowed alive by a wet black mouth. Even with two powerful flashlights, there's not enough light.

No one says what they're thinking. That we're going to find the hostages dead. That Mast won this little war and we should chalk up another one for the bad guys. . . .

Our feet are nearly silent on the ancient brick and dirt floor. Tomasetti has to walk at a slight stoop because of his height.

'Where the hell does it go?' the deputy asks.

'The slaughter shed,' I tell him. 'There was another turnoff, which might lead to the barn.'

Flashes of my blind run through this tunnel nudge the back of my consciousness. I remember feeling my way along the brick walls, stumbling over unseen obstacles, knowing an armed Perry Mast was closing in and bent on killing me. I suspect I'll be making that run in my nightmares for some time to come. . . .

Twenty yards in, the unmistakable sound of footsteps reach us. Someone is running toward us.

'Shit.' Tomasetti raises his weapon and drops into a crouch. 'Police!' he shouts. 'Stop! Police!'

Beside me, the deputy drops to a shooter's stance, raises his weapon. I pull the Glock from my waistband and do the same.

Both men shine their lights forward.

'The hostages were bound?' the deputy asks.

'Yes,' I tell him.

I see movement ahead. Out of the corner of my eye I see the deputy take aim. 'Stop right there!' he shouts. 'Sheriff's office!'

On instinct, the three of us move closer to the wall, but there's no cover. A figure appears out of the darkness. I see a tall, thin silhouette, a pale face and dark hair, dark clothes.

'Stop!' Tomasetti shouts. 'Stop right fucking there!'

A young man dressed in tattered Amish garb stumbles to a halt a dozen feet away. His arms flap at his sides. His mouth is open. His eyes are wild. He screams something unintelligible and falls to his knees.

'Get your hands up!' Keeping his sidearm poised center mass, Tomasetti approaches the man. 'Get them up! Now!'

'Get down on the ground!' the deputy screams.

The man stares at us, his expression terrified as he drops to his hands and knees and then onto his belly. He's muttering words I don't understand – an old Amish prayer I haven't heard in years.

We rush forward as a unit. Tomasetti pounces on him, puts his knee in the man's back. The deputy withdraws cuffs from his belt and secures the man's hands behind his back. My hands shake as I pat him down for weapons. I pull the pockets of his trousers inside out. As I run my hands over his chest, I discern the sharp edges of ribs. He's little more than skin and bones.

'He's clean,' I say, trying to ignore the sick feeling in the pit of my stomach.

Tomasetti gets to his feet, brushes dust from his slacks, slants a look at me. 'He one of the hostages?'

'The hostages were female.' I turn my attention to the young man. 'What's your name?'

The deputy helps the man to his feet. I guess him to be in his twenties. He's breathing hard, his concave chest heaving with each breath. He looks at me as if he doesn't understand.

I repeat my question in Pennsylvania Dutch. '*What's your name?*'

'Noah,' he blurts. 'Noah Mast.'

A shockwave goes through me with such power that I take a step back. I glance at Tomasetti. He's not easily surprised. But I see shock in his eyes.

'You're Noah Mast?' he asks.

'*Ja.*'

The deputy's eyes widen. 'Holy shit.'

'Are you the son of Irene and Perry Mast?' I ask.

The man nods. 'They are my *mamm* and *datt*.'

I'm so taken aback by the revelation, it takes me a moment to find my voice. 'What are you doing down here?'

'This is where I live.'

'What do you mean?'

'I live here. This is where they keep me.'

'You mean here? On the property?' I ask. 'With your parents?'

He looks at me as if I'm dense. 'No. I live here. In the down below. *Here.*'

If I wasn't hearing this with my own ears, I wouldn't believe it. My brain sorts through the information, but I still can't get my mind around it.

'Where are the others?' I ask.

He looks at me. Even in the dim light from the flashlights, I can see he's not healthy. His lips are dry and cracked. His face is so pale, I can see the veins through his skin. The hair at his crown is thin and dry-looking.

'They are here. I hear them scream sometimes.' He says the words as if living in a tunnel where people scream is a normal, everyday occurrence.

'Are they alive?' I ask.

'Some of them,' he says matter-of-factly. 'The good ones.'

I glance at the deputy. 'Can you take him topside?' I hear myself ask. 'I'm going to get the hostages.'

'Sure thing.' He glances at Tomasetti, who nods, then at Mast. 'Let's go.'

The deputy and Mast start toward the hatch. Tomasetti and I watch them go. Mast turns his head and smiles. In that instant, he looks like a frightened teenager.

'What the hell was going on here?' Tomasetti mutters.

I look at him and shake my head. 'I'm not sure I want to know.'

Shaking his head, he shines the beam down the tunnel. 'Let's go find those hostages.'

Neither of us holsters our weapons as we begin walking. I look around for some familiar landmark. A step-up or alcove or door. But there are only brick walls and the oval of the tunnel. It's as if I've never been here.

We've only gone a few yards when a scream echoes from the darkness. It's the same voice I heard when I was down here earlier. It's a bloodcurdling sound that rattles my nerves. But it also fills me with hope, because I know at least one of the hostages is alive.

I break into a jog. Tomasetti quickens his pace to keep up, holding the beam steady and ahead. We've gone only a few yards when I see the door.

'That's it,' I say.

'Careful. He could have booby-trapped it.'

But I'm already pushing it open. I see two girls lying on the floor. Sadie is standing, one hand shading her eyes from my beam. I see terror in her eyes in the instant before she recognizes me.

'Katie!' she cries. 'You came back!'

'Is everyone okay?' I ask.

The girl's face screws up. 'I heard the gunshots,' she chokes out. 'I thought he'd killed you.' She lowers her face into her hands and bursts into tears. 'I thought he would kill us, too.'

'It's going to be okay.' I go to her, put my arms around her. The chain binding her to the wall rattles as she throws her arms around me. She begins to sob uncontrollably, her body trembling against me. 'It's over,' I tell her. 'You're going home.'

TWENTY-FOUR

Two hours later, the Mast farm is swarming with sheriff's deputies, local police, paramedics from the volunteer fire department, and a slew of state Highway Patrol troopers. The coroner's SUV is parked outside the slaughter shed. Midway down the driveway, out of the crime-scene perimeter, is a television news van from WCVK, out of Cleveland. A young reporter in a lime green raincoat is finger-combing her hair while the cameraman sets up lights.

I'm about to go in search of Tomasetti, when I see him coming out of the house. The scowl he's wearing softens when he spots me, and he starts toward me. 'You're getting wet, Chief.'

The fact that I hadn't noticed tells me something about my frame of mind. I'm unduly glad to see him – for myriad reasons – and it takes a good bit of self-discipline to keep myself from putting my arms around him. 'Anything new?' I ask.

'Going to take a while to figure this one out,' he tells me. 'How are the hostages?'

I've spent the last hour in the tunnel with Sadie Miller, Bonnie Fisher, and the third girl, who, we believe, is Ruth Wagler, while the local locksmith dismantled the shackles.

'Sadie Miller and Bonnie Fisher are in relatively good condition. Physically anyway.' I look at Tomasetti and sigh. 'The third girl is in terrible shape. She's emaciated and weak. Nearly catatonic.'

'I called the Waglers,' he tells me. 'Sheriff's deputy is driving them down from Sharon.' He pauses. 'Did you speak with the Miller girl's family?'

'I called Glock and had him run out to my sister's farm. They were . . . ecstatic. And thankful.' I grin. 'Gave all the credit to God.'

'Ah . . . the bane of being a cop.'

We watch an ambulance pull away. I find myself thinking about the body I found. 'Any more remains?'

'One of the deputies found bones in the hog pen,' he tells me. 'Two skulls.'

'Jesus.' I stave off a shiver, trying not to think about what that means.

'We're going to search the entire property. Sheriff's office is going to bring in some cadaver dogs.'

I sigh, wondering if we'll ever get the full story of what happened and why. 'Have you talked to Noah Mast?'

He nods. 'One of the troopers and I did while we were waiting for the ambulance. Kid's a mess. Doesn't even know what year it is.'

I struggle to wrap my brain around that. The conditions were truly horrific – dirty, unsanitary, damp. The hostages were malnourished and filthy. I can't imagine the psychological toll nine years would take.

'Does he know his parents are dead?' I ask.

'Not yet.'

A snatch of memory pushes at the back of my brain. 'All of this makes me wonder what really happened to the sister.'

Tomasetti nods. 'We asked Noah about her. Evidently, the parents blamed him for her death.'

'But it was a suicide.'

'Maybe. We'll need to take a look at the autopsy report. Maybe even exhume her body.'

I'm still thinking about the parents and how they could lay blame on their son. 'Did Noah say why they blamed him?'

'We didn't get that far. EMS took him to the hospital in Mayfield Heights. He'll probably spend at least one night there. Once they get him set up in a room, we'll do the interview.' His face darkens. 'You get anything from the girls?'

'Not much. They were pretty shaken up.'

'We need to talk to them.'

'They took Bonnie Fisher and Ruth Wagler to the same hospital as Noah. Sadie went to Pomerene, in Millersburg, so her family could be there.'

For a moment, the only sounds are the crack of police radios and the patter of rain against the ground. 'Tomasetti, what the hell was going on here?'

He shakes his head in a way that tells me not only does he not know but the depravity and insanity are so far beyond his grasp, he can't imagine.

'The Masts seemed so fucking normal,' I say.

'Except they kidnapped at least five teenagers, killed at least three people, and imprisoned their own son for nine years,' he growls.

We fall silent, our thoughts zinging between us, and watch a trooper in a yellow slicker turn away a young reporter. But my mind is still on Bonnie Fisher, Sadie Miller, and Noah Mast. Tomasetti's right: They're going to be our best source of information. Our only source now that the Masts are dead.

I hope they know enough to tell us why.

There are innumerable rewards that come with the closing of an investigation. First and foremost is the knowledge that a dangerous individual – in this case, two – has been taken off the street and won't be harming anyone else. But there are other rewards, too. The personal satisfaction of knowing you did your job to the best of your ability; that the time and energy you'd invested paid off. Then there's the intellectual reward of finally having the question of 'why?' addressed.

That, more than anything, is the engine driving us as Tomasetti and I walk through the emergency entrance of Hillcrest Hospital in Mayfield Heights, a small community east of Cleveland.

We don't speak as we ride the elevator up. The doors whoosh open to a brightly lit nurses station. A heavyset woman wearing pink scrubs sits at the desk, staring at a computer monitor. She glances up when we step off the elevator. She doesn't speak, but her mouth firms into a thin, unpleasant line, and I suspect she's not happy about the police questioning her new high-profile patients.

Beyond, a wide tiled hall is lined with doors. We don't have to ask which rooms belong to the victims. Two Lake County sheriff's deputies and a state Highway Patrol trooper stand outside rooms 308 and 312, drinking coffee and talking quietly, eyeing us with the territorial glares of a pack of dogs. Another local cop sits in a plastic chair, reading a magazine.

Since the crimes were committed in rural Lake County, the case falls under the jurisdiction of the sheriff's office. But Tomasetti and I have been part of this investigation since the task force was formed. I don't think there will be a problem with our sitting in on the interview.

All eyes fall on us as we approach. I recognize two of the deputies from the scene at the Mast farm earlier. Their expressions aren't hostile, but they're not friendly, either, and I'm reminded they've lost a fellow officer today.

Tomasetti slides his badge from his pocket, and I do the

same. The deputy I don't recognize steps forward and extends his hand. 'I'm Ralph Tannin with the Lake County sheriff's office.'

He introduces the other men, one of whom is with the Monongahela Falls PD, and then addresses me. 'We want to thank you for what you did, Chief Burkholder.'

'I was at the right place at the right time,' I tell him.

'No one could have imagined what was going on out there at that farm.' He rocks back on his heels. 'Goddamn middle-age Amish couple.'

'You talk to any of them yet?' Tomasetti asks.

'The doc's with the Fisher girl now.' Tannin indicates the room directly behind him.

'You guys find anything else at the scene?' I ask.

He shakes his head. 'Just those two skulls. But we've got a lot more to search.'

The door behind him opens. I look up and see a tall, thin man emerge. He's wearing a white lab coat over SpongeBob scrubs and glasses with small square lenses. He's young, maybe thirty, with a five o'clock shadow and circles the size of plums beneath his eyes, telling me he's been on duty for quite some time. His badge tells me his name is Dr. Barton.

'How's she doing?' I ask.

The doctor looks at me over the top of his glasses. 'She's dehydrated, exhausted, traumatized. But she's going to be okay.' He glances at Tannin. 'Are her parents on the way?'

The deputy nods. 'They got a driver and should be here within the hour.'

'Good,' the physician says. 'She needs them.'

'Can we talk to her?' Tomasetti asks.

Barton gives a reluctant nod. 'She's been sedated, so she can get some rest tonight. Keep it short and try not to upset her too much.'

'What about Ruth Wagler?' I ask.

Dr. Barton shakes his head. 'She's not going to be talking to anyone for a while.'

Tomasetti jabs a thumb at Noah Mast's room a few feet away. 'We need to talk to him, too.'

'I'm going to examine him now,' the doctor replies. 'I don't think it'll be a problem. Same rules apply. Don't upset him and keep it short.' With that, he walks away and disappears into Noah Mast's room.

Tannin looks at me. 'I understand you spent some time with this girl in the tunnel.'

'Just a minute or so before I went for help,' I tell him. 'And I stayed with the hostages while the locksmith cut off the shackles.'

'Did I hear right when someone told me you used to be Amish?' he asks.

I smile, but the expression feels tired on my face. 'You heard right.'

'I'm not opposed to your taking her statement.' He looks from the deputy to Tomasetti and back to me. 'She might be more comfortable if you ask the questions tonight.'

'I'm game,' I tell him.

He motions toward the door and the three of us walk into Bonnie Fisher's room. She looks small and pale and vulnerable lying in the hospital bed with an IV hooked up to her arm. It's a vast improvement over the wild-eyed, desperate girl I discovered in the tunnel. Her hair is still damp, and I suspect a nurse must have helped her shower after leaving the ER. The only physical signs that betray the ordeal she went through in the tunnel are the sores on her mouth and the purple bruises on both wrists.

But while the girl's physical wounds are minimal, I suspect the damage to her psyche is significantly worse. Bonnie Fisher now possesses the face of a victim. There's a shadow in her eyes that denotes a certain loss of innocence, and I know she no longer believes the world is a safe place or that people are fundamentally good.

'Hey.' She offers a tremulous smile when she sees me and lifts her hand. 'It's you.'

'Call me Katie.' I give her hand a squeeze. 'How are you feeling?'

'Like I just took a shot of tequila,' she tells me. 'Less the burning throat.'

'The doctor told us he sedated you. He said it would help you sleep.'

'I'm afraid to go to sleep.' She looks out the window at the rain and darkness beyond and a shiver moves through her body. 'I'm afraid when I wake up, I'll be back in that place.'

'You're not going back into the tunnel. You're here and you're safe. Okay?'

She nods.

'Did the doctor tell you that your parents are on their way?'

'The nurse told me. I can't wait to see them.' Her eyes fill with tears. 'I want my *mamm*.'

'I know, honey.' I reach out and squeeze her arm. 'Do you feel up to answering a few questions?'

She looks beyond me at Tomasetti and Tannin, but her gaze drops away quickly. 'I guess.'

I pull up the chair next to the bed and tug out my notebook. 'Bonnie, we need to know how you got into the tunnel. Can you tell us about that?'

She reacts to the question as if trying to avoid a physical blow, sinking more deeply into the bed, pulling the sheet and blanket up to her chin. 'It seems like a long time ago.'

I nod in understanding. 'Take your time.'

The silence stretches for a full minute before she finally

speaks. 'I was riding my bicycle to work at the joinery,' she begins. 'It was just starting to get light. I was late and in a hurry. There was a car behind me, following too close. I kept pedaling, but I remember being annoyed that a driver could be so rude when he had plenty of room to go around. You know how the tourists are. Always in such a hurry. . . .' Her voice trails off and she looks out the window.

'What happened next?' I ask.

'The car hit me. The back wheel went out from under my bike and I lost control, went into the ditch.'

'Were you injured?'

She chokes out a laugh. 'I was angry and set on giving the driver a piece of my mind.' Her expression sobers, and I know her memory is taking her back.

'The old man was just standing there,' she whispers, 'looking at me with this creepy expression.'

'Who was the old man, Bonnie?'

'Deacon Mast.'

'Perry Mast?'

She nods. 'We were only allowed to address him as "Deacon."'

'What kind of car was he driving?'

She shakes her head. 'It was old and blue, I think.'

I think of the old Ford LTD I discovered in the shed and continue. 'What happened next?'

'I accused him of driving like a maniac.' A breath shudders out of her. 'Deacon Mast . . . the old man, he made like he was sorry and wanted to help me. When he was close, he stabbed me with the needle.'

'What kind of needle?'

'The kind we vaccinate the calves with.'

'A syringe?'

She nods. 'I thought he was crazy. I screamed and tried to

get back on my bicycle. But whatever he put in that syringe made me sleepy, and no matter how hard I tried, I couldn't move.'

He drugged them, I realize. 'Was he alone?' I ask.

'I didn't see anyone else.'

'What happened next?'

'Everything was kind of like a dream after that. But I'm certain he put me in the trunk. I remember riding in the dark.'

'Did he bind your hands or feet?'

'My hands were tied. I remember because my wrists were raw when I woke up.'

'Where were you when you woke up?'

'I was there.' Her face crumples and she looks down at the bruises on her wrists. 'In that awful tunnel.'

I press on, suspecting she will soon reach a point where she's either too upset to speak or succumbs to the sedation. 'Was there anyone else in the tunnel with you?'

'The crazy girl. I think her name was Ruth.' She raises her gaze to mine. 'Did you save her, Katie?'

'We did.'

'There was another girl, too. Leah.' She slurs the name, and I realize the sedative is pulling her down. 'But she never woke up, and they took her away.'

I think of the body I stumbled over, and I wonder if that's the girl Bonnie is speaking of. Perhaps she succumbed to the physical and psychological stress and fell ill. I wonder if Mast dragged her aside like a bag of garbage and left her to rot in the cold and dark. . . .

'Did you see Mast's wife, Irene, at any point?' I ask.

'The old lady. She brought us food. Scrapple, mostly. And bread. She's not unkind, but my *mamm* is a better cook.'

I smile. 'Did you ever see a young man?'

Her brows knit. 'No, but I heard male voices sometimes.'

'Did Deacon Mast tell you why you were there?' I ask. 'Did he ever say why you'd been taken into the tunnel?'

'He said we were there to pay penance and confess our sins. He said he was going to save our souls.' She stares at me, her expression stricken, as if she can't quite believe the words she has just uttered. 'I think he was crazy,' she whispers.

'I think you're right. I close my notebook and slide it into my pocket. 'Get some rest.'

'Mast used the car to make contact. He used it as a weapon or to stage an accident. Then he shot them up with some kind of drug to subdue them, threw them into the trunk, and took them to the tunnel.'

Tomasetti, Deputy Tannin, and I are standing outside Noah Mast's hospital room, preparing to go inside for his statement.

'To save their souls.' Tannin makes a sound of disgust.

Tomasetti narrows his gaze on me, poses a question that's been eating at me since the beginning. 'But how did Mast know about these teenagers? How did he find out they were troubled?' he asks. 'These kidnappings are fifty to one hundred miles apart. The Amish generally don't use phones. How did he find out about these so-called troubled kids?'

'He was a deacon,' I tell them.

Tannin nods. 'I knew he was some kind of elder.'

'Is that relevant?' Tomasetti's gaze is sharp on mine.

'Deacons are usually the ones who convey messages of excommunication,' I tell them. 'The bishop sends them into the church district to find out who the transgressors are.'

'Because of his position within the church district,' Tomasetti says, 'he was able to find out who was breaking the rules. He considered these kids transgressors.'

'Even though they weren't baptized,' I tell them.

'Being the insane son of a bitch he was, maybe Mast decided

that didn't matter. He took it upon himself to save their souls, the rules be damned.'

'Probably the best explanation of motive we're going to get,' Tannin says.

'I'll double check with the bishop tomorrow to see if Mast was indeed an ordained deacon,' I tell them.

Tannin motions toward the door of Noah Mast's room. 'Maybe his son will be able to shed some light on all this, too.'

TWENTY-FIVE

Noah Mast watches us enter, wary as an animal whose den is being invaded by predators. He's wearing a hospital gown. A stainless-steel IV stand next to the bed holds a bag of clear solution, which drips steadily into his arm. The lower half of his body is covered, but despite the blankets, I discern the boniness of his legs and the sharp points of his knees. His hands are clean, but they're dotted with scabs. His skin is so pale, I can see the blue of his veins. The sight of him reminds me of photographs I've seen of Holocaust survivors.

'Hello, Noah.' Tomasetti stops a few feet from the bed. 'How are you feeling?'

'Fine.' His eyes are the color of pewter. They're glassy and rheumy, like an old man's. 'I don't know what the fuss is all about.'

I'm aware that Tannin is moving unobtrusively to the wall adjacent to the bed. He leans against it, his arms crossed in front of him. I move beside him, giving Tomasetti the floor.

'I'm John,' he says, showing his badge. 'I'm with the police.'

'Am I in some kind of trouble?'

'I'm just here to ask you some questions.'

Noah's eyes flick to me and Tannin, then back to Tomasetti. 'Where are my *mamm* and *datt*?'

'I want to talk to you about your parents. But we need to get some questions out of the way first.' Tomasetti lowers himself into the chair next to the bed, leans forward, his elbows on his knees. 'I understand you were living down in the tunnel on your parents' farm. Is that true?'

'*Ja.*'

'How long have you been living there?'

Noah glances out the window, where rain streaks down, as if he wants to scramble out of bed and take a running leap through the glass. 'I'm not sure. A long time, I think. I didn't have a way to mark time.'

'How old were you when you started living in the tunnel?'

'Eighteen.'

'How old are you now?'

'Twenty-seven.' He offers a tentative smile. '*Mamm* brought me German chocolate cake for my birthday.'

I hear Tannin's quick intake of breath. I feel that same shock echoing through me. It's inconceivable that his parents kept him in that tunnel for *nine years*.

'Did they force you to live down there?' Tomasetti asks.

'I reckon so.'

'Did they tell you why?'

'I fell prey to sin.' The matter-of-fact tone makes his answer all the more bizarre.

'How so? What did you do?'

'Once, I was with a girl – you know . . . doing things. Bad things.' The Amish man's eyes drop and he searches the sheets covering him, as if he's too ashamed to meet our gazes. 'You know . . .' His left leg begins to jiggle. 'I kissed her. Touched her. We . . . you know.'

Tomasetti nods. 'You had intercourse with her?'

'*Ja.*'

'What's the girl's name?'

'Hannah Schwartz.'

I take out my notebook and jot down the name. In the back of my mind, I wonder if she's missing, or dead.

'Did your parents find out?' Tomasetti asks.

He looks down, nods. '*Datt* came into the barn and found us.'

'What did he do?'

'We prayed and then he made Hannah leave. Then he took the buggy whip to me.'

A sigh hisses from Tomasetti's lips. 'He hit you with the whip?'

'He made some marks is all. On my legs, my rear end. You know.'

'How old were you at the time?'

'I dunno.' He shrugs. 'Fourteen or fifteen. It was a long time ago.'

Tomasetti nods. 'What else did your father do to you when you were bad?'

'Sometimes he took me to the tunnel. Put me on the wall.'

'What do you mean by "put me on the wall"?'

'With the chain, you know.'

'He chained you to the wall?'

'*Ja.*'

'How long did he make you stay there?'

'Well, it depended on how bad I was. Sometimes an hour.' He shrugs bony shoulders. 'A week.'

'How often were you bad?'

Noah looks down at his hands, picks at a scab. 'All the time. I tried to be good. I tried to abide by the *Ordnung* and God's laws. But sometimes I could not.'

'Why did your *datt* move you into the tunnel permanently?'

The Amish man raises his hand and bites at one of his nails. His leg jiggles faster beneath the sheets. 'He blamed me for what happened to Becca.'

'Is Becca your sister?'

'*Ja.*'

I write down the name, then the word *sister* beside it.

'What happened to her?' Tomasetti asks.

'She killed herself.'

'Why did your parents blame you?'

'I don't know. I didn't do anything.'

'Did Becca ever misbehave?'

'No. Never. Becca was perfect.' He lowers his face into his hands and begins to cry. 'She was like an angel.'

Tomasetti gives him a moment. 'So, after Becca died, they moved you into the tunnel and you lived there permanently?'

'*Ja.*'

'Did they ever let you out?' he asks.

He raises his head, rubs at his eyes with the heels of his hands. 'They brought everything I needed down to me. Meat and bread. Water. Milk. *Mamm* read the Bible to me.'

Tomasetti stares at the calluses on the man's wrists. 'Did they keep you chained?'

'Most of the time. But only because I tried to leave.'

'Were there others down there with you?'

Noah doesn't answer immediately. It's obvious he's trying to protect his parents, despite the cruelty they inflicted upon him, the years they stole from his life. 'I never saw them. But I could hear them sometimes. You know, crying.'

'Do you know any of their names?

The Amish man shakes his head.

'Were there girls and boys?'

'Girls, I think.'

288

Tomasetti nods. 'Do you know why your parents put them there?'

'I figured they did something bad and needed to be brought back. Same as me.'

'How did your parents find the girls?'

'I dunno.'

'Do you know how they got the girls into the tunnel?'

'I think God brought them.'

Tomasetti looks down at his hands, laces his fingers, unlaces them. 'Noah, about your parents . . . I'm afraid I've got some bad news.'

'What do you mean?' The Amish man pushes up in the bed, propping himself up on his elbows. The gown shifts, and I see a swirl of hair on a sunken chest and shoulders that are bony and sharp.

'Your parents were killed earlier today. I'm sorry.'

'What? *Killed?*' His mouth opens. I see yellow incisors and molars in the early stages of decay. 'You mean they are dead?'

'I'm very sorry,' Tomasetti says.

'But how can that be? I saw them this morning. *Mamm* brought me milk, like always. They weren't sick. Why are you saying these things?' He looks at me as if expecting me to dispute the words. When I don't, he collapses back into the pillows and looks up at the ceiling, his chest heaving. 'I don't believe you. They would not leave me.'

Without looking away, Tomasetti reaches for the plastic pitcher of water on the tray and pours some into a cup, hands it to Noah.

The Amish man doesn't look at us as he sips. When he finishes, he relaxes back into the pillow and closes his eyes. 'I cannot believe they are gone. How did they die?'

'Your father was sick—'

'But he was fine!'

Tomasetti touches his temple. 'He was sick inside his head, where you couldn't see it.'

Noah Mast puts his face in his hands and begins to sob.

The Whistle Stop Tavern in Monongahela Falls is nestled in a warehouse district between the Grand River and a busy set of railroad tracks. In keeping with the train theme, the establishment is housed inside an old railroad car. The interior has been renovated and made into a bar and restaurant – heavy on the bar – and reeks of fried onions and cigarette smoke. The smell should repel me, but I have an affinity for places of disrepute and I've spent too much time in dives just like this one not to be attracted to it now.

Six booths line the left side of the car. The benches are the requisite red vinyl; the tabletops are Formica, with chrome strips on the sides. The bar itself looks like a ramp that was once used to schlep goods onto railway cars. It's a massive slab of scuffed wood and runs the length of the car. The lower part of the bar, where red and chrome stools are lined up like colorful mushrooms, is covered with gum – the chewed variety – and I realize that at some point over the decades, it became a weird kind of tradition for patrons to stick their gum to the wood.

It's after midnight and the place is deserted. We find a booth at the rear and order coffee. The bartender is a large bald man with arms the size of tree trunks. He has a spiked dog collar around his neck, and there's a tattoo of a pit bull on his right bicep. But he's fast and friendly, and within a couple of minutes he delivers two steaming mugs.

Tomasetti smiles as he picks up his cup. 'You think there's a matching leash?'

'I'm betting his wife keeps it in the night table next to the bed.'

'There's a thought I don't want in my head.' He tips the mug. 'Here's to interesting characters.'

'There are plenty of us to go around.'

We sip coffee, comfortable with the silence. The last hours have been intense, and we both know it will take some time to decompress.

'You haven't talked about what happened in the tunnel,' Tomasetti says after a moment.

The truth of the matter is, I haven't had a chance to think about the time I spent underground with Perry Mast. Now that the adrenaline is flagging and exhaustion is setting in, I realize those minutes were probably some of the most terrifying of my life.

'The worst part was having to leave those girls behind,' I tell him. 'They were terrified I wouldn't come back for them.'

'I guess they don't know you as well as I do. Remind me to give you shit later about risking your neck, will you?' But there's no rancor in his voice.

'Bad habit of mine.' The smile feels phony on my lips, but I don't bother trying to disguise it. Maybe because I'm tired. Maybe because I trust him, even with the part of me that isn't always on the up-and-up.

I think about the case and all the strange places it has taken us. I think of the body I found in the tunnel, and I wonder if the parents know of their dead child yet. I wonder if the news will give them comfort or closure, or if the not knowing was better because they still had hope.

'Did the coroner have any idea how long that girl had been dead?' I ask.

Tomasetti shakes his head, gives me a reproachful look. 'You couldn't have saved her, Kate.'

'If we'd figured this out sooner, we might have—'

'Cut it out.' He softens the words with a smile. 'Those three girls are alive because of you. Because of what you did. You listened to your gut and you went into a dangerous situation. A lot of cops wouldn't have done that, so stop beating yourself up.'

The television above the bar changes to a newscast, and the bartender reaches for the remote and turns up the volume. Neither of us looks at the TV, but we listen.

According to the Lake County sheriff's office, a local Amish man shot and killed his wife this afternoon and then turned the gun on himself. The sheriff's office isn't releasing details, but according to reports, a number of hostages were being held in an underground room. The hostages, several of whom have been missing for quite some time, are recovering at a hospital in Cleveland. No names have been released. . . .

Tomasetti sets down his mug and walks over to the jukebox, digs change from his pocket, and makes a selection. A few seconds later, Red Rider's 'Lunatic Fringe' rattles from the speakers, drowning out the newscaster's voice.

Neither of us wants to talk about the case. But it's part of the decompression process. I sense the weight of it between us.

Tomasetti breaks the silence. 'I heard from the CSU earlier,' he tells me. 'They found more remains. Bones. In the hog pens.'

The hog pens. The meaning behind the words creep over me like a snake slithering around my neck. 'Have any of them been identified?'

'I don't know if the lab will be able to extract DNA from the bones. We're going through cold missing-person cases, but I think identification is going to take a while.'

I nod, thinking about the Masts, what might have driven them to commit such horrific deeds. 'We talked to them, Tomasetti. Why the hell didn't we know something was wrong with them?'

'Insanity isn't always obvious.'

'How did it get to this point?'

He shrugs. 'Taking into consideration everything we know, I suspect it started when their daughter committed suicide.'

'They snapped,' I say, venturing a guess. 'Went off the deep end.'

'Or maybe they were just a couple of fucking lunatics. Fed off of each other.'

Bitterness resonates in his voice, and for the first time I grasp fully the ironies of the case. This is about kids, our most precious resource, and the way we treat them. How out of touch parents – even good parents – can be. But this case is mostly about the lost ones who fall through the cracks, both Amish and English. Some of the children were loved; some were ignored. Others were looked upon by their parents or society with a sort of detached disdain.

I look at Tomasetti and wonder how he has fared. So many times I've tried to imagine him with a wife he loved and two little girls he doted on. It's a difficult image to capture. I suspect he's a different man now than he was before.

'I can't imagine how difficult it's been for you to deal with a case like this,' I say after a moment.

He looks down at his coffee, but not before I see the walls go up, and I realize even after three years, the deaths of his wife and children is the one topic he won't broach.

'Tomasetti?'

He looks at me. 'Yeah?'

'If you ever want to talk about it, I'm a good listener.'

His expression softens. 'I know.'

The sound of a train whistle drowns out the final notes of 'Lunatic Fringe.' The liquor bottles above the bar rattle as a train passes. The tabletop shakes, and I feel the vibration through the floor beneath my feet.

Across from me, Tomasetti slouches in the booth, staring

at his coffee, his face revealing nothing of what he's thinking or feeling. It's a battle-scarred face, though it bears not a single mark. I want to heal him, but I don't know if I can. I don't know if he'll let me.

'I got a room,' Tomasetti says. 'The old hotel by the river.'

'The Petry,' I say slowly. 'I noticed it when we drove past.'

'I figured we could both use some downtime.'

Even after so long, it unsettles me that I want him with such intensity. That I'm vulnerable to him in that way. That I'm vulnerable to my own needs and that we're sitting here as if any of it makes sense.

I reach across the table and take his hand. Surprise flashes on his face when I tug him toward me. I lean across the table and touch my mouth to his. His lips are firm and warm against mine, and my only conscious thought is that I want more. I smell coffee and the fading redolence of aftershave, and something profound stirs inside me.

Not for the first time, I wonder where our relationship will take us. I wonder if two people with as much baggage as we have can get past it, make a go of something good. I wonder if our demons will allow it. And I wonder how long this precarious happiness will last.

After a moment, I break the kiss and move back slightly. But I don't let go of him and our faces remain close. 'You make me happy,' I tell him.

He stares at me as if I'm some puzzle that's unexpectedly baffled him. It would be just like him to spout off something flippant or crude. But he doesn't, and his silence leaves me stammering.

'Are you okay?' I ask.

'That kiss helped a lot.'

'Maybe this relationship stuff isn't as complicated as we thought.'

His mouth curves. 'You're complicated. I'm screwed up. That's probably a bad combination.'

I start to pull away, but his hand tightens on mine. Pulling me close, he kisses me hard on the mouth. It's completely inappropriate for a public place, but it feels good, and I'm too caught up in it to stop. After a moment, he pulls back and contemplates me. It's as if he can see all of those jumpy places inside me – the ones I spend so much time trying to hide, especially from him.

I try to tug my hand from his, but he doesn't let me. He's so close, I feel the warmth of his breath against my face. His dark eyes are level on mine, and for an instant it's as if there's nothing between us. Not my secrets. Not his baggage.

That's when the reality of what I've let happen strikes me. The realization staggers me. Terrifies me. A rise of panic is like a steel clamp around both lungs. I feel my mouth open, but I don't dare utter the words. But I feel the tangled mess of them piled up in my chest.

I wonder if the truth is pasted all over my face. I wonder if he can see it in my eyes, in the way my hand is tight and wet within his.

'Tomasetti . . .' I begin, but I run out of breath and my voice trails off.

'I know,' he whispers. 'I know.'

TWENTY-SIX

No matter where I travel, how long I've been gone, whether it's for business or pleasure or something in between, there's something special about coming home. It's midmorning by the time I pull into my parking space at the Painters Mill police station and shut down the engine. For a moment, I sit there, taking in the facade of the building – the ugly red brick and the circa 1970s glass door. I see my office window with its cracked pane and bent miniblinds, and a few leaves from the ficus tree I've been nursing back to health sticking through.

It's not the visual that grants me such a powerful sense of homecoming, but knowing what lies beyond those doors – and my utter certainty that I'm part of it. Lois's Cadillac is parked a few spaces down and, as usual, I can tell her husband spent much of the weekend detailing it. Glock's car sits a few feet away, waxed and lined up within the parking stripes with military precision. Mona's still here – four hours after the end of her shift – and not for the first time I wonder if she's got a life outside her job. There's no sign of Pickles or Skid, but I know they're on their way. T.J. has already gone for the day, but I'll see him tomorrow. That's something else I can count on.

Tomasetti was gone when I woke at just after seven this morning. There was no note. No good-bye. In typical Tomasetti fashion, he slipped out the door without waking me. He's good at that, leaving without so much as a kiss.

God knows, I'm no expert on relationships, but I do know when something's good. And this thing we've created between us is precious and rare. I only hope it's not fleeting, because for the first time in my adult life, I've given someone the power to hurt me.

I get out of the Explorer and start toward the front door. Suddenly, I can't wait to get inside. I want to talk to my team and get caught up, not only on any police matters but on the small pieces of their lives they occasionally share. I want to sit in my office and listen to Mona and Lois argue over something mundane. I want to fret over that stupid ficus and procrastinate when it comes to archiving those old files that have been sitting on the floor in boxes for the last three months. I want to talk to my sister and brother and find a way to repair all the broken things between us, things I've let the past and my own pride destroy. I want to call Tomasetti and say the words I couldn't say last night.

The smells of coffee and old building laced with the redolence of something that smells suspiciously like lemon wax greet me when I walk in. Tracy Chapman belts out a bluesy tune from Mona's radio. There's no one in sight, but I hear Lois and Mona talking somewhere nearby. I cross to the reception desk and look over the top of the hutch. The switchboard has been shoved aside and a can of Pledge with a dirty white cloth draped over the top sits next to it.

Lois is on her knees beneath the desk, a power cord in her hand. 'I don't know where it goes,' she snaps.

'Plug it in to the surge protector.' I see Mona's red stilettos sticking out from beneath the desk, and I realize she's on her hands and knees. As usual, her skirt barely covers her equipment.

'What if it starts smoking again?'

'Do I look like a freaking electrician?'

I clear my throat. 'Do you guys want me to have the fire department stand by?'

'Oh. Crap.' Lois crawls out from beneath the desk and gives me a sheepish look.

'Oh, hey, Chief.' Mona backs out from beneath the desk, a Swiffer duster in one hand, a power cord in the other.

'Phones up and running?' I ask, only mildly concerned.

'Never unplugged the switchboard or dispatch station.'

Lois plucks a dust bunny from Mona's hair and the two women break into laughter. I laugh, too. It starts as a small chuckle and then turns into a belly laugh powerful enough to bring tears to my eyes.

'What's so funny?'

I turn, to see Pickles and Skid standing just inside the front door. On the other side of the room, Glock leans against the cubicle divider, his arms crossed, shaking his head.

'We're not rightly sure,' Lois mutters, and we break into a new round of laughter.

Skid studies the tangle of wires beneath the desk. 'That shit looks like a fire hazard.'

I cross to the coffee station and fill my mug. The Mast story made the morning news shows. Anchors from Bangor, Maine, to San Diego have been carrying it ad nauseum all morning. I know my team is wondering how much is true and how much is sensationalism.

'Everything quiet on the home front?' I ask as I turn to face them.

Skid makes a sound of annoyance. 'Garth Hoskins ran a stoplight out on Hogpath Road and T-boned old man Jeffers's pickup truck last night.'

'Anyone hurt?'

He shakes his head. 'I cited Hoskins.'

Garth Hoskins is eighteen years old and drives a 1971 Mustang fastback that has more horses than the kid has brain cells.

'I'll talk to him,' I say.

The room falls silent, all eyes landing on me. I tell them everything I know about the case. 'Apparently, Perry and Irene Mast suffered some kind of breakdown after their daughter committed suicide. For reasons unknown, they held their son responsible and imprisoned him. They began preying on troubled Amish teens.'

'How many dead?' Glock asks.

'Four,' I tell him. 'Coroner's office is still there.'

'How's Sadie Miller doing?' Lois asks.

'I'm going to drive over there and take her final statement in a few minutes,' I tell her.

My cell phone vibrates against my hip. I see Tomasetti's name on the display and hit TALK as I start toward my office. 'You make it home okay?'

'Been here a couple of hours,' he tells me. 'What about you?'

'Letting myself into my office now.' I toss my keys on my desk. 'Any news?'

'Noah Mast is missing. He left the hospital this morning and no one has seen him since.'

'That's odd. They checked the farmhouse? The tunnel? Sometimes people go back to the places they're used to, even if those places are unpleasant.'

Tomasetti makes a sound that tells me he's not convinced. 'If he doesn't turn up in the next hour or so, the sheriff's office is going to put out an APB.'

'You don't think he hurt himself, do you?'

'Nothing would surprise me at this point.' He pauses. 'Have you talked with Sadie Miller yet?'

'I'm heading out to the farm now. I'll send my report your way as soon as I get everything typed up.'

I find Esther Miller in the backyard of her farm house, hanging trousers on the clothesline. A wicker basket full of damp clothes sits at her feet. She smiles around the clothespin in her mouth when I approach.

'*Guder mariye,*' I say, wishing her a good morning.

'*Wie bischt du heit?*' *How are you today?*

She looks like a different woman. Her eyes are bright and alive, and I can tell she's truly happy to see me. Dropping the trousers back into the basket, she crosses to me, throws her arms around me, and clings.

'*Gott segen eich.*' *God bless you.* She's not crying, but I feel her trembling against me. 'Thank you for bringing her back to us.'

After a moment, feeling awkward, I ease her to arm's length and offer a smile. 'How is she?'

'Good. Happy, I think.' She blinks back tears. 'She's to be baptized in two weeks.'

'I'm happy for you.' But I feel a pang in my gut. I think of Sadie's passion for her needlework and the part of her that will be lost when she takes her oath to the church, and I realize something inside me mourns its loss.

'I need to get a final statement from her, Esther. Is she busy?'

'She is in the barn, feeding the new calf.' Bending, she reaches for the trousers, pins them to the clothesline. 'Go on, Katie. She'll be happy to see you. I'll be out as soon as I get these clothes hung.'

I take the crumbling sidewalk to the hulking red barn. The big sliding door stands open. The smells of fresh-cut hay and horse manure greet me when I enter. An old buggy in need of paint sits in the shadows to my left. I hear Sadie singing an old Annie Lennox song, and I head toward where the sound is coming from.

I find her in a stall. She's holding an aluminum pail with a large nipple affixed to the base. A newborn calf with a white face sucks greedily at the nipple, his eyes rolling back as he gulps and nudges vigorously at the pail. The sweet scent of milk replacer fills the air, and for an instant the familiarity of the scene transports me to the past.

'He's cute,' I tell her.

Sadie looks up from her work and grins. She's wearing a light blue dress with a white apron and *kapp*. There's no sign of the girl who was fighting on the bridge just a few days ago. The transformation seems to go deeper than clothing. There's a peace in her eyes I didn't see before. 'He is a she and her *mamm* has decided she wants nothing to do with her.'

'She might come around.'

'Maybe.' She looks down at the calf and smiles. 'I kind of like bottle-feeding her, though.'

We watch the animal in silence for a moment and then I ask, 'How are you doing?'

She doesn't look at me. 'Fine.'

'Your *mamm* tells me you'll be getting baptized soon.'

'After everything that happened with . . .' Her words trail off. 'I think it was God's way of telling me the path I should take.'

'That's good, Sadie. I'm happy for you.'

The calf's mouth slips from the nipple. We laugh when she makes a slurping sound and reattaches.

'I need to ask you some questions about what happened,' I say.

Sadie nods, but she still doesn't look at me. 'Are they in jail?'

'They're dead,' I tell her.

Her mouth tightens. 'They were crazy.'

'I know, honey.' I pull my notepad and pen from my pocket. 'I need you to tell me what happened, Sadie. From the beginning.'

She continues to watch the calf nurse, but all semblance of pleasure is gone from her expression now. 'I was walking on the road, down by that old horse farm.'

'The Reiglesberger place?' I ask.

She nods. 'I was standing by the bridge when I noticed an old car parked alongside the road. The man was walking around, calling for his dog. He told me the dog's name was Benji and that he'd jumped out the window and run away. He asked me to help him find it.' A breath shudders out of her. 'So we walked the ditch for a few minutes, calling for him. When my back was turned, he rushed me and stabbed me with something sharp.' Using her right hand, she reaches around and rubs her left shoulder. 'At first, I thought it was a knife. I thought he was going to kill me, so I ran. But I got woozy – I mean, like I'd been drinking or something – and I could barely walk. The next thing I knew, he got back in the car and he rammed me with it.' She indicates her right hip. 'Bumper hit me here, and I went flying.'

She takes a deep breath, as if to garner the full force of her determination, and keeps going. 'He dragged me to the car. I tried to fight, but by then I could barely move.' She shrugs. I guess I passed out after that. When I woke up, I was in the tunnel.'

Her breathing is elevated. Beads of sweat coat her upper lip. She's no longer paying attention to the calf, but lost in a nightmare I suspect she'll be dealing with for quite some time.

Everything she has said corresponds with Bonnie Fisher's statement and the evidence found at the scene.

'Thank you,' I tell her. 'I know that wasn't easy.' I look down at my notes. 'I'll add this to my final report and then all of us can put it behind us for good.' I smile at her. 'You can concentrate on your upcoming baptism.'

She chokes out a laugh. 'I still have two weeks to misbehave.'

I open my arms. Setting down the pail, she steps into my embrace. I squeeze her tight. 'You'd better get back to your calf.'

I'm closing the stall door behind me when I think of one final question. 'Was Irene Mast with him?' I ask.

Sadie looks up from the calf. 'His *mamm*?'

'His wife.' Even as I say the words, something cold and sharp scrapes up my back.

I pause outside the stall, my heart pounding. 'Sadie, how old was the man who accosted you?'

She's already turned her attention back to the calf. 'Older than me,' she says matter-of-factly. 'At least twenty-five years old.'

For a moment, I'm so shocked that I can't speak. I think of the way Noah Mast looked lying in the hospital bed, as pathetic as a dog that's been neglected and brutalized by a heartless owner.

Not wanting to upset Sadie any more than I already have, I leave the stall. Disbelief trails me to the barn door. Once outside, I dial Tomasetti, praying I'm wrong, refusing to acknowledge that my hands are shaking.

He answers on the second ring.

Epilogue

Two months later: Lancaster County, Pennsylvania

The party was in full swing by the time he arrived. The Amish teens, most of them on *rumspringa,* had been gathering at the trailer home for going on a month now. Everyone, it seemed, was always broke. But somehow, someone always managed to wrangle a few six-packs of beer. On a good night, someone would bring a bottle of whiskey or tequila and everyone would sit in the living room and do shots until it was gone and everyone was so shit-faced that they were lucky to make it to their vehicles. Most simply passed out where they were.

As usual, the front door stood wide open. As he parked behind Big Dan Beiler's pickup truck, he could hear the bass thrum of Nirvana's 'The Man Who Sold the World' blaring through the open windows. Two Amish girls wearing dresses and sneakers sat on the steps, sharing a joint. They looked up when he got out of the car, but he didn't pay them any heed. They weren't the one he was looking for tonight.

He found her in the kitchen. Rachel Shrock was seventeen years old and as beautiful and intelligent as she was headstrong. He'd met her here three weeks ago and he'd thought of little else since. She'd charmed him with her sense of humor and gentle way. When he was with her, it was as if he were the only man in the world and the very center of her universe. He'd taken her to one of the bedrooms that same night and they'd made love until the sun streamed in through the window.

He knew it was wrong to lie with her before marriage. They'd discussed it, in fact, and Rachel felt the same way. She was a gentle soul, after all. She loved God. She loved her family. And he was beginning to think she loved him, too. It was the start of something beautiful. That was why Noah had to do everything in his power to save her soul. The way his *datt* had saved the others.

The way his *datt* had saved *him*.

Perry Mast had been an ordained deacon – an important position within the church district. One of his responsibilities had been to go into the Amish community and secure information about transgressors. He'd also been charged with meting out admonitions, usually at worship. They were burdensome duties, but his *datt* had borne them with courage and fortitude.

Noah would never be the man his father had been; he'd made too many mistakes – sinned too many times – most of which he was not repentant for. That was why he'd had to live in the tunnel, why his father had chained him and used the whip. It was why he'd been denied food and, sometimes, water. His *datt* had loved him and wanted only to ensure his son's place in heaven. Noah understood that. He'd accepted his punishment with the same strength and grace with which his father had doled it out.

As part of his penance, his *datt* had sent Noah into the Amish community sometimes to seek out the rebellious members, the ones who'd fallen into sin. Noah had brought them home, where his father had meted out the appropriate punishment.

Noah had decided early on that, while he would never be

a deacon, he could continue his father's work. His father had taught him well, after all, and Noah had been an astute student. His *datt,* he mused, would be pleased.

Noah had worked hard through the summer. Held down two jobs. But he had a place now. A little house set on two acres. He'd bought a nice young gelding for his buggy, and also a cow. By spring, he'd have a calf, the beginning of a herd.

Rachel stood at the kitchen counter with her back to him. She wore cutoff shorts and a white T-shirt, both of which hugged her female curves. He loved the way her long brown hair tumbled over her shoulders. He loved the feel of it in his fingers, the way it smelled when he brought it to his face and breathed in her scent.

Yes, he thought as he drank in the sight of her, *she is the one.* He knew she would make a good wife. She would bear him children. She could be saved, and he was just the man to do it.

'Rachel,' he said.

She turned. Her eyes widened, as if she was surprised to see him, which was silly, since he'd been coming for a month now. She held a can of beer in one hand and a cigarette in the other. Then she smiled, and he was so dazzled by her expression, he forgot all about her vices. With patience and admonition, they would be eradicated.

'Hey, Noah.' She shoved a can of beer at him. 'Want a Bud?'

'Sure.' He popped the tab and sipped, uncharacteristically nervous. 'What are you up to?' he asked.

'Just trying to cop a buzz.'

He fingered the syringe in his pocket. 'You want to take a drive out to see my new place?'

Her eyes lit up. 'I'd love to,' she said, and they started toward the door.

Sworn to Silence

By Linda Castillo

ISBN: 978-0-330-4-7188-6

Some secrets are too terrible to reveal . . .
Some crimes are too unspeakable to solve . . .

Painter's Creek, Ohio, may be a sleepy, rural town with both Amish and 'English' residents, but it's also the place where a series of brutal murders shattered the lives of an entire community over a decade ago. When the killing stopped, it left in its aftermath a sense of fragility, and for the young Amish girl, Katie Burkholder, a realization that she didn't belong.

Now, 15 years, two dead parents and a wealth of experience later, Katie has been asked to return as Chief of Police. Her Amish background combined with her big-city law enforcement expertise make her the perfect candidate. Katie is certain she has come to terms with the past. Until the first body of a slaughtered young woman is found in a pristine, snowy field . . .

Pray for Silence
By Linda Castillo

ISBN: 978-0-330-4-7190-9

The dead tell no lies . . .

The sound of a scream in the early morning dawn leads to a case that will change Kate Burkholder's life irrevocably . . .

When the police arrive at the Amish farmstead in Painters Mill, they can't imagine the horror that awaits them. An entire family slaughtered: the men shot, the young women tortured and killed. The Amish are peace-loving, gentle folk and the town is shocked by what appears to be a particularly brutal – and random – killing. But is it random?

Every family has its secrets. Kate knows that better than anyone. And as she and Agent John Tomasetti dig deeper into the victims' lives they discover a young woman who was living a lie. A girl who had to live in silence.

With her own past resonating, Kate knows she has to maintain some distance. From the case, and from Tomasetti. She knows what could happen if she gets too close. But when she puts herself in the line of fire, she realizes that, this time, there may be no going back.

Breaking Silence
By Linda Castillo

ISBN: 978-0-330-4-7191-6

Sometimes even the Amish keep secrets . . .

When Chief of Police Kate Burkholder is called to a farm in the Amish community of Painter's Creek, nothing could prepare her for the horror and tragedy she encounters. Solly and Rachel Slabaugh, and his brother Abel, have drowned in the hog pit, leaving the four children as orphans. As the investigation progresses, it seems that the Slabaugh deaths were not an accident, and the case suddenly becomes a murder enquiry.

As the case deepens, Kate develops a bond with the children, particularly the 15-year-old daughter, Solome. Maybe she is reminded of herself at that age, and maybe there's something about this case which stirs up memories for her. The events surrounding the deaths puzzle her – something doesn't feel right. As more information comes to light, a tragic incident turns into something much more shocking.

extracts reading groups
competitions books new events
discounts extracts extracts
competitions extracts reading groups discounts
books new events
reading groups new extracts reading groups
events books events
new books extracts new titles reading groups
interviews
books events extracts events new
reading groups books discounts interviews books
books extracts new books events
events new events
discounts extracts discounts interviews new books extracts
www.panmacmillan.com
extracts events reading groups books
competitions books extracts new